I0762050

Heretic Behaviour: The Lies of Midas

E.C. Glynn

Dedication

This book is dedicated to the one true God.
May she keep the fun, freedom and creativity forever flowing.

And to Bron, forever Plan A.

Authors Note

Dear Reader,

Heretic Behaviour: The Lies of Midas is a new adult dark romantic fantasy that contains mature themes and explicit content. For a full list of trigger warnings, please visit my website www.ecglynn.com.

If you enjoy the story, please feel free to recommend this book to others, and don't forget to leave a review on Goodreads. A recommendation from a friend is worth 100x anything I could possibly do to promote myself to new readers. Your words are powerful social currency and I appreciate every time you use them to help enable my dream.

Contents

The Heretical Behaviours

1. Selling one's soul to Obtain Demon Powers

The God-King alone holds the rights to supernatural powers and abilities. It is forbidden to accept the Devil's contract and sell one's soul to Viah in exchange for powers.

2. Dancing, Revelry, Festivals or Celebrations.

The nation remains in an age of contrition. This must be observed by all citizens at all times until the Divine Mercy and Forgiveness of the God-King is decreed.

3. Using the God-King's Name in Vain.

His name is sacred and powerful. Flippant or ill-considered use is forbidden.

4. Misuse of the God-King's Golden Sand.

All that is created by the God-King's holy power remains an extension of his divinity. Any use of his Golden Sand must be approved by the God-King himself. It is expressly forbidden to use it in any form of trade or financial transaction.

5. Idolatry.

All gods worshipped before the arrival of the Almighty God-King were false gods. Worship of any but the One True God-King is forbidden.

6. Disrespecting the Church.

The Church is the Arm of the God-King. It implements his will. Its authority and personnel must be respected at all times.

7. Harbouring a Heretic.

Any person found to be harbouring one who is known to have committed a Heretical Behaviour will be considered to be colluding in that transgression and punished.

8. Misconstruing Dark Age History.

It is forbidden to fondly reminisce or misconstrue the Dark Ages, especially if committed with intent to cause disruption to the rightful ascension of the God-King and his Church.

Prologue

Despite Jezebel's displeasure, Christopher Culis insisted on wearing black to his own wedding. He walked alone like a man condemned, with an unfocused, unhurried step, as though he were in a dream. The blurred flurry of people around him ebbed and flowed, each of them just dimly outlined shapes that he occasionally tottered to the left or right to avoid.

Physically, he was here, pacing slowly towards the Grand Cathedral. Mentally, he was a thousand miles away, deep in a rainforest, so remote it had no name, kissing the soft lips of a heretic under a wide sky of stars.

It was only by focusing on that memory and not on her disappearance that he was able to keep placing one foot before the other.

The plan had failed.

He could not crumble.

If he was to ever find Mila, he needed to do this. The fledgling resistance needed him to do this...

As he walked up the steps of the Grand Cathedral and passed under the archway he became acutely aware of how different everything now seemed.

The Culis of a year ago would have scanned the room with his whip-sharp mind, analysing every guest to the nth degree. With Jezebel being the God-King's only child and the Second Heretical Behaviour suspended for this occasion, their wedding was likely to be the largest celebration the nation would ever be permitted. A guest's choice of companion to share the historic moment was important, particularly if they brought their mistress or beau instead of their spouse. The old Culis would have filed that tasty tidbit of information away for opportunities of future extortion.

An opportunist to his grave.

The old Christopher Culis would have also taken note of the fashion. Not because he cared about one design over another, but because it was important to note who was wearing something that was obviously newly made for the occasion, and who thought they'd get away with re-wearing a dated garb. Their choice would convey their support for him and this union more than words ever would.

More than anything, he would have noticed where the Priests and Acolytes positioned themselves. They made him uncomfortable at the best of times but a year ago, on an occasion like this, he would have been concerned about them imposing some religious frippery on what should have been a relatively secular event.

An entirely different version of him would have cared. One who'd never met Mila.

This version, however, was consumed only with questions and torment.

Where was she? Was she alive? Did Tarett have news?

He was vaguely aware that some of the guests tried to congratulate him as he passed, sycophants trying to take advantage of his impending new station.

He ignored them all. The only people he cared about, his trusted inner circle, were not here. Sour weather had delayed the ship on its journey back from Keras.

He was alone.

Hurry up and let this be over with.

Culis walked down the long aisle until he reached the place where he would await Jezebel's entry. There he took stock of the magnificent hall properly for the first time and saw that he now stood before the God-King Midas, who sat behind the podium on his own dais. Culis bowed to him in reverence. He'd never been this close to the deity before.

"Well, well," Midas said softly, his voice gravelly and hard. He surveyed him critically. "Wearing black to your formal surrender? An interesting last stand."

Midas knew his daughter.

Knew her well enough to know that Culis wouldn't have proposed unless the heavy hand of coercion had been involved. He knew that while Culis might be gaining the title of Consort, he'd be relinquishing any personal freedom he'd ever cherished. He knew that Culis understood that he was signing over his life to the most unpredictable, temperamental and dangerous woman in the nation.

He knew.

Culis tried to reply, but his mouth was too dry. Instead, he merely nodded, then returned to scanning the hall anxiously for his future wife as the guests filled the pews. He did not insult either of them by pretending to be the eager bridegroom.

He didn't have to wait long.

Princess Jezebel, ever impatient, barely waited until the last of the guests were seated before making her entrance.

She was always beautiful but today she looked otherworldly in her sleek, white gown that hung low from her shoulders and cleaved like a glacier through the low valley of her cleavage.

Culis barely saw her. All he could think about was Mila.

It had been five weeks of agony. Not knowing where she was, not knowing if she was alive or dead, the constant worry, the helplessness...it was corrosive, and destroying him from the inside out slowly and effectively.

When he'd woken to find her gone, there'd been a tiny moment that he'd wondered if she'd left him voluntarily. It had broken his heart to consider it – but he'd accepted it. She owed him no explanation, and he would never blame her for choosing to leave this cesspool of a nation behind. Even if that meant leaving him too.

But then he'd found the pile of her discarded clothes and seen the clear signs of a struggle. The drops of blood and hair across the rocks, the crushed foliage that can only be made by a body being dragged through it. The boot prints and hoof prints of her assailant and their steed...

She'd been *taken*.

The knowledge that someone had done something terrible to Mila, and he hadn't been able to save her had driven him mad. He'd barely slept. Barely eaten. Consumed with guilt, trawling the wild rainforests, eventually expanding the search across the entire nation for her.

But all his efforts, every favour, demand, bribe and threat had yielded nothing. No signs of life. No whisper of a clue. Mila had been whisked away with violence and never heard from again. There was no body, no note, no ransom, no gloating from anyone in his life. She was simply gone, as if she'd never existed, and the silence of where she should have been echoed deafeningly in the weeks that followed.

But she *had* existed. He knew she had, because the memory of her was stitched into his heart, into his very fibres, and he refused to believe she was dead.

He'd *know* if she was dead. Something inside him would surely cease to exist if Mila was dead, and so far as he could tell, he was still all here – weary, worried and crumbling – but still whole. Still fighting. Still hunting. So, that meant she was still alive... somewhere. And he would find her

He blinked. Jezebel suddenly stood before him.

How did she get here so quickly?

She took charge, taking his hands in hers. They were cold. Like snakeskin.

He shuddered.

Why was she making him go through with this? She didn't even look happy to see him. Oh, her eyes were glinting, and she had a smile on her face, but he knew her well enough by now to know that this expression was not what Jezebel looked like when she was happy. She wore this smile on days when she was feeling vindictive.

The low bell tolled and the hall fell silent.

The ceremony was about to begin.

Culis's stomach felt leaden and cold. He forced his mind away from what was happening, desperate to be anywhere else but right here.

He watched his betrothed scan the room and survey the opulence around them with pleasure. Then he saw her spot something that drew her focus intently. She tried to hide a smile, a true smile.

With morbid curiosity, Culis followed her gaze.

Once he'd turned his head, it was hard to miss. Something was being brought towards them down the aisle. Something gold and shiny.

A gift? An offering? A sacrifice to honour their wedding?

Whatever it was, it looked wretched. It took a moment for Culis to register that it was alive, stumbling towards them. He blinked hard through the incense that swirled around them and the thing came into focus.

A skeletal, nearly naked, twisted, limping figure. A half-dead, broken, wisp of a being, coated mockingly in slick golden oil.

Time slowed, sound dampened and for a long heartbeat, Culis only heard the roar of blood in his ears as he realised what – who – it was.

Mila.

The Housewarming

No one was killed during Jezebel's invasion of Culis Manor. In fact, considering the woman possessed all the nuance of a clod, Mila was obliged to begrudgingly acknowledge that the Princess had managed it all rather artfully. Instead of weapons, the combatants had wielded terse, muttered arguments; the battlements were made up of stilted, leering smiles; and the battering ram was the dark-haired, hawk-eyed woman, whose gaze could cut through glass.

Not a typical invasion, but an invasion nonetheless.

It was the first day of true winter and Mila's hands were icy cold despite the relative warmth inside the manor. She and Tarett watched in horror from a top window as the long procession of servants marched like ants below them, each one carrying a crate of Jezebel's various belongings into the manor. As each object crossed the threshold and Jezebel marked her new territory, Mila felt dread begin to lay itself, thick and sticky, around her heart.

Jezebel was coming. Inescapable. Barrelling towards their lives, with the inertia of an avalanche down a mountainside.

Since escaping Jezebel's clutches, Mila had devoted considerable effort to trying to erase the dark shadow of the Princess's imprint from her skin, her psyche. She didn't want to look at the other woman and break out in a cold sweat of fear, didn't want to flinch every time she opened her mouth. She didn't want to give her that kind of power over her body. She wanted to be healed from the scars that had formed during the torment she'd suffered for months, alone, at the Princess's hands. Unfortunately, in this past week, Mila had come to realise that healing didn't quite work like that. One cannot simply will oneself to be healed, especially not when the reason for the fear remained. Jezebel was still a threat. The fear she felt in her presence, Mila eventually came to appreciate, was not weakness, but a survival mechanism.

Stay as far away from her as you can, and you will live longer, her fear was telling her.

And now Jezebel was in her home.

"I...I'm not sure I'm going to survive this," she whispered to Tarett with a shiver.

Her friend nodded in grim agreement.

It had been a week since Culis's impromptu, coerced proposal to the Princess. A week that had felt like a year. In that time the nation had responded to the news like a flock of startled birds, exploding in a flurry of gossip, speculation and cautious celebration. It had only taken two days for Jezebel to announce that she could not wait until their spring wedding and would be moving into her new winter chateau, Culis Manor, immediately.

It was astounding how quickly any semblance of safety Mila had felt about the manor was wiped away by that proclamation. This had always been her place to escape. Her room had always been a sanctuary that Culis and the other members of the house had honoured as her private space. Not anymore. She knew that with Jezebel here now, nothing would be sacred.

More than once Mila had considered trying to leave.

She knew that if this wedding went ahead and she stayed at Culis Manor, she'd spend the rest of her life serving the one woman who triggered a bone-deep fear in her, the woman who wanted her dead more than anyone else in the country. She'd live the rest of her life always looking over her shoulder for the blade aimed squarely at her back, and she'd always, excruciatingly, be within reach of Christopher Culis, but never permitted to grasp him.

Intolerable.

Why, though?

She'd grappled with the question every day since the engagement, embarrassed and humiliated that despite everything, she was still so undeniably drawn to the man. Yes, he was handsome...in a roguish, slightly skinny, too aristocratic kind of way. Yes, he had eyes that were so green and clear they were nearly portals to other worlds. And yes, he was intelligent, and made her laugh, and he was interesting and a myriad of other pleasant and admirable things. Yes, his energy had felt incredible on the morning that she'd woken in his arms with him tucked around her fiercely. These things were undeniable.

But the fact remained that these traits only coloured one side of the sphere that made up the many shades of Christopher Culis. He made no secret of the fact he was a deeply self-serving man. He had declared himself to be untrustworthy many times, and Mila knew to believe him on this, despite the fact he was a charming liar. He was ruthless in his ambition and when push came to shove he always erred on the side of getting his own way. Even as it had been happening, Mila had known her gradual softening and attraction to him had been dangerous. The way he'd betrayed her in the Highlands, abducting Natalee for his own schemes, wasn't just a misjudgement of the moment. That callous focus on the plan, on making money, on gaining power was a core part of his upbringing, his values.

And yes, while it was true to say that he'd had some redeeming moments; he'd apologised, he'd come for her when he'd discovered Frank's torture, and he'd even blown up the Dusk Ball to try save Natalee for Mila's sake. Was it enough? He'd told her he was trying to change, told her he wanted *her*, and for a day or two it had all seemed true. Even when he'd first proposed to Jezebel, she'd believed it had been part of a ruse to try save her from the Princess's wrath. Now, a week later and with Jezebel moving in, she didn't quite know what she believed.

Without touching him, it was impossible to truly know.

Since the moment Jezebel had said yes, the kitchen gossip at Culis Manor had been unable to veer an inch either side from the subject of Culis's apparent new utter devotion to the Princess.

According to Petrie and Tess, lavish gifts had apparently been sent to Jezebel's apartments every morning. A new horse, a cartload of peacocks, a trio of string musicians had been employed to follow the Princess everywhere she went for an entire day. Culis apparently wrote her poetry, ordered new casks to be bottled in her vintage, had even had ten dresses ordered – each in her exact measurements and made from different and equally rare and expensive materials. If the cook and his helpers were to be believed, Culis's every waking moment had been allegedly spent either in the Princess's direct company, or loudly pining for her and planning their next rendezvous. Mila couldn't confirm any of these rumours personally. She'd kept as far away from the couple as she physically could. However, there had been one time, one day, when no other servers had been available and Mila had been forced to take them their midday meal. When she'd laid the tray of their food on the table before them, Culis had ignored her so thoroughly she may as well have been invisible. He'd not thrown her even one tiny, measly little glance.

That had hurt. Mila's insides had felt like skinned knees pressed against ragged gravel. Here was the man whose life she'd saved, who'd kissed her with fervour just days ago, whose energy had screamed, *I'm yours, I'm all yours*, on the night after the assassins. Now he wouldn't even look at her.

A week later and she now sat at the window with all that anger, humiliation and sadness finally, mercifully burned out. She just felt empty and exhausted inside. The stubborn walls around her heart were now firmly recovered from the short period she'd tested slowly, achingly, foolishly lowering them.

This is just what Culis does, she'd told herself. He uses people. He'd used her to gain her trust, her compliance in his schemes. And now he was using Jezebel to become a prince.

She should have just left the manor.

At the height of her sadness the instinct to flee had been so strong that more than once, Mila had found her feet heading for his study in the dead of night, ready to raid the room and steal the key that kept her tethered to the property. She knew he kept the vasium there, the mystic sister stone that coupled with the enchanted necklace which remained around her neck. If she had the stone, she'd be able to leave, to go anywhere, to be free of this horrible situation she found herself in.

But every time, to her own surprise, despite all the anger and hurt she was holding onto so tightly that she felt ill, she'd always stopped short before pushing open that study door.

What if it had been real?

She hated that there remained a tiny flicker, a seed of uncertainty lurking inside her. Hated it.

But what if?

What if the thing she'd felt that fateful night, that energy, that desperation she'd sensed in him – to be seen, to be loved, to love in return – had been real? Energy was a far more difficult thing to fake than words or deeds.

What if?

If anyone could manage such a deception, she sternly reprimanded herself, it was probably Culis. Yet in her weakest moments she could almost persuade herself it had been real.

"*Here,*" he'd said, opening himself to her. *"I want you to read it all."*

What if it was real?

That question was the one saving grace that kept her in the manor. That and the thought that, if she knew Culis at all (and she considered that she did) then if their connection had indeed been real, Culis would have some sort of plan up his sleeve.

He was the master of plans. He must have a plan, surely.

As she sat by the window watching Jezebel's cherished household belongings invading her world, that shakily held belief suddenly felt even more foolish.

She sighed.

It was all so complicated. On top of all her pain and confusion surrounding Culis, she also hadn't heard a peep from Natalee. Not that Mila had necessarily expected her to visit, or even write a full letter, but surely a short telegram saying she was alive and safe was within the realms of possibility for a fugitive. Arran, Culis's spymaster, had assured her that so far as he knew, Natalee hadn't been injured in the blast at the Dusk Ball, and the jesu hadn't recaptured her after the explosion. Surely that meant she'd made her way to safety, to freedom?

Knowing the reclusive woman, it was entirely possible she'd simply gone back to the Highlands and would remain there, in disguise for the rest of her life.

Still, Mila wished she could know that with absolute certainty.

Tarett sensed where her mind had gone and tried to lighten the mood.

"Where are they going to put all that...crap?" He inclined his head towards the fifteenth statue of Jezebel that was passing below them – this one carved from crystal, which flung blinding rainbows over the pavement wherever the sun touched it.

"Do you think you'd be able to fit each of them in your pockets?" Mila asked, grateful to think about something else, something less soul-crushing.

"I'd be able to fit them all," Tarett said confidently. "But it depends on how heavy they are. Remember, it's just the size of an object that my power affects, not the weight. By the looks of how they're struggling to carry them in, I'd say the weight of one statue would be enough to weigh me down considerably."

Mila studied the man, her fellow ikarei, and wondered how he would fare over the next few months.

After the Dusk Ball she'd decided to come clean to him and Marie about everything that had happened with Natalee. To say the two of them had not been at all happy to learn that Culis had abducted Natalee from the Highlands, and that this had been the start of the series of events that had seen her served up as sacrifice at the Dusk Ball, was a serious understatement.

"You told us this contract to serve was a choice," Tarett had said, his usually light and joking face gone. Mila could clearly picture the cold anger that had taken over his handsome features, Marie bristling, her energy a black ball of fury, beside him. "You said we were free to come and go as we pleased, told us we were signing a contract of servitude, but doing so in exchange for a life of freedom. But now apparently when an ikarei resisted, she was taken by force anyway. Am I hearing you correctly, Mila?"

"I..." Mila's stomach had felt so tight that she'd found it hard to breathe. She'd never in her life been so ashamed. "I didn't know it was going to go that way," she said softly. "But yes. That is how it played out, in the end."

Next, Tarett and Marie had directly confronted Culis, threatening to leave the manor and abandon the venture altogether.

Mila hadn't been privy to the specifics of that conversation. They'd sternly ordered her to wait out in the hallway as they'd cornered the merchant in his study. She'd obeyed, wringing her hands anxiously in the shadows, alone.

What happened next was not what she'd expected. Tarett and Marie had eventually emerged from the study still looking angry, but their energies were mollified somewhat. Whatever had happened in there, whatever magic Culis had weaved, had convinced them to stay. They didn't share with her what had transpired, but they did make a point of telling her that she shouldn't expect their forgiveness or trust anytime soon. She didn't blame them. If she'd been in their shoes, she would have done the exact same. Knowing this made it all the more meaningful that, despite his anger and hurt, Tarett had come to find and sit with her today, a day he'd known would be especially difficult for her. She was touched. She wondered if this was a gesture to tell her that the rift between them could be mended over time.

She desperately hoped so.

She liked Tarett. He was interesting and unusual. She watched his eyes track the movement of people and goods as they passed below. They glittered as the priceless objects entered Culis's house, and Mila noted the hint of greedy energy that she could sense seeping out of him. She wondered if recent conversations about the art of smuggling with Black Berran had been rubbing off on him.

"I'm sure when the dust settles after a few months, no one will notice if one of the four hundred priceless statues goes to...a better home. Especially if they disappear one at a time." She offered him a half-hearted smirk and he responded with a sly grin. "I knew there was something in you, Mila, that enjoyed being part of a criminal enterprise." His voice now had a cutting edge to it and the smile turned sardonic. "For all your apologies and your saint-like attitude...You do secretly love breaking the rules."

She grimaced at the barb.

Clearly not yet forgiven after all.

She turned back to the window, resuming the task she'd given herself for today - scanning the faces of the servants and guards. There was only one she wanted to see. One friend amongst the sea of incoming enemies.

She waited and watched all evening, peering down at everyone until the last of the sun's tendrils dipped below the mountains on the horizon and rolled a soft purple carpet out across the sky to seduce the incoming stars.

He hadn't come.

Her stomach dropped and she finally pulled away from the window.

"You've been waiting for someone?" Tarett asked.

"Jahan, Jezebel's guard. He's been part of Jezebel's court since he was ten years old." Mila explained. "There's no reason he wouldn't be part of this entourage. Not unless something was amiss."

She'd been worried about Jahan since the morning of the proposal, since Jezebel had arrived without her bodyguard in tow to confront

Culis for the perceived slight he'd given her at the Dusk Ball. Jahan's absence then had been the first hint that Jezebel had punished the kind man for being seen with Mila at the decadent event. Now, Jahan's absence today only fed that harrowing suspicion.

She felt a cold pit begin to grow in her chest.

She should have done more for him, she chided herself. She should have sought him out the very day after the ball to ensure he'd be safe from Jezebel's retribution. And now, was it too late? Was he imprisoned somewhere, injured? Had Jezebel fully blinded him and left him somewhere cold and quiet. Time seemed to slow as she considered this in a panic. She had to know.

Her relationship with the man was complicated. On one hand, she liked him. He'd saved her life, several times now. He'd helped her stay safe from Jezebel, and even comforted her in her times of need. His energy was good, kind and strong. On the other hand, he was also a devout follower of the God-King. He fervently believed that Mila was a demon, a heretic, and because of this he would obediently take her to her death the moment Midas decided her temporary abscondence from sacrifice was over. The dual nature of his regard for her was confusing to say the least, but she certainly didn't want any harm to come to him. She owed him too much to simply let him rot away in some dungeon for the rest of his life. Finding him was imperative.

Beneath her worry for his wellbeing, Mila was also curious to know if Jahan had seen the important moment at the Dusk Ball when Midas's power had failed. Had he been watching in that split second when Midas's finger had touched Natalee's forehead and nothing had happened?

That nothing was the most important 'nothing' that had ever happened in the past forty years. It was the moment Mila had conclusively proven that rubane-infused oil would block Midas's powers as surely as it blocked her own. If Jahan had seen it he would now know that the God-King was, almost certainly a fraud, an ikarei just like her – albeit one that was wildly more powerful. Had Jahan had seen it? She wouldn't blame him if he hadn't. The ensuing explosion had occurred so quickly afterwards.

She sighed deeply.

Where was he?

"We should go," Tarett said gently, breaking the spell of her rumination and taking her by the elbow. "Surely someone in Jezebel's retinue can tell us what happened to him."

Mila took a deep steadying breath and tried to convince herself that Tarett was right. The housewarming for Jezebel's new life at Culis Manor was tonight. Perhaps the excitement of a new environment and abundant alcohol would loosen the lips of Jezebel's staff sufficiently enough to yield helpful information about Jahan's fate. Surely people would be gossiping and talking about it. Surely.

Together, they headed away from the alcove, down the staircase and into the grand entry hall of the luxurious homestead. Here the last of Jezebel's statues were being placed, and the rest of the servants and household staff waited expectantly for the housewarming celebration to commence. Despite the festive decor of the room, Mila sensed the energy of the crowded space as tense and uncomfortable. Two full households now stood crammed into the entry hall, which, while not small, was no ballroom, and none of its occupants were accustomed to the casual way this occasion flirted with heresy. Other than Jezebel, of course. Pushing the Church's boundaries was a pastime she loved to indulge in.

The uneasy chatter hushed as Culis and Jezebel emerged from the dining room hallway, hand in hand, and took their place in the centre of the room.

Mila hated that she found herself drinking in the sight of him.

Culis was lit from above by a grand chandelier adorned with beautiful green draping vines that matched the green of his long shirt and eyes. He looked stunning...and exhausted. Battle weary already from his week-long fight in the trenches of Jezebel's obsessive love.

As Mila studied the numb and despondent notes in his sad eyes, it occurred to her in horror that maybe there was a third option she hadn't considered.

Maybe this was it.

Maybe this *was* the plan. Maybe this was the only thing Culis could think of that would protect her from Jezebel, that sacrificing himself, his life, was the only way.

No. Surely not.

Beside him stood the triumphant Jezebel, who clutched his hand, her prize, in proud determination. Her skin-tight golden dress gleamed in the candlelight.

"Welcome, all!" Culis said, abruptly shaking the invisible sad cloak from his shoulders and embracing the people in the room with a grand, sweeping gesture of his free hand. His voice boomed, and Mila heard the forced jolly tone it took as it bounced off the pillars. She wondered if anyone else did too.

"We welcome all those who are friends, all those who are foes, and all those who sit somewhere in the middle."

The folk in the room gave a chuckle, then collectively seemed to breathe a little sigh of relief. It was incredible the way a light acknowledgment of the many competing loyalties within this gathered group could deflect some of the tension. Culis, for all his flaws and misgivings, was ever the master of a crowd.

"Welcome to Culis Manor, soon to be baptised as Winterhaven," he said with a smile. "We are all so pleased to have you here."

He cast his eyes about the room and, for a sliver of a moment, it happened. His haunted gaze found Mila. It snagged on her where she stood at the top of the stairs, like a thorn on delicate pantihose. Her heart stuttered as that gaze seemed to rip her open.

He blinked. It broke the spell. He moved on. His smile did not falter, not even for one second.

Mila felt both heartened and saddened by the gesture.

It was finally an acknowledgment of her, of them, of their predicament. The most he'd given her in a week, and she knew he couldn't have done anything more. Not in a place as public as this. Not at the moment Jezebel was formally making his house her new home. And yet, that tiny pause meant something enormous. It was an affirmation that he knew she was confused and uncertain. Perhaps a promise that he was indeed brewing up some scheme to save himself, save her.

Or perhaps she was reading into it too much. Perhaps it had just been a glance to say goodbye?

Again, she wished she could just touch him, allow her power to read him and show her the truth.

Jahan is missing.

This, she reminded herself, trying to tear herself from her sadness, was worth her focus. It was the only thing she could do anything about tonight. Not Culis. Not Jezebel.

Find Jahan.

She and Tarett would interrogate Jezebel's household tonight. For a moment, Mila desperately missed her friend Flue, who – with the power to draw infatuation – would have undoubtedly been an asset in this plan. But Flue was gone, working now at The Harem for the ambitious Marcina. Mila felt a twist in her gut as she considered that situation. She hoped she'd get a chance to reconnect with Flue soon and ensure that particular path had worked out well for them.

In the meantime, she and Tarett would try their best alone tonight. Surely it couldn't be too hard. Jahan was an established and well-respected member of Jezebel's retinue. His absence was noteworthy. Someone must know something.

With this decided, Mila turned her attention back to the goings-on below and watched as Jezebel finished a toast to herself.

"...and may the value of these halls be ever increased by my illustrious presence." The Princess beamed her radiant smile around the room and gently clinked her own glass with a tiny spoon, prompting the obedient tinkling of two hundred others. The musicians struck up.

The housewarming had officially commenced.

Seducci

There were so many people in attendance, more people than she'd ever seen before at Culis Manor, and while there were some faces Mila recognised, most she did not. She extended her horns fully and used her power to sift through the differences in the energies of the guests around her. Enemies she quickly identified and avoided. The distinctively bitter residue that she knew it left on a person's energy always caused her face to pucker slightly, as though she'd just bitten into an unripe grape, but unpleasant as it was, tonight it was helpful to know exactly who they were – so she could avoid them like the plague. There were very few friends; the kitchen staff, Nemecca, Lyria, Baird and a few others, but they wouldn't know anything about Jahan's fate. No, the ones she deliberately sought out were those from Jezebel's court, whose energy towards her was neutral.

It was easy to identify them. Culis's staff were all wrapped in a jovial air, each enjoying the celebration and relishing in the unusual night away from their chores. Jezebel's staff, on the other hand, all felt wafer thin, adorned with polite smiles, frightened eyes and tense shoulders under their festive garments. It was as though whatever sense of life and fun and joy they'd ever had was now pushed far below the surface. Mila didn't remember Jezebel's servers feeling like this during the time she'd lived at the palace, but perhaps she'd been too preoccupied with her own struggle to notice and take pity on them.

Mila identified her first target and approached a maid whose frightened, mouse-like energy gave her away. As Mila approached her, she realised she recognised her. She was one of Jezebel's trusted inner sanctum.

Perfect.

"You're Trinity." Mila grabbed the woman by the sleeve and tugged her slightly to the side, into a shadowy corner.

The redhead, who had once been dangled upside down from a window for Jezebel's amusement, flinched slightly at the contact and grimaced. Mila felt the fear flowing cold and fast from her.

"Don't talk to me." Trinity lifted her bubbling flute of golden liquid to her lips and looked away from Mila, trying to sidestep her.

Mila did not let her go. "I just have one quick question for you, please."

"I do not want to be seen associating with you." Trinity's voice was hard but there was no hatred in her. She was just frightened. She looked anywhere but directly at Mila. "Let me go."

"Jahan," Mila insisted in a firm whisper. "Where is he?"

Trinity's fear tripled at the mention of the former guard's name, and Mila felt her spine grow cold at the confirmation such a response offered.

Something terrible had happened, or was still happening, to Jahan.

Mila let the woman stumble away and sent her power out again, hunting for the right person with the right energy. Someone who could give her a clearer answer. But for all her scanning and reading, her efforts only yielded similar, vaguely threatening results from anyone she spoke to. No one wanted to be seen anywhere near her, no one had answers for her about Jahan's welfare. After a few fruitless hours of asking, all Mila knew was that Jezebel's staff thought that something terrible had happened to Jahan after the Dusk Ball, and that Mila was to blame.

"Well, well." A cutting and vaguely familiar voice sounded in her ear. "Still alive and it's nearly been a full year. I'll have to let the High Priest know the latest update, he'll be...overjoyed."

The speaker was a woman Mila had seen with Jezebel many times. An older dame who was always flitting around the outskirts of the Princess's inner sanctum but never quite seemed like she was permitted inside. Lady Meredith. The proud woman was rake thin and wore her jutting clavicle like a prize. She surveyed Mila with the arched brow of a judgemental peacock, her thin lips crooked in disdain.

Mila refused to be cowed by the threat.

"Please do give him my best," she replied icily. "And look at you, Lady Meredith. Moving into Culis Manor with the Princess and her court? Funny. I wouldn't have considered you to be her first choice of companion."

Mila watched with interest as Meredith seemed to flinch. She hadn't expected her petty insult to strike the dissonant chord that it seemed to in the woman.

"I go where I please," Meredith hissed in reply. "*Not* at the heels of the Princess."

"And you chose to come here?" Mila asked now with genuine curiosity. Why was Meredith so angry at the implication? What nerve had been struck? Mila wanted to dig deeper. She began to send her power into the strange woman but before she could read anything she was interrupted by a hand that reached out and grabbed her forearm with such force it made her jump. It was cold. Mila didn't need to look to see who it was. The way the nails dug into her skin was answer enough.

Jezebel.

"So much skulking around tonight, demon," she hissed, her beautiful, cold face filling Mila's vision as she yanked her around to face her directly. "Don't think I haven't noticed the sly way you've been approaching my staff, one by one, this evening. What are you doing to them? Poisoning their goblets?"

For a moment, Mila was frozen in her vice-like grip, like a rat in the clutches of a python. She tried not to let her fear show, but as surely as she knew Jezebel, Jezebel also knew the effect she had on her. She luxuriated in Mila's fear.

"No? Something else? You want their attention, do you? Is that what this is? You're so used to being the *special* one and tonight isn't going your way. Am I correct?" Her tone was mocking and condescending.

"No, Princess," Mila rasped out, desperate to derail wherever the conclusion of this speech was taking them, but Jezebel could not be stopped. She pulled Mila like a teacher dragging a child towards the cane, away from the crowd and into a side room where they were alone.

"Well, answer me, demon! What are you up to?"

Mila didn't answer immediately, didn't want to grant Jezebel the satisfaction of a stuttering, panicked excuse. A considered, calm response was one of the few things still in her control, and she wouldn't cede it.

She took stock of the situation. Jezebel was pulsing with malice. The jealous rage she directed at Mila was nearly all-consuming. Mila also knew that Culis, even if he was indeed just playing the role of besotted fiancé and wanted to help, was in no position tonight to save her. If he'd seen Jezebel drag her away from the crowd there was little he could have done to intervene. He was as trapped as Mila was when it came to letting Jezebel have her way.

Trying to keep her fear at bay, Mila decided she had nothing to lose by answering the question truthfully. In fact, she realised, it could bode well for her if Jezebel could again be convinced that she was infatuated with Jahan rather than Culis. A tactic she'd once tried all those months ago when she'd first been caught in Jezebel's angry, jealous crosshairs.

"I'm trying to find Jahan, Highness. I did not see him with your retinue when you arrived."

Jezebel looked down at her silently for a long moment, and then a slow smile began to spread across her beautiful face. "He's gone."

"Gone?" Mila fished, letting her power explode out of her to read the Princess's next words as deeply as she possibly could.

"Dead," Jezebel crowed. "I had him killed for his treason."

All those painful months Mila had spent fine-tuning herself to the minutia of the Princess's energy paid off.

Jezebel was lying.

Jahan was definitely alive.

Her heart soared. Now that she knew this, Mila was even more determined to find him.

"You had him killed?" She repeated Jezebel's words back to her, feigning anguish. "For being seen with me?"

"In case it wasn't already clear," Jezebel hissed. "Let me spell it out. I know my betrothed needs you alive for his current ambitions, but as soon as I get even the tiniest whiff that you're dispensable, you'll be joining him. If I see any of my staff sparing you similar sympathies, they will not be spared either."

Mila let the sadness she felt show on her face. *Let Jezebel believe it is for Jahan.*

She did, and noted it with cruel delight.

"Has that upset you, demon? Well now that won't do." Her tone suddenly sickly sweet. "I can't have anyone unhappy on the eve of my housewarming." Jezebel pulled a small vial from her pocket. As she unstoppered it, Mila realised that the interrogation about her actions tonight had just been circumstantial. The Princess had always planned to pull her aside, to do something terrible to her tonight.

"What is that?" Mila asked, trembling now, unable to help it.

"It's just a little bit of seducci," Jezebel said with a leer, pushing Mila up against the wall and holding the bottle to her lips. "Something to ensure you have a wonderful evening, and ensure you get all the attention you desire." In sudden panic, Mila racked her brain to see if she'd heard the name of the potion before. She hadn't. What was it? She knew without a doubt that she should not imbibe this mystery tonic, but she also knew she would not be permitted to refuse.

"Drink up," Jezebel ordered.

"Please don't make –" Jezebel didn't wait to hear the end of Mila's plea. She took advantage of her open mouth, catching her jaw with her strong hand and holding it open as she poured the seducci in. Then, she tilted Mila's head up to ensure she swallowed it.

The tonic was delicious. It slid easily down Mila's throat like oiled honey, and quickly nestled into her empty stomach, then spread swiftly up, shooting a pleasant, tingling heat straight into her head.

"There," Jezebel said with a smile. "That's better, isn't it? Tell me you feel better."

"I feel better." Mila agreed, and realised, with horror, that the words hadn't come from her own volition. Whatever this seducci was she could feel its grip, its influence overriding her brain, seducing it away from its own faculties.

"Good. Now spin around ten times."

Mila instantly obeyed. As she did so she rifled through her mind, looking for the thing that was doing this to her, trying to find something to fight. But there was nothing. Nothing to latch on to, nothing that registered as foreign in her brain that she could try to unhook or push out. The seducci had taken her mind and simply made it not her own. Had imprisoned her ability to override orders somewhere.

"You didn't need to do this," she croaked, clasping at her head once she finished spinning. "I would have obeyed you anyway."

"Oh, I know, demon," Jezebel leaned forward and kissed her. The press of her lips was surprisingly soft. The smell of her vanilla and lavendile perfume was strong. "But this one is not for me," she whispered. "It's for you. Now go. Have a marvellous night. Put a smile on your face and tell every man you come across that you want their special attention. Tell them...tell them that you offer yourself up as a housewarming gift and that you'd be happy and willing to do whatever they order," she smiled again, before adding, "and I mean, *whatever* they order."

No.

"Oh. And you're not to tell anyone what I've done to you either. Just go out there and have the happiest night of your life. Go on now."

Mila's mind railed for one second against the order, but then all resistance and fear vanished. Her traitorous face lit up into an obedient smile and her feet turned her around as a huge load suddenly lifted from her shoulders. Why wouldn't she want to go back into the throng of people waiting for her in the hall? She was having the happiest night of her life!

She waltzed into the hall, humming a little in delight, and scanned the room.

It was beautiful, so beautiful, with greenery and statues and gold everywhere. She couldn't remember why she'd been so unhappy earlier. Who could be unhappy here, surrounded by all this beauty? By all these people? It was the happiest night of her life! Tears came to her eyes. How odd. Why was she crying? It must be from joy. Where were the servers? Where were the musicians? She wanted a drink, then she wanted a dance.

Something in her drove her to walk away from the men she saw. She wasn't sure why but there was an inkling lurking within her that she'd have a better night if she found a woman to dance with. She steered herself towards a female figure she recognised.

Someone safe.

What a strange thought, she observed, then pushed it aside and continued walking towards the woman. It was Nemecca.

"Mila!" The lovely tall blonde was clearly happy to see her. "How are you?" Mila laughed delightedly, seized her hands and spun her around. "Nemecca! Come get a drink with me, and then let's have a dance. This is the happiest night of my life!"

Help me.

Her mind wouldn't let her think the words, but they still existed in her. Somewhere.

Nemecca grinned back.

"Oh? Did you and Jezebel make peace?"

"Jezebel?" Mila was confused. What did she have to do with anything? "Why would I care about her? I'm having the happiest night of my life."

Nemecca leaned forward with a frown now and studied her. "Mila, are you drunk?"

"I'm having the happiest night of my life!"

"So, you've said." Nemecca seized Mila's wrist, all frivolity now gone. "Come with me, you jolly little thing." Mila happily obeyed and followed. She barely noticed Nemecca calling out to someone else to join them as she trotted behind the tall warrior woman. To her surprise, they left the party and went outside. A shock of cold air hit her. It was freezing. Why had they come here? No matter. There was still joy to be found in freezing to death.

"Now." Nemecca turned to her, her face coated in concern. "Are you still having the best night of your life?"

Mila opened her mouth to tell her that she indeed was, when the second person joined them, closing the door as they stepped out into the cold. It was Arran, Culis's spy master.

"Arran!" Mila was overjoyed to see him, and also, strangely terrified.

"'lo Mila." He turned to Nemecca with a raised brow. "What's up?"

"This." Nemecca replied grimly and gestured at Mila who began to speak without knowing how her mouth even formed the words. "I'd be honoured to have your special attention tonight, Arran. To be your housewarming gift, if you'll have me."

Arran and Nemecca's jaws dropped. Mila simpered. "I'd be happy and willing to do whatever you want." She leaned in close to his ear. "*Anything.*" She meant it. Sincerely meant it. She also felt vaguely nauseous. Strange.

Arran turned his head and brought her face close to his. Mila closed her eyes, expecting him to kiss her.

"Open your eyes," he ordered and she did so. He studied her intently for a long moment then sighed.

"Mila," he said. "Clap your hands three times and tell me how much you love the God-King."

Mila clapped. "The God-King is illustrious. The God-King is wise. The God-King is – "

"Alrig' enough," he ordered, and Mila's mouth clamped shut.

"What's happened to her?" Nemecca asked.

"Seems like seducci," Arran replied.

"What?"

"Compulsion tonic. We use it sometimes in interrogations. Bu' basically, Mila's been drugged. Seems she'd been ordered to 'ave a wonderful night and also...what was it, Mila?"

"I'll do anything you want, no matter how depraved," Mila said with a beaming grin.

Nemecca swore, then sighed. "I'm sensing the Princess's mind behind this one."

"I reckon yer right," Arran agreed. "It's okay. It's pretty easy ter counter. We can jus' take 'er down to the kitchen an' I'll crush up some rue bark."

"You sure?" Nemecca asked. "That'll help?"

"Should do. I don' know 'ow much Mila's been given but, we'll figure it out."

Mila skipped merrily along behind them as they led her to the kitchen, and sat obediently on a stool while Arran crushed rue bark in a mortar and pestle. Nemecca watched on in concern. When the concoction was ready, Mila opened her mouth willingly and slurped it down.

She coughed, it was bitter and tangy.

"All of it." Arran ordered.

"I don't need any more." Mila bit back, and then sharply registered that she was arguing with an order – her faculties had returned. "I'm back!" she announced in relief, but the feeling was short-lived. One instant later, the weight of every stress and worry she usually carried came crashing back down.

"And," Nemecca said grimly, "I'll assume that you're actually not having the best night of your life."

"No," Mila said slowly. "Not in the slightest." She heaved a deep breath and tried to take stock of what had just happened, what could have *nearly* happened.

"Jezebel?" Nemecca asked, wanting her suspicions confirmed.

"Who else?" Mila sighed. "Thank god I came directly to you. What if I'd bumped into one of Jezebel's men first..."

"It was a clumsy application of the potion, at best." Arran explained. "'er orders were prob'ly vague and incomplete. There would 'ave remained a part of your free will that knew to avoid men, and even though you were told to be 'appy, you still knew to look for 'elp. If an expert practitioner 'ad been administering the order, you'd 'ave suffered a far worse evening."

Mila looked at him carefully. Fellow ikarei or not, she still wasn't sure she entirely liked Arran. "Have... have you done that to others?" she asked.

"Used seducci to humiliate my enemies?" he gave her a stern look. "Nah. But I've used it to make folk want to tell me wha' they know. It's a far more effective interrogation stra'egy than torture. But, seducci is pretty rare to come by, and expensive to ge' your 'ands on. So nah, don't really use it much."

"Well...thank you. For curing me." She turned back to Nemecca with a big sigh. "And thank you for realising something was amiss."

Nemecca pulled her into an unexpected hug. Her arms were warm and strong. For a moment, Mila felt like a small child in the embrace of a big sister. It made her want to cry and unexpectedly miss her own little sister – someone she hadn't allowed herself to think about in years.

"Of course." Nemecca released her, then looked her up and down with a teasing smile. "I know you well enough by now to know you're pretty much miserable all the time, especially whenever you're not frolicking through a dense, leech-infested rainforest."

"Hey!" Mila protested. "I'm not miserable all the time."

"Sorry. When you're around Culis is also the exception."

Mila punched her arm. Nemecca didn't even flinch.

"And you're weak too," she mocked playfully. "Weak and miserable. Of course, I knew something was up when you were swinging me around and telling me how happy you were."

Mila laughed, but there was also something true about the statement that rankled. A note that rang irritatingly true.

"Thank you," she said to them both again. "I...I might just go to bed now, if you think that'll be fine?" she cast a look at Arran who shrugged.

"Should be. You'll prob'ly 'ave a 'eadache when you wake up, but that's about all you need to be worried abou' so far as aftereffects and all tha'."

The two of them left the kitchen and Mila remained on the stool for a few minutes longer, alone.

If she could put aside the rage she felt about the seducci and the way it had essentially made her a docile little puppet, she could appreciate that tonight had been a relative success. She'd learned something big from Jezebel and it was important that she consolidate it now that her mind was her own again.

Jahan wasn't dead. Not yet, at least.

But Jezebel's staff certainly thought he was, and Jezebel wanted her to believe he was. Why? If it was torture, why not just say as much?

Surely, Jezebel would know that the idea of Jahan being tortured somewhere would hurt and upset Mila equally as much? Why lie?

She stood up as she pondered the mystery, and in the process disturbed the grey house cat who'd been licking at a pan of grease. He perked his ears in her direction and hissed in vague discomfort at what, to him, must have been disembodied shuffling in his kitchen. A consistent phenomenon for him ever since Mila had become a permanent resident of the house, but one he still hadn't quite accepted.

She reached for the door handle to her room that was adjoined to the kitchen and let herself in, closing it behind her in relief.

Darkness. Solitude. Blessed silence.

Still pondering this question, she moved towards her bed, stripped out of her clothes and put on her nightslip. Then, as she turned back towards the bed she caught a glint of light from the back corner. She yelped when she realised someone was in the room, lying in wait for her, on her bed none the less.

"Surely the little demon isn't afraid of the dark?" A soft chuckle. The taunting, soft velvet voice instantly made the hairs on the back of her neck stand upright and a small fire alight in her belly. "Get over here. We don't have long."

It was, of course, Christopher Culis.

Forbidden Things

"Culis!" Mila was suddenly hyper aware that she wore nothing but a thin, nearly translucent slip of a dress. She reached self-consciously for her warm gown, which hung from a set of deer antlers on her wall, and threw it over her shoulders, covering herself quickly. "What are you doing here? If Jezebel knew..."

"I know." He sat up, his playful expression turning serious in the moonbeam that threaded through her window. "I can't stay long. But I had to see you. Had to give you this."

She looked down at his outstretched palm and gasped when she saw what lay cradled in it.

He was holding out the sister stone. The object she'd nearly raided his study for just two nights ago. It glinted black and silver in the moonlight that shone through her window. Mila reached out a trembling hand to take it. It felt both light and heavy in her palm.

"Why?" she asked, turning it over as she inspected the item. It was a powerful, unassuming little thing. The memory of when she'd been taken by Frank far away from the stone, and how the necklace around her neck had responded to that distance, nearly killing her with its weight, was not easily forgotten.

"Jezebel knows about the power of the necklace and the stone," Culis explained. "She asked me how I was preventing you from running away."

"So, you can't take it off me." Mila concluded.

Culis sighed heavily and closed his eyes in regret. "I can't. Especially not now with her living amongst us." His eyes flew open again. "But I can't leave you to her mercy either. I don't know how she, or my father, might try to use that necklace against you, but if you have the stone in your possession, at least you will be somewhat protected. Keep it safe and secret at all costs."

"What about you?" she asked breathlessly, unable to believe she was finally holding the mechanism for her escape, that he'd given it to her willingly. "Won't Jezebel want to know where you keep the stone?"

"I replaced it," he said. "I have a pretty pyrite stone wrapped safely in a silk scarf in the top drawer of my desk that will do the trick nicely, especially if you can keep this one discrete."

Mila turned the true vasium rock over and over in her hand. Culis was standing so close she could feel his body heat, but he was carefully not touching her. As though he wasn't sure he was permitted to...didn't dare. She looked up at him.

"Mila." His eyes had lost none of their intensity. "You must know...all of this, this engagement, the slap, the act. It's all to save your life. You know that, don't you? Her jealousy would have had you killed."

"I...do," she lied quietly, then decided in a moment of reckless abandon to be honest. "Actually Culis. I've got no idea what is going on. If you'd have asked me a week ago, maybe I would have had a different answer, but this?" she gestured towards the door and back in the direction of the housewarming. "If it is an act then I wasn't expecting to half believe it myself. I have no idea anymore what's real and what's a lie."

"Little demon." Culis's smile couldn't be contained. "You know I'm a good liar, and whilst I don't *always* lie, when I am lying, and I *tell you* I'm lying...you should trust me."

She knew he was trying to lighten the mood, but she was too sad, too angry at him. She shook her head.

"You're not yet forgiven."

"That's fair enough." He accepted it. "It hasn't been easy for me either."

She was in no mood to hear about how difficult it was for him to bed Jezebel every night. Her voice was cold and stern when she said. "Do you know what she did to me tonight?"

Culis's face turned thunderous. "She touched you?"

"Worse," Mila said bitterly. "She made me a vulnerable, willing plaything for anyone who might have the mind to take advantage." She told him about the seducci and Culis's expression went from dark to murderous.

"But despite all that," she finished with a miserable croak. "Despite the uncertainty of what's true and what's an act, somehow, the worst thing is knowing that you're in her bed. How am I supposed to reconcile myself with that?"

Culis took in everything she was saying with deep seriousness, but at the last his expression became somewhat impish. "Well, I'm...not, actually." He bit his lip, to restrain a laugh, suddenly looking more than half proud of himself.

"What on earth do you mean?" Mila snapped.

"Well, I told her that I've contracted the scrot."

She blinked at him for a full moment then, despite herself, couldn't help the laughter that burst out of her. "The *what*?"

"The scrot." He grinned through the darkness, then tutted, "truly, a terrible disease of the lower half. Makes any kind of *excitement* excruciatingly painful. The only way to cure it is time, and the occasional orange, apparently. Some cases are known to take months to heal."

"*Oranges?*" Mila tried to keep up. "I don't...are you? Is this true?" she blustered.

"You tell me," Culis purred softly, raising an eyebrow and encouraging her to look down and see the very clear evidence that it was not.

Mila felt a deep, mortifying blush take over her face and he chuckled in delight, his eyes savouring every detail of her expression. Eventually he grew serious again.

"The seducci is unacceptable. Your safety can never be in jeopardy while you're in this house. I'll have Odin assigned as your body guard."

Mila considered his words for a moment, then shook her head.

"How's Odin supposed to stop Jezebel doing whatever she wants? Interfering with her whims will just get him killed. No." She took a deep breath. "All I actually need is to know that you have a plan to get rid of her. To end this engagement. I can withstand anything from her for a time if I know there is an end in sight."

"There is a plan," Culis assured her confidently. "It's coming together a little slower than I would like. But it exists."

"Okay..." Mila prompted, waiting for him to elaborate. Culis glanced at his pocket watch and sighed.

"It's complicated, and I don't have time to go through every detail right now. But it involves all the normal things you'd expect. You know...an ambush, decoys, the love of a foreign prince, an abduction, a fake death...Lots of moving parts." Mila blinked dumbly at him for a whole three seconds, trying to process what she'd just heard.

"What?!"

"I told you," Culis shrugged unapologetically. "It's complicated. And step one is getting you as far away from Jezebel as possible to keep you safe while all of that is going on."

"Hang on. No. Wait," Mila interrupted, realising something important. "You can't send me away." If she was sent away to some remote, isolated little village to escape Jezebel while Culis deconstructed his engagement, how would she ever find Jahan?

"What do you mean?"

"I need to find Jahan."

"Jahan?" Culis's previously expressive face became carefully neutral now. "The guard?"

"He didn't arrive with Jezebel's retinue. I'm afraid he was punished after the Dusk Ball. I need to find him."

Culis released a long, slow controlled breath. "Let me get this straight. You won't let me assign Odin to you, and you won't accept being sent away for your own safety. You want to stay here and torture yourself, watching me pretend to be in love with Jezebel, because you need to find Jahan and ensure his welfare?"

"Yes," she said firmly.

"Okay," Culis accepted it, nodding simply. "I don't like it, but we can make it work. And I will have my team help you. We're already looking for Natalee, it can't be too much extra effort to include Jahan in that search."

"You're looking for Natalee?" Mila demanded, suddenly wary. "Why?"

"Of course we are. To ensure she's safe," he replied, but Mila felt a flicker of worry in her gut. Natalee's freedom and the threat that she would spread the word about how she was treated by Culis, was the man's worst nightmare. If it got out it would be a reputational disaster.

He might have been able to smooth things over with Tarett and Marie in private, but if Natalee went public and started telling every ikarei she could find about what had happened to her, Culis's dream of the demon trade would be killed.

Was his motivation to find Natalee sincere? Or was she just an escaped asset that needed to be contained?

Culis seemed unaware of the sudden shift in Mila's demeanour.

"Once Jahan is found, you're going away, somewhere far away from Jezebel until this is sorted. Agreed?"

"Agreed." Mila extended her hand, determined to read him and ensure he was being truthful about his intentions with Natalee. Culis beamed as he reached out and shook it.

He was.

In fact, to her great surprise, he was being truthful about everything. There was not an ounce of calculation or deception in his energy, it was the reassurance she'd been desperately needing. Her shoulders relaxed. The feel of his warm palm and hard callouses wrapped around her hand sent a jolt of hot, white fire to her gut.

"And in the meantime," he said softly, not releasing her, "while you must remain around us, observing my pretence, here's what I'll do: whenever you're unsure of the intent behind my words or actions, watch my hands. When I put one finger to my lips, like this" – he demonstrated with the index finger on his free hand, gesturing as though he were absentmindedly scratching his lip – "I'm saying, I miss you."

Mila smiled, relaxing further, sensing where this was going.

"Whenever I put two fingers up" – he held his index and middle finger to his lips, brushing them with the lightest kiss as he passed his hand swiftly from left to right – "I'm asking if you are okay. And whenever I do this" – he reached up and adjusted his collar, then finished the motion by smoothing his hand down over his heart – "it means, whatever is happening, whatever you think you're seeing, regardless of what looks true…I'm yours, please don't doubt it." His energy flared, matching his words.

I'm yours, I'm yours, I'm yours.

He ate up her smile with his eyes, then he simply breathed, "Mila."

And there it was. The desperation that lay just beneath the surface reared up. Her name rasped in his throat like a rusty hinge, and Mila felt the gravity of it reverberate through her bones. With it came a yearning vulnerability that bombarded her through their touch. Not lust. Something more. Culis thrummed with a desire that ran deeper than the core of the earth, the hunger of a man who had wanted to give his love to something, someone, his whole life, but had never been allowed to. Not without conditions. There had always been conditions…

Before she knew what she was doing, she stood on her toes and placed her lips to his. He did not hesitate, responding so instantly that, for a moment, she wondered if she'd indeed moved first.

He drew her deeply against the hard planes of his body, one hand clasping her hair to the nape of her neck, the other locked around her waist, pulling her into him as though he could fuse their bodies together. His mouth was soft but commanding. He worked her lips open, and she readily submitted to the insistence, gasping as his tongue delved deep, claiming her as his own, devouring her. Mila felt heat roar through her entire body, from fingertip to the burning furnace between her legs. *Oh…this was…*

"Culis," she gasped into his mouth, losing her ability to think, to rationalise. This was dangerous, she tried to remind herself. Jezebel would notice their dual absence any moment. It would all come crashing down. She'd be killed. He'd be killed.

She could not pull herself away. She drank him down like he was water and she an arid plain, desperate to be consumed by him but...she could not. Not here. Not like this. Every second they stole away like this was another second of risk, another second closer to mutually assured destruction.

And yet.

Ultimately, it was Culis, his energy pulsing with regret who finally tore himself away. He chuckled faintly at the disappointed sigh that escaped her.

"Don't worry, little demon," he whispered against her lips, cradling her face. "The plan is coming together and when it does, we'll have our moment. Many times over."

"Is that a threat or a promise?" Mila whispered back.

"Both." His eyes glittered with amusement and desire. His usual aristocratic poise suddenly cast aside, shattered and dishevelled, laid to waste before her, by her.

"When?" she demanded, raking her fingers up through his hair. It was the golden question. When would they be free of Jezebel? "Why can't the plan come now?"

"The *plan,*" Culis's eyebrow raised playfully, "has to wait. And will come when I'm ready for it to come." There was a dark tease to his words as he ran his hands from her face and down her back, her bottom. Her whole body was now humming with need.

"Is that so?" she played back, a little breathlessly. "Well, when that happens, just know, *this* plan," she indicated to herself, "won't come quietly."

"Oh," his smirk was evil as one hand rolled forward and gently traced over that hot space between her legs. "I'm counting on it."

Her stomach nearly exploded in flames.

"I have to go." His voice was hoarse, his breathing now ragged, his eyes gleaming like expensive green jewels. He regretfully withdrew his hand and became serious once again. "I promise, I will find time and space to give you all the details. I will find a way to make this better. Please, just...trust me."

I want to.

"Go," was all Mila could say, her body already feeling cold and empty without his connection, and Culis obediently departed, but not before stealing one last, comparatively chaste, kiss.

After the door closed behind him, Mila slumped with a heavy sigh onto her bed and groaned. Her body still felt like it was on fire. This was torture.

I will find a way to make this better, he'd said, but what he hadn't said spoke louder. He hadn't said, *I have a plan to stop the wedding*, or even, *this is a mess, let's escape this place together*. Christopher Culis worked in the grey chasm between expectations and Mila suspected that, for all his talk about ambushes and foreign princes, the cold hard truth of the matter was that Jezebel had him under lock and key, and this faux engagement had secured the shackles.

I will find a way to make this better, he'd said, and he'd been close enough that she'd sensed it was the truth. But what did it *actually* mean for her? Did he think he could somehow make Mila's life under Jezebel's thumb bearable? Perhaps he wanted to send Mila away and live two lives bouncing back and forth between the two women? A merchant prince could certainly justify travelling constantly and long stretches of time away from home. A man like Culis could easily juggle two separate lives, especially ones that were unfolding an ocean apart. What evidence did she truly have that he had had become less self-serving since knowing her?

Trust me, he'd all but pleaded with her. *I'm yours,* his energy screamed.

But...only hers?

She turned the sister stone over in her hand.

There might be no way out of this for him, but maybe...maybe there is now one for me.

With a flash of understanding, Mila realised that Culis wasn't just protecting her by giving her the stone. He had knowingly given her the key, the option to leave. With it, there was nothing physically tethering her to this place, to him, anymore. If she wanted to, she could leave tonight, head to Traders Bay, and find someone to remove the necklace for good.

Keras.

The option to flee to that faraway nation, where ikarei were not thought of as demons, but as the children of gods, was now truly within her grasp. To go to the land where someone might be able to explain to her what the hell had happened to her on the night the assassins had attacked, the night her power had *morphed* into...into something else. She shuddered and pushed away the memory of how it'd felt to suck the energy from another living being. It was too complicated to deal with tonight. Tonight she had to decide what to do: trust Culis, or take the key and find her own freedom?

Still sizzling with adrenaline from the kiss, Mila found that this conundrum made her restless. She stood up, pacing back and forth around her room, imagining what she'd pack and take with her if she were to leave now, to have that kiss be their last. Their unknowing goodbye. Perhaps it was better like this.

Please trust me.

He'd known what he was doing when he'd handed her the sister stone. Knew she'd come to this decision tonight. Could she stay, even if it was just for a little while longer? Give him a chance to elaborate on what he'd meant by 'make this better'? Give him the chance to truly prove himself worthy of her trust?

And Jahan.

If she left now, she'd never know what happened to him. If he was imprisoned somewhere she'd never be able to help him. She owed him at least an attempt to find out if he was safe.

What about bringing down the Church? Saving the other ikarei? The call to take on such a momentous task had been in the back of her mind since the Dusk Ball, uncomfortable in its insistence. The secret of the rubane was heavy and could not be denied. It'd been just over a week since she'd acquired the fresh knowledge that it could block Midas's powers. Midas was not a god. Midas was an ikarei. Someone needed to do something with that information. Someone needed to expose Midas, to bring the Church crashing down, and unfortunately, the list of candidates available and willing to take on such a venture was short.

There was only her.

Exhaustion crashed into her like a wave. It had been a huge night. She lay back on the bed again, sighing once more under the burden of what was quickly becoming apparent. Whether or not she decided to trust Culis's plan, escaping to Keras right now was not an option for her. Not while Jahan was missing. Not while Midas still reigned and Abbott continued to slaughter ikarei in his name. Not while the people of Artor remained content to sit back and let it all happen, while good people like her family were happy to give up their beloved little girls to the glittering hands of death in the name of their religion. As much as she hated to admit it, it seemed there were bigger, more important things to worry about than whether or not Culis was truly capable of turning over a new leaf.

Seems as though I'm choosing to stay, at least for a little while longer.

She looked down at the sister stone in her hand and turned it over between her fingers again. Then she sat up, reached over to her coverlet and tore a small square of fabric free. She wrapped the stone in it and closed it up with a knot of twine. She cut another length of twine and twisted it into a longer strand, one she wrapped around her neck. Now the small parcel that held the sister stone bumped gently against her sternum. It was a reassurance she didn't know she'd been missing until now. The necklace that was welded to itself around her neck seemed to hum with delight at being so close to its counterpart.

She lay back down and closed her eyes.

Just before she fell asleep, it came to her.

In that sacred moment between one's last conscious thought and the mysterious, irresistible call of the dark kingdom of slumber, something big loomed up in the back of Mila's mind. It felt familiar in a way, as though it had been lurking there for some time and was now choosing this moment to reveal itself. A shadow version of herself perhaps, as constant, yet distant, as the dark side of the moon. The thing, the presence, whatever it was, brought with it a deep sense of foreboding. It felt so strong and real that it was almost like a premonition – a knowing that, one day, she'd look back at this moment, when all doors had been open to her, and she'd regret not leaving.

She shuddered, and despite her exhaustion, she could only fall asleep by clenching the sister stone tightly in her hand.

The Makings of Midas

The God-King Midas didn't often dream.

When he did, it was in the dying weeks of the passing season, when his anticipation for the upcoming Sacrament grew and his body began to ache and beg for the release of his power. In those weeks, sleep came to him like a shy kitten; slowly, cautiously, tauntingly elusive. When he managed to catch it, it still always felt as though he was perched on the cliff's edge of his consciousness, braced, waiting to be tipped over into wakefulness again. The dreams were exhausting and, on this night in particular, in the shallow prison of his unconscious mind, the images that flashed behind his eyes were more memory than dream.

Golden sand.

His home hadn't always been sand.

Once it had been a large rainforest island, and the background tapestry of his childhood memories had been green, not gold. Full of ancient trees that reached to the heavens while still cascading thousands of brown roots down from their branches in a waterfall display of terrestrial dominance.

There once had been a house, a roof that his mother had tried desperately to raise him and his siblings under, a bed he'd shared with his brother and sister, a mouldy wooden wardrobe she'd pushed him, Talbot and Alice into when their father's constant, crushing shadow of disappointment reared its head and transformed into violence.

He remembered the devastating artwork of purple and black against his mother's skin, bruises that were always present, always in varying stages of greening. He remembered other things too. Nicer things. The smell of hot fog in the mornings, the way the dripping humidity poured from the fat leaves of the ground plants, no matter the time of year. He remembered how, across the inlet, he could see large green mountains rising up in the distance. Kings, giants, gods, shrouded in mist, forming a wall between the mainland, the ocean and the island where his family lived.

It had been a good life as a child. He'd been shielded by his mother and brother from the worst of Father's rages, and he and his siblings had spent most of their days exploring what felt like their personal island kingdom. The beach was a constant source of washed-up mainland treasures. Rusted metals that could be bent and shaped into crowns and swords, floating cargo crates with all manner of secrets still trapped inside. Once, a sunken ship's torn flag found its way into Aidas's private collection. These treasures gave Aidas everything he could possibly desire by way of entertainment, and the towering forest behind the breach provided the gift of great danger, a superb opportunity for a young boy to prove his mettle.

There were other families with children on the island, but they had little to do with any of them except Merry, a skinny, dark-haired young thing, who just turned up one day and stuck to his younger sister Alice like dogwood sap.

Together, the four of them spent their childhood years combing the beaches and forests under the canopy of grey, hazy skies and dripping green leaves. Learning about one another and the world around them so intimately that, at times, their bond felt more pack than human.

Tight knit and territorial.

Talbot always led the group, and Midas – or Aidas, as he'd been known back then – didn't mind. Despite the fact they'd always been competitors, as different to one another as water is to stone, he'd always looked up to his older brother.

As they entered their latter years of childhood, their differences were only emphasised. Talbot was hard-edged and thin-lipped. Fair and skinny. Far more like their father than their mother – a comparison he'd never liked, but especially hated after he became too big to hide in the cupboard anymore. Aidas had been a far softer child. Always with a far darker complexion, dark eyes, dark hair. And tall. Very, very tall. His height could have been intimidating if he hadn't been so quick to laugh, to create, to be carried away by his imagination and entice the other children in the gang to follow suit. Aidas was always the one to lead them all into mischief, and Talbot was often the one to step up and take the punishment.

Aidas was content to let him.

When Aidas's thirteenth summer arrived, everything changed. He awoke one morning to find horns growing from his head, and everything he touched shone more brilliantly, as though a beam of sunlight was striking it directly – even in the dead of night. Their father had been ecstatic.

Another ikarei in his family, he'd rejoiced. Another superior being like himself.

And just like that, the family beatings ceased. There was no more rage, no more disappointment. He was a changed man. For a time, Aidas's father now sat at the dinner table with them, smiling contentedly, staring into the middle ground, as though the night air and fireflies that mobbed them were vaguely amusing. He'd join the boys on the rocks as they fished, his horns casting shadows on the sand behind him, laughing from his belly as the grey waves hit the rocks and spat droplets of water onto his face. He twirled their mother about the cabin, making her giggle and laugh with delight.

"You did it after all," Aidas heard him whisper to her as he kissed her cheeks over and over. "You gave me one."

A bat screeched in the night and roused Midas from his shallow sleep. He cursed at it before rolling to his side, pummelling his pillow into another shape. It didn't help. His body ached, no matter which way he lay, no matter how comfortable the bed.

In desperation, he crawled out from beneath his canopy and laid on the smooth tiled floor. It was far harder, but the coolness of the terracotta against his overheated skin was a blessing.

Please, he beseeched his exhausted brain. *Sleep.*

Another memory (or dream?) accosted him. This one far more recent.

Lexia.

Never far from his mind.

Coy, smart, tantalising Lexia.

She who had loved his anger and his rage, for it matched her own. They were a pair, a mirror to one another. Unique in their fierce fury towards life. Both tangled in their need to inflict their pain and disap-

pointment on others. Lexia, who demanded he unsheathe his rage on her whenever they tousled in the silken sheets of his parlour.

He could never hit her though. Not in the way she wanted him to.

Lexia who had birthed his child, Lexia who never scolded him, but taught him to laugh in the face of criticism and taught his ego to fear no ridicule.

Lexia, who had loved and trusted him so wholly that she'd accidentally orchestrated her own demise. He remembered vividly the way she'd tied his gloved hands above his head with her silken scarf, rubbed her perfect, svelte form over his body, ready for him, always ready despite birthing their child only a few months earlier.

Her curtain of thick, black curls had draped over his face as she'd leaned in close and whispered, "I want to hold your hands in mine," and then, without warning, slid her thin fingers under the lip of his gloves and inside them.

It happened so fast that Midas had barely had time to cry out "No!" before she was gone and he was left alone, in a haze of horror, unsated lust and the shimmer of nothing but golden sand...

He rose.

There would be no sleep tonight.

The Compass and the Conundrum

Find Jahan.

Mila woke to find the demand whirling around her head like an incessant fly.

Find Jahan.

It was a simple enough statement. Harder indeed to execute. Made harder still by the unfortunate arrival of the storm cloud that was Frank Culis to the manor that morning.

The original serving staff of Culis Manor tried to avoid him as much as possible. The new staff, those who had just arrived as part of Jezebel's retinue, learned the hard way that Culis Senior was not a man to be trifled with.

On this particular morning, he seemed to be in a far worse mood than Mila had ever seen him. She was sitting with Tarett and Marie in the kitchen when they heard the sound of a whip cracking in the hallway and a serving girl's cry of pain.

Tarett and Marie looked shocked and grimaced in unison in the direction of the sound. Mila kept her head down, remembering that Frank Culis had put considerable effort into wooing them on his first meeting with them. Today, perhaps, they'd see his true colours.

"He seems...angry today," Tarett ventured.

"He is," Petrie the cook muttered, handing Mila a bowl of flour to sift. "He didn't receive an invite to the event this year."

"The event?"

"The housewarming last night," Petrie explained. "That spectacle wasn't just for the Princess's benefit, even if she tried to make it appear so. We hold a housewarming every year at the start of winter. An age-old tradition of turning Culis Manor into 'Winterhaven'. For a few months."

"Oh, really?" Marie said, leaning forward to accept another bowl full of eggs that required beating.

"Of course! The heavy lifting to prepare the building for winter will start today."

"Heavy lifting?" Tarett asked warily.

"Well, for example, the tender plants that can't survive a heavy frost must be brought inside. The maids will buy hundreds of tall candles and affix them to every wall and corner. You'll see. Not a single corner of the house will be permitted to be dark and droll. And around the candles, they'll arrange pretty things like...oh, I dunno. Ornately painted animal bones, golden bells, decorative candies...anything and everything they can find."

"You'll all be required to help with the firewood," Tess chimed in merrily, her forearms taut with strain as she kneaded a huge lump of dough. "The giant fireplaces around the manor will now be kept burning all day and night, and it's the kitchen staff's job to monitor them. Oh, and even without the Princess's court here, there would have been plenty more folk around than usual, children too, because the workers who are usually housed in the workers' quarters on the property are now invited to stay in the northern wing, and bring their families with them on the very cold evenings."

Mila was shocked by the generosity. "This happens every year?"

Petrie nodded, stirring the biggest pot Mila had ever seen him use. A cauldron. "It's been the way ever since Master Culis came of age. More people means more food, too," the cook added in response to her pointed stare at the pot. "It's only sensible that we transition to more stews, soups and stroganoffs."

"What's a stroganoff?"

"You've never heard of stroganoff?"

"No?"

"Heathen!" Petrie threw his hands up at the ceiling in mock outrage.

"Heretic," Mila risked the cheeky correction.

"Both," he rolled his eyes. "And you're missing the point. It doesn't matter exactly what a stroganoff is. What matters is that the dishes are hearty, warm and go a long way amongst many mouths."

"And delicious with some fragrant rice and crusty bread," Tess interjected. "Oh! And Tarett?" She turned to the young man with a sweet smile. "I'll be needing your help on the entertainment committee."

"The what?" Tarett looked like he didn't know whether to be excited or apprehensive.

"Well, as the sun rises later and sets earlier," Tess explained, "the dark nights of winter are long, and with so many more people within these walls, Master Culis tasks us with finding ways to entertain the household. So, myself, Hannah, Bola, and Quentin are on the committee. And we come up with some great events. Card tournaments, darts competitions, puppet making...all things that are still in line with the Behaviours, of course. No festivity." She added the last as an afterthought, as though she had been scrutinised about the particulars of these 'entertainments' before and was forgetting she was speaking to demons.

It was wilful ignorance, Mila thought. This whole 'Winterhaven' thing was heresy. A winter festival that directly contravened the Second Heretical Behaviour, the one that forbade festivity, revelry or celebrations of any kind. Culis had been getting away with it for years because he disguised it as preparing the house for winter and his servants had gone along with it willingly because it directly made their lives more pleasant and easier during the harder months.

He'd always been a bit of a heretic, Mila smiled to herself.

"So much effort," Marie marvelled.

"Yes," Tess agreed cheerfully. "It's the perfect recipe to make the place feel homely and cosy, even in such droll weather and a crowded environment."

A concerted effort, Mila realised, made by Culis, to both protect the welfare of the staff who worked for him, and replicate all the life, heat and sunlight that were about to be sucked away from the outside world by the change of season. More evidence, she thought, as to why his people liked him so much.

Their pleasant conversation was ruined by Frank's voice punching angrily down the hallway. His words were muffled, but the irate tone was obvious.

"Well," Mila said brusquely. "I, for one, am glad Frank wasn't present last night."

"So am I." Petrie chuckled and then went out into the garden to fetch some more rosemayne. Tess followed him.

Temporarily alone, Mila turned back to Tarett and Marie.

"So, Jahan..." Tarett kept his voice low. It wasn't that they didn't trust Petrie and Tess. It just seemed safer to not involve them in these types of conversations, for everyone's sake. "Neither of us could get a peep out of anyone at the party yesterday, but you don't think he's dead. You think Jezebel is lying?"

"I could *tell* she was lying," Mila corrected. "I'm certain of it. I'm just not sure why she would lie. If he's being held by her somewhere, surely she'd relish the opportunity to gloat."

"What if..." Marie suggested in her soft, high voice, "she doesn't actually know where he is?"

The longer Mila dwelled on this, the more certain she became that Marie was onto something.

"He might have left. He might have gotten out..."

That would certainly give Jezebel good reason to lie. She'd never want to admit such a thing to anyone, let alone to Mila, that her longest serving, most trusted guard had abandoned her. Of course she'd lie. Of course she'd convey to the rest of her staff that something terrible had been done to him.

She doesn't know where he is. She doesn't have him. Mila's chest lightened at the thought of Jahan living free somewhere.

He got out.

Mila turned to Marie with a big smile. "I think you might be right."

"Excellent," Tarett said swiftly. "So we don't need to stage a rescue mission? That makes life much easier. Especially as we know how well the last one you attempted went for you. Tell me, how is Natalee these days?"

Mila flushed at the barb, a reminder that, while they both seemed inclined to forgive her for her deception, they certainly weren't about to let her forget about it any time soon.

"I'm not sure where she is either," she admitted. "But Culis assured me that so far as his spies know, she got away unharmed."

“Well that's reassuring” Tarett said. “Because we care about where she is too, right? About what’s become of her?”

“Of course.” Mila said sharply, hurt by the implication. “As if I wouldn’t be.”

“Just checking that you’ve decided your ikarei friendships still warrant the same amount of effort as your human ones.” Tarett said cuttingly before he turned away. Mila bit down on her lips and held in her retort.

Despite yesterday, despite being willing to help her find Jahan, they were both still angry with her and she couldn’t do anything more than she already had to appease that anger. She’d apologised. She’d tried to make amends. All she could do now was wait. and hope time could mend the rift between them.

It was bearable. Mila far preferred the undercurrent of tension to carrying the weight of a dirty secret.

Time was on her side though. Tarett and Marie wouldn’t be able to stay angry at her forever. They all needed one another these days. With Jezebel’s household now amongst them, friendships and alliances within the old network were more important than ever, and both Tarett and Marie would recognise that.

In one of her efforts to extend the olive branch and earn back Tarett’s trust, Mila had brought him in on the secret of the rubane and the fact it could block the power of Midas’s touch. She’d hesitated to tell Marie, only because Marie had become far too close to Arran – and despite his help the previous evening, Mila was all but certain that, at this point in time, to tell a secret to Marie was to tell Arran, and to tell Arran was to certainly tell Culis. Despite all her complicated feelings for the man, she wasn’t quite sure she wanted him knowing about the rubane's ability. That felt like a secret about ikarei and should only be known by ikarei.

She was brought out of her reverie by another yell and whip crack in the hallway, followed by the sound of smashing crockery.

Frank.

She sighed. His presence was another blight in a household already filled with too many shadows.

She didn't want to think about Frank. She needed something good, something invigorating to think about. Something enlivening.

The plan, *her* plan. The one that would see Midas and the Church brought to their knees.

"I'll get the firewood," Mila offered and slid from the bench to commence the long walk out to the forest. She wanted thinking space, and she did *not* want to run into Frank.

"Be our guest!" Tess said enthusiastically. "You'll get sick of that soon enough. It's constant. Back and forth from the woods. You don't appreciate quite how much a fireplace can burn through until you're on firewood duty."

"I'll be okay," Mila said confidently. "I need the exercise."

"I'll come with you," Tarett offered.

"And I'll go see if Arran needs help today." Marie said. "Let's catch up at lunch."

***

It was dusk and Mila was alone in the courtyard, carrying her last armful of wood. Her arms ached, but it was a good ache. The ache of well-used muscles and the innate pleasure of using one's body to accomplish a satisfying task. Tarett had kept her company until lunch, but had moved onto kitchen chores in the afternoon. Mila hadn't minded at all. Solitude was something she was used to, and it'd given her plenty of time to think.

She was going to sabotage the Spring Sacrament.

It would take a bit of planning, and probably some help, but she'd broken the ambitious mission down into key tasks, and for the time being, that seemed like enough of a start that she felt thoroughly invigorated.

This was going to happen. She was going to bring down the Church.

First, she'd have to collect enough rubane to infuse at least four buckets of oil. Enough for each of the impending sacrifices to douse themselves thoroughly because she had no way of knowing who'd be offered up to Midas's touch first. Then, she'd need to get the infused oil to the ikarei, which meant she'd have to somehow break into the palace dungeon and access them on the day of the Sacrament.

Finally, she needed to make sure that there was an audience. If Midas's touch failed in private then there was every chance that Abbott, with his inexplicable hatred for ikarei, would simply order them killed by the sword and pretend nothing had ever happened. She knew that Abbott had seen the way Midas's touch had failed at the Dusk Ball – so she knew his continued obedience wasn't simply rooted in belief. There was something more to it. So there needed to be an audience to witness Midas's power failing on a grand scale because ultimately, it'd be that audience who would spread the word of what they'd seen.

If she could do these three things before the Sacrament, this plan would work.

She was mulling this over and beginning to fine tune some of the details when Frank cornered her.

He loomed out of a dark crevasse in the side of the building with a timing and expectancy that told her he'd been lying in wait.

An ambush.

"You might be the answer," he said softly. No greeting. No acknowledgment of their past. He saw her as nothing but chattel and made no secret of it.

Mila felt a cold shiver trill down her spine. She *hated* this man.

"All day, I have wrestled with an unsolvable problem." His piercing green eyes raked over her body. They always made her want to recoil. The opposite effect of his son's. "But now..."

"Leave me alone." She tried to sidestep him, but he blocked her.

"I cannot."

"What do you mean you *cannot*?" she bit at him scathingly. "You despise me."

"They're not mutually exclusive things, I'm afraid," he sneered. "I don't have to like you to need you."

For a moment, Mila considered throwing her bundle of wood at him and using that as a distraction to flee. It would buy her a moment of time, but where would she go? Back out onto the manor grounds? Into the darkness alone, with Frank Culis chasing her? No, at least here she was close enough to the manor that light spilled out from the tall windows and illuminated them. With light there was always the possibility of witnesses.

She drew a deep breath and found her courage. "What do you want, Frank?"

She could have never, in a thousand years, predicted his answer.

"I have an opportunity to offer you, demon. If you succeed, then you'll prove your value and usefulness to me so much it'll make it worth my while to see you continue living unharmed for as long as possible."

Mila waited for the axe to fall.

"I want to employ you. I want you to use your power for me."

If Mila hadn't been holding herself so tightly in check, her jaw would have hit the cobblestones. "On who, and why?" she replied curtly, proud of the unyielding tone she managed to fire back at him.

"On my son," Frank answered quietly. "Because I think he is going to kill me."

Deal with the Devil

Silence hung between them like a noose for a long, long moment. "Explain," Mila finally demanded.

Frank didn't hesitate. "I acquired this cursed thing on my recent trip." He drew out a battered-looking square object from his pocket.

"Acquired it? You bought it?"

"I stole it," Frank snarled. "My need was greater than its previous owner's."

"I don't think that's quite how a moral compass works, Frank," Mila said, forcing out a scathing laugh, trying her very best to appear unafraid of him.

"Very funny," he sneered. "This compass is special. It was made in Keras, by a zoi of great power. Its magic points the needle towards the person who will be responsible for the holder's downfall."

"I find it interesting that you'll readily associate with zoi," she shot at him, "but remain very happy to persecute me as a demon."

Frank merrily grinned at her outrage. "When in Keras," he shrugged, infuriatingly.

His words stoked the smouldering anger that was never far below the surface. The rage she felt at the injustice constantly perpetrated by Midas, the Church and their entire twisted operation. She also considered the implication of what it meant that a device such as the compass even existed. She'd never known an ikarei who could imbue their power into an object. If 'zoi' was simply another term for ikarei, then she didn't believe such a thing to even be possible.

"What exactly do you mean by downfall?" she asked.

"That's just the question, isn't it?" Frank gave her a grim, close-lipped smile. "And, ultimately, however you define it, the fact remains that whenever I hold this infernal thing, the needle points directly at my son. He will be the one responsible for my downfall. He wants full control of the company, and the only conceivable way he can achieve that would be to orchestrate my death."

"You think...you think he'd kill you?" Mila grappled with the idea without success. "Why?"

"Because he's marrying Jezebel, who he hates." Frank's eyes were wide. "Without informing me prior! Without consulting or sharing a single snippet of reason or logic! I've demanded answers, and all he does is insist it's because he loves her." Frank sneered at the word. "He's lying. He's posturing to be prince consort." He spat the title with derision. "How *boring*. False power. Life as an emblem and little else. And eternally betrothed to that brat? It makes no sense. None at all." He held up a long, white finger. "Not unless it was all about the long game. The game to seize control of the company."

Mila blinked at him incredulously

"It's obvious," Frank snapped. "Even if you're too stupid to see it. This engagement rigmarole is only to deflect suspicion away from when he eventually comes after *me*."

"When...when..." Mila spluttered. "When has it ever seemed like...like that is something he wants to do?"

"Well, I certainly don't think Martin's death was an accident." The implication was clear.

"I don't..." Mila wondered how to formulate her response. She was so shocked by what she was hearing that her brain was struggling to form full sentences. She didn't think that Culis had killed his brother, or that he would ever try to kill Frank, but she wasn't sure if she should tell Frank any of this. She finally settled on saying, "I think your son has more pertinent things currently on his mind than orchestrating your downfall."

"*Currently* is the key word in that sentence," Frank replied ominously, and that was when Mila realised there was something different about his eyes.

She studied them and noticed, as he spoke, that his gaze seemed to slip in and out of focus, that his hard, wide stare didn't correspond to the other twitches of expression on his face. There was a detachment to it somehow. A disassociation that chilled her.

"The compass doesn't give time frames," he continued. "It could be in a year, or it could be in ten years' time that he turns his ambitious gaze towards me and decides to remove me."

"He's going to inherit anyway, isn't he?"

"Perhaps." Frank gave a shrug. "But if current trends prevail, there's every chance that I'll decide to outlive him."

He didn't want to be talked out of this idea, she realised. This delusion the compass had planted in his mind had taken root, and while Mila acknowledged that there was at least a small possibility that Culis might try to dethrone his father at *some* point in time, the idea that he would ever *kill* him? Highly unlikely. They had a complicated relationship, to say the least, but she knew that, deep down, Culis loved his father.

"And this compass, it definitely points to him?" she tried again.

"I'm certain of it. I've tried every room in this house, every angle, surrounded by all manner of people. It always points directly at him."

"Well, what do you want me to do about it?" she asked.

"What I want – " he took a deep breath, then said with an unexpected flash of vulnerability crossing his face, " – what I *need* is for you to monitor his energy with your power, and alert me when it becomes ambitious or unsavoury towards me. So I can make...preparations."

"So you can kill him first," Mila guessed. She felt a chill down her spine when Frank did not confirm or deny.

"Preparations is all I'll say." His eyes were still too wide, too hard. "If we can catch the plot early enough, in its infancy, I might be able to confront him and shepherd away any danger before it matures into a true threat. But I can't make these plans if I don't know how he feels about me, and acting too soon could easily be a misstep that acts as the catalyst. I'm not a fool. But this is why I need *you*."

"You want me to spy for you," Mila clarified, and contained a shiver when Frank nodded. She could barely believe the next words were about to come out of her mouth.

"Why should you trust me to do this? You know I despise you, and this task...it could go on for decades. Not to mention, you're asking me to betray someone I...someone I care about."

"I don't trust you," Frank agreed. "But I trust that your sense of self-preservation is strong. Do this well for me and you'll be securing your safety for the rest of your life". The way he was dangling safety made her feel like a fish staring at poison bait on a rusty hook. "I go to great efforts to keep my spies alive," he continued, "and I have powerful sway with the elites in Artor. You won't be sacrificed anytime soon if you're my spy. And you wouldn't be betraying him," Mila recognised the greasy, placating tone that now entered his words. A true snake oil merchant. "You'd be *helping* him." Frank said, then added. "Always remember this. If I can't find a way to keep this threat in check, I'll simply have it removed."

Removed. Mila knew exactly what he meant by that word.

"He's your son!" she exclaimed quietly.

"I can always make more." Frank replied with a shrug.

"Urgh." Mila was truly disgusted. "You are...vile," she spat the words at him.

"I'm also alive," Frank said, unperturbed at her outrage. "Despite many attempts over the years to achieve the contrary. So...if you're finished being appalled, tell me. What's your answer?"

Pretending to go along with him was the only way she could keep Culis, and herself, safe. She wished she could read his energy to determine the right course to steer this conversation, but in the fuzzy absence of those answers, she instead carefully watched his strange and frighteningly intense face.

As she opened her mouth to reply, she saw something else flash across his expression that gave her pause. Powers or no powers, she knew that look.

He was expecting her to lie.

She changed tact. Something she'd learned from watching Culis in his negotiations was to never let someone bully you into giving a direct answer when you didn't want to give one.

"You're asking a lot from me," she said. "It'll require almost constant work on my part. I'll need to read his energy with nuance in almost every interaction I have with him. My powers won't be able to tell me something specific such as, '*I'm angry at my father and want to overthrow him.*' The only way this will work is if I monitor him with my power constantly, and if I feel a general sense of anger or ambition coming from him, I would then have to utilise our trusted relationship to determine the cause. Not to mention that I have to find an inconspicuous way to report this all back to you. It's a lifetime of work for me, so if I agree, my return price is high."

"Name it," Frank replied. His face was still hard, but his suspicion temporarily defused. He might actually believe her answer now.

"I want the full might of the Artor Trading Company available to me, once a year, for any task or favour of my choosing."

She saw Frank's throat bob as he swallowed hard. It was an enormous request. She knew he wouldn't accept it. *Couldn't.* He would have to justify unjustifiable journeys and potentially put the future of the company at risk to appease Mila's demand.

"No," he finally said. "Not the whole company."

"This isn't a negotiation," Mila said coolly, trying to force her face to mimic the way Culis's face sometimes appeared when a negotiation was souring. Hard and unyielding eyes, a flat mouth.

"The whole purpose of this discussion is for me to *save* my company," Frank protested. "I can't promise it away to you, to use on whatever whim you think is worthy. What I can offer you is..." He took a deep breath, "is me. You have full access to my power, influence, contacts and efforts for one favour every year, for the rest of my life. No questions asked."

Mila hadn't expected that.

For a moment she considered the power and influence she'd be able to wield by having Frank working for her just as surely as she was working for him. It was tempting. She pretended to think long and hard about it. "Deal," she finally said. "And my first favour starts now – "

"Wait," Frank interrupted. "How will you report back? We cannot be seen to be colluding, and Christopher certainly can't suspect you are spying for me. It'll negate the whole purpose. He has to trust you implicitly."

"I'll write you an unsigned letter," Mila said. "Once every six months. And I'll hide it in the stables in the top left-hand corner. The one under the angry magbill's nest."

"Once a month," Frank countered. "Mailed to me directly."

"Once every three, and you get swooped every time you come here to retrieve it. That's my final offer."

Frank mulled it over then said, "Deal," and stuck out his hand.

Mila took it. It wasn't often that she was given the opportunity to touch Frank Culis and read his energy. The family resistance to her power was eternally fascinating and frustrating.

His grip hurt and his energy struck her like a bat, determined and bullish. Underneath that, though, Mila could sense a creeping shadow of fear and paranoia. And something else. Something that revolted her power and made her want to shrink away, like rancid milk. Something unhealthy had grown in Frank since she'd last touched him. A seed of madness perhaps. She released him quickly.

"Now," she said. "My favour."

"Yes," he said, his tone abruptly switching. "I'm indeed curious to know what the demon who hates me so bitterly could possibly need me for."

"I need you to track someone down for me. I want to know their whereabouts."

"Oh?" He looked intrigued. "Who is it?"

"He's a former guard of Jezebel's. Tall, very muscular, cropped brown hair, one eye, tanned skin."

"Ah, I know the man, Jahan Batu, Abbott's foster."

"Abbott's *what*?" Mila couldn't believe what she was hearing, and although she didn't want to give Frank an ounce more information than she needed to, she couldn't hide her surprise. "His foster?"

"Yes." She watched him note her unexpected interest and mentally file it away for future use. "I was visiting the palace on the day the priest brought him in. Abbott and I were talking. He said he'd found him somewhere up north and believed he'd make a good acolyte. It stuck with me. It was an unusual thing for Abbott to do. I like to make a habit of noting when people act out of character, you see, and back in those days Abbott was far more inclined to set his feet on fire in the city square or flog himself bloody to demonstrate his convictions. Not really the nurturing type. The fact that he'd ventured out to the Highlands and brought back a little boy to care for...well. I found it odd, to say the least."

The Highlands?

She wracked her brain and tried to remember what Jahan had told her about his childhood on the night of the Dusk Ball.

I was taken from my mother young and raised as an acolyte in the Church.

He'd never mentioned that it was Abbott who'd taken him, or that he'd come from the Highlands. He'd said his mother had come from the Village of Truth. Where was that? Surely not in the Highlands – Mila would know about it. Had he lied to her? What else didn't she know about him?

Probably quite a bit.

"Well, I'd like to know where he is," she said, trying and probably failing to contain that this information was a huge revelation to her. "He saved me multiple times when I was living at the palace. I'd like to ensure he's safe."

"Consider it done," Frank said. He stepped away from her, indicating that the conversation was drawing to a close. "And I'll look forward to reading your winter summary about my son's innermost workings."

"Yes," Mila said, feeling a little ill at the idea, despite the fact she had no intention of actually betraying Culis in this way.

Frank nodded briskly. "One other thing," he said, his voice now falsely light.

Mila's suspicion flared, and she watched cautiously as he held out his hand towards her, the compass nestled securely in his palm.

"Do you want to hold it?"

Mila eyed the thing like it was a poison chalice. It screamed danger, and yet she couldn't deny the intrigue that surrounded it. Her mind swirled irrepressibly with questions.

Where had it come from? Did she want to hold it? Did she want to know the person who would be responsible for her downfall? What if it pointed to Frank Culis or Jezebel? She already knew they were threats. Would the compass just reinforce the fear she already felt around them? What if it didn't point to either of them? What if it spun around aimlessly, then pointed in an ambiguous direction? What if it pointed at a friend? The person responsible for her downfall could be miles, countries, years away. Holding this compass would not give her any answers or closure. It would only add to the list of things weighing on her mind.

Yet still...tempting.

"No," she finally said, with effort.

"Wise girl." He gave a grim smile and then the gravel crunched beneath his boots as he turned and disappeared back into the beckoning warm light of the manor.

Mila was left standing alone in the cold. She considered everything that had just transpired with a deep, bracing breath. When the dark curtain of night finally fell and forced her inside, she left the courtyard with the distinct, unsettling feeling that she'd just made a deal with the devil.

The Engagement Party

"Mmm, a tattoo I think." Jezebel's smile was the jaws of a closing trap. "On your forehead. One that reads, 'I displeased the Princess Jezebel.' That should help your future memory."

The serving girl could not have been more than fifteen. Her pretty face was fresh and unblemished, promising great beauty to come. Her watery eyes could not hold back the dam that burst at the Princess's words.

"Oh, fates no, *please*!" she sobbed. Her knees buckled out from under her at the horror of such a threat. "I'll do anything."

"Anything except serve my breakfast at a suitable temperature apparently!" Jezebel hissed, throwing the porridge against the wall. The white crockery bowl smashed into ten pieces. "Sort out your staff, Cook, or you'll all receive the brand! I don't usually give warnings. Consider this my first and last one for you all."

The kitchen door slammed shut behind her but then abruptly reopened as she poked her head back in. "And I want a fresh batch of oranges delivered upstairs. Immediately!"

The door slammed again, and she was gone.

The kitchen staff released a collective breath at her absence, and Tess moved to comfort the serving girl.

Petrie turned back to the huge pot of porridge he'd been stirring. "No wonder you were a shell of a thing when you arrived here," he said quietly to Mila, who'd been leaning back and hiding behind the protruding fireplace. Any mere glimpse of her made Jezebel irate, even on a good day, so she made a special effort to hide herself when the Princess was in a bad mood.

Today was Jezebel's engagement party, although in an effort to at least try and pretend they weren't directly disobeying the Second Behaviour yet again, it had been formally dubbed, A Solemn and Respectful Observance of the Princess's Future Union.

Despite the fact that the day was all about her, Jezebel was in an especially sour mood because she'd been obliged to invite the people she hated the most – her friends – to come to Culis Manor and celebrate. Midas would not be attending, not would Abbott.

Mila had been hoping to avoid the party altogether and hide away for the day. Her heart sank when she found out that Jezebel had specifically demanded her attendance. In fact, when Tess appeared at her door later that morning and broke the news, Mila had frozen in fear. She now knew, all too well, what having Jezebel's special attention at a social function meant for her. She couldn't stop her fingers from trembling as she donned the ridiculous outfit that Tess had insisted they were all required to wear. It was an extravagant white serving dress, styled to look like snow, with long, pillowing skirts and short sleeves. Entirely impractical for both their duties and the weather.

Wonderful.

A few hours later, from her secret vantage point in Culis's library, Mila watched the elites of Artorian society arrive at the manor. The theme of the event was 'White and Gold', and everyone had seemingly gone to extensive lengths to meet it. Mila was astounded by the creativity, but none looked more extravagant than Jezebel, who always refused to be outdone, but most especially at her own Solemn and Respectful Observance.

She was wearing a dress that was, for all intents and purposes, an icicle. Somehow, over a sheer, skin-tight slip, Jezebel had managed to freeze ice into a perfect cast over her body. She must have been freezing but Mila begrudgingly appreciated that she refused to show an ounce of discomfort, smiling broadly and twittering with Culis gleefully once the guests began to arrive. In fact, perched together on the threshold of their magnificent house, Jezebel and Culis looked every inch the picture of the perfect couple in love. They greeted each and every guest by name, Culis with his arm around Jezebel's waist, despite how cold the ice must have made his hand, and hers clutching possessively at his chest.

"Eliza! So nice to see you." Mila could hear Jezebel's insincerity even through the glass. "Lady Meredith. Welcome."

Mila deliberately held back from reaching out with her power to read the guests. Her day was bound to be difficult enough without exposing herself to their toxic energy.

When all the guests had arrived and the party started in earnest, Mila couldn't justify her absence any longer. She descended the stairs warily and tried to make herself as small as possible as she joined the other servers, in what was bound to be a marathon of a day.

Despite her apprehension for the event, Mila couldn't help but admit that the household staff had done good work to make the manor look incredible. Not only was Winterhaven now in full swing, but the back courtyard had been transformed into a decadent winter garden, with ice sculptures and lights in every corner and a hedge maze that had been imported from across the country. A strip of lawn had been set aside for a game called skaldi. It involved throwing an ornate stick into a pile of skittles. The number carved into the side of each skittle was akin to the number of points received by the thrower of the stick. The aim was to get as close to twenty-one points as possible, but any throw in which the total sum went over twenty-one would result in a score of zero. It was simple enough but elicited fierce competition from the guests and dominated the activity of the afternoon.

The day was long, cold and windy, and despite her best efforts to avoid them, Mila still found herself unwillingly bombarded by the energies of the fools and sycophants who surrounded the Princess. Worse still, she had to watch Culis dote on Jezebel and endure her simpering back at him.

Christopher Culis was, to any observer, by all accounts, a man deeply in love.

Every time Mila glanced over at him, his eyes appeared to be firmly glued to his fiancée. He attended to her every need swiftly and would not let anyone but him serve her. Her drink was constantly topped, his hand constantly on her waist. He laughed at her jokes and twirled her around the ice sculptures.

Watching them together caused a shadow to form in Mila's already heavy heart, and the pinpricks of doubt and distrust that always seemed to lurk in the background began to rise in her mind.

What if he decides he wants to be a prince? What if he decides he actually likes this life?

Then, without looking, but as if he felt the power of her gaze and the nature of her silent worry, Mila watched as Culis reached up and adjusted his collar, then let this hand drift down and caress his heart. It was such a deliberate motion. A message, meant only for her. Mila felt a knot of tension in her stomach loosen slightly.

I'm yours. Whatever you see, whatever else is happening. Remember, I'm yours.

Mila moved around with the other servers, balancing a silver tray with six pewters of hot, syrupy alcohol that smelt like cinnamon apples. She tried to blend into the background and was successful for a short time, particularly when the game of skaldi became vigorous. For a moment it seemed that Jezebel had forgotten her original demand that Mila be in attendance all together.

Mila's mistake was getting drawn into the game.

She couldn't help but edge closer to watch Culis toss the stick into the skittles with a well-balanced hand. She grimaced as his teammate, Jezebel, cheered him on. She noted begrudgingly that for all their differences the two were well-matched when it came to this game. They were both competitive and very physically capable. Paired as a team, they dominated the competition and won many of the rounds. This moved Jezebel's mood from happy to outright triumphant, and as the alcohol began to take hold, she reached new levels of obnoxiousness. She flung herself around the courtyard jubilantly and to Mila's horror, caught her eye as she stood quietly by one of the ice sculptures nearby.

"Demon! Attend me!" Her shrill cry cut through the chatter of the gathered guests like the nick of paper against skin. Mila's blood ran cold at the threat of promise in it.

She hadn't been forgotten after all.

"Highness." Mila weaved her way through the crowd towards Jezebel, her stomach plummeting with every step.

The Princess's cold eyes fixated on her face as she approached, like an arrow on its target. The ensuing smile was equally as devoid of any real happiness. Just cunning and expectation.

Mila cast her gaze about, searching for a shield.

Culis, for all the shadowing he'd been doing of Jezebel all day, was suddenly, inexplicably, nowhere to be seen, as if he'd chosen that very moment to relieve himself or, and perhaps more likely, Jezebel had chosen the very moment of his absence as her chance to summon Mila. She must have known, deep down, that Culis would not suffer Mila's torture. It had to be done in his absence.

Despite the courage she tried to muster, Mila felt herself begin to tremble. Jezebel saw it. Her smile widened.

"Good to know I can still make you shiver, demon," she taunted. "It does seem to me that you're entirely too comfortable here otherwise."

She surveyed Mila who stood, head bowed before her, dressed in the white, plump, ridiculous snowball gown she'd been commanded into. She seemed to be waiting for an answer but Mila refused to speak. This, like most of the situations Jezebel put her in, was a trap. To admit she was happy would warrant punishment, to say she was unhappy could be just the excuse Jezebel needed to send her some place worse. Silence was the only safe refuge.

Around them, the party buzzed on. Those closest tossed the occasional curious glance in their direction, but it suddenly seemed like Mila and Jezebel were in their own bubble.

Jezebel noticed it too.

"And how was your evening on the seducci, demon?" she probed. "I didn't see you lurking around much after that."

Mila still chose silence.

"The lesson is always the same." Jezebel's eyes were glittering, delightedly assuming the worst had occurred. "Don't cross me. Don't betray me, and don't, for even one second, forget that you are still on borrowed time because of my mercy."

Mila's cheeks began to hurt from the way she was biting down hard on them.

"Do you ever miss me, demon?" The unexpected question caused Mila to look up at her sharply and shoot her power deep into the Princess. Jezebel's eyes were glinting, but her energy wasn't quite what Mila had expected it to be. Jezebel exuded very little hatred today, and instead, was a complicated mix of envy and hurt.

Hurt?

There'd been a time, Mila remembered, that Jezebel had relied on her, confided in her. Was it possible...did she miss that...connection?

"I..." Mila again had no idea how to answer the question.

"Don't." Jezebel cut her off. "Don't lie. It's fine. I know you don't, you ungrateful brat. I know you're determined to think only the worst of me." The hurt in her energy swelled. Mila couldn't have been more shocked to hear Jezebel's next words. "I know we've had our run-ins. But it truly pains me that you've never looked back and appreciated the many times I saved your life. I fed you, I let you sleep by my bed, on a soft cushion. I kept you alive and safe and healthy and all you'll ever consider me is vain and cruel. It's quite unfair really."

The unpredictability of Jezebel never ceased to catch Mila off guard. The Princess had gone from mocking her about the seducci, to feeling genuinely hurt that Mila didn't like her, all within the space of a second. "You...you kept me as a pleasure pet," Mila challenged quietly. "And cut out the eye of the guard who was kind to me."

She never expected her words to land with Jezebel, and was surprised when she sensed a tinge of regret enter the woman's energy. It never showed on her face though, or in her words.

"You're a demon," she hissed. "I can do whatever I want to you, without recourse, and all I ask is that you're grateful that I didn't, and still haven't, had you killed."

"Of course." Mila dropped to all fours and bowed her head, sensing that her subservience was exactly what Jezebel's satisfaction required.

"I am grateful, immeasurably. Thank you, Highness." The words tasted bitter leaving her mouth, but Mila's pride wasn't above doing what she needed to do to stay alive. She was powerless against Jezebel.

Or was she?

For the first time ever, Mila wondered what would happen if she got Jezebel alone again, in a safe, quiet place. Could she use her new power on her as she'd used it on the assassin? Drain her of her hatred, her malice? Would there be anything of her left?

She pushed the thought away. She had no idea how that unexpected version of her power worked, or how to summon it again. It hadn't emerged since that night with the assassin. Sometimes she tried to convince herself that she'd imagined the whole thing.

But she knew that wasn't true. The euphoria that had followed could not have been imagined, and it had hung around for two days afterwards. Strong and pulsing and irresistible. It had made Mila feel invincible.

She could use some of that feeling now. She felt utterly vulnerable and alone, kneeling at Jezebel's feet.

"Get up," Jezebel ordered, and when Mila stood again, Jezebel reached for her chin. Mila let her, trying not to flinch away as the nails dug in, she knew they'd leave tiny half moon imprints in her skin. The energy had shifted again. Hard. Dangerous.

Oh no.

"I had plans for you at this party, demon. Plans you would most definitely not enjoy."

Where was Culis? Where was anyone who would intervene? A distraction, anything. Someone to come save her...

"I have no seducci remaining, unfortunately, but I had intended to order you to perform a foot cleaning service for all my guests today."

Mila remembered with horror the last 'foot cleaning' she'd been required to give at Jezebel's behest and didn't respond. She didn't need to. Jezebel's gaze was inches from her own. She'd be able to see the fear, the hate.

"Let it be known, demon." Jezebel's voice was like ice. "That I could do this, and more to you, and not a soul in the world, not even my sweet, protective Culis, could stop me." Her words were a sneer again, her energy terrifying. Mila felt the ice of the Princess's dress pushing into her, making her already freezing skin even colder. She felt the cold clamp of despair rush in and take her. With Jezebel in the house, this was forever to be her fate. Humiliated and degraded for the woman's pleasure.

Then, utterly unexpectedly, Jezebel's energy shifted yet again. Something else rose up within the Princess. Something Mila had never sensed in her before.

Restraint.

"But," Jezebel said softly, contemplatively, more to herself than Mila now. "I won't."

"Why not?" Mila's voice was barely a croak, she didn't know where the courage to speak had come from, but apparently it still existed somewhere. "Why not have your fun?"

"Because," Jezebel released her and stepped back abruptly as if Mila were toxic. She surveyed Mila up and down with a hard eye, then turned away, now bored. "I'm trying something new." She stalked away without a second glance and Mila's legs gave way. She fell, trembling to the ground.

Mila felt ill.

Enough of this.

As soon as she was able to move again, Mila slunk away from the party. She hoisted her ridiculous skirts and tried to suck in deep breaths as she ran. Desperately trying, and failing, to hold back tears. She was overwhelmed.

The fear, the threats. Jezebel. *Culis.*

She retreated to the kitchen and was relieved to find it blissfully, mercifully empty.

Stepping into the warm, quiet room after a day of enduring blustering cold wind and the indolent, self-absorbed chatter of the party guests was like stepping into a lover's embrace. She let the warmth wash through her and sucked in a deep breath before letting out a huge sigh. She crossed the room and sank down on one of the benches, her silly dress ballooning around her, up to her shoulders. She did, indeed, feel like she was trapped in a snowbank with this thing on.

I'm trying something new, Jezebel had said.

What did that mean? Was she planning something far worse than what she'd threatened? Worse than the seducci? Or perhaps she meant she'd decided not to indulge those base, cruel fantasies? Was being in love with Culis changing her? Was that even possible?

Mila got up and ladled herself a glass of warm mead that had been simmering in the cauldron over the fire and drank deeply. She wasn't usually a big drinker, as it affected her ability to keep her power under control, but this afternoon, of all days, she needed it.

As Mila finished her third big sip, she heard a small click sound across the room and raised her head towards the sound.

"Any left for me?" The exhaustion on Culis's face was evident as he stumbled into the kitchen towards her. Her heart squeezed at the sight of him.

"You shouldn't be here."

"No one's coming," he assured her, and reached for his own glass.

She ladled the mead out for him, and he took a deep, bracing swallow, steadying himself against the table as he swayed a little.

"Are you drunk?" she asked, astonished. She'd never seen him drunk before.

"Did you expect me to get through this spectacle sober?" he tried to make a joke of it, but his exhaustion showed. Mila realised then the toll that this play-acting was costing him. She gestured for them both to sit at the wide kitchen table that stood beside her.

"How did you get away?"

"Jezebel decided to give a horseback tour of the grounds to her guests. There weren't enough horses for all, so I gave mine up. We have time."

A long silence sat between them after that. Eventually Mila broke it, her voice quiet and sad.

"I'm beginning to think I overestimated my ability to endure this. Perhaps I do need to leave."

Culis nodded at her words, deeply serious. "Can you bear it for just one more week? I'll organise for us to go away to Traders Bay for business. We'll get some space. We'll be alone. I'll be able to fill you in on the details of the plan."

"So there really is a plan?"

"Of course there's a plan! I told you there was a plan!"

"The plan sounded...made up!" Culis couldn't help but chuckle a bit at that.

"Mila, the plan is already in motion. It's just... it's slower, more considered than my usual style."

"Why?" she demanded.

"Because," he replied, a little frustrated now. "Because for the first time that I can remember, I actually give a damn about the outcome!" He tried to stay calm, but whether it was the alcohol or something else, all it took was another glance at her for his next words to spill out, seemingly of their own accord. "Mila. I may have lost this particular battle to Jezebel, but I'll be damned if I lose the war."

"The Culis I knew from a month or two ago," she said softly, "would have simply told me to perk up and put on a good show for the Princess, perhaps to go prepare for our next demon hunts. The Culis I knew would have tried to convince me that he'd be better able to protect me if he" – her voice cracked – "if he were Prince." He flinched slightly at the picture she painted. Then he nodded slowly in agreement.

"Perhaps you're right, and perhaps he wouldn't have been wrong." Mila held her breath and waited for him to continue. When he spoke again his voice was clear and certain.

"That man has been outgrown. I've no use for him anymore."

"Oh?"

"It's very simple." His eyes burned hard into her. "I've never met someone more fearless and intelligent and determinedly themselves in my entire life. You're a demon, you're a woman, you make me laugh, you challenge me, you're loyal, you're conniving... you even smashed an assassin's face in with a saucepan for me. I've told you once before and I'll say it every day for the rest of my life if that's what it takes for you to understand – you're perfect for me. I'll do whatever it takes to have you. You've also done me the great favour of making it quite apparent what you will and will not accept from me. You want me to be different when it comes to matters of power and status. To be kinder, less self serving. I understand. I'm trying. I'm not saying I'll be perfect or that I'll find it easy, but I think you can safely consider me to be... very motivated to want to be different. For once."

As if to put the seal on his words, he reached out across the table and ran the back of his fingers along the side of her face. Through that touch, her power found his energy swiftly, and the world suddenly softened, narrowed.

It was all focused on her. All of him.

Despite the nature of the day and everything Mila had feared about Jezebel's new tactics, this touch revealed his inner truth.

No one existed for him but her.

"So -" her next words were interrupted by voices echoing down the hallways outside the door.

People were coming to the kitchen.

Culis flashed her a look of utter panic as he glanced around the room, looking for somewhere to hide. His anxiety morphed into a fearsome grin when it quickly became evident the only place someone wouldn't be instantly spotted was under her voluptuous dress.

"No."

He quirked an eyebrow at her. "You prefer to be caught together and suffer a lovely, romantic, dual execution?"

"Oh, damn you, go on," she hissed and raised the left side of the fabric enough for him to slide neatly under and nestle between her knees. Mila's breath hitched.

It was not a moment too soon. Petrie, Tess and Tarett burst into the room. Petrie was swearing, Tess and Tarett were laughing. Tarett was holding Tess as she stumbled, and she was clutching greedily at him in return, one arm slung around his neck.

Was everyone drunk except her?

"What's this?" Petrie exclaimed when he saw her. "Sneaking off alone, Mila? Decided to leave early and risk her wrath, did you?"

"Yes. I'd had enough. I just need some peace and quiet." She hoped they'd get the hint and leave the room, anything to give Culis enough time to slip away out the back door.

She could feel the cheek of the man in question, nestled against the inner wall of her right thigh, his hot breath warming her. She jumped a little as she felt his other hand reach up to caress her left thigh, and let out a long breath as he ran a finger along the length of it, skimming tantalisingly close to the centre of her, which sat open and oh so exposed in front of him.

She tried to shut her legs, but his head sat stubbornly between them. And then he placed his palms on either side of the inside of her thighs and parted them even wider.

Oh no.

"I'm not surprised." Infuriatingly, Petrie missed her suggestion completely and, instead of leaving her, he instead ladled himself some of the mead and came and sat directly opposite her in the seat where Culis had been only moments before.

No, go away!

"It's not easy dealing with the likes of *her* in any capacity." There was no question as to who he was referring to. "Let alone the special attention you always seem to receive. She's a beast. I don't know how Master Culis does it."

"I'd say he's in love," Tess said from the side, picking at some left-overs. "I've seen how he looks at her." Mila saw her cast her gaze at Tarett. "Like he's so in love he's having an out-of-body experience."

"I'm about to have an out-of-body experience," Tarett mumbled, suddenly looking very pale and reaching for a spare pot, retching into it. Tess winced and rubbed his back sympathetically.

"You owe me a new pot, demon." Petrie muttered, then continued. "I dunno. It all seems far too soon after that attack to me. I reckon he suspects her of sending those assassins and proposed to her to save his own skin." He turned to face Mila, expecting her to contribute her thoughts – which Mila might have done if she wasn't being *thoroughly distracted* by the man between her legs, whose light stroking on her inner thighs had now securely found and focused on the place that burned hottest between her legs. His finger pushed against the thin, wet fabric of her undergarments with determination, rubbing up and down, over and over.

Fates. Christopher.

"I...uhh...I'm not sure. He hasn't said anything to me about it," Mila managed to get out. "I think he likes difficult women, though." That earned her a pause, a slight reprieve and the sting of a gentle flick of his fingers against the inside of her thigh. She almost chuckled. Almost.

"Well, I hope he has a plan to rectify this disaster," Tess said, pushing back Tarett's fringe from his sweaty face. "It's going to be hell to live here with her otherwise."

Culis's fingers against her soaked underwear were now insistent. In a confused haze of panic and lust, Mila tried to shift her hips to try dislodge him, but he was merciless. His free hand reached out to grasp her thigh, pinning her firmly in place. Escape was impossible.

Fuck.

"Speaking of hell," Petrie stood and moved over to inspect Tarett. The sick demon was still bent over, holding his stomach. The Cook joked, "when are you going to your new household?"

Mila barely heard their conversation. Culis's breath was hot against her skin, her own breathing was becoming ragged, and then she nearly jolted out of her chair as he placed a firm little bite on her inner thigh.

"Beats me." Tarett groaned and accepted Petrie's helping hand, then came and sat at the table. Tess poured him a water and herself some mead then joined them.

Dear fates, no. Can't everyone just leave?

"It was all arranged," Tarett garbled. "So far as I understand. But Culis hasn't pulled the pin yet. I think Marie will be the next to go before I do."

"Hmm." Dimly, Mila recognised that this was good news for her. If Tarett was going to be around for a while longer, then perhaps she could use him to procure all the rubane she'd need to save the demons at the next Sacrament. That seed of an idea began to plant itself in her mind, but was swiftly driven away by the abrupt movement of her undergarments being pushed to one side and Culis's hot mouth pressed against her core.

He was licking her.

Mila gripped her glass and the table for dear life, knowing that her face was reddening, knowing that her breath was hitching, her mouth opening in a way that would surely, *surely* give them away in the next second. But she couldn't help it. Her stomach felt on fire, the heat between her legs was unbearable. Culis's wet, strong tongue was laving against her with desperation. She was building to a release she was not going to be able to withstand, let alone disguise.

"Sweet mercy," she breathed in agony.

"What did you – "

A large crash from the hallway saved them. The unmistakable sound of multiple serving trays hitting the ground at once. Petrie, Tarett and Tess all turned their heads towards the din and jumped to their feet. Two of them ran, one stumbled, out into the hallway to investigate, abandoning their drinks. Mila and Culis were left alone for a moment, but they wouldn't have privacy for long. They needed to move.

"You devil," Mila gasped, panting as she pushed his head away and out from under her skirts. "Are you trying to get us killed?"

"If that was my death sentence, I'll take seconds," he whispered wickedly, then with grim determination he gathered her up and bundled her into her adjoining bedroom, locking the door securely behind them before he all but threw her onto the bed, pried her legs open again, and bowed his head between them, finishing what he'd started.

Mila somehow forced herself to stay silent as her vision went black and stars burst behind her eyes. The orgasm was glorious and left her bones feeling like liquid, but she remained aware, all too aware, that the trio of her friends could come back into the kitchen at any moment and hear the scream she was so desperate to release.

So she held it in, restrained herself, and when she found she could finally breathe again she drew him up to eye level, kissed him and whispered. "I need more. I need you." The orgasm had only stoked the fire that had been smouldering inside her.

He nipped at her neck. "I know," he said between kisses. "So do I. Desperately. But...We will have to wait." He pulled away reproachfully. "I need to return to the party before my absence is missed."

Mila groaned and her body burned. "This is torture."

"No," Culis said with a grin. "This is just a waiting game. Believe me. When I'm torturing you, you'll know it."

He opened her window and regretfully, slipped back out to join the party.

That Damned Compass

Culis moved quickly after that.

The reliable stream of household gossip brought the morning report downstairs to the kitchen while Mila was eating breakfast. It revealed that now the engagement formalities were all concluded, Culis had told Jezebel that he would be leaving to attend to business in Traders Bay that week. The second half of the story came a little later. Apparently, the Princess had surprised everyone by refraining from a tantrum and begrudgingly acknowledging that this was a part of his work.

At mid-morning, formal word was sent that Marie would be required to join Culis on his trip as her buyer had been secured and they'd be conducting the exchange. Mila would also be required to join, as her presence and powers were necessary for some essential meetings that Culis had planned for later in the week. Finally, in the dying stages of the afternoon, Tarett was informed by messenger that he would also be required to join them. Culis apparently intended to introduce him to a number of merchants who ran goods on the black market. It had been less than 24 hours since Culis's promise to Mila, and he'd made good on that word. They were suddenly all set to get out of Culis Manor, and away from Jezebel.

She should have known it was never going to be quite that easy.

Since her unexpected encounter with Culis's tongue the night before, Mila's entire body was captured in a constant, thrumming state of anticipation. She lay in bed that following night achingly hungry and wanting more, like a starving prisoner who'd been fed merely a crust but knew a banquet waited around the corner. She was restless and agitated, and tossed and turned in her small bed all night. Her feelings were only heightened by her eagerness to get on the road and away from Jezebel.

The next morning, Mila was up before the sun with her small bag packed. She wasn't bringing much. One dress and a coat would do. A pen, some paper and her pocketknife that she'd previously purchased from a shop in the city. She didn't actually know how long this trip was meant to go for, but she didn't really have much else.

As she waited for the sun to rise and the servants to prepare the carriage, she paced the kitchen cobbles so determinedly that Petrie joked she'd wear a path in them. She barely heard him. She was so desperate to get away from the Princess and be with Culis alone again that she felt as though she were itching out of her own skin.

And then, one hour before their scheduled departure, the Princess got wind that she was missing out on something.

She met them in the courtyard with her green winter travel coat bunched around her shoulders, and her servant beside her, bowing under the weight of her six large travelling bags.

"My Princess?" Culis was surprised to see her.

"I don't want to be separated from you for a single moment, my love," she cooed and stroked his face in a manner Mila found sickening.

"Are you sure?" he asked. "It's nothing but a few dull business appointments." He tried to keep the tone of persuasion from his voice. Tried to seem nonchalant about whether she came or stayed.

"I've never been more sure," she simpered, and Mila had to turn away, knowing that she'd be unable to disguise the red hot fury burning through her veins.

Culis could not object.

So, with that, the secondary carriage was brought round. Mila and the demons alighted into it, while Culis and Jezebel took seats in the main, and they set off to Traders Bay in a procession, rather than together.

Mila sat in the plush, red velvet seat and seethed.

Was it not enough that Jezebel had *everything* else? Had she really needed to come on this trip too? Had she known what she'd been foiling?

Mila suspected she somehow did.

***

Mila had always found the long carriage ride from Culis Manor to Traders Bay uncomfortable, but she'd never done it in an entirely separate carriage from Culis before, and despite the fact that Tarett and Marie were with her, she couldn't help looking out the window every few minutes, seeing the shadow of the black carriage rolling out in front of them, and feeling the sick jealousy rising in her gut.

Beside her, Marie also sat in stony silence. She was being sent to live with her new household today, and although Mila knew she was looking forward to her new life – serving the manager of the national archives – she was upset because, that morning, Arran had broken off the fledgeling romance that had been budding between them.

"He said it was too far to travel," Marie eventually shared with them, after quietly seething for nearly an hour. "And that his work comes first. He said he wouldn't be able to guarantee time away from his duties to come see me often enough."

Mila both felt sorry for her and relieved that she was away from Arran's influence. She regretted that she'd had to hold Marie at arm's length because of it and hoped that, in time, without the threat of Arran lurking over their shoulders she'd now be able to bring Marie into the same confidence she held with Tarett and Flue.

"I'm sure you'll still see him," Tarett tried to comfort her, wrapping an arm around her shoulder. "Maybe he's simply trying to...manage expectations? Who knows? Sometimes the heart grows fonder with a bit of distance."

"That's often true," Mila agreed, grateful for the distraction from her own heart-sick stomach-ache.

"I'd give him a few weeks." Tarett continued. "During that time, he'll either figure out that he's being a fool or if he really is finished with you. And if it's the latter, well, at least we'll know he's a bit cracked in the head. And Traders Bay is a big place. I'm sure it won't be long before you find someone else wonderful."

Marie nodded, but continued to stare at the carriage floor with a sour expression.

"Oh, and Mila?" Tarett changed the topic. "I nearly forgot. Frank Culis found me this morning and directed me to give you this." He handed her a small package, wrapped in an ornate, orange-and-purple handkerchief.

Mila took it cautiously. She gasped in horror and outrage when the silky fabric fell away in her palm, and she saw what she now inadvertently held.

The compass, that *damned* compass.

She thrust it away, determinedly not looking at the needle. "Take it back!" she cried out.

"What? What is it?" Tarett's brow deeply furrowed.

"It's the compass." She covered it back up in the handkerchief and continued to press it towards Tarett, who did not accept its return.

"What does that mean? What's wrong with it?"

"Frank thinks it shows you the person responsible for your downfall. Take it back."

"Well, why would I want it?" Tarett exclaimed, looking equally as horrified now, still refusing to take back the package she held out to his nose. "He said to give it to you. I don't want it!"

"Oh for the love of the God-King."

"Mila!" Marie chided, horrified. "Do not use his name in vain! Especially not where we might be overheard."

"Overheard by who, Marie?" Mila snapped, at the end of her tether now. "We're in a carriage."

"We're *about* to be in Traders Bay," Marie shot back. "What a stupid habit to decide to start."

Mila bit back a cutting reply and sucked in a deep breath, trying to reestablish calm in the carriage. She reluctantly withdrew her hand, and the compass, from Tarett's face. It was Jezebel and Frank that she was upset with. Snapping at Tarett and Marie was unfair.

"Just keep it somewhere hidden," Tarett suggested. "You don't have to look at it if you don't want to."

Mila laughed bitterly. "Tell me honestly that you don't want to look at it now that you know what it shows," she challenged.

Tarett thought about it for a second, then begrudgingly agreed. "Well, I suppose, now that you mention it, I do. Here, pass it back."

Mila considered it and then to everyone's surprise, said "No."

Tarett's eyes flew up into his hairline. "What do you mean, no?"

"Well, the more I think about it," Mila said slowly, "the more I think this is a trap. There's no proof this compass does what Frank thinks it does. In fact, the only thing I know it does for certain is generate paranoia. What if you hold it and it points to one of us? Would you ever look at us the same?"

Her friends fell silent, considering her words.

Finally, Tarett nodded. "If you're right, why do you think he wanted you to have it?"

"Probably to achieve exactly this. To sow division between us."

"Why would he do that?" Tarett asked again. "Why would he want us not to trust you? Are you plotting my downfall, Mila?" He said it with a laugh, but Mila could sense a seed of burning curiosity beginning to take hold in him.

Perhaps she was giving Frank Culis too much credit, but if this was, indeed, the beginning of an insidious plot by the Culis family patriarch, it was working. The man was a damn snake. If he managed to get Tarett and Marie to ostracise her, then she'd be more isolated than ever. Without friends, and with Jezebel still as unshakeable from Culis's life as a blood sucking leech, Mila would be more reliant on Frank for favours and help in the future. What a bastard.

"Oh, goddammit," she hissed, ignoring Marie's indignant *"Mila!"* as she realised the only way to stop Tarett's curiosity and suspicion from building over time was to risk letting him hold the damn thing.

"Here. Look at it if you must. But promise me you won't take whatever it says to heart."

She held it out again, and Tarett slowly leaned forward and plucked it from her palm. He stared at the face of the compass, his expression unreadable and his energy held tightly in check. He shifted his seat around a few times, facing the back of the carriage and side to side as though needing to be certain of the direction the needle was pointing.

"You were right," he said finally, with a carefree smile and almost a disappointed energy. "Frank did give it to me to try orchestrate this exact dilemma between us."

"What do you mean?" Mila said.

Marie's eyes were saucers as she stared at the two of them.

"Well, the compass does what you suspected it would," Tarett said evenly. "It points at you."

"As in...it says I'm the one who will be responsible for your downfall?"

"Yes."

Mila didn't know what to say, but she was relieved that she felt nothing in his energy shifting against her.

"But now that I've held it, I can tell it's nonsense," he continued. "For starters, how can we know for sure that it does what Frank says it does? What if it just points to the last person who...I dunno...ate an apple or something? And secondly, even if it *does* point to the person responsible for my downfall, well, that in itself is just so subjective, isn't it? What does downfall even mean? And what if it's referring to something in my past? For example, perhaps you *were* responsible for my downfall, because I'm now, in a technical sense, less 'free' than I was before I met you." He shook his head in disdain. "The whole thing is foolish. Frank is a fool if he's letting this affect him."

A fresh wash of relief fell over her and, feeling almost silly about her earlier fear, Mila took the compass back and allowed herself to look at it.

The needle was still pointing at her, and did not waver an inch once it touched her skin.

"Well?" Tarett asked.

"It's still just pointing to me," she revealed.

"Maybe it's broken?" Marie piped up.

"Do you want to hold it?" Mila offered.

But Marie shook her head. "I'm happy in my ignorance, and I'll just assume you're responsible for my downfall too."

For some reason, this made everyone laugh, and diffused the tension between the group.

Mila tucked the compass away in a pocket and was very grateful for Tarett's interpretation of the thing. She felt relieved that she was no longer so disturbed by the object, although it still weighed heavy in her pocket.

The Flying Fanny

It took a few hours but eventually, they arrived at Traders Bay. As they disembarked, Mila, Marie and Tarett all burst into a fit of giggles at the sight of the signage for their first stop: The Flying Fanny.

Jezebel let out a disapproving huff and spun violently on her heels. "I cannot stay here," she said primly. "We need to stay at the royal travelling apartments, Christopher."

"I can't, my love," he replied in a voice that was both sad but firm. "This is how I do business in this city. It's the cornerstone for my success. I stay at different taverns during my travels and mingle with folk of all backgrounds."

"I...well...I also have very important business in the city," she said indignantly. "And my reputation! I cannot be seen staying at this..." She waved her hand in the direction of the shabby establishment to their left.

"Of course not," Culis agreed pragmatically. "You should go stay at the apartments. I will come find you each morning, and we shall break fast together, while the demons move my suitcases and belongings to the next tavern."

"What about the evenings?" she demanded.

Culis shaped his face into a believable look of reproach. "My business is often conducted at night, with talks that bleed into the wee hours. If it finishes early enough, I will come to you. But I cannot promise it."

Jezebel huffed. Unimpressed.

"I'm sorry," he said, giving a believable grimace. "This is why I didn't make plans for you to join us. I didn't think you'd enjoy coming on a business venture with me."

"And *her?*" The look she shot at Mila was so filthy that she had to fight the urge to scrub her arms.

"She's essential for my negotiations," Culis said calmly. "But I brought the other two along to keep her occupied, so she doesn't inconvenience us with her presence a moment more than she has to."

That seemed to mollify Jezebel, who nodded, accepted a kiss and returned to the carriage that took her away from The Flying Fanny's courtyard.

With Jezebel finally gone, Mila released an audible breath and turned to face Culis, who looked as though a large rock had just been rolled off his chest. He smiled broadly at them all.

"Well, now that that's sorted. Come inside all of you. I have organised for you each to have your own room, and Marie, your buyer will be joining us this afternoon."

***

Jezebel's absence changed everything about the trip.

A new lightness fell over the group. Tarett started joking again, Marie whistled as she pulled her luggage up the stairs and Culis finally felt free to look at Mila directly, his eyes bright and sparkling. His gaze and the promise within it made every last particle of her body feel alive.

Would they finally be able to have an evening alone together? Unhurried? Uninterrupted? Unrestrained?

God.

Mila's mouth felt dry at the thought of it. She was *buzzing.*

Not quite as buzzing as the taproom of The Flying Fanny though. As soon as they walked in, the energy of the place bombarded Mila and drew her reluctantly out of her fantasy about what Culis would do to her in the rooms upstairs.

It was so lively, so loud. The floor was so wet and sticky. Perhaps she shouldn't have expected otherwise for a venue with such a name.

Culis took a seat and gestured for Mila to sit in one of the booths nearby while the other two made their own entertainment for the afternoon. Mila didn't mind that she was being asked to work while the other two played. She loved watching him negotiate, even if he had to yell to be heard over the ruckus that emanated from the gambling table where Tarett had decided his time would be best spent. Mila sat in a booth a few yards to the left of Culis, nursing an ale and using her power to read the men and women who visited him throughout the afternoon, communicating with him in their agreed silent language of blinks, finger taps and hair twirling.

Mila watched as one negotiator paid Culis in a handful of pearls before he departed. From her vantage point she saw the gleaming white spheres roll about on the dark oak table, flashing brilliantly against the sunlight. She watched as Culis's quick and sure hands bundled them up and secured them into an oilskin pouch. All except one, which nested securely in a hole in a knot of the wood grain. Culis did not seem concerned that he'd missed it. Instead, Mila watched, transfixed, as he unhurriedly reached out and caressed it, savouring its silky smoothness, then ran his middle finger up, down and around it in slow, languishing circles.

Up, down, round and round and round. Almost as if it was...

Her face burned with heat and a hot vice gripped her insides as she realised what he was doing. She raised her eyes and found him already staring back at her, penetrating, a knowing glint of hard amusement written on his face. Half promise, half threat. Mila's entire body suddenly felt as though it might explode. In that moment, she wanted nothing more than for him to stand up, walk over, bend her over this table and take her – and damn anyone else in the room.

The look in his eyes told her he was considering it.

Just then, Marie's buyer arrived and broke the torturous spell. Mila breathed a devastated sigh of relief. He was a stout, fat man named Barnabus Pricely, who had a kind face and blushing cheeks. With difficulty, Mila turned her focus away from Culis and onto Barnabus. She sensed eagerness and awe from him when he appraised Marie. He seemed like he might be a little overexcited to see how he could use her powers in his employ, but Mila certainly did not pick up anything cruel or unkind from him. And, to everyone's surprise, he informed her she'd be receiving a small stipend for each manuscript she correctly transferred from the mouldy, rotting old scrolls onto the new, fine parchment. It was a small amount, but it was something that Mila and Culis had never even considered – that masters would be willing to offer a wage to their demons.

"The work we do is critically important," Barnabus said in response to their astonished faces. "I know humans work best when there is an incentive to do the job right. I assume demons are much the same."

Marie beamed, very happy with her choice.

***

When it came time for them to say goodbye, their farewells were tearful.

"We won't lose touch," Mila said, trying to reassure herself, almost as much as she was trying to reassure Marie. "We will visit often. Our network will remain strong."

"If you're unhappy," Mila heard Culis add quietly, "you let me know. Immediately."

All in all, despite the bubble of shame that still always hung over Mila about these contracts, she retired to her room that night feeling safe and grateful.

She changed into a soft, white nightgown and poured some boiling water into a waiting bed of tea leaves. The aroma of lavendile and rosemayne rose up to meet her, and she breathed in deeply before taking a small sip.

She wondered if Culis would visit. Would he risk it? There were so many people around – any one of them could be a spy for Jezebel.

A small tap on her door interrupted the thought and her heart nearly exploded with the thrill of anticipation.

"Come in."

It was Tarett, and he easily read the disappointment on her face.

He grinned as he closed the door behind him. "Just me," he teased.

"I don't know what you're talking about." Mila threw a cushion from the simply furnished room at him.

He caught it and threw it back. "Don't accost me. I've come to make plans with you."

"Plans?"

"Yes. Plans." He sat cross-legged on the floor by her bed. "We're going to need to get a move on if we're going to save the demons of the next Sacrament."

Mila sat up.

She'd been expecting to have to approach him and ask him to help her. Hadn't anticipated that he'd seek her out and volunteer. The gratitude and relief she felt was immense. She was not alone in this. It was unusual, and nice, to have a co-conspirator in a plan that felt so enormous, so world-changing. Unusual and nice to have a friend, even if that friendship came with some baggage.

Tarett continued. "If tonight is anything to go by, I'm going to have a lot of free time on my hands this week while you and Culis are at work. Now, I could spend it earning my fortune night after night at the tables..."

Mila snorted in amusement, Tarett had been *fleeced* that evening.

"Or, I could make myself useful. But to do that we need to have a plan. So, here are my questions: How are you going to get enough rubane for all the sacrifices? How are you planning to transport it? And how are you going to get access to them all and apply it?"

"I only have the answer to one of those," Mila said, feeling excitement flow through her. "I was going to see if the markets here have enough rubane, but if they don't, I know for certain that there's enough growing near my house in the Highlands. I'm just going to need either an excuse for Culis to go there and take me with him, or permission to go alone."

"And how are you going to bring it all back?"

"I...That's as far as I am with my planning so far."

"Mila!" His disappointment was palpable.

"Don't *Mila* me. I've never claimed to be some kind of tactician or schemer!"

"Well, perhaps if you wasted less time pining after Cu – "

"*Alright.* I get it," she snapped. "Look, to be honest, I was intending to ask you for help, but I wasn't sure you were ready to accept. Not after..."

He nodded, understanding. Then he said, "of course I'd help. I'm angry at you - but this is about something far bigger than us. As if I'd leave you to figure it out alone."

Mila wanted to cry. She was so grateful.

"Besides," his mood lightened and he offered her a little smile, "Unfortunately for both of us, you're going to need me and my power for almost every step of this plan."

He was right.

From covertly transporting vast quantities of rubane from the Highlands, to sneaking the oil into the palace grounds, to getting that oil to the would-be sacrifices, Tarett, with his unique power that meant he could shrink anything – literally anything – and carry it in his pockets, was the only way to do it.

"You're right," she agreed.

"And so..." he said slowly, as though leading her to a conclusion he'd long ago reached, "we're going to need to spend this week convincing Culis that he doesn't want to sell me, and that maybe he wants to make another trip, with you and I, up to the Highlands to go find more demons to sell instead."

When he laid it out in front of her like that, it all became so clear. "You know," she said, "when you actually use that brain of yours for good rather than evil..."

"I know," he laughed. "I honestly astonish myself sometimes."

"Truly."

They grinned at one another, and Mila poured him his own cup of tea.

"And, just to confirm, we don't want to tell Culis the real reason for the visit?" Tarett asked.

Mila thought it over again and then nodded in agreement. "As much as I want to tell him, and I think he'd help us if we did...I...I think the rubane needs to stay a secret about ikarei, for ikarei only."

"So, by that you mean, all ikarei except Arran and Marie, or any other demon who might tell Culis?" Tarett confirmed, teasing again. "Because then Culis will probably find out."

She sighed. "Yes, I guess so."

"So really, it's just a secret from Culis."

"No..." she said slowly. "It's a secret from humans. And Culis is a human."

"Fates, Mila. You still can't quite trust the man, eh? Even though I see you and your doe-eyed lusting – "

"For the love of...*stop it!*"

"Who is doe-eyed lusting after what?"

Mila's stomach seized at the sound of the new voice that had joined the conversation. How had she not heard the door open?

Culis stood resting against the doorway, dressed in his long-sleeved, billowing white shirt and a pair of grey slacks. His green eyes sparked in the candlelight, and he looked comfortable and jovial. Not at all like he'd just overheard his two demons plotting to manipulate him. But who could trust how this man presented himself to the world? Mila ached to touch him, both to feel his warmth beneath her palms and also to determine what he knew.

"I might leave this one for you to explain, Mila," Tarett said with a grin, slipping away out into the hallway. Traitor.

Culis watched him go, then closed the door behind him gently.

They were alone, finally.

Mila knew she needed to be sensible.

There were things she needed to say to him that she'd been holding onto for days – waiting for precisely this kind of solitude. She needed to tell him about her plan to disrupt the Sacrament, she needed to warn him about Frank, his paranoia, the compass...but right now it was finally just the two of them, in a warm, clean room, with no Jezebel or spies to be seen. Mila had a flashback to the way his fingers had been rubbing that wayward pearl on the table earlier in the day, the way his hot tongue had felt between her legs only a few days ago, and suddenly she'd never been more aware of the way her nipples showed through the thin, white cloth of her nightgown. She trembled with anticipation.

"Doe-eyed lusting, ey?" Culis drawled with a laugh in his voice, stalking over to her and catching her chin in his hand, forcing her eyes to his. As if she'd want to look anywhere else. "You're not a doe, little demon. You're something far more dangerous. Something that's going to end up being my destruction, I can just tell."

He swept up her mouth in a deep, commanding kiss, and Mila relinquished herself to him, allowing herself to be reeled in like a fish that well knew the danger of the lure but still couldn't help itself. She leaned into him and let herself be consumed and to consume in turn. His energy was full of passion, frustration and desire. It flooded into her like a broken dam, making her ache between her legs. That scent of rich tobacco, leather and *him* was potent. She felt her blood rising and his responding in kind. There was not an ounce of distrust or suspicion in him.

He hadn't heard the secret about the rubane.

When he finally broke away, it was with a sad smile. "I spotted one of Jezebel's spies downstairs. He just left," he said regretfully, stroking her cheek and the back of her neck. "No doubt on his way to report to her that I finished my business early tonight. So, I can't stay, even though it's..." He raked his gaze up and down her silhouette. "All I want is to..." He seemed to catch whatever he'd been intending to say next, ate down the words with difficulty, and instead said, "I actually just wanted to come give you this before I went."

He took Mila's face in his hands again, this time holding her as gently as if she were made of porcelain. He kissed her first on the forehead, then his lips moved down to her nose, her cheeks, and then finally her lips.

The way she demanded more again was almost involuntary, done on instinct rather than conscious will. She pressed her chest hard into him, and what he'd intended to be a short and sweet farewell press of lips was deepened into another full, gasping kiss. Culis groaned into it, hands clutching her to him, roaming over her back, her shoulders, her arse. She could sense every part of his desire, the commanding urge to take her and claim her on the bed then and there. She felt herself spiralling into it. Overcome.

"Culis..." she gasped between kisses. "You have to...Jezebel will..."

She felt his anger flare in response to that name. He growled in frustration, pulling away from her for just a split second, long enough to spin her around and pull her against his chest. His hands reached around her, delving under the nightgown and capturing her two small breasts in his calloused palms. He rolled her nipples between his fingers as he bit down on her neck.

Mila's legs nearly gave way.

But he wasn't done.

With his left hand firmly on her breast, his right hand found its way down between her legs and...

Bang, bang, bang!

The hard knock at Mila's door made them both jump apart. The abrupt separation felt painful, the thrill of fear that spiked through her, even worse.

Who would be knocking at this time of night?

"Culis," Mila heard Tarett's voice urgently whisper through the door. "Jezebel's man is downstairs asking for you."

Culis swore roughly. He walked over to the door and threw it open. Tarett jumped back from him in fright but then glanced into the room and looked relieved to see that everyone was still fully clothed.

"Thank you," Culis grunted, and barrelled down the hallway, throwing Mila a tiny, despairing, apologetic glance on his way out.

Mila's heart crumpled.

Tarett stood still and watched her face in concern. "You fool," he finally said quietly.

Mila stalked to the door and slammed it in his face.

A Hairy Situation

The day that followed did not offer any better opportunities. Although Jezebel, thankfully, did not insist on attending the daily business negotiations, Mila could easily sense the spies she'd ordered to shadow their every movement. Their loathing of her and their fear of Jezebel, punctured her awareness constantly. This was the reason she initially attributed to the discomfort she felt as she, Culis and Tarett walked to the next tavern, but after they turned down one busy street to the next, it became swiftly apparent that something else was afoot.

Something was deeply wrong in Traders Bay.

There was a general aura of violence and paranoia around them. It had never been a particularly safe city but today, every corner brought a lingering sense of menace. Even the rats of the city seemed to sense the unease of its citizens and hung back in the sewers rather than roam freely as they might have done. It only took one more turn into one of the main streets to reveal the reason for the disruption.

Traders Bay was swarming with jesu, Abbott's chosen warrior priests. There were hundreds of them.

Despite her inherent protection as Culis's employee, Mila still felt exposed and threatened every time a pair of them glanced in her direction. Their cold gazes made her want to stay as close to Culis as possible, to tuck herself under his cloak and hide like a baby bird under a wing. She could not do that, of course. Not merely because of what Jezebel's spies would make of it, but also because of what it meant for ikarei. It was in circumstances such as these that she had to truly be the symbol for the change in status quo that they were trying to achieve. This integration of her kind into society was the whole point, the thing that was supposed to make Culis's demon trade worth it. Freedom in the streets. Protection from sacrifice. Being out and proud and visible as a demon because she was bound in a Church sanctioned contract to a human. She had to walk with her head held high and force herself to meet their gaze proudly. Otherwise, what was the point?

She forced her horns to rise high above her head for the day and swallowed down the nausea and discomfort that came from the constant buzz and overstimulation of the bustling city's energy.

"What are they all doing here?" she murmured to Culis from the corner of her mouth.

"Hunting," Culis replied grimly and steered her into the Hungry Eagle to avoid yet another pair of jesu coming their way.

"Hunting what?" Mila whispered.

"Probably the Children of Midas," he replied. "They've been more active since the Dusk Ball explosion. They took credit for it."

"And you're letting them!"

"Well, I hardly want to be arrested myself."

"Huh," Mila said, sliding into a booth. "So, they're aspirational liars. Interesting."

"Definitely liars" Culis agreed, following her and ordering them both drinks. "Although I'd hesitate before calling them aspirational."

"What do you mean?" Mila asked. "From what I've heard of them, they're quite progressive. They want the same thing you and I are trying to achieve, equal observance and weight of the Heretical Behaviours."

"On one hand...yes," Culis agreed slowly. "But I'm sceptical. I've seen enough swindlers in my time. Anyone who tries to implement religious change by using force upon a population is only truly seeking power. If they were simply preaching their views in an attempt to influence others, then maybe I'd believe this movement came from a pure place. But I've heard rumours –"

He was interrupted by a bang, as a body hit the window beside them and rattled the glass panes. Mila and Culis watched in surprise as a man was aggressively pressed against the glass by one jesu, and another stood in the street, holding a woman tightly by her chin. The jesu reached into her hair and plucked out three strands, surveyed her for a few seconds expectantly, then, as if nothing unusual had just occurred, the pair of jesu let both the man and woman go, and continued walking down the street.

"What was that?" Mila said, instinctively retracting her horns in fear.

"Oh hell." Culis rubbed a hand over his eyes in exhaustion. "This can't be happening."

"What can't be?" Mila hissed.

"They're not hunting the Children of Midas," he whispered under his breath. "They're hunting for *Natalee.*"

"What?!"

Culis rubbed a hand over his eyes, as though this new development of Church stupidity was exhausting to process.

"The day after the Dusk Ball," he finally shared, "Abbott summoned me before Midas and the two of them demanded to know what Natalee's power was." He kept his voice low. "Obviously, I lied –"

"Here we go." Mila's forehead met her palms. Culis closed his eyes and sighed.

"Yes, well. I told Abbott that if one of Natalee's hairs was plucked, she would shrink or grow a few inches."

"That..." Mila burst out laughing. "That's a *terrible* power! I'm sure if Natalee ever finds out, she'll be offended."

"Well, I had to think on my feet!" Culis exclaimed. "The question caught me off guard and it's not quite so easy to think up benign, useless demon powers as you might think! Never in a million years did I think Abbott or Midas would care about what her powers were. Up until now their focus has always singularly been simply destroying you all."

"True," Mila agreed. "I wonder why they want her so badly."

Secretly, she knew exactly why they so desperately needed to find her. Natalee was – so far as Abbott and Midas knew – the one person in the world who could resist the God-King's power. Of course they'd be desperate to find her. The preservation of their secret relied on determining exactly how and why Natalee was immune to the deathly touch of the false god.

Mila kicked herself for not thinking of this earlier. She hoped Natalee was lying low, somewhere safe. She hoped she wasn't anywhere near Traders Bay.

"She's definitely in Traders Bay," Culis said, as if reading her thoughts. "She was spotted here a few days ago. I got a report."

"Your spies?" Mila asked.

"A spy in every pie results in less burned fingers," Culis chanted back to her with a grin, then looked up quickly as the small, brass bell at the top of the door to the tavern tinkled. The barkeep looked up, too, and also acknowledged the new patron.

Culis smiled at him and stood up from his seat, gesturing at the seat opposite him, which Mila was readily relinquishing. She found a different, more inconspicuous place a little further away from which to watch the negotiations that were about to ensue.

The first merchant of the day was a gruff man with dark hair and olive skin. By the bold skull and crossbones inked clumsily into his forearm it was quickly revealed that he was no merchant, rather – quite unashamedly – he was a pirate. He had come to negotiate free passage through some of the straits that the Artor Trading Company man-o'-wars usually dominated and promised their protection to.

"Not for huntin', I swear," he insisted to Culis. "Jus' safe passage. Leave us be as we get where we gotta go. We'll find huntin' grounds to the north and south of the Hollis Strait. Bu' we need access to it to reach 'em."

"Forty silvers per pass," Culis said, leaning forward, and Mila saw the pirate go white.

"We pass through it twenty-five times a month! That's robbery. Ten at the most."

"Those ships you rob," Culis showed no mercy, "pay us good money to protect them. What kind of protector would we be – what would become of our *reputation* – should we allow a hunter into the very straits they must use, notwithstanding the fact that they're often transporting *our* goods?"

Mila never ceased to be fascinated by the back and forth, and the light that seemed to emanate from Culis as he wriggled his shoulders and effortlessly sank into the role he was born to play.

Negotiator, dealer, merchant prince.

She was fascinated by it, inspired by it, loved it.

She studied the way his lips pursed as he bit down on a smile, the way he leaned forward with eagerness, and that constant, errant golden lock that flopped rebelliously forward onto his forehead. It was the one thing about him that insisted on being untidy despite his otherwise immaculate presentation.

One tactic that stood out to her was the way that Culis nearly always spoke first when a new trader approached his table, but was never the one to first suggest a price. He'd set the tone and ensure he was seen as both the leader and the member in the conversation who wanted the best deal for both parties, but would go to great lengths to ensure he was not caught in the far weaker position of bartering first. Very occasionally, when his counterpart brought a bullish, confrontational attitude to the table, Culis would barely speak. He'd draw the silences out and force the other to hear their own tone echoed back to themselves. Both tactics always put Culis in a position of dominance and meant he almost always ended up getting what he wanted.

He always got what he wanted, she reflected, except with *her*.

Culis had not come out on top in the negotiation with Jezebel. At its rotten core, that's what this engagement had been – a negotiation wrapped in assassins, obsession and manipulation. In fact, not only had he not won it, he'd outright lost. He'd been backed into a corner and had come out with barely a bargaining chip for himself, or his company.

And he'd done it willingly, to save Mila.

She considered this as she listened to the conversation before her eagerly. All the while she took mental notes as she scanned the pirate's energy and silently communicated back what she'd found to Culis. Back to their usual dance.

Tarett was another story entirely.

Mila was vaguely aware of him operating his own scheme behind her. To all outward appearances, he appeared to just be a young man practising a game of pool and enjoying the company of the occasional challenger. But Mila caught enough snippets of conversation and energy to know that he was concocting his own machinations. She wondered if Culis was also aware. She wondered if she should tell him.

It was a smart move on Tarett's part – shoring up his own contacts and supporters, other than Culis. The wily ikarei was learning from his mentors that having a second plan in the back pocket was not a luxury, but a necessity in these uncertain times.

Her musing was broken by the commotion at the front of the bar. Two jesu had barged in and were plucking hairs from every woman in sight, causing quite the commotion.

"On order of the High Priest," was all they barked by way of explanation, over and over, while the women they harassed squawked and flinched under their administrations. Eventually, they approached Mila.

"No need to pluck her hair, boys," Culis called out in a tone that was both playful and curt. "We already know this one's a demon. She belongs to me."

But either the jesu didn't quite understand what he was saying, or didn't care, because it seemed that they only heard Culis say the word "demon," and that was enough for them to accost her.

One of them leapt at Mila, as though she were trying to escape rather than sitting quietly in her seat. He forced her violently to the floor, tearing a handful of hair from her scalp before anyone could react.

Mila screamed in pain at the unprovoked assault, and then the weight of the hands pushing her down into the floor vanished as swiftly as they'd descended. She looked up, confused, and saw Culis, eyes blazing, with a *sword* drawn and pointing directly at the heart of the jesu who'd hurt her.

For a moment, her heart stopped at the magnificent sight of him bristling with fury in her defence.

"One reason." His rage was palpable. "Give me one reason I shouldn't extract reparations with a pound of your flesh."

"How dare you!" the jesu shot back at him. "Drawing a sword on the Church." The jesu, clearly humiliated, had his own sword still securely clipped at his belt.

"Accost her again," Culis snarled, "and you'll find my sword in *far* more lethal places than merely *drawn*, I assure you." His voice could have cut a stone. Suddenly, he stepped forward and, in one fluid movement, as graceful as a cat, he stood beside the jesu, forcing the man to his knees, his sword positioned at the man's throat as though about to execute him.

The entire tavern fell deathly silent.

"You will regret this!" the second jesu said, moving to draw his own sword.

"Uh, uh, uh," Culis tutted with a tilt of his head, pressing the blade harder against his prisoner's skin, drawing a visible trickle of blood. "Don't be stupid. Not if you value your friend's life."

The second jesu paused, frozen in indecision.

"What do you want?" the first man gasped from the floor.

"Repayment," Culis said coolly. "For the hairs you stole."

"What?"

"You heard me. Repayment. Rip them out. Now. A handful of them."

Unable to hide the incredulous shake in his hand, the jesu reached up and plucked a few hairs from his own head.

"Pah," Culis mocked. "Coward. Let me show you what I mean." He withdrew his sword from the man's neck at the same moment that he shoved his fist into his short hair and gave a hearty yank.

The jesu cried out in pain, hands flying to the site of the injury, and Culis dropped him, letting him fall forward as he sprinkled the bits of hair and scalp that he'd collected on top of him.

"You'll be strung up for this," the second jesu barked, helping his companion to his feet.

"Maybe. But only if the High Priest can convince Princess Jezebel that her betrothed's life is worth less than a few hairs on this idiot's head. Now get out of here." He turned his back on them with disdain.

The two jesu retreated from the tavern. There was a long pause as every occupant in the place absorbed the event that had just transpired.

The silence was broken by the pirate, who belched long and loud before proclaiming, "Well that got a bi' hairy."

The barkeep barked out a huff of laughter in response and, within a moment, the usual noises and bustle of the tavern resumed.

Culis bent down and grabbed Mila, helping her back into her seat. "You okay?" he asked, gently taking her chin in his hand and inspecting her head.

"I'll live," she replied. "But I'm less certain you will after that display. And since when do you carry a sword? And where did it *come* from?!"

"Since my fiancée tried to have me killed," Culis replied with no small grimace and answered the second question by replacing the blade in a hidden sheath along his spine.

Fair enough.

"Now," he said, wiping his hands clean of the last few hairs that still stuck to his palms and turning back to the pirate, who waited for him with a broad grin. "Unless anyone else has any further objections or disruptions planned, I'd like to get back to business."

Riverside

Aidas raced through the jungle.

He could feel his hands were growing cold from the lack of oxygen, his lungs screaming in protest. But he could not stop. Talbot was right on his heels. If he won, it would be the first time in sixteen years he'd ever won anything over his older brother.

Go, go, go.

He urged his tough feet onward as he leapt nimbly over slippery logs and treacherous creek beds. Lithe and quick despite his huge size.

Win, win, win.

Almost there. He was *almost...*

But, as he always did, Talbot seemed to find something from deep within himself, something almost superhuman, to win. With a burst of speed, he powered past Aidas for the final few steps and lunged victoriously into the deep rainforest pool.

Aidas's momentum propelled him into the pool too. He assumed the ensuing splash must have been enormous, because when he surfaced, he caught glimpses of a panting Merry, sopping wet and sporting a *very* unimpressed expression.

She'll get over it, Aidas thought, knowing that his little sister's friend's infatuation with him ran deep. He floated on his back and eyed her lazily as she stripped down to her undergarments and dived gracefully into the water. Alice was the last to arrive. Poor slow, fat Alice. She looked to be on the verge of tears when she finally pushed her way through the dense undergrowth.

"I nearly got lost!" she yelled at them all, the panic making her angry.

"Don't worry, Alice," Talbot called back gleefully. "It's not as if you would have starved to death anytime soon."

"Tal!" Aidas chided his older brother as Alice burst into tears.

Merry narrowed her eyes at Talbot, who seemed to think himself funny, and Aidas watched as she swam quickly to the edge of the water and pulled herself out, hugging Alice tightly.

"Don't listen to him. I'm sorry I left you. I thought you were just behind me."

Aidas tuned out the rest of her soothing words by doing a flip under the water. The muffled silence that met his ears was glorious.

Sometimes I just wish everyone would shut up. Talbot, Merry, Alice, Father...

Aidas knew that Talbot hadn't truly meant to be cruel to their sister. He loved her, and he protected her from many things, in his own way. But Father was in a sour rage today, and therefore Talbot, freshly bearing the external bruises from the strikes, and the internal scars from the quiet, cruel, barbed words, was also in a bad mood.

"Weak, deformed, useless squint of a human. Nothing like your mother or brother. Polluting the line... Wait until your sister comes of age. Then you'll truly see what a disappointment you are to the family. Should cast you out now..."

"Herman –"

"And you! Don't scold me when you have the gall to give me a first-born son with no powers. What a farce, what a joke. You're lucky Aidas's breeding came through. I was this close to cleansing this entire family and starting again."

Aidas tried to release the stress of the morning and emptied his lungs fully into the water, watching the expulsion of bubbles rise to the top before following them and drawing a sweet breath of air. He was a strong swimmer. They all were. Had to be when you grew up on an island surrounded by treacherous currents.

"Can you reach the bottom?" Merry asked from right beside him as he surfaced.

Aidas started. He hadn't been expecting for her to be so close. Her pretty blue eyes danced happily across her brown, freckled face.

"I don't know. Should I try?"

"Go on then." Her smile was so pretty, and she'd readily handed him an opportunity to do his favourite thing: perform.

As if she knew his thoughts about her friend, Alice scowled at him from the bank where she sat, her toes skimming the water. Aidas stuck his tongue out at her, then turned back to Merry and gave her a grin before taking a deep breath and delving down, down, down. Down to where the sun could not reach, and the cool bite of the water constricted his lungs, stealing what little breath remained. He reached a hand out in front of his face, blindly groping into the darkness, and stumbled across the smooth riverstone rocks on the bottom. He seized one in the palm of his hand, and it lit up with his power, glowing brilliantly in his grip, and lighting his way back to the top like a torch.

Aidas heaved in a deep, gasping breath as he surfaced, holding the stone above his head like a trophy. "Made it!"

"Wow!" Merry's eyes were wide in admiration. "You were gone for ages. It must have been deep."

"It is deep," Aidas said. "And dark. Kinda scary."

"Pah," Talbot scoffed.

"Go on then," Aidas challenged, turning towards his disagreeable older brother. "You do it then."

"I will, and twice as fast as you."

"Oh really?"

Quick as a whip, Talbot duck-dived down, and Aidas, never one to let his brother's challenge go unanswered, followed him down again. His lungs were still burning from his first descent. He kicked hard, sensing more than seeing Talbot to his left. Now that he knew what to expect from the pool, it wasn't quite as frightening as it had been the first time. He plunged down into its murky depths bravely, watching as his fingers vanished into the inky darkness before him.

He touched the bottom, grabbed for another stone, but as his fingers closed around it and he went to lift it, he felt Talbot's hand close over his. They'd reached for the same stone!

Neither of them was satisfied to relinquish it and simply grab another. They tousled together down in the darkness. The only light punctuating through the gloom was the abrupt blips of golden light that shone from Aidas's palm whenever he managed to get a firm grasp on the thing. He was nearly choking on water by this point, but still stubbornly refused to yield.

Finally, Talbot gave up. He pushed up towards the surface – with a different rock. Victorious, Aidas prepared to follow him, black spots already beginning to appear in his vision.

Just as he bent his knees to make the leap, Talbot's kicking leg came crashing out of nowhere, striking him square in the jaw. Aidas instinctively gasped in shock and his lungs heaved in a rush of icy river water.

He dropped the stone.

His vision swam. Everything hurt. His lungs screamed, his mind rebelled and then...nothing hurt. And everything went black.

The Riot

It was mid-morning on their third day in Traders Bay when Culis returned from Jezebel's apartments looking sad and exhausted.

"I can't do much more of this," was all he said when Mila and Tarett asked him about it and while Mila wanted to reach for him, to comfort him, she felt her own throbbing ache in her chest too fiercely.

After they finished breakfast the carriage was called and the three of them ascended the small, black steps into its body. Culis sat opposite Mila and gazed at her intently as the driver clucked the carriage into movement.

Tarett surveyed the two of them for less than a minute before letting out a deep breath and rolling his eyes. "Well," he clapped his hands, "I reckon that's my cue to get some fresh air." He opened the carriage window and slithered up and out to sit beside Bruce, who was driving them.

They were alone together. Again.

Focus, Mila.

"There's something you must know," she began abruptly, not wasting any time or allowing him to distract her.

He quirked an eyebrow. "You have my rapt attention."

"Well, there's a few things. Firstly, your father doesn't trust you anymore."

"I doubt my father has ever truly trusted –"

"This is different," she cut him off. "He acquired a compass that was crafted by one of the zoi. It's...enchanted somehow and supposedly points to the person who will be responsible for your downfall."

"I already know that's you."

"This isn't a joke," Mila insisted. "Whenever he holds it, it points at you, and that knowledge is eating him alive. It's only a matter of time before he does something about it."

Culis's face grew serious as he recognised what she was implying. "I..." He processed this information. "How does he know that it points to the person responsible for your downfall? What if it's a trick?" He thought about it for a moment more before clucking his tongue in disappointment. "It sounds like a trick, like something I'd do if I wanted to make mischief. Find a compass that points to the holder's closest family member and then tell the holder it points to the person responsible for their downfall."

"I don't know," Mila said, shaking her head. "Perhaps there's a way to find out, or disprove it. But either way, I guess the most important question right now is what Frank *believes* it does. Because that's what he's preparing for and plotting against."

"How do you know this?"

"He came to me and asked me to spy on you for him."

She'd debated whether or not to tell Culis this part. On one hand, it could seriously backfire and set into motion the very events that could make Frank's delusion come true. On the other hand, hiding this information from Culis and reporting on him to Frank would constitute *actually* spying on him for his father. And she had no intention of doing that either.

Culis sat back and released a deep whoosh of breath, processing her words.

"It's imperative that you don't change your behaviour around him," she warned. "It'll start him off on a path that we might not be able to change."

"Agreed," Culis said, scratching his chin. "I'll need to consider all this more carefully some other time. He's chosen an awfully inconvenient time to make me prove I'm not a traitor." He sighed heavily. "Doesn't he know I'm *busy?*"

"I mean," Mila said dryly. "I did try to tell him as much."

"It seems," Culis said eventually, "and I may change my mind on this in the future but for now, it seems like the best way forward is simply for you to report to him honestly. I have no desire to be his downfall, so obviously, my actions will never reflect that I do."

Mila nodded in agreement, although part of her wondered how far Frank's paranoia had gone, and if he was even in a position to still believe the truth.

"We can try that," she said, "and see how he responds."

"Yes," he agreed. "I think that's all we can do for now. And loath as I am to rush through the topic, I'd like to make the most of this rare chance to talk to you alone and tell you about the plan to extract us from this mess with Jezebel."

The relief that hit her was stronger than she'd been expecting.

This was the Culis she knew. The Culis with a plan.

"Well," his tone became matter of fact, "the crux of it is this. Jezebel is fixated on me for a few reasons. To dissolve these fixations, we have to get to the root of them."

"Well, the first is because you've been baiting her for as long as I've known you."

"That's one." Culis nodded, not flinching from the barbed criticism. "Another is that she's jealous of you. And finally, she's competitive, and while she thinks she's winning at something, she'll continue to latch onto it."

"And she thinks she's winning against me?" Mila clarified.

"Exactly," Culis confirmed. "So, theoretically, all we have to do is erode these fixations and the problem will solve itself."

"And if it doesn't," Mila added with false lightness, "and you end up married to Jezebel anyway, surely you'll be able to make it work in your favour."

"No, Mila. I would not." There was no space for argument in the sharp, anguished look he gave her. The silent words in his gaze struck her as forcefully as if he'd said them aloud.

Because of you.

Once again, she was reminded that something in him was changing. Her stomach buzzed.

"So," Culis finally proceeded, "we start with taking away the element of the game. I want to show her what a boring, conventional and somewhat neglectful relationship it is to be married to a trader. She'll grow tired of me when I'm distracted and busy, as she's grown tired of every other suitor that's ever come into her life."

"The wedding is in a few months!" Mila argued. "You really think she'll get bored of you so soon? I think you underestimate your magnetism."

"Oh. Believe me. I don't." He grinned. "I'm not that far reformed."

"Still arrogant and vain then? Thank heavens."

"I prefer charismatic and pragmatic," he challenged.

"We'd all prefer that." she teased back.

His eyes flickered with dangerous, green fire. "You've grown quite the bold mouth these days, little demon." He slid forward and reached across the carriage to her knee, then began slowly walking his fingers up her thigh.

"What are you going to do about it, Master Culis?" Mila's breath hitched as he slid entirely over to her seat and moved his mouth up against the curve of her neck.

"Nothing...yet." She could feel his hot breath against the sensitive skin under her ear. "Not while you still have that necklace on. But when it's off..."

Mila felt her eyes rolling back into her head as his hand found its way to the centre of her legs and held herself still in delicious anticipation as his fingers danced there for half a moment.

"But in order for us to get there" – he drew back, pulled his hand away and forced his voice to become businesslike once again all in an instant and Mila's eyes flew open as she shot him a daggered glare of frustrated fury, "someone new needs to enter the scene," he continued as if he hadn't noticed her reaction. He definitely had. "I have Nemecca and Lyria working on it right now. In a week or so, they'll return from their trip with the most handsome, articulate tribesman from Escillion that you've ever seen. Barberos is the heir, and he is the most cultured, impressive man I've ever met. Jezebel is going to love him."

"Sounds like I might too," Mila's tease came out a little rougher than she'd intended and Culis shot her a look of mock anguish before saying, "The final thing that needs to happen is that you're going to need to disappear. Mostly, because I can't have you also falling in love with Barberos..."

Mila chuckled.

"But also," he was sincerely earnest now, "because, for this to work, Jezebel needs to forget all about you and the threat you pose to her.

You cannot be a shadow constantly lurking in the corner of her mind. So...I'll be sending you away. I know you didn't want to go when I mentioned it back at the manor. But I've thought about it a lot since then, and... it's become apparent that you must."

She still hadn't found Jahan, but now this proposed absence tied in perfectly with the plan to return to the Highlands and collect the rubane. Spring would be here before she knew it. She had to get started on this rubane collection, and with the unexpected boon of Frank now committed to helping her track down Jahan, she could leave the south with somewhat of a good conscience. Frank had far more resources and access to places than she did. If either of them were going to find her missing friend, she reasoned, it'd be him. This was perfect.

"You look relieved," Culis noted with a little sadness perched at the crook of his lips.

"I think I'd like to go home. I want to see my house again."

Culis's face fell even further at that.

"What's wrong?" Mila asked.

"Well, nothing. I just...I'd hoped to come with you when you went back to your home."

Mila's heart suddenly ached a little at those words and the picture of earnestness on his face. She wanted to bring him into her confidence about the rubane and Midas's secret completely but...she couldn't. Could she? It was a secret just for ikarei...wasn't it?

She opened her mouth to say something, and for the first time, was uncertain about what words would come out.

"It makes sense," Culis spoke again before she could. "Your old home is probably the safest place you could be right now." He surveyed her with a sad smile, then said, "I've a ship leaving for Keras in three days' time. It'll pass the Highlands on its way out. I'll ensure you and

Tarett are on it and organise for you to be disembarked near your home."

"Tarett too?" she asked, now suddenly suspicious that all this was coming together a little too neatly. Perhaps Culis had indeed overheard them plotting the other night.

"I'd prefer you not be alone," was all he said, revealing nothing that further fed her suspicions. "Will you be able to find your way home from the coast?"

"I'd be able to find my way home from Ocianna," Mila said, referring to the major port of the Highlands.

"Perfect," Culis said with a sharp nod. He still looked upset though. "The ship leaves in three days. Between now and then let's – What the...?"

He pulled sharply away from her and moved to the window.

Mila glanced towards the other window and saw Tarett shimmying through it, back into the cabin.

"We're surrounded by them," he said a little breathlessly.

"By who?" Mila could suddenly hear the noise of people yelling and chanting outside.

"How distracted have you two been?" he shot Mila a look of frustration as he explained, "The Children of Midas have gathered in the street, and they're not letting the horses through."

Outside, Mila could now hear the driver trying to calm the horses, who were clearly distressed amidst the river of overexcited people they'd inadvertently found themselves in. She could feel it now in the air, the frustration and excitement, the potential an energised group of people always had to morph into a mob if the environment was just right. She'd felt that threat in the air once before when she'd been dragged from her home in the Highlands. It was unnerving to feel it again.

"I'll go up and help Bruce," Culis slid past Mila and Tarett, and leveraged himself up through the window and into the driver's seat above.

A moment later, Mila could hear the stressed hum of his voice through the carriage roof above them but couldn't make out the actual words.

"We're going back to the Highlands on a ship in three days," she told Tarett quickly, who took the seat opposite her.

"We are?"

"Culis is going to help us," she said.

"You told him the plan?" he accused.

"No, it's part of his own scheme to get out of this engagement."

Tarett looked pleased. "So you were getting actual work done back here, nice."

A loud bang suddenly shook the carriage. Mila felt a thrill of fear run through her.

"We've managed to end up right in the middle of this," Tarett hissed, looking worriedly out the window.

Mila gazed outside too, the disruptive, aggressive energy was growing stronger as more people began to encircle them. Others were obviously eager for something more, some action. Suffocating under their heavily regulated lives, this was a moment to explode, to express themselves. They were not going to miss this chance.

Some started chanting and yelling. A cry that was quickly picked up by those around them. "Abbott is corrupt! Abbott is corrupt!"

It was far too late for the carriage to backtrack now. Another bang hit the side of the vehicle, and then another, as wave after wave of people started to crash and pool around it. Their energy was difficult to block out – a frenzy of mindless rage, confusion and even fear.

"Abbott is corrupt! Abbott is corrupt!"

Another blow struck the side of the carriage and echoed throughout. Mila caught the eye of an angry blonde woman with hawk-like features, roaring in the crowd, her hair flowing loose and wild, her forehead scrunched up in a picture of fury. She held a stone in her hand and levelled it at the carriage. It missed, but Mila still shrank back from that window and looked out the other side.

"This is not good," she said to Tarett. "We have to get out of here. This is about to get ugly."

Just as she spoke, a handsome, freckled, redheaded man from the street climbed up onto the front wheel. He used it for leverage as he tried to mount one of the panicking horses and yelled over the heads of the protesters.

"Abbott's Church has been misinterpreting the Holy Text for decades!" he bellowed. "They gatekeep the word of Midas and act as the barrier between the people and our God-King." He now sat fully astride one of the horses as he yelled, "Down with the Church!"

"Down with the Church!"

"Down with the Chur –" His voice broke as, at that moment, Culis reached down and gave him a hearty shove, propelling him face down onto the ground.

That was a mistake. It seemed the crowd had been waiting for precisely this excuse to change gears and become a riot.

"Heretic!" the man bellowed, pointing a stern finger in Culis's direction.

The square exploded into violence.

"Heretic!"

The cry was taken up, and the carriage began to rock as more and more of the crowd tried to clamber up onto it. Mila's heart was hammering in her chest. The energy had completely shifted now. The crowd had become a rabid beast, and this carriage and its occupants its easy prey, an outlet upon which to unleash their grievances.

"Mila..." Tarett's voice reflected her own concern and fear.

The carriage was rocking, they were surrounded by shouting, so loud it had become a dull roar. Mila couldn't see the sky out the windows anymore, all she could see were bodies and leering faces pressed against the glass, people trying to wrench open the door, people trying to reach up and pull Culis and Bruce down into their swirling, violent midst.

They want to kill us, Mila suddenly realised.

It had all happened so quickly, and they were utterly helpless to change it.

She gripped the seat with white knuckles, trying to keep from tipping over as the carriage rocked violently again. A window beside her smashed, and the volume crescendoed, the deafening roar of noise from outside now spewing into the cabin.

"Heretic!"

"Come 'ere!"

Grabbing hands reached for her, uncaring of the jagged glass that scratched and tore at their forearms until they bled.

"Get the heretics!"

Mila heard a yell from above. Culis and Bruce were unable to help her, caught up in their own struggle. The horses were screaming. Mila could sense their pain and distress, tangled in their reins, unable to move properly, unable to flee, being bashed from all sides by the crowd. Tarett was beside her, fighting to hold the door on his side closed, but the hands that reached through the broken window were grabbing at him, punching him, seizing him, and half dragging him out.

"Mila!" he screamed, throwing his hand out, begging her to save him, to pull him back into the cabin. She lunged for it, and for half a second she held him tightly. But then he was gone, torn away by the force of the wave of furious people.

The door on her side burst open and people tumbled inside, falling on top of her. There were too many people, too much violence, too much noise, too much energy. Mila was being crushed and drowned all at once.

We're going to die here. Like this. I can't believe it.

She closed her eyes, heaving for breath beneath the bodies that piled atop her. Someone grabbed her ankle and tried to drag her free, but whether it was to save her or lynch her, she didn't know. She couldn't breathe, couldn't breathe, couldn't...

I'm going to die.

As her mind screamed for oxygen and black shadows crept into her vision, her power suddenly acted, as if of its own accord. It expanded out from her body and acknowledged those closest to her. Acknowledged their rage, their ferocity, their fear, and drew them into her sphere.

Without knowing quite how she did it, her power flew through those bodies, and into the bodies touching them, and the bodies touching them...and on and on, until upwards of thirty people were caught in its web.

Less, her gasping, panicking mind commanded them, more as an instinct than conscience thought.

And in the next instant – incredibly – she was obeyed.

Mila clearly felt the exact moment that the crowd's frenzied energy dissipated. It was as though a vacuum of space was instantly created in the air, and nothing remained to fill it. Like the eerie silence of the eye of the storm...all noise, all energy, drained away from everyone in her vicinity, as the people who'd been caught in that energetic web of her power were suddenly leeched of something of themselves.

Mila distinctly knew the moment the humans around her ceased being lush, life-filled beings and became hollow shells instead. The man on top of her rolled to the side, off her, and let out a deep, bone-bruised groan. The pressure on her lungs loosened. She heaved in a huge, life-affirming breath...

And then.

I'm alive.

The wave of power, of life, of what she'd taken from them, hit her.

In a flash of blinding white light, it filled her everywhere, all at once. Every pore, every sinew, every molecule of her body was suddenly filled to the brim, overflowing with the live energy she'd just extracted from thirty others. It was too much for one body to contain. She felt as though she would explode. She screamed in agonising ecstasy as this new energy pumped into the marrow of her bones. She writhed on the floor of the carriage like a senseless puppet.

Mindless, feral, intoxicated. She would never come down from this high, would die if she ever came down.

"Mila."

Something was making a noise beside her. It meant nothing to her. It was another language. The idea of a name, of speech, an entirely foreign concept.

"Mila!"

Someone was forcing her eyelids open. The light was painful, she roared in agony and snatched her head away.

"She's alive."

Nothing. The words meant nothing to her. Nothing existed but her. There was no one else in this world but her. Nothing. Nothing. Nothing. She *was* the world, the universe. The stars and the sky and Aluah and the Rotting Muds of Hell. She was everyone and everything in it.

"What's wrong with her? What happened here? What happened to all these people?"

"I don't know."

"Where's Tarett?"

"Let's get her out of here."

She briefly experienced the sensation of being lifted by strong hands, but it felt like it was happening to someone else. It was boring for her to notice.

She turned her attention back inside herself. Back to the pulsing, glowing light of energy that was filling and living in her body. This light was all that mattered now. This feeling was all there was. There was nothing else, no truth, no reality, nothing except this feeling, this enlightenment, this...divinity.

"Less"

When Mila woke, she was in a dark room.

She smelled her surroundings before she saw them. Clove incense gently wafted throughout the air, a fireplace crackled to her left, the faint smell of smoke and ash making her nostalgic for a childhood back in Prious that she barely remembered. A slightly musty woollen blue rug lay on the floor. A vase of fresh yellow flowers sat in slightly stale water. Outside, she could hear bells and people bustling around. A child laughed, a horse whinnied. There was a distinct aura of peace and calm around her, as though the rage and fear of the riot, the scene she last remembered flashing before her eyes, was a fever dream.

She lay still and took stock of her body, mentally running through her limbs, her body, her face...

She felt...*amazing.*

Her arms and legs felt powerful and tough. Strong and ready to leap to action at a moment's notice. Her mind felt clear, unencumbered by fears or doubts or general discomfort. Without opening her eyes, she knew her skin was glowing and healthy. She felt about ten years younger.

"Mila, are you awake yet?"

Her eyes snapped open at the voice.

Culis sat beside her, a plate of sliced fruit and yellow cheese on his lap.

"Hello!" she chirped at him brightly, registering the exhausted cast of his face and the grey shadow that covered him. "Yes, I'm awake. Is that for me? I'm ravenous."

"Yes...it is." He hesitantly handed her the plate, and she ate the fruit so quickly she may as well have inhaled it. "Mila...you seem...okay?"

"I feel fantastic," she said between bites. "What happened?"

"Well, you've been unconscious for two days."

That gave her pause. "I have?"

"Yes."

"Why?"

He scratched his chin. "Good question. I'd also like to know. What do you remember from the riot?"

"I remember things were looking pretty dire," Mila said, casting her mind back. "The carriage was invaded, Tarett was being dragged out, I was being crushed, and then I..." She stopped chewing. The memory returned. "I used my power."

"I suspected something along those lines," Culis said grimly. "What do you mean 'used' your power?"

Mila didn't understand why he looked so concerned. She was alive, wasn't she? And she felt incredible.

"Culis, this is all very boring. Let's do something fun." She felt drunk.

"Mila. I need you to concentrate. What do you mean you used your power? I thought your power was the ability to sense energy?"

"Well yes, I thought so, too, but something new happened on the night when those assassins came for you." She paused for half a moment, wondering if there was a reason she'd not told him about this earlier. If there had been one, she realised now that she didn't care. She felt reckless and invincible now. Nothing mattered.

"Something happened to your power when you were being attacked," he guessed.

"It did," she chirped happily. "It morphed somehow. Evolved. I was able to command the man strangling me to feel less rage. It was almost as though I drained him, and his energy flowed into me instead. It felt...amazing." She couldn't help but laugh. "But it was only a snippet of exhilaration compared to how I feel now. I feel..." She looked down at her hands, surveying them. "Incredible. And the feeling isn't going away."

Culis looked deeply troubled. "Mila," he said softly, "I think you may have drained and absorbed the energy of the thirty or so people who were in and around the carriage."

"I think I did too," she said with another laugh, running her hands through strands of her hair as though feeling it for the first time. "Wow, it really saved my life. And Tarett's. And probably yours and Bruce's too."

"It's impressive."

She didn't understand why his voice remained so low, why his expression was so grave, until he said. "But I think it nearly killed you."

Mila knew she should care. But she was finding it very hard to care about anything other than how amazing she felt. That and Culis's proximity, their current privacy, and his beautiful eyes.

Fates, she felt good, and he *looked* amazing. And they were alone in this room...

"I'm okay now," she said, reaching for his strong forearm.

"Are you?" His energy was full of black dread. It burst the bubble of her good mood abruptly.

"I told you, I'm fine," she snapped, drawing her hand back. "Now, how about you stop nannying me and let's use this opportunity to do something far more...fun." She reached out again and trailed a bold finger up his arm to his shoulder. She felt no fear, no inhibitions. Just this zest for life. It felt incredible.

"Mila, gorgeous." Culis winced and stepped back ever so slightly from her advance, still within her grasp, but barely. "I'd love to. But, right now, I think we need to explore and understand this power of yours a little bit better. In fact, I'd say we *urgently* need to understand it."

The inch of fear that poked into his energy through her fingertips made her pause. Culis was frightened. That was unusual and warranted her attention.

"Why? What's wrong? I promise I'm fine."

"I know you feel fine," Culis said. "But Tarett doesn't."

Mila blinked. "What's Tarett got to do with my power?"

Just then the door to the small room opened. Tarett stood in the doorway, making no secret of the fact he'd been listening in.

"Everything."

Mila's power flew across the room and assessed him. What she felt gave her pause.

Tarett's energy was...less. Diminished somehow, as though something were missing. As though part of his *soul* was missing. She scanned him once, head to toe, and couldn't find it, then scanned him again, far more frantically, urgently.

Where was he?

Nothing.

The bright, bubbly energy that usually preceded him before he even entered a room was now just a flicker of a light, a dying flame in a dark cave.

"Where are you Tarett?" she asked in quiet panic.

"I don't know." His voice was deadpan, his eyes empty.

Mila's stomach plummeted. She'd done this to him somehow, drained him of his life's energy.

Could she give it back to him?

"Come here." She reached out her arm, and Tarett crossed the room to take her hand. She reached inside herself, found her power, and tried to visualise sending a spear of it into him.

"Anything?"

Tarett shook his head.

Mila closed her eyes and tried again, urgently trying to harness this light, this euphoria she was experiencing and pour it back into him. Even just a thimble-full would be enough. She desperately tried to tip it into the space where she could sense Tarett's weak energy, add kindling to that tiny, struggling flame.

But she couldn't. It was as illusive and effervescent as trying to hold onto a bubble.

"Tarett...I'm...I'm so sorry."

Tarett's face was a stone. There was no light behind his eyes, not even a flicker of grief for what had happened to him. The lack of *anything* was painful for Mila to sense, as though someone was driving a dagger into her chest.

She'd done this to him.

She sent an anguished look at Culis, who stared back at her hopelessly. "What do I do?" she begged him for an answer. "How do I fix this?"

"I have no idea," he replied, watching Tarett who stood still beside her, his face now permanently etched into the saddest expression she'd ever seen. "Your power has evolved into something else. Something destructive."

"Maybe it won't be permanent?" she said softly, hopefully.

"Maybe." Culis gave a slow shrug, then he stood and moved over to where Tarett stood, placing his hand on the demon's shoulder.

"And it didn't affect you?" she asked anxiously. "Or Bruce? How?"

"We're both unscathed," Culis replied. "Thankfully. It must have been sheer luck that whoever was grabbing us wasn't linked in some way to those touching you, because whatever you did, you caught a huge swath of others as well. It was quite the morbid sight. Thirty people just...flopping to the ground with little more life in them than a rag doll."

Tarett let out a hollow groan at his words, and Culis grimaced. "Come. Let's get you back to your room."

With the weary movements of an old man, Tarett stood and shuffled out the door, taking his thin, despairing energy with him. Mila watched him go, feeling bitterly ill.

The compass, she suddenly remembered and felt her throat constrict. *Tarett's downfall.*

Culis shut the door behind him and turned back to face Mila, just as she retched and threw up her recent meal onto the floor.

"Oh," she gasped, clutching at her head, "what have I done to him? I'm a monster!"

"No," Culis corrected sternly, crossing the room to sit beside her again. "You didn't do this to him, or anyone else, on purpose."

"What if I can't bring him back? What if I can't reverse it?"

"Well...as with anything unusual, I think we should try not to panic until we have all the facts."

His calm pragmatism helped her steady her breathing just a little.

"First things first." He went to the windowsill and picked up a plant, bringing it over to the bed. "Here. Try use your new power on this."

Mila turned her attention and power to the plant. She could sense its happy, thrumming energy running through its highways of stems and leaves. It was well watered and in a prime position. This plant wanted for nothing and was bursting with potential for growth.

Mila touched one of its leaves and tried to command it with her mind. *Less,* she ordered it, and sucked in her breath, as if she could physically draw the plant's energy out of itself.

Nothing happened.

"Nothing," she said with a sigh, drawing away her hand. She wasn't sure if she was relieved or frustrated. "Both times that it's happened, my life has been in danger. It felt more like an instinctive response rather than something I'm consciously deciding to do."

"Try again. Take your time," Culis implored gently. "There's no rush. We have all day."

Mila looked at the plant a second time and steadied herself. This time, she took a few deep breaths and tried to focus on slowing her heartbeat, silencing her mind. She tried to push away the fear of what might happen if she succeeded, or failed, and instead tried to simply be neutral about the action. There was nothing inherently good or bad about what she was trying to do. It just was.

Less, she said to the plant, this time almost imploring it, and she watched with eyes wide as one of the leaves relinquished its energy to her command and shrivelled at her touch.

She shot a panicked look back at Culis, who blinked back at her.

"Well, well," he said softly. "Look at you go."

Mila turned her gaze back to the plant and, for a moment, she saw Tarett, in her hands, standing shrivelled and small.

"What is this?" she whispered in horror. "What am I?"

"I suppose," Culis said grimly, "you're an ikarei." He stated it factually, and his face was carefully neutral, but as Mila considered this new power and what she was now capable of doing, she wondered if he'd have been more correct had he said she was evil instead.

Tryst

The next morning was a 'drink a tankard of dark ale for breakfast' kind of morning for everyone apparently. Culis arrived early, saw Mila and Tarett with their heads bowed miserably over their swirling pints, and ordered his own before even touching the hot breakfast that awaited him. He sat down without a word, uncharacteristically quiet, and Mila didn't need to touch him to know he'd also had a bad night. In the back of her mind she wondered if the 'scrot' excuse was still holding up between him and Jezebel.

"I won't accompany you to meetings today," she told him. Her stomach roiled with guilt every time she glanced across at Tarett's husk. His condition hadn't improved overnight and his hollow, depleted state was one of the most frightening things she'd ever seen. It significantly sobered the ecstatic feeling of power and energy that had been roaring consistently through her since she'd awoken yesterday.

Now she was trying to ignore that part. It felt terrible to be feeling so good now that she knew it came from the stolen energy of Tarett and others.

"I need to scour the city," she continued. "Try see if there's some kind of cure for..." She gestured at the shadow hunched over his tankard in the corner. "For this."

Culis let out a sad breath but nodded. "Of course. If a cure exists, Traders Bay is the place you'll find it. But do you still want to take the ship to the Highlands? It's leaving in two days."

Mila mulled over the question, then nodded. Collecting the rubane to interrupt the Spring Sacrament was too important to delay much longer. If they didn't find something to help Tarett in the next few days, then the hunt for his cure would unfortunately have to wait. "Yes."

Culis nodded unquestioningly. "I'll organise it then. Baird is in charge of the voyage. He will be expecting you both. The ship is called *Leone's Fury*. You can't miss her. She's spectacular. And, of course, in the meantime, if you get a whiff of anything that will help Tarett, let me know. I'll have the might of the Artor Trading Company's procurement team hunting it down to the ends of the earth for you. Anything you need."

"And what if we don't?" Mila said softly. "What if there's nothing that will help?"

"Well," Culis said eventually, "you can still head to the Highlands as planned, and continue your hunt there. There's plenty of rainforest wisdom and exotic plant properties that can't be found this far south. Perhaps the answer is up there, but you may as well start closer to home." He forced himself to sound energetic and cheery. "See what the hawkers and pharmacists of the Porters Lane Market can do for you today, yeah? Make a start?"

"A start on what?" Tarett asked suddenly from beside them. Mila jumped. He hadn't spoken at all since those few words the day before.

Mila felt a cold chill in her chest. "Finding something to reverse this, to restore you," she reminded him. "We're going to try find something to help you"

"Oh." Tarett heaved an exhausted sigh and bitter sound choked out his mouth. A laugh? A sob? Whatever it was, it grated like scratching chalk.

Mila wanted to cry. The decay of everything that made Tarett himself was a devastating thing to witness, and she was the sole cause. "Tarett...I'm...I'm so sorry –"

Tarett held up his hand to stop her but said nothing, as though talking was too much effort. Mila and Culis exchanged devastated looks once more, then finished their meals in silence.

Eventually Culis needed to leave to attend business. With a leaden heart, Mila watched him return to his carriage and when he reached the bottom step, he turned to face her.

"Any spies about?" he asked.

Mila did a quick scan with her power through the courtyard around them. "There's one," she replied. The maid tidying their rooms up inside the tavern was keeping a keen eye out the window as she replaced sheets.

Culis sighed heavily and turned his back to the window so the maid wouldn't see his lips. "I don't know when I'll next get to see you," he whispered sadly. "If you find something for Tarett before the ship sails, come find me and say goodbye properly. Otherwise, this might be it for a little while."

Mila itched to touch him, to kiss him, to give him a proper goodbye. He was right. She might not see him again for months. She burned with the misery of the thought but showed none of this outwardly. Instead, she sighed and nodded. "Get the plan in motion. I'll come see you as soon as I can."

***

The Porters Lane Market was a world of its own. It was one of only two permanent markets of the city and the only one that specialised in jewellery, knick-knacks and trinkets. Mila didn't hold much hope that something earthly could restore whatever had happened to his energy, but...if something could, surely they'd find it here.

Vibrant and hawkish, Porters Lane was filled to the brim with sellers ceaselessly advertising their wares, eager to snare an easy sale. Mila could not cast even a side glance at a vial or chain at a stall without being dragged in and urged to try, sip, don, touch and, ultimately, buy everything. The constant pulsing, frantic, greedy energy was exhausting to battle, and try as she might, in this proximity, she could not block it all out. It wore at her, like ocean waves against a sandbank.

There was also a dark, murmured rumour that lurked amongst the streets like a plague. News of what had occurred at the riot had spread quickly and Mila caught whisper after whisper about the fates of some of the unfortunate others who'd also been in attendance at the riot.

"Animated corpses," she'd heard one seller tell another in hushed tones. "Walking the streets, haunted and groaning."

"I reckon it's the God-King's punishment," the other had replied. "By all accounts those rioters were committing the Sixth."

"He can do that to them? From afar?" the first seller had gasped. "I didn't know he could do that!"

"He is God!" the second had exclaimed. "He can probably do a great many things that he doesn't specifically tell you, Trent."

Mila shuddered and tried to block it out but Tarett's presence indeed felt like a dead weight. He shadowed her every step like a silent, crushing boulder, with no ability to inspect the items around them and provide any insight about whether he thought they might help. He had no consistent awareness about where they were or why. Every step with him felt like another weight added onto her chest and, after hours of hunting for his cure, without even knowing what exactly she was looking for, Mila realised she needed a break.

So she took Tarett to Tryst, the pleasure quarter of the city. She'd been meaning to organise a time to meet up with Flue and find out how they'd been faring at The Harem. Now seemed as good a time as any she was going to get.

Mila navigated the winding streets of Traders Bay, reaching into the archives of her memory from when she'd lived here for those few awful months, as a teenager. When she felt like they were close to Tryst, she asked a passerby for directions. The woman turned and pointed to a set of rich, black gates that stood proudly on the hill on the street above them.

They were admitted through the gates without fuss and Mila was dazzled by the garden they walked through to reach the building. It was a large plot of land to have in such a densely populated city, a sure indicator of the kind of money that flowed into this establishment. Behind the high stone walls, most of the bustling sounds from the street outside were dimmed, creating an artificially calm and tranquil space.

Mila and Tarett walked along a flat stone path that led to a beautiful, square townhouse. Two tall streams of water fell down on either side of the arch they walked beneath to enter, and once inside, they were seated upon two plush velvet settees while they waited for Flue. Mila read the energy of everyone who entered and left the place, customers and servers alike, and found them all to be happy and light and enthusiastic. She wondered how Flue found it, with a trill of worry in her gut. What would she do if Flue was unhappy here? What *could* she do?

When Flue pushed through the many silk curtains that fell from ceiling to floor, Mila gasped. They looked glorious. Wearing a sleek, silver jumpsuit that clung to their body and emphasised their long, silver hair, they let out a squeal of joy at the sight of Mila and Tarett and ran over, hugging them both fiercely, then leaping back in concern and studying Tarett's face intently.

"What's happened to you?" Flue demanded.

"It's a bit of a story," Mila said with a grimace. "How long do you have?"

"I have an hour until my next client," Flue said softly, their eyes never leaving Tarett's face. "Come, sit. What happened?" Mila sat back in the settee Flue was gesturing towards and used the opportunity to run her power thoroughly through her friend, noting with relief and interest that Flue was happy, safe, engaged and had seemingly grown in self-confidence. *Interesting.*

"I'll try be succinct." Mila began. "My power evolved, and there was an accident. I accidentally drained Tarett of some of his energy."

Flue's eyes widened in horror, "I think I heard about this," they said softly. "Word arrived earlier today that one of my clients was cancelling as he is...not himself after an incident at a riot. That was you?"

"It was an accident," Mila repeated, desperate to be understood as she explained the whole story as swiftly and painlessly as she could. Tarett's eyes never left the white marble floor and he did not react at all to her words. Finally, when the summary was over, Flue sat back with a heavy sigh.

"So you're looking for a cure?"

"Yes," Mila confirmed. "And I realised we were close to Tryst, and now...here we are."

"Well, one of you is here," Flue corrected coldly, giving a pointed look towards their friend. Mila felt a strangling cold, invisible hand clench her gut. She knew that her power, what she'd done to Tarett, was abominable. She'd had thought, however, that Flue of all people, might be sympathetic to what it meant to have a power that seemed to act of its own accord.

"You're happy here?" Mila asked, trying to change the subject.

"I am." Flue agreed and accepted a lute of elderflower cordial from a passing serving boy. "Treated like an honoured employee in fact. I've single-handedly doubled the madam's income this quarter, and I have full control over my own engagements and...I'm being paid a generous wage."

"Really?" Mila was surprised but overjoyed to hear it. "A wage? That's...so unexpected. So is Marie."

"So should we all be, Mila," Flue admonished sternly. "Being here, working for an employer like the madam, it has opened my eyes. We aimed too low on these contracts with Culis. For the next group he brings in, you must renegotiate them. There's an opportunity here we can't ignore."

"What do you mean?"

Flue spoke slowly, as if worried Mila's fear would prevent her from understanding the importance of what they had to say. "I mean, the people who engage with Culis, in this venture, in good faith, are not scared of ikarei, nor do they hate us. They are used to skirting on the edge of morality in society and employing ikarei would, yes, be a taboo, but also not a taboo they'd shirk at. Our powers are *valuable* to these people."

"I understand that," Mila said. "That's why this trade is able to exist at all."

"Yes, well, perhaps *dear* Culis would be able to fathom a trade where he acts only as the intermediary. Connecting such humans and ikarei under the nose of the Church for mutually beneficial employment, rather than as part of a trading scheme. It'd mean that he would accept a whole lot less on his upfront asking price, charging only for his services, and the coin he would have charged as a purchase price becomes a wage for us."

Mila thought about it and looked at Flue carefully. "You really think society is ready for that?" she finally asked. "In my experience, most of them hate us. Most of them fear us."

"That might be true in the backwaters of the Highlands and in Jeralusah. But here, in Traders? From what I've seen so far, it's not the case. Everyone who comes here and learns I am a demon is curious about me, titillated even. They've always been polite and kind. Some have expressed that they could use their own demon companion."

"Yes, but Flue, your power ensures that *everyone* loves you," Mila reminded them. "And a companion is not the same as an employee." She didn't know how to say the next part without seeming rude, but it had to be said. "This is just a pleasure house, Flue. People don't come here to be the best, morally upstanding versions of themselves. Things they might accept within the walls of this house are not the same as things they'd accept out in the streets."

Flue looked hurt and angry. "This is not *just* a pleasure house," they snapped. "It's the most prestigious pleasure house in the city! It's a melting pot of the elite from around the country. I'm telling you, there's something here to explore, and you're ignoring me because it's more comfortable for you to just go along with Culis's plan and not rock the boat, because you're scared – as usual."

"I just want to be careful!" Mila protested. The accusation stung. "This demon trade sits on the thin edge of a knife that Culis is balancing us all on, while the Church throws fireballs at him! One misstep and Midas removes his endorsement, and we are all rounded up and slated for the next Sacrament. Is that what you want?" She took a deep breath and tried to calm herself. "Look. I'm not trying to say that what you're suggesting doesn't have merit. I'm just not sure the rest of us would have such a positive and welcoming reception that you've had."

"And Marie," Flue rebutted, not backing down. "And even you, with Culis. Think about it, Mila. Every ikarei who has gone to live with a human as a slave has *swiftly* had their status elevated. Stop selling humans short. Stop selling *us* short. In fact, find your backbone and stop selling us at all."

***

Mila left the Harem feeling both disquieted and invigorated by the conversation.

Flue's accusation that she was acting from a place of fear roiled within her chest and festered. She didn't want to be fearful anymore. She'd resolved not to be. Was Flue correct? Was she missing an opportunity to lift the demon trade above the bones of this original form and evolve it into something better? Something she could actually be proud of?

Her mind whirled as they walked on. Around them, the streets grew even more crowded, particularly as they approached the Buxton-Canal Market, the farmers market of the city. Mila didn't have high hopes that she and Tarett would find anything of use there, especially after they'd failed at Porters Lane, but to not even look felt like giving up before they'd begun.

She grasped her friend's hand firmly to ensure they remained together as they pushed through the throngs of people. Tarett didn't seem to care either way. His hand hung limp in hers like a dead fish.

As they manoeuvred through the crowd, Flue's words still rang in her head.

I'm not just 'going along' with Culis's plan, Mila argued with the imaginary Flue in her head, but her impression of what her friend might have said in response was interrupted when Mila bumped sharply into the chest of a man who had deliberately stepped into her path. The strength of the contact forced Tarett's hand to slip free from her grasp.

Violence, hardness, cruelty.

The man's energy struck her almost as forcefully as his body had. She backed away quickly, staring up at his face. He looked brutish, with cauliflower ears and a face made angular from being on the receiving end of one too many strikes in his lifetime. He stared back down with a scowl that made her stomach curdle.

"Sorry, my mistake," she said, although she knew it hadn't been. She also knew he was not about to let her slip past him and go on her way.

He stepped menacingly towards her.

"Who are you?" she demanded, backing up away from him, realising in horror, as another man flanked her left, that she was being herded towards an alleyway.

He paid her question no attention and continued to advance.

"Tarett!" she screamed, searching desperately for him over the tall man's shoulder. But all she saw of him was a dejected lanky shape staring down at the gutter – totally oblivious to what was happening to her.

She tried to dodge away, but an arm as thick as a tree trunk shot out and smacked her across the jaw. Mila saw stars and stumbled. The giant man took the opportunity to grab her by her collar and drag her the final few steps away from the main street.

When she came to, she was deep in the alley and away from the bustle of the market. Away from prying eyes, she realised, away from any witnesses.

Mila tried to blink through the pain in her jaw and understand her surroundings. There were three more men with her in the alley. Two of them were also huge and brutish. The last one was a thinner, older man. One whose shrewish, red face looked oddly familiar. Where did she know him from?

Then it clicked. He'd been at the demonstration at Central all those months ago. Kurt Featherstone, from the Guild of Merchants – the Artor Trading Company's greatest competitor.

This was not good.

"Well, well," Featherstone said, as he surveyed her with a big beaming smile, his jovial tone completely at odds with the coldness she felt emitting from him and his cronies. "If it isn't the merchandise, traipsing about alone on the streets."

"What do you want from me?" she hissed, scanning the alley, desperately hoping that Tarett was rallying some help somehow, but knowing, deep down, he was not.

"Oh, you know. Just want to see what all the fuss is about," Featherstone replied, still looking mightily amused. "Where's your Master?"

"Culis? He's around the corner. We're heading back to him now. Let me go."

"Liar, liar," he tutted.

They're all the same, these merchants, she realised, with fear seeping into her blood. *Frank, Featherstone. They're all slimy and cruel.*

"You can't hand me over to the Church," she told him with false bravado. "They already know all about me. They know I'm in Culis's employ. It's been approved by the God-King himself."

"Oh my," Featherstone said with condescension. "I wasn't going to hand you over to the Church, demon. I've only just acquired you."

Mila shivered at the words. "You've acquired nothing," she hissed. "You're holding me under duress. I belong to the Artor Trading Company. I belong to Christopher Culis. And when he finds out –"

"What, demon? When he finds out what?" Featherstone stroked her chin with an oily finger, just as Cauliflower Ears grabbed her forearms roughly and wrenched her arms behind her back. "What will he do when he finds out we've all sampled the goods to determine if your kind is worth an investment by our Guild?"

His hideous intent slammed into her. "Let me go!" she screamed, thrashing in her captor's tree-trunk arms. It was ineffective. The grip that restrained her was like a vice.

"What will Christopher think when he finds out he now possesses soiled goods?" Featherstone mused as he unzipped his trousers and, to Mila's horror, began to stroke himself to firmness. "I wonder if he'd sell you back to me at a discount."

"Help me!" she screamed into the alley as he approached her. The giant who held her cut off her screams with a sweep of his humongous mitt.

This is not happening. This is not about to happen.

"If it's of any comfort," Featherstone said, his eyes gleaming as he fought off her bucking, kicking legs and pushed them apart. "It's not personal. I just *so* hate that arrogant cunt. And this is too good of an opportunity to pass up."

Mila struggled ferociously, her strangled scream caught behind the brutal hand that stayed smashed against her lips. Harsh fingers dug into the skin of her arms, bruising deeply as they held her helplessly in place. As the finality of what was about to happen hit her, a sheet of white panic flooded her vision.

Mila's rational mind fled and all that remained in its place was a snarling, hissing animal in a cage. Her power reared up inside her like a coiled snake, ready to strike, but before she could command it a masked entity, more beast than human, tore out of the shadows and descended upon them.

Featherstone was taken down with a hit that seemed to stop time. In slow motion, Mila gaped at the whirlwind that was, from what her power told her, human, but her eyes would not believe it. She watched in awe as the masked thing systematically worked its way through the gang, slicing, punching, whirling, destroying each body in his path with pinpoint precision. Her attackers were felled one by one, like trees by loggers, each crying out in shock and pain before being left in a crumpled, useless heap on the ground.

Even with his mask on, Mila recognised him. There was only one person in the world she'd ever seen move like that. She'd watched him train for weeks when she'd been bound to Jezebel's side. Only one person who'd dedicated his entire life to perfecting the art of protecting a woman against any and all attackers.

When he'd finished with them, he was left standing amongst a small circle of bodies, his shoulders heaving.

He turned, faced her and let out a wry smile. Still shaking from the near encounter, but forcing her legs to stay upright, Mila returned the grin.

"Hello, Jahan."

Reunion

Reminisciary was unrecognisable in the light of day.

The underground dance room of sin and decadence was closed, and the upstairs tavern that faced the street was just a quiet, somewhat dingy room with an unloved, twangy piano. Alita was not an owner of an illegal dance club, with walls adorned with iconography and tributes to the old gods. She was just an unassuming, short sighted older woman who stood, gently wiping a glass with a clean rag behind the bar.

When Mila, Tarett and Jahan entered, she looked up, mildly surprised to hear the sound of the small bell on the door at this time of day. She took one look at the exhausted expression on Mila's face, the blank slate on Tarett's and the grim expression on Jahan's, and let out a deep sigh. She moved to the door, ushered them in and turned the sign at the front to 'Closed'.

"Again, Jakob?" she scolded.

"This wasn't planned," Jahan said quietly, as if justifying something.

Mila also registered his use of a false name. *Smart.*

"I promise," he insisted. "I just happened to be in the right place at the right time."

Alita sighed again, but as she looked Mila up and down, her face softened. "Come dear, come inside." She took Mila's trembling hand and led her to a booth. "You're safe here." She poured three big mugs of red ale and placed them on the bar.

"You two," she said pointedly to Mila and Tarett. "Take as long as you need to recover, but you," she looked back at Jahan, "I'll need you back at work within the hour, Jakob."

"Of course, thank you," Jahan said solemnly, and gestured to a booth to the side. Tarett slid in first and leaned against the wall, closing his eyes instantly. Jahan barely spared him a glance. He never drew his eyes from Mila's. "Can we talk?" There was a hungry, desperate look in his eyes. *I need to talk,* his energy screamed at her.

"I *definitely* need to talk to you," she replied.

For a moment, they just stared at one another intently across the booth. She anxiously scanned the bare skin she could see on his arms and neck for signs of Jezebel's torture. There were none. Oh, he certainly bore signs of injuries; a black eye that looked a few days old, a cut on his ear that had scabbed over and a graze along his neck that seemed fresh from the fight he'd just come from. But all things considered, he seemed well. In fact, there was a brightness to him, an openness to his energy that had not been there before. The tension between them broke and suddenly, despite everything, despite what Featherstone had nearly done to her, Mila found herself grinning at him like a happy child.

"You're alive! You made it out of there!" she exclaimed in a hushed but ecstatic whisper.

"Of course I did! I had to," Jahan said. His energy was now like a fresh pool of cold water, invigorated and pure. "Jezebel was...murderous after that night, and I'd seen something I could never unsee."

"You did see it then," Mila said softly. "I wondered if you had. It was such a short instant, such a tiny moment."

Jahan's smile faded a little, and he stared into her eyes as if he wanted to fall into them. "It was," he said. "And yet it brought everything crumbling down in an instant." His voice was now deathly quiet, and his face became taut and angry. "My life, my *whole* life was built around serving the Church and its elite. They took me from my family. I was forced into acolyte training by Abbott, and then served Jezebel for decades...for what? It was, it was..."

All a lie? All a waste? Painful and cruel and unfair? Whatever his answer, he didn't need to finish the sentence. Mila could feel the outrage and deep, burning pain emanating from him. It was brutal. She ached with sympathy, and yet also found herself deeply awed by him. Jahan was a man who'd just discovered that his entire belief system was a lie, something most people would never be able to confront, even when presented with irrefutable truth. And yet here he was, making the best of the next stage of his life with this new information.

"So, you left Jezebel."

"I had to. I've never seen her like that before. I knew there would be no surviving that wrath."

Mila remembered it clearly. The way Jezebel had looked at them when they'd come tumbling down from the roof together, the rage in the Princess's eyes when she'd realised that Culis had offered up a demon other than Mila to be sacrificed at the Dusk Ball.

"I waited until she'd returned to her apartments," Jahan continued, "and just...didn't follow her inside. I turned around and walked out the gates. Never looked back. It's funny...no one stopped me. I was a fixture of that household for so long that I was basically part of the decor. No one thought to limit my movements, or assume that, if I left, I wouldn't be coming back."

Mila shook her head at him in wonder. "And you came here? To Reminisciary of all places. How did you even know about it?"

"I...I asked around when I arrived and kept my ear to the ground. I needed to find something that was the opposite of the Church. The opposite of everything I'd been ordered to build my life around. So" – he gestured around them – "here I am. Alita took me in like I was a stray cat. I help her out around the bar and provide security when required. And for the first time, there are no rules to follow. No one telling me what I can and can't do."

"You've gone from one extreme to the other," Mila said with a laugh.

"I rarely do anything by halves," Jahan agreed, and she was relieved to see him smile again.

"Well, I'm...I'm just glad you're okay. Jezebel told me you were dead."

He huffed with laughter at that and looked away for a moment, staring into the middle distance. "It's strange being away from her," he said slowly. "She provided such a constant source of...stress that I barely recognise myself without it. I feel as though, by being away from her, I'm ageing backwards, and yet, in some ridiculous way...I miss her."

"What?" Mila was dumbfounded.

"I grew up alongside her," he tried to explain. "And I know her probably better than anyone else. For all her faults, she is still smart and creative and engaging. I've never met a presence like her. It's just such a shame she was never taught to channel that energy for anything good or healthy."

Mila considered this quietly. She remembered there'd once been a time she'd also found something redeeming in Jezebel, or at least something to be pitied. Since Culis's proposal, though, she'd put that aside. All she felt now was anger and hatred towards the woman.

"I suppose so," she muttered, still unwilling to be gracious.

Jahan noticed her shift in mood. "Let's not talk about Jezebel. Let's talk about you. And where's Culis? How did you escape from under his thumb?"

Mila took a deep breath. "There's a lot to tell. How long do you have?"

Jahan smiled back. "If you'll help me wash dishes then you have me for as long as you want me."

Mila stood up. "Okay. Well, throw me a rag and let's start back when Jezebel sold me to Culis."

***

Alita generously provided rooms for Mila and Tarett to stay in for the night, and in exchange, Mila helped Jahan in the kitchen and at the bar for the entire evening. This allowed them to talk for the entire afternoon privately, while they worked side by side, their conversation hidden from prying ears by the clatter of pans and general hum of tavern noise around them. Meanwhile, Tarett retreated to his room, tucking himself away from the hubbub for his own comfort. Privately, guiltily, Mila felt grateful for the distance. Tarett's deteriorated, hollowed condition could not be ignored. When present he hovered listlessly over her shoulder like a vulture of death, reminding her of the terrible new power she now wielded, a constant reminder that if she couldn't find a way to fix this then she might indeed be a monster.

She didn't tell any of this to Jahan. Instead she sat and listened to him, letting her power flow so she could fully understand what the handsome man was saying and how he'd changed since he'd witnessed the failure of Midas's power against Natalee's skin at the Dusk Ball.

"Mila," he said as he passed her a stack of dirty plates. "You have no idea what that did to me. I just feel so destabilised. I used to have such a sense of certainty in my life, the belief that no matter what I chose to do, so long as I was not committing one of the Heretical Behaviours, I was doing the right thing, that I was a good person. Now that I know it's a lie, there's nothing for me to hang my moral compass on." He gave a bitter laugh. "Apparently I just have to figure out how to be a good person all by myself." He shook his head, his energy felt pained and fearful, his face was scrunched up in contempt. "And it doesn't help that I am just so... angry all the time. So angry that it's eating me alive."

"Angry at what?" she asked. "At who?"

"At everyone and everything," he raged. "It shadows me day and night. Sometimes, I wake up sweating, roaring and ripping at my bed sheets. Sometimes, I'm so restless that I can't sit, can't talk, can't eat. I just need to run, to fight," he looked up at her when he said the final word.

"You've been fighting?" she asked softly.

"I have this irrepressible urge to hit something," he admitted. "I try to ignore it but...it's impossible. And even when I indulge it, even after I've gone out and found someone who I think deserves a battering, when I lie alone in bed afterwards, my knuckles bruised and bloody, it's still all I can think about. Like an itch I can never quite scratch to satisfaction. Something has been pent up inside me for so long, Mila, and it now is screaming to be unleashed. I barely recognise myself. And with no religious laws to fall back on, to guide me, I'm worried that this anger is going to consume me."

Mila listened intently and felt the energy he was talking about pulsing from him, so strong it seemed to form a shadow entity of its own. One made from a sordid concoction of rage, fury and humiliation.

"I always prided myself," he continued, "on having this iron-strong self control. On being obedient and tolerant of Jezebel, even when she was at her worst. Now, a few weeks away and with my eyes open to the Church's lie, I just see that being tolerant of evil acts is its own kind of evil. I'm worried about making wrong decisions and becoming...evil."

"I know exactly how you feel..." she said slowly when he'd finally exhausted his words and sat staring at his hardened, clenched fists. "And I want you to know something," she reached out and placed her hand softly over his. Jahan looked up at the gesture and met her eyes with his own. "You are, at your core, a good person. Your scar," she gestured to his missing eye, "will eternally be testament to that. When you feel like you need somewhere to turn for guidance, just take a deep breath and remember the time you didn't need any religious doctrine to tell you how to behave. You listened to your heart and helped someone who desperately needed it."

Jahan took a deep shuddering breath at her words. She continued, "As for the anger? That seems normal to me. Not only are you unpacking a life of deception, you've also been repressed for most of it. If you're unleashing it on bullies and thugs? Well... I, for one, will never judge you for anything you need to do to process what happened to you." She felt her words send a flood of relief through her friend. The sensation washed through his body and up onto the shores of his good eye, materialising as brimming tears.

"And, as someone who spent most of their young life being told they were evil," she continued, "please trust me when I say there is a big difference between being angry and being evil. There's even a difference between doing terrible things and being evil."

"What do you mean?"

"Well, do you think I'm evil?"

"Not at all."

"Okay then, well brace yourself." She took a deep breath and told him everything, all the terrible things she'd done to survive since she'd left Jezebel's service. She told him about the idea of the demon trade, about Natalee's capture and Culis's betrayal. She told him about the necklace, how she'd attacked Baird, and Frank's brutal punishment.

It was a confession, an acknowledgment of how far she'd been driven to betray her morals and her innate sense of goodness simply to try and survive. To be selfish. To put her life before others. She'd never said it all out loud before, had never summarised each of her betrayals in such a way. She had barely been able to acknowledge them all to herself, but it seemed important to do it now. With Jahan, who was grappling with his own newfound sense of sin and was desperately reaching out to her for support and guidance. As she spoke, she used her power and knew that Jahan was not judging her. He understood her now in a way he might not have just a few weeks earlier.

The only shift in his energy came when she told him how Culis had come for her after he'd discovered Frank's barbaric punishment. How he'd confessed his feelings for her and been determined to earn back her trust.

When she'd mentioned this, she'd felt a pang of discomfort from Jahan, it took her a moment to register it as an emotion she'd never expected to feel from him. Jealousy.

She noted this development with silent curiosity. She knew that she and Jahan had shared something while in the nook in the roof at the Dusk Ball. A small flirtation, an acknowledgment of attraction. She wondered if now, with the shackles of religious authority removed, he thought of that moment as something more.

She pushed the thought away and continued with her story, sharing with him the secret that Culis, in his efforts to repent and save Natalee, had been responsible for the explosion at the Dusk Ball. With reluctance, she also told him about the assassins, about how her power had morphed, about what it had done to Tarett. Of everything, this was the only news Jahan flinched at.

"That is... terrifying," he said quietly, a low note of deep concern in his voice.

"I know," Mila agreed sadly and found she had nothing more to say about it. What could she even say? Her new power and what it could do to people was an abomination. It didn't make *her* evil though. At least, that's what she was desperately trying to convince herself.

She waited until he'd processed this news and his energy had returned to that familiar steady and solid rock.

"So now you know everything," she said finally. "Everything there is to know about me. Every rotten, selfish, violent decision I've made in the past year. And you know why I've made all of them."

"I do." Jahan nodded.

"And?" she prompted, already knowing the answer.

Jahan sighed and scratched at his stubbled chin. "I think you're right. Without the Church of Midas at its core, the concept of good and evil in this world is far less simple but," he closed his eyes and leaned his head back, "perhaps, ultimately, it's a far more forgiving and understanding place."

"Perhaps we'd all be far better off without that core," she said gently, testing the waters with him, wondering how ready he was to hear the next part of her life. His eyes flew open. A light shone in them that hadn't been visible before.

"Perhaps we would," he agreed.

So Mila told him about the plan she'd made with Tarett to expose Midas publicly at the next Sacrament. The one thing she still withheld from him was the name of the secret weed that they would need to collect, the weed she'd told him about at the Dusk Ball. Jahan wasn't bothered by the specifics though. At the mere mention of a plot to expose Midas he seemed to truly come alive.

"I will help you," he said firmly, then paused for a moment, seemingly to try to rein himself in before asking, "Wait. Do you *need* my help? Do you want it?"

Mila was truly grateful for the offer. "I'll take all the help I can get," she admitted. "Tarett and I were supposed to go to the Highlands alone, but after what happened to him, I'm no longer sure he could actually help me if I needed it."

"Absolutely not." Jahan had been outraged to learn that Tarett had been standing dully around the corner of the alleyway while Mila was being attacked. At least now he understood why.

"And it's too dangerous for me to go alone," Mila continued. "Too many people now know I am a demon up there. Without Culis's protection, it'll be dangerous."

"Well consider it done." Jahan said with a firm nod, then cracked a smile. "Bodyguard first to a Princess, now a demon. A new set of morals, ones I devise myself. How my mother would cry."

Mila smiled back at him, a warmth spreading through her chest at the thought of Jahan being by her side for this upcoming adventure. The lonely, heavy cloud that had been weighing on her since she and Culis had said their goodbyes now suddenly didn't seem quite as oppressive.

"I'll also need your help when it comes to getting into the palace," she told him. "Tarett will need access to all the sacrifices too, to get them the oil. Can you help me do that?"

Jahan nodded again. She could feel a real fire burning in him now. Determination tinged with the thrill of breaking the Church's rules, of crafting his own for the first time ever. Perhaps this was what he needed to be free of the anger.

"Of course," he said. "I know the palace grounds and its security better than anyone alive. I helped put it together."

Mila realised then that even without Culis with her, with Tarett and Jahan's help, this plan to douse the sacrifices in rubane for the Spring Sacrament and expose Midas as a false god was fast becoming less of a suicide mission. In fact, it might actually be achievable.

She had friends. She had help.

Maybe, just maybe, this was going to work.

They talked and plotted until the early hours of the morning. There, the decision was made that Mila and Tarett would return to Culis the following day and tell him that Jahan would be joining her and would also need a bunk on the ship. Then, just before sunrise, Mila decided to come out from behind the bar and go below, into Reminsciary, to join the dancing throngs of heretics below. She was not willing to miss this rare opportunity.

As she had on her first visit, she threw herself into the music with utter abandon. She danced until her feet hurt, until she felt drunk off the vibrant energy of drumbeats and ecstatic revellers. As the night drew to a close and she watched the guests depart into the white light of morning, she felt a deep pang of sadness. She missed Culis. She wished he was here with her, in his mask, spinning her with abandon across the room, bending her backwards in his arms, kissing her, running his hands up and over her back...

"Mila?" Jahan appeared beside her. He'd finished his shift and was holding out a hand to hers. "I think the musicians have one more song in them...do you want to? Will you?"

Mila looked at the outstretched hand of her friend, and knew from the hopeful energy, the rising excitement flowing from him, that this was a request for more than just a dance. It was a question of whether there was a chance for something more between them. Liberation from his beliefs had opened something wild and free in Jahan, and he wanted to share it with Mila, explore it with her. This was not just a question of a dance. He was asking if she wanted something more than a friendship with him, something deeper.

Mila looked at the hand again. For half a second, she saw a flash of an imagined future with Jahan. A good man, with a kind heart, who would jump at the chance to protect her. A far simpler path than the one she currently found herself stumbling down. A quiet life, without intrigue or suspicion or plots around every corner.

She surveyed him, with love in her eyes, but shook her head. "I'm sorry," she said. "I think I'm all danced out for the night."

She felt Jahan's hopefulness drop. "Is it because of Culis?" he asked gently. "You told me earlier that he declared his feelings for you, but you never clarified whether you shared them or not."

Mila bit her bottom lip and nodded. She'd never quite admitted it out loud before.

"I know he's not perfect, and there is an uncomfortable past that I'm still trying to work through, but...when I think about it, I just...cannot imagine being with anyone else."

Jahan drew a deep breath. "Mila," he said, stepping closer, "I respect your decision, but I will feel restless and like I'm doing you a disservice if I don't at least say this." He took another deep breath, and Mila braced to hear what he had to say. "I'm... I don't pretend to be an expert about relationships." He stumbled a little over his words, clearly awkward and uncomfortable, but determined to see this through. "But...just...I assume that Culis is the first man you've met in recent history who didn't seem to be repulsed by the fact you are a demon."

Mila's stomach nervously clenched. Suddenly unsure she wanted to have this conversation.

Jahan continued. "In fact, he saw it as a gift, something of value." He cleared his throat. "I can understand why that would endear him to you, why you would feel like he really sees you and cares about you. And I know that he also had means to protect you. I also understand, *completely*, why you might think that's a good choice for your future."

Mila could barely believe any of this was coming from Jahan. Her heart felt so full, especially because she could feel the sheer earnestness coming from him, so honest and strong it was nearly blinding.

"I just want you to know," he continued, "that I," he cleared his throat. "I also accept and embrace you for who you are. You don't need to be with Culis if...if that's the reason you're choosing him."

"I know," Mila said softly. "Thank you. I appreciate the courage it takes to say something like that."

"It's *true*," Jahan pressed. "You're an intelligent and capable and beautiful woman. Demon or otherwise. Any man who doesn't see and appreciate that is a bloody fool. And..." he really hesitated now, but still somehow found the courage to push through. "It would mean a lot to me if...if before you truly decide that you are set on Culis, you promise me that you will think about it. About...me."

Mila didn't quite know what to say. For a moment his gentleness nearly moved her to tears. She couldn't believe she was hearing this from the man who'd once told her he merely tolerated her existence at the God-King's pleasure. He'd come so far since the Dusk Ball, had changed so much. He truly saw her now, for who and what she was. And he was not balking from it. He was leaning in.

She turned away and glanced around the now empty room.

Again she saw, almost like a premonition, a life with Jahan that gave her everything that she'd imagined from a relationship, a partner. There was a hint of something here that could be real if she just let it. And then the shadows of the room morphed into Culis's silhouette and Mila felt a deep, primal yearning for the other man. The man who'd also seen her, who also loved her. The man with whom life would never be easy, with whom there would always be some new plot, some intrigue, some ambition to chase. Would she always come first to Culis? Or did he just want her now because he couldn't have her? Would the passing of time corrode his feelings, his attention? Life would never be stagnant. Something else newer and shinier would always emerge. Would Culis's roving, scheming brain be forever satisfied with just her?

Jahan was right. It was worth considering.

"Thank you." She turned back to her friend, took his hand and clasped it hard. "Truly, thank you. And yes. I promise to consider what you've said."

"That's all I ask." He smiled a sad sort of smile, as though he knew what her answer would be, but at least he'd alleviated himself of a burden he'd been carrying. "And just know that, whatever you decide, I'll still help you with this task. I'll still be by your side throughout it all."

Mila reached out and touched the unscarred side of his face with the palm of her hand. As she felt the pain and pure determination welling even more strongly within him, she wondered what she'd ever done in her life to deserve a man like this at her side, and for a split second, considered that maybe there was a god up there, somewhere, and that in friends, at least, she'd been blessed.

The Children of Midas

The following morning, Mila's hands were trembling and she had a pounding headache. She felt weak and shivery, and regardless of the warm blanket and insulated room, she could not seem to get warm. Surely, she thought, surely this was not from the few shots of liquor she'd shared with Jahan the night before? These felt more like withdrawal symptoms than anything else.

Impossible.

What could she be withdrawing from? It had been months since she'd overcome her addiction to rubane, and though that withdrawal had been uncomfortable, it hadn't been coupled with the crushing wave of despair that accompanied this powerful discomfort. She rolled over and groaned. She needed a cup of tea and a piece of dry, toasted bread brought up to her. She was rarely sick, but this felt like a very sudden onset of a flu. Perhaps she'd caught something while dancing last night? It seemed implausible. The last time she'd even remotely felt unwell had been before the riot...

Then it hit her. The stolen energy, she realised sharply. That ecstatic, powerful feeling she'd felt after she'd drained the energy from the rioters a few days ago was fading, leaving in its place something in her body that felt heavy and murky and...off.

Mila sighed. It seemed there was no such thing as using enormous amounts of power without consequence. She could hardly be surprised. But this wasn't the first time she'd dealt with withdrawal symptoms.

She could endure this too, she told herself. It would pass.

As she made her way downstairs to the main tavern room for breakfast, the nerves she felt about seeing Jahan added to her discomfort. His words at the end of the night had sat heavy within her and caused her to sleep restlessly. She'd lain awake in bed as the early white tendrils of morning had crept into her room and visualised the life she'd briefly imagined having with him, the life he was offering her. It seemed undeniable that it would be a good and easy life. At least, as easy as surviving as a demon in this world could be.

But maybe, just maybe, she didn't want easy.

She'd had to hide her true nature for so long, it had been easier for the entire nation when she just pretended she didn't exist. The one time she'd allowed herself the slightest indulgence and fallen for the thick red hair and long slim legs of Cari, her arrest had swiftly followed. Now, she didn't want to choose the easy route. She wanted the path that was far more convoluted. The path that any sane person, anyone who knew her and Culis's history, would look at and scoff.

And yet. It felt right. *He* felt so right for her.

The ruminations were driven from her mind when she descended the stairs and entered the main room of the tavern. There the energy of the room hit her sharply and she instantly registered that something was wrong.

Alita was exuding a tight, nervous energy, and she wouldn't look directly at Mila. Instead, she kept throwing harried glances towards the only other two patrons in the room. A middle-aged couple who sat together in one of the booths.

They looked up when Mila took her seat, and for a second, they openly appraised one another. They were a man and woman, both in their early fifties, the breakfast they'd each ordered laying before them, untouched. Their energy was alike, curious and wary and prickly somehow, as though she'd lightly run her fingers over a cactus and still come away with fibres in her skin. They'd been waiting, she realised. Lying in wait. For her.

She looked away from them nervously. They looked vaguely familiar. Her mind tried to place where she'd seen them before for a full minute, and then she remembered. It had been here. In Reminisciary, when she'd last come with Culis. They'd been talking animatedly in the booths, about religion and politics, drawing a crowd to them.

They were members of the Children of Midas, and after the riot, Mila was not foolish enough to think that, although they opposed Abbott, they'd be looking to be her ally.

She tried to sink down in her booth unnoticed, but when they stood up and walked over it was apparent that they'd been waiting for her. She regretted that she hadn't retreated immediately to her room the instant she saw them.

"You're the demon the God-King has allowed to live," the woman said as she approached. Her eyes were grey and sharp and not kind. More accusatory than anything else. Mila did not respond.

"My name is Imogen, and this is my brother Raoul." The woman waved her hand in his direction, and he nodded solemnly, looking at Mila cautiously. They both had thick brown hair, although Imogen's was streaked with grey.

"May we talk to you a moment?"

It was posed as a question, but Mila wondered if she was allowed to refuse. They were already moving in, their energy stern and unyielding.

"I don't usually like company before I've had my morning tea."

"That's fair enough," the woman said, cracking a small smile and departing, only to return with a steaming teapot and another mug, sidling into the booth opposite Mila, as though she'd been invited. It was intended as a friendly gesture, but Mila still felt the hairs on the back on her neck raise up.

"What do you want from me?"

From across the room, she could see Alita watching out of the corner of her eye. It didn't make her feel any safer. The barkeeper would be able to do very little to help if these two suddenly decided to do her harm. Alita seemed to recognise the same thing and suddenly turned her back and slipped away.

Mila's stomach plummeted. They were alone.

"Answers," the woman named Imogen said simply. "We want to know why the God-King has decided to let you live."

Despite feeling incredibly uncomfortable, Mila forced herself to consider the question. It wasn't something she'd ever wondered about too deeply back when she'd been living at the palace with Jezebel. She'd assumed that Midas had let her live because Jezebel wanted her alive, and he was happy to indulge his daughter. It did, however, seem to be true that he was continuing to suffer her existence, despite opposition and the numerous opportunities that had since arisen where he could have demanded her death. Why had he not condemned her at the Dusk Ball explosion as Abbott had?

There were many uncertainties, but one thing was clear – telling these two that she didn't know why she was still alive wouldn't help keep her, or other demons, safe.

Imogen registered her discomfort. "You don't need to be afraid of us," she said, her tone turning gentler, although Mila registered that her taut, cold energy did not shift one iota. "If the God-King sees value in your life, well, then we do too. We want to better understand his stance on demons, so that we might be more loyal servants."

"Not blinded by false doctrine and teachings," Raoul added with a fervent nod.

"Here's a better question," Mila countered, trying to shift the attention away from herself, as she'd seen Culis do when negotiations went down a path he was not willing to take. "Why does any of this matter to you? These semantics about which of the Behaviours are worse than others. Why do you care? Neither of you are demons. It barely affects you."

They seemed shocked and offended by her questions.

"We serve *God*," Imogen said indignantly. "You might be a heretic, but surely even you can understand why it is important to us to deeply understand his doctrines and follow them obediently."

"Well, what about the sixth?" Mila challenged. "Disrespecting the Church of Midas? Isn't that what the Children of Midas do day after day? What you do when you preach against Abbott and inspire protests?"

"Abbott's Church is false, a perversion of the message of Midas," Imogen hissed, now starting to get angry at Mila's accusation. "We alone understand the true interpretation and are *trying* to spread the true word, create the *true* Church."

"By force?" Mila challenged.

Imogen's silence was answer enough.

Yes.

"If you're correct," Mila challenged, "then why hasn't Midas denounced Abbott?"

She felt the way her question took the wind out of Imogen's sails just a bit, but the woman still replied with grim determination, "He hasn't condemned us either. Neither he nor the Princess have. We believe, by keeping you alive, he's sending us a message that he approves of our cause."

"No, no." Mila was horrified. "You can't use me being alive as justification for your actions."

"Why else then?" Imogen said, leaning forward. "Why else are you still alive, if not for the God-King to send the message that Abbott is incorrectly interpreting his word?"

Mila hated that she had no answer, and her silence elicited a beam of sickening righteousness from the siblings.

"So, what are you going to do?" Mila challenged. "Continue to push your message until Midas orders Abbott to step down? What if he never does?"

"Oh...don't you worry yourself about that part." Imogen's smug smile was simultaneously condescending and that of a pariah.

"Of course I'm worried! I've already nearly been a casualty of your machinations, nearly crushed to death in a riot just a few days ago!"

Imogen opened her mouth to reply but was interrupted by a sound from the side, a door banging open, which made them all turn. Jahan had entered the room and was moving swiftly toward where they all sat, his face a picture of concern. Alita was a shadow on his heels.

She'd gone to get him, Mila realised, and she felt tears burn at the back of her eyes at the unexpected demonstration of care.

"Mila, are you okay? What's going on here?"

"Calm down, Jakob," Raoul said with annoyance. "No one is hurting anyone. We simply wanted to talk to" – he registered that he now knew her name –"Mila."

Jahan ignored them completely. "Mila, you know who these people are, don't you? They're –"

"With the Children of Midas, I know."

"They're the leaders."

Mila's blood ran cold, and she turned back to face them. "The leaders?"

Imogen and Raoul stared resolutely back. Mila felt righteous pride roiling in their energy.

"How do you know one another"

"Jakob has only been in the city a few weeks and has already made a name for himself as a heretical thug." Raoul snarled. "We serve with purpose, and unlike you, Jakob, we actually give a damn about the truth. That's all we're here to do. Not accost or arrest or hurt anyone. We're not here to threaten or hurt anyone."

"Nothing traceable at least." Mila could feel Jahan's inner calm boiling over. As one who had so recently been amongst the most devout, she could feel his fury at being spoken to as though he were some fool who'd never thought to determine the truth for himself. The condescension in their words was oily.

"What gives you the right," Jahan growled, his anger causing the words to come out fast and hard, "to interpret the Holy Text for yourselves? You're just as fallible as the rest of us."

Raoul nodded as though he understood. "Generally, I'd agree with you, Jakob, and it is good and right for you to be suspicious of those who claim to know better than the Church. But Imogen and I are different. We were raised in the very shadow of the God-King himself. Our mother was scribe to his initial sermons."

Jahan rolled his eyes and scoffed. "Is that so? Well...so was mine, and let me tell you now that what my mother *thought* she knew, and what I now *know* to be true, are very different things..."

"Jakob..." Mila warned. She felt strange using the false name he'd adopted, but she needed to interrupt the conversation before it got too out of hand. Jahan couldn't go blurting out the secret of Midas's lie to just anyone, especially not the leaders of the Children of Midas. He'd probably get himself, and just as likely her, killed.

"Yes," Raoul agreed. "Listen to the demon and stop talking, you're just embarrassing yourself. We're here for her, not for you, anyway."

"I don't have anything more to say to you," Mila said, standing and pushing the still full cup of tea aside.

"Talk to us, Mila," Imogen entreated, mirroring her, as though she'd block Mila's retreat.

"No," Mila argued back. "One bloodthirsty religion is enough to deal with, let alone imbeciles who would start a religious war over a doctrinal interpretation. You're just as hypocritical as the rest of them."

"We're not – " Raoul started, but Mila cut him off.

"For all his faults, I've never seen Abbott and his priests downstairs in Reminsciary's room of sin." She let the accusation linger in the silence.

Imogen's face went red, just as Raoul's paled. Each of their garbled excuses drowned the other's out.

"We don't go there anymore – "

" – den of iniquity, full of heretics and barbarians – "

"A mistake – "

"Look," Mila cut them off. "You might delude yourselves into thinking yours is a righteous cause and that you're better than Abbott, but" – she went in for the kill – "the reality is, at the end of the day, you're all just power-hungry hypocrites. Wearing different clothes but all cut from the same cloth, same as him."

She wondered if anyone had ever confronted them in this way. By their vehement response to her words, it had clearly been a very long time since they'd associated with anyone outside of their inner circle, anyone who didn't bow and scrape at their feet as though they were some kind of prophets. "And not only that," she continued, "you seem too cowardly to actually take Abbott and the Church on! You're all words. All bark and no bite."

"I can see we've caught you at a bad time," Raoul said stiffly, his energy now radiating hot hatred.

For half a second, Mila wondered if she had made a mistake by offending them so deeply. At the start of this conversation, they'd been curious, and although she'd known their intentions had been to use her for their purposes somehow, they hadn't directly viewed her as an enemy. Now that perception was shifting. She could see it happening before her eyes and realised she'd let her temper get the better of her.

"Wait," she said. "Look. I think we got off on the wrong foot. Maybe I'm wrong. I'm just...I'm frightened."

"As all heretics should be," Imogen said, her energy icy steel. She pushed away from the booth. "Come, Raoul, let's not sully ourselves amongst this kind any longer."

Mila watched them leave with a sick feeling in her stomach. Jahan placed a hand on her shoulder in comfort.

"I shouldn't have said any of that." Mila groaned in regret, sinking back down into her booth. "I let my anger get the better of me."

"It's not your fault," Jahan said with a sigh, joining her in her seat. "They're insufferable. They make everyone angry. They're full of hot air and angry words about the Church. But you were right. At the heart of it all, they're still cowards. They pick on the weak but would never be game enough to make real change."

"I just don't understand how they can think themselves so mighty and untouchable, when I've literally seen them downstairs, engaging in the heretical conversations, and witnessing sin all around them, without flinching!"

"They don't come anymore," Alita said grimly. "In fact, if I didn't have their fingerprints on file from their previous visits, they'd probably have reported us."

"And they know you by name?" Mila asked Jahan.

"We've had a few run-ins," he said grimly.

"You've only been here for a few weeks!"

"I... It's a long story."

"The Children of Midas have small gangs in the area that have taken to policing the streets at night," Alita explained. "And Jakob has taken to...intervening."

Mila shook her head. "That's who you've been fighting? The Children of Midas?"

Jahan shrugged. "They deserve it."

"You're getting hurt, and putting yourself in the firing line of some very dangerous people!"

"Courage is knowing something will hurt, but doing it anyway."

"Yes, Jahan," she shot back. "But so is stupidity."

"Well, I guess that distinction is what makes life so complicated, isn't it?"

"Ah yes." Mila rolled her eyes. "Of course."

Jahan ignored her concerned look and began eating his sausages and mushrooms. "So," he said, changing the subject. "I'll be meeting you at the docks tomorrow night, on Culis's ship?"

"You will," Mila agreed. "I'll have to let him know, so that Baird expects you."

"You're leaving?" Alita asked him in surprise. "What about Reminsciary?" She didn't actually look upset with Jahan. In fact, her face beamed as she glanced between the two of them, sensing something was afoot.

"Helping you with Reminisciary will be my priority on my return," Jahan assured her. "I'll never forget or be able to repay the kindness you've shown me over the past few weeks, and I owe you so much. But," he said with a swallow of his food and an invigorated gleam in his eye, "for the moment, I must go with Mila. There's a Church that needs destroying, and it turns out that I'm just the one to do it."

The Beginning of the End

The inky purple of dusk was leaking from the foot of the city buildings by the time Mila and Tarett made it to Jezebel's royal apartments. Mila hadn't dared time their arrival any earlier – she'd known that Culis would be knee deep in business meetings all day, and she was loath to inadvertently stumble across Jezebel in her apartments alone. So she and Tarett had instead waited at Reminisciary until the late afternoon, assisting Alita and Jahan, and enjoying the pleasant company of friends until the time came that Mila knew Culis would likely be wrapping up his dealings and heading home for dinner.

When Mila and Tarett arrived at the apartments, they did not go in. Rather, she bade Tarett sit on the gutter in the street outside with her and, together, they waited for Culis to arrive and come to them.

It was well timed. Culis's carriage arrived less than an hour after they'd sat down, and the look of relief and happiness on his face when he saw them was palpable.

"You're back!" He grasped Tarett's forearms with vigour, looking deeply into his eyes, inspecting them for signs of life.

"I'm not," Tarett said with a flat expression.

Culis's lips thinned in dissapointment, and he turned to Mila. "What happened?"

"A lot," Mila said with a sigh. "But we didn't find anything to help Tarett. What we did find, though, is Jahan."

"Jahan?" It was clearly the last name he'd been expecting to hear. "He's alive then?"

"Yes, and he wants to come on the ship with us tomorrow."

"Does he now?" Culis did not try to disguise the narrowing of his gaze.

"I'm going to need protection in the Highlands, Culis," Mila told him simply. "And Tarett is...he isn't capable of doing that right now."

Culis looked at Tarett and then back at Mila again, sensing then that something had gone amiss. "What happened?" he demanded. Mila heard anger and panic in his tone. "Are you okay?"

"I am," she said. "Thanks to Jahan."

For a moment she debated telling him about her encounter with Featherstone, but then changed her mind. The last thing she needed was for Culis to start a trade war on behalf of her honour. Things were already complicated enough.

Culis took a deep breath. His eyes travelled back across to Mila's face, and he drank in the sight of her. Mila bathed in it, feeling soft bubbles rise in her gut at just the thrill of seeing him again after days apart. The intensity of her feelings shocked her.

She smiled tiredly at him and then caught the clack of a heel on the pavement.

Jezebel's energy smashed into them from behind like a runaway train. There was no more time to talk.

"My love. You're home!" She spun herself into Culis's arms and ensured she pushed Mila onto the cobbles as she did so.

Things had returned to their awful version of normal.

Mila and Tarett slept in the barn.

***

The next day, Mila woke to more shivering and trembling. Her head throbbed and she found it hard to rouse, even with Jezebel's servant impatiently knocking.

"What?" she snapped as she flung open the barn doors, interrupting the fifth round of booming knocks, grimacing at the harsh mid-morning sun that streamed in.

Fates, was it that late in the day already?

"You're required inside the main residence," the servant haughtily informed her but infuriatingly, would not tell her why.

With a feeling of dread rising in her gut, Mila went back into the barn and found Tarett who was sitting listlessly, staring at a wall of the barn, and asked him to start packing their things while she went to find out the reason for her summons. Then, massaging her temples to try relieve the pain, she reluctantly walked towards the imposing front door of the luxurious building and entered it for the first time since she'd been freed from Jezebel's service. She made sure to raise her horns as she entered. Jezebel liked everyone to be reminded that Mila was not human. Mila hated the way that it forced her to be on the receiving end of every flutter of energy in the room, especially when her head was already feeling so sensitive.

She found both Culis and Jezebel in the dark sitting room. The thick curtains had been drawn across the windows, creating a screen of privacy, and Culis was stoking the fireplace. Jezebel sat beside him on a plush cushion. She was sipping a tea that smelled fruity and spiced. Her energy was calm and as peaceful as Jezebel's energy ever got. Culis's remained the unreadable empty space in the room. He looked up when Mila arrived. Jezebel determinedly ignored her.

"You require me, Master?" Mila asked, bowing her head, the picture of subservience.

"Yes." His response was curt. "Ensure your belongings are packed and you are ready to travel. I'll be sending you and Tarett away this evening, to assist my father with his endeavours for a month or two. He has need of your powers."

"Your...your father?" Mila feigned fear. This was phase one of the plan coming to fruition.

"Yes," Culis snapped. "Objections?"

Mila didn't consider herself a skilled actress, but it wasn't hard to follow Culis's lead and fall into the role of downtrodden slave. "N – No."

Culis opened his mouth to speak again but was interrupted by another knock at the door. A different footman, this time with a letter in hand.

As Mila glanced up at the interruption and with her horns up his energy hit her in a sharp shock. This footman was an ikarei!

She stared at him, completely dumbfounded, as he moved swiftly across the room. *How* was there an ikarei here, in Jezebel's service? Hiding in plain sight?

Dimly, she remembered sensing another ikarei in the crowd at Lady Picory's party all those many months ago. Could this be the same person? Perhaps. Or was this another ikarei Culis had recruited for his demon trade? But, no, she pushed that thought away as swiftly as it had come. Surely he'd have found some way to tell her if he'd acquired another one? And he never would have willingly sold an ikarei to Jezebel. What was going on?

"I have a letter for you, Highness." The handsome, mysterious footman extended the envelope to Jezebel, who snatched it away from him and ripped it open.

She read the missive quickly and rolled her eyes, dismissing him with a flick of her hand. As he departed the room, the footman's eyes slid knowingly across to Mila's and met her wide, astounded ones with what could only be described as a look of recognition. And then he was gone, and Mila was left frustrated that she'd not been able to probe him with her power more deeply. There was something shockingly familiar about him.

Who was he?

"From my father." Jezebel waved the letter in the air towards Culis. "I wonder if it's an update about his wedding."

"*His* wedding?" Culis's shock was not an act.

Mila bit down on her own.

"Well, perhaps the word wedding is a stretch. But that's what he's calling it," Jezebel amended. "The finer details are restricted, but in essence, he's hunting that demon who got away from the Dusk Ball. Something about wanting to punish her by eternally binding her to him."

Mila's mind erupted at this news. She knew Midas and the Church were hunting Natalee, but she thought it was to kill her, to protect their secret. Now it appeared Midas wanted her alive. To...marry her?

"As you can imagine," Jezebel continued as she ripped open the seal, "Abbott is less than impressed."

Midas wants Natalee for himself, Mila realised in sudden horror. *Because he thinks she's the only woman he can touch.*

Jezebel's eyes continued to scan the page. "Well. Nothing to do with the wedding. He has summoned me to greet an envoy, a prince from some foreign isle. Someone of diplomatic importance apparently, although I can hardly see the need. Artor has been diplomatically isolationist for, well, since well before I was born. But anyway, he requires it, apparently. So we'll go. You'll attend me, of course."

"Ah. Well, actually," Culis interjected, smooth as silk, pretending not to notice the dark cloud that came over Jezebel's face at his words, "the timing isn't immaculate. Frank requires me to captain one of the Artor Company Ship fleets to Keras. So, I'll be away for a little while, with work."

Mila's heart nearly stopped beating at his words. Culis was coming with her on the ship? Leaving Jezebel? That wasn't part of the plan.

"But..." Jezebel's eyes widened in panic. "What? No. Where's Keras? I've never heard of it."

"It's three seas away," Culis said. "It'll be a few weeks of travel, at least."

"Weeks!" Jezebel spluttered. "But...that's...that's so long. So far away!"

"It is." Culis nodded gravely. "I'll be back for the wedding, of course. But necessary circumstances over this past year have kept me away from the sea far more than is good for business. So I must go."

"But you'll be back...for the wedding?" Jezebel repeated slowly.

"And then away again soon after, I fear." Culis shook his head with remorse.

"This is the nature of my business, my love. This is who I am."

Mila could feel Jezebel's energy plummet in despair. Then, she suddenly turned to face Mila. Mila's heart leapt into her throat, seized by an intense fear that the disappointed woman would find a reason to level her anger in her direction.

"Get out." Jezebel threw a finger towards the door with a hiss, and Mila gladly obliged, running from the room, but halting in the hallway, leaving the door open a crack so she could hear the conversation.

"My love," Jezebel was saying in a soft, low voice, one Mila had never heard her use before. "Can I...could I come with you...please?"

Mila felt what it cost Jezebel to say the words. For the smallest heartbeat, she felt a tiny bead of pity for the woman well in her chest. Being in love had softened her, was making her experiment with vulnerability. This was a new frontier for Jezebel, and she was navigating it tentatively.

"You cannot," Culis said. "There simply isn't enough space on the ships for tourists." The way he spoke to her was direct and pragmatic, without sympathy.

Mila felt Jezebel's hope plummet for a split second before she mustered up the full strength of her might and drew her inner walls back up, rehardening them with her pain.

"Fine then," she snapped. "Good riddance to you. I was getting bored of you anyway."

Culis proceeded to talk as though she hadn't rebuked him. "I'll be leaving the demons in the employ of my father. No room for them either."

Mila felt Jezebel perk up just a little at this, as though she knew Frank was likely to make Mila's life miserable and was mollified by that idea.

"If you must."

After that, night fell swiftly. Mila had no opportunity to see the footman again, or ask Culis about it. She was returned to the barn by the staff and, soon after, was bundled into an old and clearly irregular carriage with Tarett. From there, they were sent in a direction Mila could only hope was the port, as Culis had promised, and not wherever he'd told Jezebel that Frank was allegedly waiting for them.

Leone's Fury

When the carriage arrived at the dock, it was quiet. There were very few people milling around in the darkness and the ships sat nestled quietly beside one another, jostling side by side like familiar bedfellows. Their lanterns threw a dim, orange mist of light onto one another and illuminated the few duty sailors still moving around on the decks.

In contrast to the relative peacefulness of the dock, a chorus of raucous yells and bellows echoed down a small laneway to their right from a brightly lit street around the block. The tavern on the closest corner was the Mermaids Bounty. It was perhaps fifty steps away and marked the edge of where one would begin to find the vast and sprawling streets of taverns, hotels and brothels that made up Traders Bay.

Mila surveyed all the ships, unsure of where to go next, which one was Culis's. It didn't take more than a moment of scanning before the ship made itself known. *Leone's Fury* stood apart from the others, tall, regal and unusual. Its dark wood seemed to suck the moonlight out of the air itself and create an uncanny shadow upon the water.

As she stared closer at it, she noticed that perched proudly on its prow, ready to cut the waves at a moment's notice, was not the bust of a woman or mermaid as so many ships had, but a bold and snarling lion. It looked so lifelike that Mila instinctively reached for it with her power. But it truly was nothing but dead, carved wood. Exceptional craftsmanship.

From the ship, a shadowy figure suddenly detached itself from the body of gloom and made its way down the gangplank and towards them. It took Mila a long time to identify their face, and when it finally became clear, she gasped. It wasn't Baird, or Jahan, or anyone she'd been remotely expecting to receive them. It was Jezebel's footman, the ikarei she'd sensed earlier. And he was stalking towards them menacingly. Grinning wickedly from ear to ear.

"Who's that?" Tarett mumbled.

Mila untucked her horns and threw the full might of her power at the figure.

What she read made her knees buckle. It wasn't. It couldn't be

"Oh!" she gasped and ran towards him. Her. Her friend.

It was Natalee.

"You're alive," she whispered, grabbing Natalee's shoulders, the broad shoulders of the man whose features Natalee's power had copied, an illusion that could only be achieved in low light. Mila wanted to fling her arms around the disguised woman but knew that despite the seemingly empty port, people were still undoubtedly watching.

"Alive and surprisingly well, for someone who's been the object of a nationwide manhunt for a few weeks." Natalee grinned back. "Come on board. I'll catch you up."

Mila couldn't believe the wave of happiness that crashed over her as she followed Natalee's lead. Her friend, her mentor was *alive.*

Then Mila saw Jahan waiting for her on deck, standing beside Baird, who stood with his arms crossed, not quite able to deny himself a tiny smile at the sight of Mila's elated face.

"My friends," she breathed in wonder. "You're all here." She turned to Natalee. "How?"

"Jahan found me about a week ago," she said in her male voice. "It was pure coincidence. I was being dragged from hiding by jesu, who were determined to pull out my hair. They pulled me into the midday sun and, of course, I lost my glamour. Things started to get hairy from there, no pun intended."

"I recognised her from the Dusk Ball," Jahan said softly, in a hard voice.

"He saved me."

"I did what needed to be done." Jahan was pragmatic.

Mila wondered what exactly he'd done to them. The same thing he'd done to her attackers in the alleyway? He'd be in far more trouble from the Church for injuring jesu than a gang of merchant bruisers.

"You didn't think to mention this to me at any point during our conversations over the last two days?" Mila asked.

"It wasn't my secret to tell," Jahan said simply. "And she wasn't around to tell you. She was on a mission."

"A mission?"

"She found *me* yesterday." Culis's voice came from behind them, and Mila whirled around in joy, her heart lifting so high it might burst out of the atmosphere. He ascended the steps and joined them on deck, beaming back at her.

"Welcome aboard all." He gave a halfhearted grandiose swish of his tails and brushed the rebellious, errant lock from his forehead. His eyes lingered on Mila. "I wish it were under nicer circumstances that some of you were meeting her. But permit me to introduce the second love of my life, *Leone's Fury*." He looked at Natalee with a grin. "And when I say yesterday was the happiest I've ever been to have someone hold a knife at my throat, I mean it."

Natalee didn't look remotely abashed, and Mila didn't blame her. She didn't know where the relationship between her mentor and Culis sat now, but she assumed it was still strained at best. Mila didn't know if Natalee was even aware that Culis had tried to save her from sacrifice by orchestrating the explosion at the Dusk Ball.

Natalee seemed to understand the question in Mila's mind and nodded. "I know now," she said. "And it doesn't repair every transgression. But it goes far enough to get me here, with him – and you."

Mila turned back to Culis. "What are you doing here? You're supposed to be at home boring Jezebel to death."

"I realised you were right," he said with a swift grin. "It was an impossible task. I'm many things, and can pretend to be many more, but boring, fortunately or unfortunately, is not one of them. I realised that it was better to play the absentee fiancée instead. Much more convincing. And this way, I follow wherever you lead."

"So long as no one sees us together."

"We'll deal with that if it happens." His smile was so childlike in its happy abandon that it was impossible to feel worry. He was just so pleased to be here with her, and now coming on this trip.

In response, Mila's body felt like it might explode with happiness. She turned back to Natalee, Baird and Jahan. "So you all now know one another. And you know the plan. And you're all prepared to come to the Highlands with me?" she asked incredulously. "You'll help?"

"No, Mila," Jahan said, his voice low and determined. "Not just help. We're here to fight."

Natalee nodded vigorously in agreement. Mila took in their determination and enthusiasm with delight. She suddenly became fully aware of how she was holding her body. She was standing with both her hands firmly on her hips, her back tall, her chin up. Was this how she stood when embarking on an adventure with trusted friends?

She nearly laughed at herself.

Apparently so.

But it was true. She'd never felt like this before. So strong. So supported. She was invigorated. She was leading this motley crew and for some reason they all seemed inclined to follow her.

This is happening.

"And you're happy to work with Culis?" she confirmed.

"I'm about as happy to work with Culis as I am to bathe a rabid jackal, but I'll endure it," said Jahan.

Culis's spirits were too high for him to be offended. He laughed loudly and seemed genuinely delighted by the barb.

"I had no idea you had a sense of humour, guard. Or that I ever insulted your sensibilities. What do I need to apologise to you for?"

Jahan just turned back to face Mila. "No apologies required. I just worked at the palace for a long time. I've seen enough."

"Fair enough." Culis shrugged, unbothered.

Mila turned to Baird. "And you're okay with working with me?"

"I am," he said in his low, gruff tone. "For whatever it is we're doing. Although I don't know if I'm turning my back on you anytime soon." He said the last with dead seriousness, and Mila felt his energy wash over her. Cold and distrusting. She realised that she might never get a better moment than this to make amends with him.

"Baird, I...I'm so very sorry for what happened, for what I did."

Baird did not let her off easily. "What did you do, Mila?" His voice was calm, his energy unwavering.

"I...I attacked you, to try to free Natalee."

"No," he said firmly. "What *exactly* did you do? If you're trying to apologise for what happened, I want to know that you understand exactly what you did. And you may as well tell everyone here, so they know exactly who they're dealing with and pledging their loyalty to."

Mila swallowed. Her strong posture threatened to crumble again but she held firm. If she was going to be a leader – trusted and followed – then she needed to own up to her mistakes. This would be awful. But, she knew, necessary. The point of an apology wasn't to make the one at fault feel better about themselves.

Knowing this didn't make it any easier.

"I...well..." She gulped, starkly aware of the hard gazes of Jahan and Culis on the back of her head. "I tricked you," she began reluctantly. "In the basement at Culis Manor, I used your concern for myself and Natalee, to draw you close. So that I could...I could knock you out and steal the key."

"You bashed my head repeatedly against the iron bars of a cage," he whispered, his voice like ice. "You broke my nose. You knocked me out cold. Both of you did." He flung his hard gaze at Natalee, who also withered a little under it. It was impossible not to.

Mila couldn't respond. She hung her head in shame, but Baird wasn't finished with her.

"You didn't even think to ask me any questions," he continued. "Even though you know I'm Master Culis's best negotiator. You knew I'd just spent weeks at sea befriending Natalee, and you knew I was unhappy about the situation she was in. If you'd just *spoken* to me, I would have told you that I had Philomena, my *wife*, working on a secret prisoner swap from the palace. We were mere hours from approaching Master Culis with the solution. But not only did you not talk to me, you didn't even use your power to determine where my conscience lay on the matter."

Mila's blood went cold as the full force of her rash mistake hit her.

Baird continued. "You lumped me in with Frank and simply decided to try remove me, in the most immediate, violent and easiest way that came to mind, and damn all the consequences."

Her mouth felt like ash and she had to look away from him. She burned with shame. Natalee's face was white. How could she have even presumed that Baird would want to hear her apology, let alone that he'd ever forgive her for what she'd done in her panic and thoughtless desperation? She could barely forgive herself.

Suddenly, there was a firm grip on her forearm. Her head shot back up.

Baird was standing close. His stern face yielded a grim smile. "I understand, Mila." His voice was quiet now, so quiet that only she could hear him. "I understand that you were dealing with exceptional circumstances, and we all do things we're not proud of when we're stressed and under pressure. But, for the love of god, next time, instead of beating me senseless...how about just asking for the key?"

Mila burst into tears, overwhelmed with shame. "I'm so very sorry, Baird," she gasped.

"I know." His tone was still grim and cold. He released her forearm. "And while I'm still not sure I'll ever quite be able to turn my back on you in the near future, the nice thing about forgiveness is that it is a choice, not a feeling. So, Mila, I forgive you." He turned to the small group and raised his voice again. "I forgive her. And now, let's move forward from this. We're both on the same side." He looked at her over his glasses with an arching eyebrow. "Are we not?"

"We are. We are," she said from behind her tears, truly moved by his graciousness. "Thank you, Baird."

He smiled. It was still a pained expression, but a little warmer this time.

"Well now," Culis said, looking pleased. "Now that that's been sorted. I think we're nearly ready to go." He looked around at the small group and laughed. "Look at us. Mila and Baird on partial speaking terms; an obnoxiously muscular ex-guard who has come up with some poorly thought out reason to hate me; Natalee, who can barely look at me; and Tarett, who is in the twilight zone. It seems like we've got all the brains, muscle, talent and wealth we need to succeed at forming a poorly scripted melodrama. Have we got all our immediate grievances out of the way?"

"Actually," Mila said. "There is one last thing." She rounded on Culis now. "We need to talk about the demon contracts."

Culis's surprise registered only slightly but he just nodded curtly. "Indeed? Well, if that's the case, how about we all move this conversation to the privacy of my captain's quarters? It's far more comfortable there anyhow."

He led the way up the stairs toward the cabin. The rest of the deck was empty, save two duty sentries in the crow nest. The other sailors were all off enjoying their last night on land for the foreseeable future. As they entered the cabin, Mila's mouth dropped open, although in hindsight she wasn't sure why. She should have expected nothing less.

The Captain's cabin was huge and busy. It was decked wall to wall with paintings featuring scenes from Culis's travels; a sunset on an open ocean, a rainforest that backed onto a white sand beach, towering white cliffs that had long veins of jutting pink crystals running through them. Mila had never seen anything like them before.

The floor was dominated by rugs. Some thin and evidently long-worn, others made of reeds and fibres, so exotic and intricately patterned that they must have been gifts from other lands. There were so many. Some round, some rectangular and some with no defining shape at all. It was nearly impossible to see the black floorboards that lay beneath them all.

In the centre was a huge, dark dining table. A four-poster bed lay in the back corner. Two huge desks were pushed up against either wall, one covered in papers, books, trinkets and stains, the other immaculately clear of everything except a tiny inkpot and quill pen. The entire room was topped off with an extravagant, multi-armed crystal chandelier that swung gently from the ceiling like a giant, tinkling cherry.

Mila heard Jahan scoff a little from behind her when he surveyed the space, and the noise wasn't missed by Culis.

"Magnificent? Extravagant?" he challenged. "Yes, I know."

"I was leaning more towards ridiculous," Jahan rumbled.

Culis rolled his eyes. "Just because your preference is a hard pallet in the spartan guards' quarters doesn't make this ridiculous. This is tasteful decadence topped with a hint of – "

"The contracts please, Culis," Mila said, plopping into a chair and keeping him on track.

"Ah, yes. Please. Discuss away," he said, sitting opposite her and staring intently.

The others sat around her, Natalee on one side and Tarett on the other.

"Well," she started, "I want to renegotiate."

"Oh?" Culis's eyebrows flew into his hairline. He clearly hadn't been expecting this line of approach.

"Yes," Mila boldly continued. "Both Flue, Marie and myself have been very effective test cases thus far and prove that the clientele who are interested in purchasing a demon in the first place are also happy to pay them a decent wage and treat them more like trusted servants than slaves. We" – she gestured to Natalee and Tarett on either side of her – "want the contracts to formally reflect that same treatment, that status."

Natalee fiercely nodded in agreement, despite the fact it was her first time hearing this proposal. Tarett just stared at the ceiling.

"We could try."

Culis's utter lack of argument floored her, and Mila felt something that had been coiled tight in her chest release. Despite the trust she'd decided to put in him, despite the rampant attraction she felt towards him, she still hadn't expected him to be so amenable to the idea so quickly.

"We could try," he repeated. "I don't disagree with the premise of your proposal. But the risk is that if the Church should get wind of it, we'd be shut down for good and any protection this scheme has given demons thus far would be lost."

Mila nodded, appreciative of the constraint. It was exactly the same argument she'd made earlier to Flue. There was something about the subjugative nature of the contracts that made the Church amenable to the unusual arrangement at all. But she'd been thinking about it since then and realised she might have the solution. "I don't think you should change the language you've used to advertise them. Not yet, at least. But in the quiet moments with the buyer, and the actual paperwork they need to understand that this is not a slave they're getting. It's actually a rare opportunity to earn the trust of a valuable aide, but someone who ultimately remains in the employ of themselves."

"So they pay for a trusted advisor, not a slave?" Culis summarised.

"They pay for the services of an ikarei. A loyal consultant and magical aide," Mila corrected. The room was silent as he mulled this over.

After a moment, Mila reached her hand out across the table to him. With an abashed, hesitant little smile, Culis extended his pinkie finger in return, bridging the distance between them and allowing her to sense him.

He was feeling open, curious...and something more. Some excited energy was bubbling deep in him, searching for an outlet. Like a disused muscle being stretched after a long sleep, Culis's desire to do good was straining to get out. He was being truthful, being honest. He *wanted* to do this demon trade differently, wanted to make things better for ikarei.

Knowing this emboldened her.

"What if...what if you charge *nothing,*" Mila said into the space, feeling the gravity of her suggestion hit Culis immediately. "Charge nothing," she repeated. "Make no money, for once, from the trade of ikarei, but instead, do something you'll be remembered for forever. Just think. If we can embed as many ikarei as possible into trusted roles of society in the next ten years...that would *actually* change the status quo."

Culis blinked at her. Still connected by their fingertip, she felt within him, a wave of fear crash against an exhilarating thrill of interest. He liked the idea, was very tempted by it...but...there was something holding him back.

"My father," he said softly. "When Frank sees the books and sees no money being exchanged for the demons, the...ikarei. He...he won't allow it."

Despite the hesitancy of his words, the welling of determination and fortitude that Culis was mustering within himself made Mila realise that he might do it anyway. And if he did, this very well might be the beginning of the moment Frank's compass foretold.

A cold shiver ran down her spine.

Culis would bring upon Frank's downfall, because he would find a way to achieve this. For her.

And Frank would try to kill him for it.

Maybe. Maybe not. Maybe the compass is wrong. Maybe Frank will have a change of heart. You can't know the future.

"You'd do this?" she said softly. "You'd truly help us?"

His green eyes burned into hers. She'd never seen him like this, so serious, so intense, earnest that she should understand him. The usual air of teasing aloofness was gone. She felt the heat and love and trust come flowing through him into herself and, in that moment, she knew, truly knew, that he was a good man. That she'd made the right decision. That she could trust him. That he was on her side.

It was a relief beyond measure, like stepping into a cool waterfall on a hot day. The relief and joy ran through her. She wanted nothing more than Culis in that moment, to fling herself into his suntanned arms and wrap her arms around his neck, to kiss him, devour him, to bring him into her confidence, have him know everything about her. She wanted him. To have him know and understand the great deception with Midas. Everything.

He was with them.

He was with them.

He was with *her*.

She had his allegiance, completely. It was a dizzying feeling.

Suddenly, she forgot they were surrounded by people. It was as if they were the only two in the room.

He was hers, and she was his. And that was all that mattered.

Cabin Fever

Mila awoke the following morning in her own cabin on *Leone's Fury* with the sun shining through the small glass window above her head and the soaring calls of seabirds being fed fisherman's scraps on the dock.

As romantic as it was, Mila couldn't appreciate any of it. Her symptoms were worsening and she awoke with a head pounding so badly that she felt nauseous. How was she going to manage once they were actually at sea?

Baird had shown her, Natalee, Jahan and Tarett to their separate cabins last night after their conversation, and despite the fact she'd had every intention of sneaking back into Culis's cabin once the voices in the hallway died away, she'd fallen fast asleep on top of the gold-embroidered, deep-purple coverlet before she even realised what was happening.

In the white light of the new morning, fighting her body that ached as though it were fighting a fever, she roused from the bed and cracked open the door into the hallway. It was empty, but she could hear boots clomping on the floorboards from the level above her head, and the shout of voices calling over the wind outside. She closed the door and returned to her room, forcing herself to drink two big cups of some fresh water and try make herself presentable for the day.

With her hair neatly brushed, face washed, and feeling far more alive than she had felt when she'd first woken, she made the short walk back to Culis's cabin and knocked lightly.

There was no reply.

She pushed open the door and found no one. He must be somewhere on the deck with the rest of the crew.

That was infuriating. She'd wanted to see him before she encountered the rest of the crew. She'd also wanted to confront him about why the wardrobe in her cabin was filled with clothes that were exactly her size. Boots, caps and cloaks included, and why she'd found half a dozen half drawn sketches of her eyes in his wastepaper basket...

She decided to wait for him in his cabin instead of her own. It had windows that faced out onto the deck below, which gave Mila a good vantage point from which to watch the morning goings-on of the ship.

They were still in port, but today was the day they were expected to depart. It had never occurred to Mila before that moment that she might want to go on a ship's voyage someday, but as she watched the bustle of excitement occurring below her, she was suddenly filled with unexpected anticipation and excitement for it to commence.

The enthusiasm of the sailors was infectious. The large deck of *Leone's Fury* was full of men and women, each of whom seemed to consider their individual task the most important thing in the world. As she observed them, it didn't take long for Mila to identify three distinct types of sailors.

The first type were young – barely more than children – and they'd evidently been recruited for their dexterity, agility and fearlessness.

They all but flung themselves around on the rigging and scurried up and down the main and foremast like rats.

Speaking of which, she watched in amazement as neat rows of actual rodents could be seen scurrying across the ropes that kept the ship tied firmly to the dock, seemingly undecided whether they wanted to stowaway on board or try their luck in the city sewers instead.

The second caste of sailor moved around below the agile ones at a more grounded, but no less intense pace. They were evidently employed based on their experience. Mila could see it even from here – crooked fingers, leathery skin, scars and a swagger to their walk that indicated they were more comfortable when the floor was rocking beneath them than when it was still. These were the men and women being ordered and tasked by the leadership, the third type of sailor. From her current position, she could only see one of these. Baird was up and about, ordering a small group to load crates from the gangplank to the hold. Jahan was with them, shirtless in the warm mid-morning sun. For half a moment Mila was hypnotised by the sight. His huge forearms rippled as his hands moved, one over the other, across the rope, hauling it up.

Mila pulled her gaze from him and continued to scan the crew. The longer she looked, the more she saw a few other familiar faces lurking around. Culis's trusted few, the hunting party were all on board, mingling seamlessly with the rest of the crew. They were his spies and confidants, never betraying that they knew one another or were anything more than acquaintances. Arran leaned against the mainmast and distracted a pretty, young toprider with his idle chatter. Mila assumed from the gleam in his eye that Marie was now long forgotten. Black Berran was also on board, rolling a barrel that looked suspiciously like it was full of wine away from the kitchen and towards his own cabin. To the side, she saw the women, Nemecca, Lyria and

Philomena, sorting through and coiling ropes as if they were the lowest of deckhands. Even the three men she really only knew by sight – Dabriel, Corbyn, and Odin – popped up in unexpected places here and there.

Amongst it all, the cut of Culis's shoulders caught her eye. She watched as he cruised about the hubbub with haughty confidence, as comfortable amidst the chaos as she'd ever seen him. He barked orders and gave direction, but never lifted a hand himself to help, which Mila knew was unusual. She'd seen him getting his hands dirty many times at the manor, but here on *Leone's Fury*, the dynamic was different. Here he was the captain, and these people were his crew. Mila understood from the energy pulsing from each of them that establishing this dynamic was as important to the sailors as it was to Culis himself. They wanted him to play the role of untouchable leader, needed him to do it to ensure order and harmony on long journeys abroad. Once away from land, he would become the sole point of authority for them. He had to ensure that at the beginning they found him suitable to be father, confessor, judge and jury. He would fill all roles. On a ship, Christopher Culis had more authority over them than even the false God-King had over his own Church.

Mila watched the scene below for a long time. She didn't see any of the other demons. It appeared they, too, had elected to lay low until either Baird or Culis came to get them, uncertain of the environment they were entering. They were still at shore and there was still every opportunity for something to go wrong.

Finally, the last crate was loaded, and Baird moved towards where an old iron bell hung. He rang it twelve times, deafening all in its vicinity.

It was the call for all to board. The ship would be leaving within the hour.

As she waited, Mila reflected on the night before.

A lot had happened.

After their conversation about the demon contracts, Culis had poured them each a shot of rum, and over the tink of crystal and tumble of liquid, Mila had baptised the group into secrecy and shared almost everything she knew. It hadn't been a straightforward conversation, however.

"Midas is not a god," she'd announced, studying the faces of the others as the words had left her mouth.

Under the low light, across the salt-worn table, their expressions had all been caught in shadows. Natalee and Jahan had both nodded in grim agreement. This information was not news to them. Culis, however, hadn't been able to hide his surprise, and Baird had visibly flinched at the blasphemy, even though Mila could sense him trying to compose his response. Baird and his wife were still ardent believers. She'd been hesitant to speak again, wondering if her next words would shatter the tenuous relationship that she'd just tried to mend between them, but knowing she must say them anyway.

"With the help of Abbott," she'd said calmly, "they've both deceived the nation. He's not a god. He's an ikarei, just as Tarett and Natalee and I are. He's able to destroy things with his touch because his powers evolved. I didn't know ikarei powers were able to do that – until it happened to me."

"Wait. What?" Baird interrupted. "What's an ikarei? And what happened to you?"

Mila had then gone on to explain everything. The history of the ikarei, the assassins, the riot and Tarett's current situation. Baird's eyes had flown to Tarett's face when she bitterly described the damage she'd done to her friend, what she'd taken from him by accident. As she spoke, Tarett's shoulders had slumped even further towards the floor.

"That...this is horrifying," Baird had muttered in disgust when she finished.

"Probably about the same level of horrifying as disintegrating someone with your touch, and yet you've worshipped him for it," Natalee had said with contempt, defending Mila.

Mila had watched both Baird's face and energy shift at her words. He passed through the initial burst of defensive anger quickly. As a skilled negotiator it was his job to remain calm in the face of antagonism and his muscle memory was working hard for him in the face of this new information. But then came a deep surge of denial, of disbelief. He fought to maintain his calm façade as he worked through it.

"It's okay," Mila said to him quietly. "It's a lot to process."

"Trust me," Jahan interjected. "I understand. I tied my whole life into the Church. At least you've *lived* your life."

For a long moment, they'd all sat in silence, watching Baird's expressions as he warred with his long-held beliefs and this new information that he'd been presented. Culis, on the other hand, suffered no such conundrum – he was all too eager and willing to believe that Midas was a charlatan. His eyes sparkled as his brain ticked over, marinating in this new information.

Finally, Culis had leaned backward, given a big sigh, and said, "I have questions."

Mila found herself unable to contain the burst of laughter that exploded at his words. "Of course you do," she'd gasped. "So do we all!"

Natalee and Jahan had joined her. It had felt good to laugh, like her nervous system was shaking itself free, a wet dog on a riverbank. She'd let the tension out freely. It was infectious.

"Well, firstly," Culis said over the chuckles at the table, "he's bald, so where are his horns?"

For some reason, the fact that this was his first question had made them all laugh even harder. Mila's stomach ached, but she'd leaned into it, trying to savour the rare moment. She couldn't remember the last time she'd laughed so hard it had hurt.

"The mystery of the horns is actually the very thing I can't quite explain. That and the question of why cats fawn about him so."

"Is it even possible to remove your horns?" Jahan had asked.

"I tried once," Mila shared. "It was excruciating, and they grew back within a day."

"I had the same experience," Natalee nodded. "But that's not enough reason to say it can't be done. He's obviously figured something out."

"And you know this for sure?" Baird interjected, there was a note of pleading to his voice and dread in his energy, but Mila wasn't able to tell if it was because he wanted it to be true, or he wanted to find a hole in their story. "You're certain this is the truth, without a shadow of a doubt?"

"I do," Mila had replied softly, recognising the significance of his question. "And I'm sorry that I can't explain to you exactly how I proved it. That test must remain a secret, because it pertains to the safety of all ikarei everywhere. But all this...the crux of what I'm saying, the lies of Midas? Every bit is true."

Baird turned to Culis. "You believe this?"

"The Dusk Ball had something to do with it." The cogs in Culis's brain were visibly whirling. "That's why you were so insistent on going, on watching."

"Yes," Mila admitted.

"I saw it too," Jahan said. "I can vouch that there indeed was a test, and Midas failed it."

"That's why I'm still alive," Natalee added softly.

At that point, Culis had slammed his fists against the hard wood of the table. His face a combination of frustration and begrudging appreciation. "Argh. I *knew* you had a plot of your own going on. I *knew it.* And you executed it perfectly, too, right under my nose. I'm losing my touch. How embarrassing." He stood quickly from his chair and began pacing the cabin. "Here I thought you wanted to watch Natalee's death out of moral obligation and a guilty conscience. But, really, you were looking for some secret sign to prove that the God-King isn't real!" He'd turned to look at her, searching for confirmation in her face, and he'd found it. "And you and Jahan saw it! And I assume Natalee and Tarett know what it is." He continued to think out loud. "It's something you're hiding at your home in the Highlands, isn't it? That's why it's our destination. But now you're saying you can't tell Baird and I?"

"No humans can know." Mila said. "It is an ikarei secret."

"But Jahan knows," Culis accused. "Why can he know, but not us?"

"Some of us are just inherently more trustworthy." Jahan hadn't been able to resist the chance to put a shot across the bow, and Culis looked delighted at the chance to argue with the man. Mila had hurried to interrupt.

"No, it's not that at all." she snapped, shutting Jahan down swiftly. "It's because he just happened to be present when it happened. And even he doesn't know all the details."

"I know all the details that count," Jahan prodded at Culis again, never taking his eyes off the man, as he bounced an eyebrow. The implication was unmissable to everyone in the room and Mila was mortified.

Culis's eyes had darkened, "The thing about lions, Jahan?" he'd replied coolly. "They don't go around telling everyone they're a lion."

"And what's that supposed to mean?" Jahan had bitten back, undaunted.

"It means that those who *actually* know all the important details about Mila, generally don't feel the need to brag about it."

"Oh, sweet mercy, save us," Natalee had sighed loudly, rolling her eyes. "Do the three of you need some privacy?"

"No, we don't." Mila said firmly. "Nor does *anyone*" – she'd shot both Culis and Jahan a stern glare – "know any *details* that they shouldn't know." Then she took a steadying breath and tried to bring the room back to order. "I'm sorry," she said to Baird and Culis. "The secret of Midas's weakness must remain a secret from humans. The less who know, the better."

"Ahhh, the secrets of demons," Culis said with a shake of his head and a slow smile, diffusing Mila's discomfort. "Will they never cease to plague me? Do you know how *utterly* maddening this is for me?"

"I do." Despite herself, she couldn't quite wipe the smile from her face. His animated indignation and amazement was unfamiliar, and highly entertaining, but what he'd said next would stay with her for the rest of her life.

"Mila, you are..." Culis stopped dead in his pacing to face her. "An utter *force* to be reckoned with." His green eyes had glowed with heat and suddenly it'd felt as though the entire room and everyone in it had fallen away from them and nothing else but those eyes existed in the whole world. He'd then walked around the table and approached her slowly, prowling like a giant panther. "I've been tricked." He'd reached for her, tucking a strand of hair behind her ear, his touch electric. "I've been outwitted." He'd placed his hands on either side of her face, cupping it possessively. Through them, she felt his admiration and awe sweep over her like a tidal wave. "In you," he'd whispered, "I have met my match." He held onto her like he was no longer the famed Christopher Culis, but merely a man, one who was clutching onto a life raft in a stormy sea. He needed her. She could see it in those eyes, feel it in those hands. Mila had felt something rooted in his energy open then. As if a deeply clutched pain or fear were uncurling itself from a long slumber and blinking its eyes in the bright daylight.

Jahan let out a huge sigh and banged his feet on the table, interrupting the moment. Natalee's face was equally as unimpressed. "Mila's just told you that the God-King is not a god, that the entire nation has been deceived, and she has a secret she's not going to tell you," she said, "and your response is to fall more in love with her?"

"Sounds about right," Culis had replied with a wry smile, and Mila's entire body had lit up at his words. He'd released her face reluctantly and turned to face the others again. "Alright," he finally said. "You're right. Enough talk of love. Let's talk plots that break the world open."

So there, hunched over the large salt-worn table, beneath the low, evening light of the gently rocking chandelier, the vague, spidery outline of the plan became a solid thing, and the unlikely group of demons, merchants, spies and a guard who'd committed treason somehow became a team.

The memory blurred back into the present.

Despite the night's sleep, Mila could still feel the hangover of feelings from the previous evening. She felt so tense in the gut whenever she remembered the gleam in Culis's eyes that she could barely breathe, so happy to have a solid plan now and a team to help her achieve her goal.

She felt so...invigorated. So alive. And now, with the bell of the ship ringing out clearly into the new morning, Mila harnessed those feelings and watched as the ship prepared to depart. They would take a few days to reach Ocianna, a major Highland port where she and the others would disembark and commence their march towards her home in Bori. All this to collect the rubane they needed to sabotage the upcoming Sacrament and bring down the God-King once and for all.

Mila watched in fascination from her hiding place as hundreds of men and women scurried down from the markets to come say goodbye to their loved ones. Her stomach twisted a little as she watched families embrace and sailors part from new or old sweethearts. It was a day brimming with emotion and vibrant, excited energy, and Mila was delighted to find herself not overwhelmed by it, but enjoying the spectacle. It was a beautiful sunny day too, although cooler than usual by Traders Bay standards. Jahan's lack of shirt was entirely unnecessary, but not, Mila noted with a wry smile, unpleasant.

Finally, they pushed off.

Mila felt a thrill of excitement run through her as she watched the sails unfurl and catch the wind. *Leone's Fury* leapt forward, as though rejoicing in her freedom after being too long restrained. She surged forward into the rocking, choppy water with fervour, taking her trusting crew with her.

When they were well underway, Culis finally returned to his cabin, still barking orders as he ascended the steps.

"Meeting on the deck in five, Baird," he called and then broke into a smile when he saw Mila's face peering at him from out the window.

"Hello, little demon. You can come out now if you like," he said through the glass.

Mila opened the door, but instead of stepping out into the wind, she drew him into the room with her and closed the door behind him, pushing him back against the wood.

"Finally!" she said with a sly smile. "A moment with you alone."

Culis's smile broadened at her words and their implication. He drew her closer against him, spinning her so that it was her back, not his, that was pressed against the thick wooden door.

"I don't think I've ever seen you be so bossy before," she teased a little breathlessly. "You plan to use that tone on me too?"

"You want orders?" A wicked glint entered his eyes. "Here's your first one. Open your legs."

Oh.

Mila obeyed.

"Very good." Culis's left hand wasted no time, running down her body and hitching up the fabric of her dress as though he'd been waiting all night and all morning to do exactly this. His grin widened as he found her already wet and ready, and his next move was merciless. He circled the slick nub between her legs once, twice, and then pushed two of his long, clever fingers firmly inside her, with no gentle ease into the pleasure, as though he knew the pressure between her legs had been building all night and her body was screaming for this. And, somewhat humiliatingly, it was true. She was aching for him, for release, for *anything.*

"This is what you've been waiting for, little demon?" he mocked gently, both amused and ravenous for her. He watched her face contort with pleasure, with sheer *relief* as he said, "Waiting to soak my hand while I make you dance upon it?"

Mila cried out at the intense response her body had to his words and he covered her mouth with his free hand and paused the movement of his fingers. She stared sharply at him in confusion and indignation.

"Here's your next order. Silence on deck." His eyes were glazed with lust, his mouth still holding a hint of wicked amusement behind it. “Mila, fraternisation on the ship is forbidden. If we’re caught, the punishment – ”

“I don’t care.” Mila wrapped a frantic hand around the back of his head. She already knew that the punishment for sailors caught fraternising was being tied naked to the mast for a day and a night. She knew. She didn’t care. She drew his mouth down to hers again and, kissing the words away, reached down with her other hand to guide his back between her legs again.

“More,” was all she gasped in demand. “I’ll be quiet.”

“Good girl,” his voice was rough and raspy as he obeyed.

Oh god.

He plunged his fingers back into her and nipped against her neck. Not kindly. Mila felt a deep, guttural moan building in the back of her throat but she held it in check while they continued like that, him, pinning her against the door with his mouth and hand, the friction between their bodies so exquisitely rough, and her, clinging to him, urging him closer, to meld to her, to fuse into her bones. He wordlessly obeyed her silent commands, his fingers rocking in and out with determination. The pleasure built inside Mila with each stroke, to a point where it was almost painful to contain. She bit hard into his shoulder to try muffle the desperate mewling noises that would betray them both if left to the air, and Culis sucked in a sharp breath, pulsing his hand faster and harder inside her.

“Culis,” she gasped into his ear, barely able to form words, her knuckles white in fists balled against his shirt. “I can’t. I’m...I’m going to scream if you don’t stop.”

“Shh,” was all he offered, maddeningly, in reply. And he did not stop.

“*Culis!*” Panic mingled with pleasure as she began to helplessly crest.

"You can do it. Quietly now, little demon. Come for me."

The command tipped her over the precarious edge she'd been teetering on, and Mila's silent orgasm wracked her, sending a deep, pulverising shudder through her body. Obediently, she held in the scream, forced it back down her throat, and banished it into her belly. It was beyond frustrating. She wanted to lose herself in total abandonment, scream her release to the heavens, and she couldn't. In every stolen moment they'd had together, she'd been forced to muffle herself, and she ached for a time when this wouldn't be necessary.

As she panted for breath, Culis's hand found her chin, tilted it up, and kissed her. "You're spectacular."

Mila chuckled, but her legs wobbled. "You had more faith in me than I did."

"Are you okay?" he asked, tucking a wayward strand of hair behind her head.

"I...hell, I...yes. I'm...yes, I'm *wonderful.*"

But unsatiated. And he knew it. He kissed her again. This time it was deep and slow and leisurely. Mila felt the heat return instantly. She was ready again. Combined with the energy of his own desire, her need was almost overwhelming.

"What about you?" She reached her hand down to the space between them and trailed her fingers firmly over the hard length at the front of his trousers. What she felt there made her stomach clench in total desperation.

Something animal awakened inside her and made its desire to be ravished by this man known. He was long, thick and so ready for her. She swore quietly, and Culis's mouth twitched at the sound of the profanity on her lips. Then he leaned forward, placing his hands on the door at either side of her head and braced himself with his eyes closed tightly, his breathing ragged as she stroked him through the fabric. Back and forth.

"Mila." Her name both a prayer and a war cry in his mouth.

He endured it for a moment then broke the distance between their bodies as he pushed her hand aside and leaned forward, biting hard at her neck. Mila gasped as sparks flew through her body. He ground himself up against her. The friction and pressure made her senseless. Would he take her here? Like this? Up against this door with the whole crew waiting for him outside?

"Culis," she panted, her fingertips scrabbling at the lip of his trousers, trying to pull them down.

She felt the way that hearing his name from her lips caused that tightly coiled sense of decorum and responsibility to unravel in him. The way his most base and primal energy roared to life and thrust aside any thought of consequence. Culis was suddenly vivid and reckless and ravenous for her, as a wolf is for hot blood after a long winter.

His arm snaked down her side and seized her arse, the other running up into her hair, taking a tight hold, making her gasp in pleasure. Her bones melted in his grip, under his hard, hungry, unleashed gaze.

"Turn around." A command. This was the captain of the ship, ordering her.

She unflinchingly obeyed. She bit down on a long moan as, a moment later, she felt the silky hardness of him pressed against her wet, ready body. She tried to push backwards, to take him into her, but he held her in place with the hand still wrapped firmly in her hair.

"Culis," she gasped again.

"Ask me, Mila," he growled. "I need to know you want me as much as I want you."

"I want you." She practically choked on the words. Her body wasn't her body anymore. It was an alien thing, a hot, heavy mass that throbbed head to toe with each beat of her pounding heart. She was nothing but wanton need. If he didn't give her this, she might explode. "Please," she begged.

Instead of answering her desperation with his own, Culis released a deep, shuddering sigh of anguish. Slowly, he turned her back around and gently touched the vasium necklace that still lay around her neck, rolling the delicate metal between his fingers.

"I can't do it. Not while this remains here."

"Remove it," Mils hissed. "You can remove it now. She's not here to see."

"The unwelder is back at the manor, in my study." His face was a picture of anguish. "If I'd known this was how this trip to Traders Bay was going to go...believe me. The moment we're in Ocianna, I'll find another. I'll make one myself if I have to."

And then, from the other side of the door came three shuddering bangs, and Baird's voice, far too close to Mila's ear, called out apologetically.

"Captain! If I may, the crew is waiting."

Mila saw Culis let out a long, slow breath.

"I have them lined up on the deck for your address," Baird continued. "But...if you want to do it later, I can reschedule. I just need to know so we can get this journey under way."

"For the love of all..." Culis muttered, and then kissed her again, a despairing apology.

"When I finally take you," he said as he held her chin tightly, his words more warning than promise, "I'm going to need at least three days of you. No interruptions. No necklaces or interfering plots or plans. Three days, at least. That's how long I'm going to need to recover from this."

Another three bangs on the door behind her.

"For fates' sake, Baird!" Culis bellowed, his temper unfettered. "I'm coming." He re-adjusted his trousers in dismay.

"Aye," came Baird's terse reply, as if he knew exactly what he'd just interrupted and didn't approve of it in the slightest.

Mila wondered if the ship's fraternisation laws applied to the Captain.

"Go on," she said. "I'll follow soon after. If you're addressing the crew and introducing the ship's company, it'll seem odd if I'm not there."

Culis nodded, then kissed her again, as though unable to stop himself. "You are...incredible," he whispered, his lips still practically pressed against hers.

"I'm a mess!" she protested with a happy laugh, catching a glimpse of her reflection in his mirror and seeing the unmistakable red flush of her cheeks and brightness of her eyes that would betray their recent antics to any passing observer.

"An incredible mess." He turned her face back to his again and deeply drank in the sight of her.

"Go." She finally pushed him away. "I'll follow you shortly. Just...give me a few minutes."

"Of course." He took her hand and kissed it like a courtier before regretfully pulling himself away and closing the door behind him.

Mila flopped onto his bed in dishevelled breathlessness and grinned at the carved wooden stars in his ceiling.

She couldn't remember ever, *ever* feeling this frustrated, or quite so happy, in her life.

Stage Fright

When Culis introduced the ikarei to the crew, he chose not to reveal their true natures. Instead, he explained that they were simply human passengers paying for transit to Ocianna. Mila sensed that most of the crew believed him without question, but the vitriolic energy emanating from two who did not was unmistakable.

One was a middle-aged woman, who stood tall and thin above most of the men. She looked hardened, weathered and fight-weary. Even if her energy hadn't been so menacing, Mila still would have found the way her sleeves were rolled up to her elbows, proudly displaying the cord-like muscles that jutted out, to be disquieting. The other was a shorter male. He was handsome, with a thick build, dark moustache and a face that made him appear naturally affable. Whether they were Jezebel's spies, Frank's spies or Abbott's spies, Mila couldn't tell, but one thing was certain: they knew her by sight. They knew she was a demon and were harbouring murderous intent against her.

When Culis finished his opening address and dismissed the crew to their tasks, Mila moved forward to tell him who she'd just uncovered within his crew, but she was too slow, and by the time she reached the top step where he'd been standing, he'd already been whisked away by Baird, who had his own energy of deep urgency about him.

It can wait, Mila reasoned, but as the morning went on, she realised that she may have misjudged that decision.

As she moved about the ship, she became acutely aware of the tall, ugly woman beadily eyeing her off. The hateful gaze and predatory energy was constant and merciless, like a hungry sandfly in a mangrove. Mila took two steps to the left and watched, a chill shooting down her spine, as the woman mirrored the movement from across the deck, positioning herself closer. Lurking. Waiting. As though Mila was being herded somewhere.

Towards the edge, she realised in sudden horror, and without any idea of how to respond, she sat herself down firmly on the hard wooden deck where she was. She'd be harder to hoist overboard if she was sitting.

Natalee came over and joined her, chatting happily, unaware of Mila's predicament.

"So, after the explosion," Natalee was saying, "I used my power to look like one of the guards who'd held me. It worked. The actual man had been crushed by one of the falling slabs."

Mila was interested in the story, but her attention was too fixed elsewhere, drawn from the female spy to the male. She watched him move around, jumping from one chore to another. Despite his kind-seeming face, she noticed him scattering poisoned words in the ears of the crew as he went. Like a wave, the energy of anyone he spoke to turned from excited anticipation to fear. Each of them, one after the other, looked over and gave Mila a side-eye that could have frozen lava.

She could see the lips forming the words that were whispered now amongst them.

Demon. Cursed. Heretic.

A hard hand landed on her shoulder and made her jump. Jahan. She relaxed.

"Ladies." He made himself comfortable on the floor beside them and reached for a slice of the apple they'd been sharing.

"Jahan!" Natalee was happy to see him. "I was just telling Mila the story of the Dusk Ball."

"Please," Jahan said affably, "don't stop on account of me."

"Well," Natalee continued, "although, initially, I assumed the appearance of a guard, to get out of the gates I needed to look more like someone who would be moving around under their own authority. I watched this bony, old woman stride past and announce she was Lady Meredith, and the guards let her pass without question. So, all I had to do was wait until the guard shift changed and mimic her..."

Mila was barely able to focus. She was overcome with relief that Jahan had joined them, reassured beyond measure by his presence. The threat posed by the tall, muscular female suddenly seemed far less imminent. The work that the man was doing amongst the crew, however, was becoming increasingly toxic.

She turned to Natalee and cut her off. "I need you to go find Culis. It's urgent."

Natalee's brow furrowed. "What's going on?"

"Something is afoot," Mila explained. "I need you to go find him and tell him to come quickly, please."

"Tell me," Natalee demanded, never one to simply obey without question.

"I'll go," Jahan offered.

"No!" Mila said, so sharply she made the both of them jump. "I think your presence is protecting me more than either of you realise," she said. "*Please.*" She turned to Natalee. "I'll explain after. I just need Culis here *now.*"

Natalee nodded, stood up and went below deck.

The woman's departure, combined with Mila's worried, furtive glances in their direction, must have alerted the threatening couple to the fact they'd been detected. As soon as Natalee's shadow vanished, they immediately made a beeline towards Mila and Jahan, who both leapt to their feet.

Jahan took a step in front of her and unsheathed his sword without hesitation. The unmistakable sound of rasping metal drew the attention of everyone on deck, and Mila watched all eyes turn their way.

"Stand aside," the woman ordered Jahan. Her voice was unusually high-pitched. "You're defending a demon. A heretic."

"This ship will sink before we reach Ocianna if we allow her to stay on board," the handsome man said, making sure his voice was loud and carried across the crew. He knew exactly what he was doing.

"Get back." Jahan brandished his sword and widened his stance. "And close your lying mouths."

Mila knew he could take them both. She'd never seen anyone fight like Jahan, and he'd been the Princess's bodyguard in another life. He could protect her from this, she had no doubt. Neither of these cowards would touch her. But the rest of the crew?

She peered over Jahan's shoulder and assessed them. Some were confused, others looked ambivalent and were settling in for some mid-morning entertainment. But there were a few – more than a few – who were filled with hard delight, already influenced by the spy's words and ready to see the demon thrown from their ship before the journey could be tainted further.

Jahan couldn't kill them all. Well, she amended, he probably could. But if it could be avoided, it should be. Besides, Culis needed these men to help sail the ship.

As if he heard his name in her mind, Culis emerged from the passageway, with Natalee and Baird behind him.

He took in the scene that lay before him. Jahan armed and braced before Mila, the hostile man and woman, now also armed and advancing on the two of them, most of the rest of the crew egging them on.

"What the bloody bollocks is going on here?" he demanded, his fury so palpable it even halted the two attackers in their tracks.

"Demon on the ship, boss," one of the bystanders called out.

"Oh?" Culis pretended to look shocked. "And how do we know this? Was a test performed?"

That set about a murmuring in the crowd.

"Well?" His tone was curt and unyielding. "Who performed the test? Or have we all just unanimously agreed to accuse a paying customer of heresy now?"

The atmosphere on deck turned uncomfortable.

"We don't need a test," the woman hissed. "We know her by sight. She was the Princess Jezebel's pet and *sold* to you."

"Is she?" Culis turned to study Mila as if he'd never seen her properly before. "I'd say she looks vastly different from the slave I acquired from my agreement with the Princess. Don't you think, Baird?"

Baird nodded gravely in agreement.

"And so either way," Culis said, turning his attention back to the two aggressors, "the fact remains that, either she is the demon who is my property and you're attempting to kill her without my knowledge or permission, which would make you both thieves – and any one of this crew can tell you that thievery on this ship is punished by a long, dark and uncomfortable stay in the brig. Or you're utterly mistaken and are about to set upon an entirely innocent woman for your own sport and ruin the reputation of the Artor Trading Company, for which I'd have you keelhauled. Which is it?"

There was an awkward pause as the pair looked at one another and then...

"She's a demon!" the man cried, pointing at Mila with his sword, disregarding Culis entirely. "She'll bring the ship down and everyone with it!"

"Keep blithering like an idiot," Jahan growled, "and I'll ensure you're not even around to learn if you're correct or not."

The commanding silence that followed his words was deafening.

Slowly, the two spies sheathed their swords, recognising that the momentum of their advance had been lost, and the tide of the crew's opinion had been turned against them. The crew knew their captain was both eccentric and ruthless. They understood that he was as likely to bring a demon on board their ship as make good on his threats. They respected him and feared him just enough to obey, even when they thought he was probably wrong.

Culis took advantage of the lull. "Baird," he ordered, "arrest these two. Throw them in the brig."

He was obeyed instantly, and Mila watched as four sailors stepped forward and took the two agents away.

"I'm happy to take a test," she said clearly, so all could hear her. She knew that the suspicion of the crew had to be abated for the rest of this journey to be peaceful. "I'm not a demon."

"Not necessary," Culis scoffed. "M'lady, I apologise that these rogues have even put you in a position where you feel the need to offer such a thing."

"Thank you, Captain," Mila replied in her best haughty voice. "But I truly don't mind. If it'll put the crews' minds at ease."

“Well” – Culis looked around at the gathered crew – “that’s very generous of you, m’lady. Does anyone here know of a test that’ll expose a demon?”

The crew members looked at one another shamefacedly for a long moment. A squeak of a boy, who, on closer inspection, was revealed to be Lyria in a cap, piped up.

“Demons can’t sing,” she said confidently. “Whenever they try, it just comes out as a hellish screech. If m’lady could sing us something...that’d...that’d go a long ways to easing the uhh...uhh, the discomfort.”

Culis grinned and turned to Mila, who could not have been more mortified. She rarely sang, even when alone. She knew Lyria knew this. They’d tried to teach her songs on the trip to the Highlands together all those months ago. She wondered if this was the woman’s way of subtly punishing her for her attack against Baird.

“A song?” she croaked, feeling her stomach twist and sweat break out over the back of her neck. “In front of all you? I think I’d rather be keelhauled myself.”

No one but Culis laughed, and she realised that the rest of the crew were taking her hesitancy as a serious indicator that she was, indeed, a demon.

“You want me to *sing*?” she confirmed, and to her surprise there was an outbreak of hearty nods from amongst the gathered crew.

“I’ve never heard someone sing anything before,” someone nearby said.

"I've heard Acolytes chant," another murmured. "Is that the same thing?"

Mila wasn’t surprised. Singing freely was barely condoned, and very few risked it. It flirted far too close for comfort with the fine line that marked the Second Heretical Behaviour – no dancing, revelry, festivals or celebrations.

"I'm not very good," she warned them, "and the only song I know is sad." It had only been deemed acceptable because it was a funeral song, one written by a woman who, despite being entirely human, had struggled not to commit the Heretical Behaviours – namely the second. "I've been born with dancing feet" Mila remembered her, sobbing as she was dragged away by the village men for yet another stint in the stocks. "How can I not dance?"

That woman had written the song for her own funeral, a day before she'd been found hanging from the rafters of her home. The Acolyte had deemed the lyrics acceptable for the village to learn and sing in her memory – a cautionary tale of resistance – he'd called it. And so, Mila had learned it and she cleared her dry throat to sing it now.

"Shapeshifter. How I've missed you,
Though I cannot remember your name.
Seen you stumbling, through the forest,
Though the city lights are bright and bold and tame.
Pull on your new skin,
Discard the clothes you've worn.
Don't make this all about you, just agree, obey, conform.

She closed her eyes as she sang, trying to block out the crew. She willed her voice to sound like anything other than a hellish screech. She wasn't sure it was working.

See the silence at the door,
and the trenches that are dug inside the mind.
See the smile, and the way that she says

'at least tonight I will be just fine.'
Take note of every piece,
The dust upon the shelf.
Do all this and still you'd never know
the war she'd lose, against herself.

She stopped, mortified and braced herself for the mocking laughter or cries of heresy. She wasn't sure, for a moment, which would be worse.

"It...it's supposed to repeat the first verse again..." Her weak words were met with only silence.

She cracked open her eyes a tiny bit and glanced around at the crew. They were staring at her in gobsmacked silence. Culis's face was heavy. Jahan looked shaken.

"Y'sure you're not a demon, m'lady?" someone from the crew called out in wonder. "That was a mite 'ypnotic."

"It's not...not..." she stuttered. "It's not *good*. I'm not a good singer. You should have heard my sister...well. Anyway." She clamped down on that memory hard.

"Well, then." Culis donned his captain persona like a well-worn cape once again. "Anyone who still thinks our guest is a demon, hang around and explain yourself to me." He made the threat clear. "Otherwise, back to your chores."

There was a rumble of feet across wood as the spell of the song was broken and the crew hurriedly scattered back to their duties.

Culis turned to Mila. "Another secret talent of yours." His expression then shifted as he then turned to face Jahan. "And what were you going to do with that?" He glared at the sword in Jahan's hand. "Cut your way through my crew?"

"Not all of us have an oily silver tongue," Jahan snapped back, sheathing his blade.

"Leave my tongue alone. Some aboard this ship appreciate it," Culis poked back, and Mila felt a deep blush rise at her cheeks. "And in the meantime, if you're able to, next time, consider trying to restrain yourself from starting a war on my ship."

"Jealous that you weren't here – again – to protect her?"

Culis was not shocked by the venom in Jahan's words. His ensuing smile was cold. "On this ship you'll address me as Captain, *Jahan*," he replied. "And unlike you, I have more in my arsenal than just brute force when it comes to protecting those important to me. Pray tell, what would your actions have achieved? You'd have cut down the whole crew and left us stranded on a crew-less ship in the middle of the ocean? Brilliant."

Jahan scoffed and looked about to retort, but Mila held up her hand. "Please don't bicker," she turned to Culis. "If you hadn't arrived precisely when you did, I would have been in a lot of trouble without Jahan by my side. Those two meant to cause me serious harm."

"Who are they?" Culis asked, changing the subject, unwilling to give Jahan's protection acknowledgment.

"Someone's agents," Mila replied. "Although I couldn't tell whose."

"I'm sure Arran can find out." Culis nodded at Baird, who acknowledged the unspoken command and departed.

Jahan decided to accompany him and Mila sensed his frustration and jealousy leave with him. She sighed as she watched him go.

"Must you?" She rounded angrily on Culis. "Aren't you grateful he was around to defend me?"

"Of course I am," Culis admitted. "But I'll never admit that to him."

"What? Why?"

"Because that man is one windswept hair toss away from being as in love with you as I am. And I guarantee you, Mila, we've got some windy days ahead." He tried to smile at her but there was a hint of pain behind the movement. More grimace than smile. "I hate to break it to you, little demon," he ensured the nickname was said no louder than a whisper. "But the role of besotted, overbearing asshole in your life is already taken. So, yes, even though I'd freely admit to you that I was calmed one- thousand fold when I saw him braced next to you, ready to fight and kill my entire crew on your behalf, I'll never admit that to him."

Mila sighed in frustration and turned away. It'd been less than twenty-four hours since they'd agreed to come together as a team on this ship, and things were already getting complicated. Not only were the withdrawals of the stolen energy making her feel unwell enough to want to stay in bed for the rest of her life, there were agents of an unknown adversary onboard, and they'd primed the crew for suspicion. Mila felt sure that, despite the apparent 'proof' of her humanity, the crew were just one superstitious sighting away from an odd looking bird or cloud or fish and they'd turn on her again. Meanwhile her unquenchable lust for Culis was making it difficult to get through the day, and now, to top it all off, he was happy to bicker with a jealous Jahan.

"I didn't think we were at the difficult part of the journey just yet," Mila grumbled as she returned to her room, seeking a dark room and cool bed for her aching head, and leaving Culis and Natalee behind her.

Scar Catcher

They were on the ship for two nights, and in Mila's opinion that was two nights too many.

There were a number of factors that had made it unbearable. After the discovery of spies in his crew on day one, Culis now flatly refused to entertain the idea of another secret rendezvous with her in his cabin which, while she understood, still infuriated her. Additionally, the warring attitudes of Culis and Jahan on either side of her during the days was exhausting and somehow managed to make a large ship feel small. When she retreated to the privacy of her room at night it only highlighted how severely the horrible withdrawals were hitting her. The rocking of the ship didn't help and exacerbated her nausea. One evening the pain in her head was so bad she vomited and blacked out on her floor. For all the positivity and excitement she'd felt when they'd started out on this journey, she was now desperate to reach Ocianna, get off the water and give the two men, and herself, some breathing space.

On top of all this, she also felt a small flutter of worry in her gut about Frank. The man would be expecting a report from her in just a few weeks. How would she provide it if she was staying away from Jezebel and the manor? Who could she entrust with the report? Who wouldn't rouse Frank's suspicion that Mila wasn't playing his game?

It would have to be a consideration for another time.

On the day they were due in at port, Mila took to the prow of the ship in the early morning and watched the sun rise over the towering green mountains before her. She deeply breathed in the sea-salt air that was just beginning to be tinged with the warmth of the choking humidity of the Highlands. Seeing her homeland again after time away was as powerful to her now as it had been on her previous visit. She hadn't realised how deeply it had imbued itself into her soul. Up here, in the north of Artor, it felt like coming up for air after holding one's breath, and for a small second just the sight of it granted her a moment of physical reprieve from feeling so ill.

The city of Ocianna itself was built on a stretch of the Highlands where the mountains flattened out, right before the ocean. This unusual geographic quirk allowed a small but bustling port to be built right at the most north-western tip of the continent and oversaw the movement of essential and eclectic supplies shipped in and out of the country. Mila had been there once before. It was larger than Brewich, and just as busy, but in a more industrial way – one was more likely to see drab warehouses stocking paper and coal than a vintage shop hoarding colourful knick-knacks.

As *Leone's Fury* moved into Ocianna's harbour in the early morning hours, Culis gathered their small band by the starboard side to prepare them for their arrival. Mila watched as Baird uncovered and prepared the rowboat they would take to shore. Mila, Tarett, Jahan and Natalee stood waiting in their newly donned walking clothes, munching on soft cheese and fresh, dark rye bread as an early breakfast. Mila made certain Tarett ate properly. He'd stayed locked in his cabin over the past few days, and she'd barely seen him at all. He'd grown alarmingly skinny.

"Tarett, what are you wearing?" she asked, suddenly noticing that his coat appeared to be an old sail and it was covered in a scattered patchwork display.

"I made it for him," Jahan said, overhearing. "He asked for it," he shrugged, then keeping his voice down so only they could hear, "It's got pockets for all the foliage you need to collect."

Mila ran her eyes over Tarett's sad face, and her heart nearly broke. For all that had happened to him, he'd somehow still had the presence of mind to ask Jahan for something that would help their mission. He was still in there somewhere. She was determined to save him from this fate. He didn't deserve this.

"Everyone ready?" Culis came over to them. The rowboat was finally ready.

Culis led the way, and the others all piled in after him, with Baird waiting until they were all comfortably seated inside before he began lowering it down the side onto the calm, light-blue waters.

"Baird will take *Leone's Fury* and the rest of the crew on to Keras and back," Culis explained. "It's a long voyage. They won't be back for a number of months."

"No chance for spies to report anything back to anyone," Mila realised.

"Exactly," he said with a smile, then picked up an oar and began to row.

Jahan snatched up the other and pulled from the other side.

The two then proceeded to ruin the otherwise tranquil morning by rowing the small boat into port at breakneck speed, both obviously trying to out-muscle the other. When it looked, for a moment, as though Jahan might have the edge, Culis slapped his oar against the water and sent a cold spray over the lot of them, causing Jahan to miss a beat in fury, then return the gesture.

"Fabulous," Natalee scowled, wiping wet hair from her brow. "My triumphant return to the Highlands marred by the petty jealous childishness of grown men."

"I'm not jealous," both Culis and Jahan chimed simultaneously, causing both Mila and Natalee to scoff.

"Sure," Natalee said, rolling her eyes then turning to Mila. "Notice they didn't deny the childishness."

When they reached the shore, the boat bumped into the pier, and Mila and Natalee tumbled out as quickly as they could. Mila watched as Jahan tied the boat off while Culis paid the harbourmaster, and seized the opportunity to sell their boat to a nearby fisherman. Mila noted with alarm that he demanded double what the boat was worth from the man, and when he returned to her side, she gave a deep, tired sigh.

"There's only one very specific situation in which I want to hear such a hearty sigh coming from you, and standing in a fishmongers village isn't it, little demon," Culis said under his breath. "What's your problem?"

"I thought you said you were changing!" she said indignantly, ignoring the innuendo. "Why did you charge him so much? Don't you think that fisherman needs that money more than you?"

"Oh that?" He chuckled. "Don't worry. He knows exactly what he's doing, and also knows, if I ever need the boat back, I'll be paying five times what he's just turned over. The Ocianna tax, as we traders call it, is real, if not strictly official. The city is remote enough that everything is at least triple the cost up here compared to down in Traders. It's all about competition and availability."

"Oh."

"So, rest assured," Culis continued, "I'm not getting pleasure from exploiting old fishermen."

"Who's getting pleasured by old fishermen?" Jahan's voice sounded to her left as the man appeared at her side.

"Not Culis, apparently," Mila said, pleased to see the playful spark in her friend, after days of hearing nothing but his grumbling. "Although, *you*, on the other hand." She stared in amazement at Jahan's shoulder, where a huge, magnificent parrot now sat, beadily glaring down at Culis. "I didn't even realise you'd snuck off, and suddenly you're back here with that thing?"

"The lady at the end of the pier wouldn't let me off without buying him," Jahan said with a shrug, the bird bobbed up and down with the movement. "I figured I'd just release him when we're in the forest, but I didn't want to get the locals offside as soon as we arrived."

Culis rolled his eyes. "Of course, but now instead you've just announced to every vendor within a half mile that you – and by association, *we* – are easy targets. You'll need a stronger constitution than that if you're going to make it through this city with a scrap of fabric left on you."

Jahan looked up at the parrot with a new wariness on his face and grimaced. The parrot on the other hand, looked overjoyed to have made new friends and he squawked so loudly that Jahan had to wince and cover his ear.

"Well, what are you going to call him?" Natalee teased.

"I'm not going to call him anything." Jahan replied. "I'm setting him free once we're done here."

"If you don't give him a name, I'm going to name him for you."

"He doesn't have a name."

"Jahan's Folly it is. Folly for short."

Mila snorted with laughter, even Culis grinned.

"No!" Jahan cried. "Okay! If I must I'll name him. His name is... Squawker."

"Squawker!" Natalee cried. "That's a terrible name for a bird! I vote for Folly."

"Me too," Mila piled on.

"He is not a group asset!" Jahan protested. "He's my bird, his name is not up for vote."

"All in favour for Folly raise your hand and say 'aye'." Mila, Natalee and Culis all raised their hands.

"Aye."

And then to their collective delight, Folly himself copied them, and cawed an unmistakable 'aye' as he observed the proceedings with his beady eyes.

"Folly has spoken!" Natalee cried triumphantly and Mila cackled. God it felt good to laugh.

"This is bullying," Jahan grumbled and Natalee linked her arm in with his, comfortingly. "Yes," she agreed sweetly. "It is. But only the gentle sort. Besides, who are you going to tell that you were bullied by a parrot?"

Jahan cracked a smile at that.

"Far be it from me to interrupt us all bullying Jahan," Culis interjected. "But it's just occurred to me that it might be worth spending a day longer here than we'd initially planned."

"Why's that?" Mila asked, confused.

"Well Ocianna is known to sell all sorts of curiosities." He gestured to Folly. "Things you can't get down south. Out of professional interest, I'm keen to find out if the gossip network here is as good as the one down in Traders Bay, but also," his tone suddenly turned a shade darker, "we should probably see if there's anything here that could help Tarett."

As one, they all turned and looked over at the forlorn man who was staring so despondently into the rockpools beside the pier, he might as well be about to plummet headfirst into them.

"That's actually an excellent idea," Mila said.

"Well, it's still early in the day." Culis said, taking charge. "Perhaps you and I can take Tarett to a few key places I know that sell true oddities, and Natalee and Jahan can see to sorting us all some accommodations for the evening."

"Wait. No." Jahan realised he was being dismissed. "I'll go with Mila and Tarett, for protection. You go with Natalee. I'm sure you have far better idea than me about which establishments here are suitable."

"I can protect them plenty enough." Culis rolled his eyes at the implication. "And you've already proven the liability you'd be in a marketplace." He gestured to the beautiful parrot again. Folly seemed to know he was being discussed in such a manner and pulled an expression that could only be likened to a face of indignation.

"I didn't know parrots could make that face," Mila whispered to Natalee, who chuckled as the two men continued to bicker.

"So," Culis finished, "I'll be the one going with Mila and Tarett."

"At this point, I think I'd rather neither of you come." Mila was frustrated with the both of them. She turned away from the group, walked over to Tarett and took his hand. "Come with me, my friend."

"Where?"

"I'm going to find something to help you."

***

Everywhere seemed busy in Ocianna.

Unlike Traders Bay, which was also perpetually busy, there were no designated market spaces in Ocianna. Rather, the entire city seemed to be some kind of market. The stalls that lined either side of every street made the already narrow laneways look even more cramped, and the wild variety of people and animals inside gave it a decidedly carnival-like energy.

Mila surveyed it reluctantly from the outside but Culis dived in and was already haggling vigorously and delightedly at a table by the time she found her bearings.

This place is a pickpocket's dream.

Ignoring her reluctance to expose herself to the swelling wave of human and animal energy before her, Mila took a deep breath, tucked her horns in firmly, took Tarett's hand and joined Culis in the crush of people, scanning stalls as they went.

"Well," Culis returned to her side, looking jubilant.

"You found something?" Mila's heart leapt.

"Yes!" Culis exclaimed, then saw her face and quickly corrected himself. "Wait. No. Not for Tarett. But I *did* find out that the gossip market here is indeed well established and reputable."

"Excellent gossip, fabulous." Mila rolled her eyes. "Focus, please. We're here for Tarett."

"Of course!" Culis exclaimed, then winked at her. "It might surprise and delight you to learn that I can do more than one thing at a time."

"I asked you to focus," Mila grumbled, "not distract me!" She continued to press her way into the crowd.

Just like it had been at Porters Lane, retracting her horns wasn't enough to stop feeling the energy of the space. The unavoidable physical contact sent jolts of alien energy flooding through her continuously.

Greed, desire, frustration, joy, lust.

All the emotions and energies were represented here, in all their many forms and shades. She tried desperately not to get distracted and keep her eyes on the wares to her side – jewellery made from glass beads that looked like frog's eyes, charms that kept away bad dreams, soaps that smelled like garden flowers, glowing blue pebbles that Mila recognised as as the same ones that sat under the bridges in Midas's palace, illuminating the running water so spectacularly. Everything and anything one could imagine was for sale – sun catchers, wind chimes, baby soothers, pranks, education aids, animal companions, travel sickness cures...

Ahh, she thought when she saw those, and beckoned Culis over from the stall behind them. *This might be getting closer to what we need.*

The woman selling the small vials was calling out, "Sea sickness and carriage gut are your enemies no longer!" She had long grey hair and a face covered in freckles. She smiled as Mila approached her. The smile broadened as she saw the pallid look on Tarett's face.

"Ahhh, another victim of the inner ear imbalance I see. Come, come. My tonic will have your head and stomach righted in no time."

"Actually," Mila corrected, "it's something else."

"Oh?" The tall woman cocked her head. "Well, I have many things here to remedy most ailments. What's troublin' him?"

"He...well. He says he doesn't feel whole. Like he's lost part of himself."

"My soul," Tarett corrected, before Mila could stop him. "I've lost part of my soul."

The woman took a moment to study them, as if to figure out if they were mocking or teasing her, but the seriousness and distress on their faces could not be faked.

"Righto," she said cautiously. "Half a soul, I don't sell. You'd best try another stall."

"Please," Mila begged, sensing she was holding back something from them. "Could you recommend someone, anyone, that might be able to help us?"

Again, Mila had the distinct impression she was being weighed by the woman's gaze, and when the silent inspection was over, she nodded and stepped to the side, pulling with her a drape of fabric that Mila had previously assumed was just decorative, but actually revealed a hole in the wall behind her.

"Someone in here might be able to help you," she said cryptically.

Mila stared at her and scrutinised the woman with her power. There was some greed in her, but also some fear – as though she was worried Mila, Culis and Tarett could turn on her somehow. There was nothing suggesting malice, which reassured Mila. Whatever waited for them in the dark hole, it wasn't bandits waiting to rob them.

She ducked her head and took a step forward into the space. It took a moment for her eyes to adjust to the gloom as she entered, dragging Tarett along behind her and shadowed by an unusually quiet Culis. She blinked heavily, trying to see beyond the shallow light of the lone candle to get her bearings.

There was something else emitting a glow in the room. It came from the back corner, where another woman stood before a number of trunks sitting on the ground. Some were open, others closed, and still others lay on their sides with their contents strewn across the floor. Mila recognised a few. Most were dark objects with an unsettling energy. Dark scrying mirrors, unrecognisable animal skulls, vials of oil with *things* in them that had clearly once been alive, snakes, lizards, toads. Mila shivered. She hated this. She cast a look at Culis whose brow was also furrowed. Clearly, he differentiated the darkness in this room from his own shrine to death, the room of Culis's intellectual interests that was hidden deep in Culis Manor.

Behind the pile of unsavoury objects came a soft golden glow, and Mila watched as Tarett headed directly for it. He moved as though he was a puppet and whatever was emitting the glow was drawing him in on a ghostly, irresistible string.

As Mila followed him, she felt the wash of death energy strike her chest. She nearly moaned aloud in horror when she saw what was making it.

The glow was coming from a small, neat pile of jars that sat on a low table in the dark corner. The jars were full of sand, Midas's golden sand. They sat quietly, emitting their low energetic hum of death like a chilling, sparking graveyard made up of ikarei Midas had once touched.

"Tarett, let's go," Mila said, tugging him back towards the door they had come in. "There's nothing here for you."

"Wait," Tarett croaked, his eyes fixated on the jars. "This feels...I want to...touch one."

Mila dropped his hand in shock and shot Culis a worried look. Tarett pulled away from her and walked towards the jars, a hypnotised mouse towards a cobra.

The woman who stood on the other side of the table looked identical to the one who sold the wares outside. Twins. Not an entirely uncommon phenomenon, but it somehow seemed unnerving to Mila under the circumstances.

"What's wrong with him?" the woman asked Mila as Tarett approached. She wore a funny, unnerving smile, as if some trap she'd set was closing, and no one but her could see the jaws.

"How do you have Midas's sand?" Mila demanded, not willing to tell this strange woman anything. Not only was the God-King's sand a pure abomination, but selling it or possessing it was blatant misuse – the Fourth Heretical Behaviour.

"The God-King's sand is the energy of living beings." The woman sidestepped the question smoothly and turned her attention to Tarett instead, making no move to stop him reaching for one of the small jars. "If anything is going to give a depressed and embattled soul a boost, it's the pure life energy of another soul."

This is so evil, Mila thought, but Tarett's gasp of relief was undeniable as he clutched the sand to his breast.

"Mila." He turned to face her, his eyes gleaming with tears. "I'm back!"

Mila stared at him in dumbfounded, horrified silence.

"It...worked?" Culis whispered incredulously. Mila moved closer to Tarett to inspect him, straining against her impulse to back away from the thrum of the horrid energy.

"Not...completely." Tarett's voice was light. "But...oh fates. I can breathe again. I can...oh. I can feel *me* again!"

The twin watched on curiously. Mila wondered if she suspected that Tarett was suffering from something more serious than just a depression.

"We'll take one." Mila said the words through gritted teeth. She hated that this was the solution. Was this truly the only counter to her power? Midas's monstrosity? What sordid irony.

"A thousand gold pieces," she heard Culis offer from behind her.

The woman scoffed. "Of course. If all you want is a single grain. But the glass of the empty jar alone is worth double that. Fifty thousand."

Mila's jaw dropped, and despite Culis's best efforts, the woman would suffer no bargaining or negotiation. She knew what she had. She knew they'd find nothing else like this on the market, and although she didn't know their exact situation, she could see what it meant to Tarett, who was currently cradling the jar to his chest and sobbing quietly in relief.

Culis did not have fifty thousand gold pieces on pocket. He offered all he had on him, which was about ten thousand, and he wrote and stamped a note with his personal seal that allowed the woman to withdraw the remainder from any ship of the Artor Trading Company that docked at Ocianna in the future. The woman snatched the note from his hand and stuffed it away into a hidden pocket of her floating robes greedily.

"Thank you, thank you," Tarett gushed to her, rather than Culis, before they left. He shook her hand and kissed the back of it as though she were a god herself. "You don't know what...you don't know what this means."

Mila's blood felt cold. Culis's face was a strange, blank mask. Whatever this solution was, it didn't feel like a good one.

As the three of them moved to depart the strange, unnerving little room, Tarett threw his hands wide, as if experimenting with the sensation of feeling in his own skin again. The unexpected movement caught Culis off guard. Startled, he stumbled, knocking into a shining, purple crystal vial that sat upon its own little table in the corner.

"Ah!" Culis cried out, lunging for the bottle as it fell.

"No!" the twin shouted, reaching out her hand as though she could somehow cross the floor and save it from impact.

It spun in the air as if in slow motion. Once, twice, thrice it flipped and then landed on the outstretched tips of Culis's fingers. For half a second, Mila thought he'd stabilised it, but at the very last moment, the liquid inside seemed to move of its own accord. It leapt from the open vial and drenched Culis's hand and sleeve.

Culis's eyes immediately rolled back into his head as he collapsed.

"Catch him!" the woman called briskly as she rounded the table and ran to them.

Mila was grateful that Tarett was now of sound enough mind to respond. His arms flew out, grabbing Culis's head and shoulders before he struck the hard floor.

Mila stared at his face in horror. All she could see were the whites of Culis's eyes, his mouth curled up into what could only be described as an expression of utter horror.

"Culis!" she shook him, then yanked her touch away from him as though she'd been burned.

That was not Culis's energy she now felt in his body. There was something else in there. Something small and frightened. Deathly frightened.

"What's happened to him?" She rounded on the woman in anger, but the strange woman did not respond in fear. She seemed annoyed, as if they'd mightily inconvenienced her somehow.

"Well," she huffed. "We can't do anything about it now. Might as well get comfortable while you wait it out. And that dash will cost you another fifteen thousand gold pieces."

"Wait what out?" Mila demanded, her panic rising as Culis began to twitch in Tarett's arms. "What's wrong with him?"

"He touched a drop of scar catcher," the woman explained. "Well...he damn near took a bath in the whole bottle. He's in for a wild ride."

"Scar catcher?" Mila was decidedly unhappy with the woman's half answer. "What in the Rotting Muds does that mean?"

"Very expensive potion," she tutted. "And yes, dear, don't look at me like that. He'll wake up. He's just going to re-live some old scars for the next hour or so. Want to see?" The look on the sharp woman's face turned devious as she held out a small, ornate hand mirror.

Mila would have flinched away from the item if she hadn't seen a flicker of Culis's open green eyes in there, instead of her own reflection. She snatched the strange object from the woman's hand and stared hard at the glass. What she saw inside was startling. It was as though she was not looking into a mirror, but a window. Except this window showed a Christopher Culis that was much younger than the man she knew. The version of him inside the mirror was a boy, probably no older than seven or eight summers.

He was heaving with the effort of holding back tears and holding a hand to his cheek, as though he'd just been struck. Mila tilted the mirror and suddenly saw another figure in there with young Culis.

Frank.

The youthful figure of Frank was no less imposing or fearsome than his matured self. He towered over his son, a horse whip in hand, slick golden hair showing no signs of the silvering that Mila had come to expect at the sight of him.

"What did you say to me?" she heard Frank say in an icy cold voice to the cringing child at his feet.

"I...I..." young Culis stuttered.

"Tell me again how you decided your time would be better spent making this?" Frank kicked something on the floor and drew Mila's gaze. It was a half-carved wooden animal. A horse. "Rather than on the problems I paid a small fortune for your tutor to devise."

"I...I..." Young Culis was clearly desperate to speak in his defence, but Frank wouldn't let him.

"Tell me again how a veritable prince of my name sees fit to ignore every luxury I have given him, to denigrate himself to a peasant's pastime."

"It...I..."

Smack.

Another blow to the face. Before her, the face of Culis, *her* Culis, flinched, as if he were feeling the strike in real time.

"Do not speak," Frank hissed in the mirror. "You insolent, ungrateful brat. Nothing is to pass between your lips until midday tomorrow." He turned to the child's attendants. "Instant dismissal is only the start of what you can expect to receive from me if I find out you've disobeyed me. No water. No food and not a peep out of him. Understand?"

"Yes, Master," the burly manservant said with a nod.

Mila was horrified. The Culis at her feet, the physical body, groaned in despair. Mila reached for him and placed a hand on his chest. His heart was hammering as though he had been sprinting. Perspiration began to appear on his brow. The energy she felt from him was frozen in terror, like his mind was locked in a nightmare.

The scene in the mirror dissolved, and was replaced by another. Culis was still a child. He could not have been much older than he'd been in the first scene. Perhaps only a few weeks had passed since then. Perhaps only days. Frank's looming spectre was present in this scene too.

"A friend?" he scoffed. "Christopher. To get anywhere in this world, you need to understand that the people you meet will either want to be you, fuck you or fuck you over. There's no such thing as a friend, and anyone masquerading as one is just a scorpion in disguise.

No friends. Only conquests and those who pay fealty. Repeat after me. Only conquests..."

Mila looked up from the mirror at the strange old twin who hovered over them nosily. She smiled a dark, witchy smile at her.

"Scar catcher," Mila said slowly. "I'm seeing all the things that have scarred him? He's reliving them?"

The woman nodded. "Clever girl."

"Why on earth does such a potion exist?" Mila demanded. "Who could have use for such a thing? And why does *this*" – she brandished the mirror before her – "exist? So someone can be a voyeur to another's pain? How sick."

"Some people use it for healing," the woman said with a shrug. "With a trusted guide holding the mirror. It can do some of us plenty good to revisit old scars and try to mend them. Others use it as a form of torture on an enemy, or to gain valuable knowledge about how to rile a foe. It has many uses." She shrugged and gestured at Tarett's vial of sand. "You're being quite judgemental for someone who just purchased some of the most contraband material in the nation."

Mila placed the mirror face down on the ground to hide the images playing through the glass. She reached again for Culis, realising the woman was right, and that she and Tarett were simply going to have to wait this out. As he twitched and cried out beneath her palm, Mila wondered if there was a part of him that was conscious she was there, if her warm hand on his chest was any comfort while he relived these experiences.

While she waited, she found it harder not to keep watching the mirror than she liked to admit. There was something morbidly fascinating about watching someone's worst moments, and she knew without a doubt that seeing them would help her understand him tenfold. *But no,* she told herself. They weren't hers to see. Not without Culis's permission, and he was in no state to give it. She knew that she'd never want someone to watch her own scars play out. Never want anyone to see what had happened in her house the morning she'd woken with horns and powers. The moment her family had not only disowned her but actively tried to have her lynched.

She pushed those terrible, aching, painful memories away and instead sat quietly by Culis's side, one hand on his chest, the other tightly clutching his hand.

"It's alright," she whispered in his ear. "This isn't real, and it will pass. We're here with you." Culis's body gave no sign that he'd heard her. He flinched and cried out again, tears starting to form in the corners of his eyes. Mila wiped them away.

Beside her, Tarett was having his own moment – the polar opposite of Culis's current ordeal. He sat beside Mila with his eyes closed, head tilted back, tears streaming down his face and a huge grin on his face.

"I feel as though I have been reborn," he whispered, pressing the hateful, glowing jar against his face, as though he could somehow meld it into himself. "I was...a shell. I was dead. An animated body with nothing to power it. But now...I have been given a second chance."

"I am...I am..." Mila struggled to say the words. "I am happy for you." It was not quite a lie, but it came out stilted and cold. She was, of course, grateful that the effect of her power had been countered. The fact that it was Midas's sand that enabled this was deeply uncomfortable and concerning. "I'd still like to try and fix you myself, if it's possible to do," she added softly.

"Of course," Tarett snapped, his sudden anger uncharacteristic and absolute. "We'd all prefer that. But until that time, if that is even possible, don't begrudge me this."

"No. Of course, I don't." Guilt swamped her. "I'm glad we found a way to bring you back into yourself."

Culis's body twitched aggressively before them, and another wave of his pained, terrified energy swept through him into her. Mila again fought the urge to look into the mirror, to watch the next scar unfolding. What she'd already seen was horrifying enough, and exactly what Baird and Arran had told her Culis's childhood had been like under Frank's thumb.

She resisted, and chose to murmur comforting words in his ear instead.

"You're safe. You're with friends. I have you." And it was true. She still did. She'd protect his privacy and his pain while he was in this state. And she wouldn't let go of his hand, no matter how tightly he squeezed it

So there she sat for the better part of the afternoon. Tarett to her left, in a state of utter ecstasy at his renewal, and Culis's limp body to her right, reliving the worst of everything that had ever happened to him in his life. This wasn't how she'd expected their day to go.

Hours later, Culis's deep groan and heave of breath was the indicator Mila needed to hear to know that his ordeal was finally over.

"Culis," she murmured gently in his ear. "It's okay. You're safe. I have you." And she did. She hadn't let go of his hand the entire time.

Culis's eyes opened heavily. They were red from weeping. He looked utterly exhausted. "What the hell was that?" he managed to croak out, his dry throat rasping.

"Water?" Mila looked at the woman, who gave a sharp nod and fetched a pitcher full.

"It was a scar catcher potion," Mila explained. "Something to make you relive your worst moments."

"You're telling me." Culis's hand cradled his head as he sat up. He groaned deeply. A weary and pitiful sound she'd never heard him make before.

"Are you able to walk?" Mila asked carefully. As much as she wanted to help Culis, she was desperate to get them out of this room.

He seemed to agree. "Yes. Let's go."

Culis barely flinched when the woman would not let them leave without taking the remainder of everything they had, and he all but threw his purse at her in his effort to leave.

"A very expensive torture," he said quietly as they walked out into the now somewhat quieter market. The sun was considerably lower in the sky than it had been when they'd first gone into the little room, and most of the stallholders were now covering their wares with thick linen tarpaulins.

Mila found herself having to keep one eye on a struggling Culis and the other on a bounding Tarett, who was now chatting happily and interacting gaily with his surroundings again.

"I'm fine," Culis insisted, but was leaning on her heavily. "Don't let me dampen his mood."

They followed Tarett into a nearby tavern and watched as he jovially ordered a round of drinks for everyone inside.

"With whose purse?" Culis said, with an attempt at a half smile. "The bank of Culis is now empty." Tarett didn't let this daunt him in the slightest, and after a few boasting remarks to the tavern owner, she seemed to accept that the Artor Trading Company would be good for the bill in the future.

"Remind me to ensure that the next ship we send is a treasury ship." Culis groaned as he slumped into a seat by the window. Mila joined him, feeling decidedly sick.

"Culis," she said softly, brushing his hair back, "are you alright?"

He took a deep breath and closed his eyes. "I have no idea," he replied truthfully. "That was..." he looked like he might burst into tears but fought them back and composed his features with effort.

"I'm not sure I can talk about it yet. Maybe not ever. I've never endured anything like that."

"I can't even begin to imagine."

"Can we talk about something else?" Culis asked, forcing his tone to become lighter and a tired smile onto his face. "Tarett's cure is...unexpected, to say the least."

"It can't be a long-term solution," Mila muttered, watching Tarett flirt with the barmaid as she poured his drinks. "It can't be. There's death energy in those vials. It might be rejuvenating him right now, but long term? There's got to be something else."

"If there is, we'll find it," Culis tried to assure her, but his face was grim.

Tarett insisted that the rest of the evening be a celebration of his restoration and continued ordering round after round for the entire tavern. Word soon spread throughout the small city, and by mid-evening, Jahan and Natalee had found them, and the tavern was packed shoulder to shoulder with drunken revellers and an absolutely obliterated Tarett.

"Madman shouting 'free drinks' at the Billy Arms," Jahan said, as he, with Folly still happily attached to his shoulder, and Natalee joined Mila and Culis in their booth. "That's the word about town."

"And that was the sign it was us?" Mila asked with a strained smile. "Madman in town?"

"Were we wrong?" Natalee replied. "You obviously found the cure."

"It wasn't what we expected," Mila replied and regaled them with the story of Tarett's recovery, but omitting the part about the scar catcher and Culis's subsequent ordeal. "Is he going to be okay?" Natalee asked once she'd finished.

"I have no idea," Mila replied honestly, watching Tarett carefully as the evening progressed. His recovery was bizarre.

Midas's sand held a potency that had always made her shudder. The energy of an ikarei's final scream, final heartbeat, and all the destroyed potential of their life. To her, it was a horrific, disgusting object that she wanted as far away from her as possible at all times. She could barely believe that, since acquiring it, Tarett had spent the afternoon with it clutched possessively to his chest and luxuriating in a renewed, hearty appetite for life. It was wrong. Off, somehow.

There was also something different about him that made her worry. Mila sensed a hardness in him now that hadn't been there before. A selfishness. Something dark and corrosive. She understood that he was elated at his returned sense of self, but still...his utter disregard for Culis's experience that afternoon was callous, and when the waitress had tripped and spilled scalding tea all over her hands, Mila had watched in disbelief as Tarett, rather than gasping in sympathy, had to try hide his laughter.

She considered saying something but ultimately decided against it. Of course Midas's sand wouldn't influence someone to be their best self, and what would be the point when she didn't have another solution for him?

She turned back to Culis and ran an assessing eye over him instead. He was putting on a grand show for Jahan and Natalee. No one would have guessed that anything was amiss with him, and with Tarett's miraculous recovery serving as the main point of conversation for the evening, his exhaustion was easily disguised. He nearly got away with it entirely, his early retirement being the only cause for a single raised eyebrow from Jahan.

Mila didn't know whether to be relieved or worried.

Sacrifice

That night, Mila lay in bed, buzzing in discomfort.The symptoms from the energy she'd stolen were now nearly unbearable, and she was beginning to worry that she wouldn't be able to endure them without help for much longer. It felt as though her veins had all transformed, expanded to accommodate the excess energy she'd taken, but were now refusing to return to their original form without a fight. Her body ached ferociously and she had to hold back moans of pain as she lay in the darkness. The nausea had also returned, this time with a vengeance, and was accompanied now with profuse sweating. Mila found herself lying in agony in the bunk she was sharing with Natalee. They were in a tiny, damp room above the Billy Arms that they were also sharing with Jahan and Culis because they hadn't been able to convince Tarett to move from this tavern with all his newfound drinking friends. Folly seemed to be the only one happy with the situation, perched securely on Jahan's bedhead, his head tucked tightly under a colourful wing. Apparently, the bird had decided on his own accord that he wasn't going anywhere.

Before they'd all gone to bed, Jahan and Natalee had pulled a fifth mattress in and laid it on the floor for Tarett, which turned out to be a good decision because when the man finally stumbled in, he was so intoxicated he could barely get out of his trousers, let alone climb a bunk.

When Tarett collapsed into the thin mattress and began boarishly snoring, everyone in the room groaned.

"Oh for fates' sake," Natalee snapped from below. "I've just about had enough of this."

"Leave him." Culis's tired voice cut through the dark. "Let a man celebrate the return of his soul however he sees fit."

Natalee ignored him. She reached down and gave Tarett a mighty push. The force of it caused the bottle of Midas's sand to roll out from his slack grip and across the wooden floorboards.

The response from Tarett was immediate. He began muttering and twitching violently, as if having a seizure.

"Oh, Tarett!" Natalee gasped in horror. She leapt out of bed and tried to shake him awake but whether it was from the alcohol or something else, he didn't respond.

The small jar of Midas's sand was continuing to roll away. Cringing, Natalee picked up a nearby boot and tapped the jar with the boot's heel, rolling it back towards Tarett until it nestled against the crook of his underarm. Once it was there, touching him again, Tarett sighed a deep breath of relief. The seizure stopped as he reached for it sharply and drew it tight against his chest.

Mila watched all this with a sinking heart.

Seeing the Golden Sand clutched in Tarett's vicelike grip drew a parallel between Midas's power and her own that she did not want to make but could no longer ignore.

Both of them so destructive. Both of them irreversible.

What was happening to her? What was *going* to happen to her? Were these symptoms ever going to abate, or would they drive her mad? And what was this shadowy, threatening dark voice that had begun looming in the back of her mind promising her reprieve from the pain if she would just use her power again. Just once. Just a little more...

A gigantic snore from Tarett cut through the silence, raking against the swollen, hot pain of her mind.

Mila sat up in bed and rustled about, beginning to don her boots. "I'm going," she announced to the others.

"Going where?" Natalee asked.

"Away. For a walk. Anywhere. I need to clear my head."

"I'll come with you," Jahan offered.

"Well, then I'll come too," Culis chirped immediately and Jahan growled in annoyance.

"Well if you're all leaving, so am I!" Natalee exclaimed. "I don't want to be left here alone!"

"Someone needs to stay here with Tarett," Culis bit back automatically. "You will stay."

"You're not the captain of this room, Culis." Natalee's tone was sharp with warning. "That better not be an order."

"Fine," Culis snapped back. "It doesn't have to be an order. It can be a suggestion, but I know you find those hard too."

"Why you –"

Mila closed the door on their bickering, already halfway down the hallway, clutching at her head and forcing back tears of pain before Jahan emerged from the room behind her, followed closely by Culis, who was still jumping into his left boot.

"Are you okay?" Jahan asked, studying her face with concern when he caught up to her.

"I'm fine." Mila brushed him off. How could she tell him what was happening to her? "Is Natalee staying behind then?" Mila asked as they all walked past the now empty bar and out the front door. "Who convinced her?"

"No one," Culis said. "I just made her the last person in the room responsible for Tarett's supervision. She won't leave Tarett alone. Not after what's just happened."

"That's cruel."

"It's not," he protested. "I'm hardly going to let you and this pining lovebird walk the street alone at night together, am I?"

"Excuse me?"

"A pining *what*?!"

Mila's and Jahan's indignation were simultaneous, and Culis just chuckled in response. Despite her distress, the sound lightened her soul a little. It was his first laugh since the scar catcher. If he was teasing again then maybe he was starting to feel better.

Culis turned to her. "Well, fearless leader? Where are you taking this merry band of night wanderers?"

"I need to see if I can reverse my power," Mila said as she walked. "I can't let Tarett's only hope be this jar of Midas's sand. I just can't. That thing is evil."

They must have both wordlessly felt the same way, for they followed her without question after that, all the way to the edge of the small city, the place where the cobblestones ended and the rainforest started, thick and wild. There, Mila reached for a large, bowl-leaf plant. *Less,* she commanded, aiming to drain it fully. To her surprise, it worked. The plant shrivelled entirely at her touch.

The subtle relief it provided her from the nearly debilitating pain of her symptoms was instant. She could not disguise the tiny sigh of relief that escaped her. Culis shot her a sharp questioning look she deliberately ignored. The nausea had lifted a little. Her hands felt slightly steadier. That was all that mattered in that moment.

So, this is an answer to at least one question.

Using her power made the symptoms better, but she assumed the relief was temporary. Ultimately they'd return, and draining the tiny flit of energy that had been present in this leaf was hardly enough to satiate her overwhelming need. She might have to drain the whole tree just to feel normal again.

"Well?" Jahan pressed.

"Well, what?" she snapped at him

"Can you bring it back?" he was looking at the leaf.

"Ah yes, of course." That had been the whole purpose of this excursion, hadn't it? Figure out how to reverse her power? It hadn't been to find a living thing to drain and abate her pain. Had it?

Hadn't it?

What had she told them? What had she meant to say? She could barely remember, like her memory was fuzzy somehow. As though her feet and her mouth had acted of their own accord and each had a different purpose. She refocused on the shrivelled brown roll of leaf that sat in her palm.

This has to work.

Culis and Jahan watched her expectantly as she tried her utmost to press the energy and life she'd taken from it back into it. She strained and heaved. She even tried blowing on it.

Nothing.

It was as though her parasitic, hungry new power, which had dragged every last morsel of life and vigour from the leaf, had barricaded her access back into the thing. She was locked out.

Permanent.

Mila turned to face Jahan and Culis in anguish, on the verge of tears. "There has to be a way!"

"There must be," Jahan assured her, reaching for her shoulder. "Don't worry. We'll find it."

Culis gave her no such false assurances. He looked at her and grimaced softly. "I don't know." He took her hand.

The energy that flowed through each of them was very different. Jahan's energy, as always, was forthright and determined. He would never stop looking for the answer, never give up. But underneath that all was a whisper of panic, of fear. A drop of worry that mirrored Mila's own – that she might, indeed, be the harbinger of something terrible into their lives. Culis's energy was no less earnest. He, too, would go to the ends of the earth to help her, this she knew. But when she probed her power into him more deeply, hunting for that same seed of fear, she couldn't find it. Instead, where it should have been was a note of calm acceptance.

He doesn't care, she realised. *He'd still love me anyway.*

Even if there was no cure. Even if she couldn't fix Tarett. Even if he knew that every touch of their skin was a risk. He'd love her anyway.

She smiled at them both, grateful for the support they offered her, but she looked directly at Culis when she said, "Thank you."

***

On their way back to the tavern, Mila and Culis were walking a step behind Jahan, who rounded a corner and stopped so abruptly they almost bumped into his back. He raised his closed palm sharply, signalling *silence.*

Mila instantly extended her horns in response and sent her power out through the streets that lay before them, searching the invisible energetic radius around them for threats. She quickly picked up on whatever it was that Jahan had seen.

A person sneaking along in the shadows of the road. A woman, her energy murderous, was moving just a few feet to the left of them and entering a particularly dark alley. What was possibly more unnerving to Mila was that the energy was familiar somehow, like she'd come across it in a dream once. But when she reached for the memory, it slid from her grasp, elusive and slippery.

"What is it?" Culis's whisper close to her ear was no louder than a fluttering moth.

"I'm not sure yet."

"This way," Jahan murmured, gesturing and leading them cautiously around the corner.

There they found themselves off the main street and at the mouth of the dark alleyway. The woman Mila had sensed was nowhere to be seen or felt. She'd vanished somehow, as abruptly as she'd appeared.

Mila peered groggily down the long alley. It held a number of doorways, each marked by a swinging, cast-iron lantern. There were a few people milling around each, but everyone resolutely avoided eye contact with one another. The energy of the space reeked of anonymity and secrets. Most of these establishments, Mila realised, were brothels and opium dens. They'd somehow wound up in the less reputable part of town.

"Where'd she go?" Jahan whispered to Mila. "Into one of these?" He gestured to the doors around them.

"She must have," Mila replied. "But I don't know which."

"Well, what are we going to do? Enter each one and look for her? That'll take all night."

"Why do we have to find someone?" Culis asked, trying to keep up.

"I'm not sure," Mila replied. She was confused by what she'd felt in the woman's energy, but something had definitely felt off and it seemed worthwhile to find out what that was. "What did you see?" she asked Jahan.

"Someone pocketing a long, nasty-looking dagger. They were trying not to be seen," Jahan replied. "Maybe I was wrong."

"You weren't wrong," Mila assured him. "There was definitely something wrong about her energy, but also something familiar."

"Familiar?" Culis became very serious. "Someone who'd recognise us?"

Mila wished she had a concrete answer for him. "Maybe?"

"Let's just give it a moment," Culis whispered. "If you both thought something wasn't right, I think we should trust that instinct. Let's wait here a minute and try and identify what the pattern of ordinary looks like in a place like this. If something is out of the ordinary, it tends to have a way of revealing itself if you hang around long enough. And," he added, "if you scan your eyes from right to left – the opposite direction of how you read – that'll help your brain to pick up irregularities in your surroundings."

"So most people scan left to right?"

"Yes, and it's easier to miss things that way. Your brain gets lazy."

Mila stared at him incredulously. "These are not things normal, law-abiding citizens know, Culis!"

"Oh, and you're the epitome of a normal, law-abiding citizen?" His beautiful smile stole the breath from her body.

She forced her gaze to return to the alleyway.

"Come with me." Culis led them out of the alley, to the next street over.

Once there, Mila watched in amazement as, in an unexpected move of dynamic athleticism, Culis used a drainpipe and some uneven bricks to scale up the side of a building.

"Culis!" she hissed up at him. "We can't do that!"

"Sure, you can," he called back. "Just pretend it's a tree."

Mila considered the pipe in front of her and realised he was right. She'd spent a decade climbing the trees around her house in Bori. Was this really so different?

Jahan shrugged and indicated for her to go next. "I'll catch you if you fall," he said.

"What if *you* fall?" she asked.

"I won't fall. Not if you don't. I'll watch where you put your hands and feet and copy what you do."

Agreeing, Mila cautiously placed one hand on the side of the pipe and the toes of one foot into a ridge in the wall, reaching up until her hand could reach the top of the windowsill to her left. She realised that, from here, she could quite easily pull herself up, and once she'd managed that, she was halfway to the top.

"There you go," Culis called encouragingly. Once she was close enough to the top, he reached down to grasp her by the collar and haul her the last of the distance.

"Whoo!" she said quietly, with a gasp of exhilaration.

"A city is just a different kind of jungle," Culis said with a smile, leaning back over the rooftop to pull Jahan up alongside them.

"With vastly more dangerous animals," Mila agreed. "How many times in your life have you scaled a building? And what are we doing up here?"

"More times than I've wanted, and we're investigating," Culis replied, and led them across the rooftops towards the back of the alley.

For a few long moments, the three of them lay quietly in the shadows, watching and waiting, but not knowing exactly what they were waiting for. Their patience was rewarded when, as Culis had said, something decidedly *not normal* caught their eye.

A new figure slunk into the alleyway. Hooded and cloaked, walking with determination past all the dens and into the dark, at the far end of the street, where they disappeared into the shadows.

"Whoever *that* was," Mila whispered to Culis, "they had the same energy as the other woman, the same ominous, murderous, anticipatory energy. Something bad is happening down that end of the alley."

"Hmm." Culis unconsciously pushed the curl back again, uselessly, and then the three of them shuffled further along the roof, away from the street lanterns and deeper into the bleary darkness, until they saw the door at the end of the alley. It was cast in shadow with no lantern lighting its threshold.

Invisible.

Mila, Culis and Jahan watched from above as a third hooded figure made its way down the alley and tapped a soft, secret knock against the black door, which opened a crack and then let them slide inside.

"I was wrong," Mila breathed to Culis. "This has nothing to do with us at all. We should leave."

"I definitely don't want to knock on that door," Culis agreed, but he pointed to a skylight that was built into the roof beside them. "But I do want to take a peek at what's going on in there."

Despite the danger of the moment, Mila loved seeing this side of him. This adventurous, curious risk-taker. His intrigue had always stoked her own, and tonight, regardless of how ill she'd been feeling and uncomfortable about Tarett's recovery, she found herself suddenly equally as curious about the outcome. Jahan was also not immune. Together, and despite the warning note in her stomach, Mila, Jahan and Culis knelt and crawled over to the skylight, then laid on their bellies and peered over the edge.

In the room below were at least thirty people. They stood tightly packed together like cattle, all wearing dark robes. It was a tavern, but it certainly wasn't currently being used as a place of drinking and merriment.

Amongst the crowd, Mila hunted to find the familiar energy of the first woman, but it was too difficult a task. The whole crowd was buzzing with that same murderous zest and clamouring around a man who stood by a counter. The counter was covered by a thick shadow, rather than glasses and mugs of ale.

Mila had a distinctly ominous feeling about what the decidedly human-shaped shadow on the counter could be.

The man standing in the centre of it all started speaking, and she had to turn her eyes away as she pressed her ear to the glass to hear him.

"...has come to dispense the justice of the God-King according to his laws. No more corruption. No longer shall a blind eye be turned against those who profess to live a life of pious observance in public, but are all too happy to break the Divine law in private. The Children of Midas will no longer shy away from the call to see the God-King's justice dispensed!"

"What is he talking about?" Jahan mouthed, his brown eye filled with apprehension, his ear similarly pressed against the glass. Mila knew. It was the same message the rioters had been yelling in Traders Bay, stoked into a frenzy by the Children of Midas.

"Down with Abbott, the Church is corrupt."

She pulled her ear away from the glass to observe the scene once more. She also hated Abbott and the Church, but the Children of Midas were not a suitable replacement. This wasn't a rebellion for the sake of the freedom of peace in Artor. This was a group of zealots seeking a violent transfer of power.

As if to confirm her fears, thirty pairs of hands suddenly extended from the dark robes, clasped together in fevered prayer. The man at the bar stood with his hands reaching out to the congregation, and before him, the dark shadow on the counter rolled to the side.

Mila gasped when she saw what it was.

Not a shadow at all, but a young Church acolyte. An acolyte with his hands bound and his mouth gagged. His face was red with the effort of straining against his bonds, his coal-black hair sweaty and plastered flat to his forehead.

"What are they going to do to him?"

As if in answer to Mila's question, the man below continued speaking.

"For too long has our nation – have our *Highlands* – been subjugated to the Church's law, rather than the laws that stem directly from the mouth and actions of the God-King himself. The Church has proved itself to be corrupt. The Church has used fear and lies to turn us from the God-King's true path for our lives."

This was met by a collective cry of outrage from the gathered.

"This liar" – the man pointed at the pitiful, bound acolyte – "claims to live among us as a way to hold our community accountable and ensure we follow the God-King's commands. But this *same* man is from the Church that has endorsed, as we've recently discovered, not only dancing and revelry amongst the elites, but the use of jars of the God-King's sacred sand as decorations." At this, he held up a vial of the God-King's sand triumphantly, as though this was somehow proof of his accusation. Having just seen the stock of them recently in the back market, Mila had no idea how anyone could verify that it had come from the acolyte's house, but none of the gathered seemed to care about the inconvenience of the burden of proof at that moment. The acolyte himself looked at the jar with bug-eyed fright.

"We know they do not enforce the demon tests in the cities with the same vigour and violence as they do up here," the man continued. "And why should they? When the God-King himself has shown his mercy to demons, when he permitted the last demon taken from the Highlands to live – and she continues to live!"

Mila shrank back a bit from the skylight at these words. They were talking about her. Perhaps she wasn't safer in the Highlands after all. Perhaps in her absence, she'd somehow become infamous up here?

"Why, when we know all this, does the Church insist on the violent tests inflicted on our Highland children?" the man continued. "Why are *we* forbidden from dancing and festivals, barred from our culture when the elites engage freely in their own decadence? I tell you clearly now – the God-King's word is the only word we must follow. The pure word, the clean word. Not the Heretical Behaviours. That list is a blasphemous Church document, and it will be used to control and subjugate us no longer!"

A roar from the crowd met his words.

Mila suddenly knew what was going to happen. Knew it by the prickly hum of energy she now recognised as violence, cloaking the air. These people were going to kill the acolyte. They were going to prove their devotion to the God-King, their hatred of the Church, by sacrificing this man, and they were using her continued life as justification, proof that they were following the God-King's commands more purely than Abbott's Church did.

She started sliding off the roof, back the way they'd come.

"Mila, no!" Culis's strong arms seized her and held her in place.

"Let me go," she whispered fiercely, her blood boiling. It didn't matter that this man was an acolyte. She couldn't let this happen, couldn't let this insanity go on unchecked.

"No." Culis's grip was like iron. "Not unless you can tell me exactly what you plan to do, how you plan to stop this."

"I'm going to go down there and – "

"And what? Barge in there and tell them they can't worship like this? That this is wrong?"

"This isn't *worship*," she hissed. "This is evil."

"It is," Culis agreed sternly. "But they'll just kill you too."

"They won't," Mila responded. "The God-King spared me."

"Why?" His question was unexpected.

"I don't know, but it doesn't matter."

"They didn't care about that when they were attacking you at the riot."

"That was different. That was random. They didn't know who I was."

"Oh, and they will now? They'll know you by sight?"

"I... I don't know. I'll tell them!"

"Tell them *what*?!" Culis's frustration and concern had turned his energy searing red. "You'll announce your presence to the whole Highlands? After all our efforts to remain undetected so far? On the off chance that somehow they'll care you're the demon Midas spared? We don't even know what that means to them. No. I won't let you risk yourself for this man."

"Agreed," Jahan said with a fast and firm shake of his head, backing up Culis.

"Since when do you two agree on anything?" she shot back furiously.

"Since now," Jahan rumbled.

"Mila, you can't go down there," Culis said again. "One on one, it might be different. You might be able to talk them out of it. But not with the whole group of them down there. They're clamouring for blood. Even I can sense it, and my powers of empathy are about as honed as a blunt stick."

Mila hated that he was right. There was a blood lust and an ugly sense of righteousness rising from the room below that was as evil as anything she'd ever felt in this world. She wouldn't be able to talk them out of doing this.

Even as she thought it, she felt a deep ache of shame in her chest at the decision. Hadn't she vowed not to be a coward again?

Culis seemed to understand her expression. "It's not...There's a difference between being brave and acknowledging a hopeless situation, Mila."

Mila just nodded and crawled back up to the skylight, forcing herself to peer over it again.

Below, the muscles on the neck of the bound acolyte turned purple as he struggled and screamed behind the gag. She watched in horror as the ringleader pulled a large ceremonial dagger from the waistband of his attire and held it above his head.

Culis sucked in a horrified breath beside her. Jahan turned his face away and scrunched his eyes closed.

Mila forced herself to watch.

If she couldn't save him, the least she could do was watch.

The dagger descended with abrupt finality. The man stabbed the acolyte in the gut and tore it free with a violence so bold, so absolute, it bordered on clumsiness. The young acolyte's eyes widened in shock and agony. He screamed through the gag, writhing staring at the new gaping hole in his body, his mind trying to make sense of it.

Even with her horns fully withdrawn, Mila could still feel his panic and animalistic fear. She fought not to let it overwhelm her.

But the leader still wasn't done. He nodded to the assistant by his side, who reached forward and tied a thick rope around the acolyte's legs. From there, they threw the length of the rope up to the ceiling, wrapping it around one of the thick beams. As the crowd followed the swing of the rope and lifted their eyes to the ceiling, Mila, Jahan, and Culis instinctively drew their heads quickly back from the skylight.

Mila was trembling and could feel Culis's cold, clammy skin against her own, his horror mirroring hers.

The leader's sickening drone could still be heard below them. "Your crimes are made all the more heinous by being committed by one with the privilege of your rank. I decree you shall not die quickly but shall spend your final hours ruminating over your sins."

"This is...I can't." Mila clasped her hands to her head, desperately trying to block the sheer evil pulsing out from the room below them. She couldn't breathe. She felt as though she were drowning in the overflow of vile energy below. "Help," she heaved. "I can't – "

"Here," Culis whispered. He took her hands and placed them on his own chest. He closed his eyes and breathed deeply.

Mila reached for him, for his essence and energy. For a short moment, it was worse, his own horror and fear fuelling her own, but then suddenly, she felt him force a slow breath out from between his lips and a hint of calm began to dribble out.

"Riding my horse with my brother through the forest. We were children," he whispered.

She glanced up and saw his eyes were tightly closed, his voice low. He wasn't talking to her. He was talking to himself, forcing happy and safe memories to override what he'd just seen and felt below. She gasped air in the space he was granting her.

"We found our way out from the trees and discovered a large, empty field. Juniper was so fast and loved being given the space to just...gallop, so I let her. Father had left on a voyage. We were alone. We felt so free, even if it was just for a moment. The smell of the fresh grass, the sting of the wind against my face. Martin beside me, whooping with joy..."

Mila closed her eyes and leaned into it.

Home. Safe. Silence.

She lost track of time and had no idea how long they stood there like that. Culis whispered the memory over and over until Mila could picture the scene clearly in her head, could feel in her body every feeling that Culis had felt.

Home. Safe. Silence.

After what seemed like an age, Jahan broke the silence with a whisper. "I think they're all cleared out. Finally."

Mila didn't need to open her eyes to know he was correct. That vile, violent prickling, that cloud of proud self-righteousness, was no longer hovering below them like a boiling pit of lava. All that remained inside the building was the acolyte and his pain.

Mila forced herself to open her eyes and crawl back to the skylight.

The young man had been suspended from a beam by his legs. He swung, upside down, like a sick mockery of a bat. Blood bubbled from the wound in his stomach and dribbled down his body, over his face, half choking him in his own entrails and gore as he died slowly from the devastating wound.

"What now?" Jahan whispered.

"Cut him down," Mila and Culis whispered simultaneously, and amidst the horror of this situation, Mila again felt the distinct warmth of knowing that, even though he'd held her back from rescuing the man, they were unified in this.

Like dark drops of dripping ink, the three of them descended swiftly and silently from the rooftop and crept towards the building. The other dandies and charlatans who'd been mingling in the alleyway earlier were now all gone, as though, even without Mila's power, they'd also inadvertently felt the sick energy radiating from the building down the alley and made themselves scarce. The alley was now abandoned, but the hair on the back of Mila's neck still stood upright.

The sound of two swords being drawn from behind her made Mila turn sharply, One was Jahan's, but to her surprise, the other came from Culis, who had drawn his from the hidden sheath. She wasn't sure she'd ever get used to seeing him with a sword, but he carried it with a comfort and familiarity that made her realise he was well practised with it.

Jahan pushed in front of them both to lead the way down the alley towards the damned tavern.

Once they arrived, Mila climbed the beam and sliced the rope that bound the acolyte's feet with Jahan's dager. Jahan held the man's bloodied head, while Culis caught the rest of his heaving, mangled body as it fell, cradling it carefully as he lowered it to the ground and laid it flat against the cobbles.

The acolyte died quickly after that.

Three Paths

When they returned to the Billy Arms, Jahan went to rouse Natalee and bring her downstairs, while Culis helped himself and Mila to a strong drink from behind the closed bar. It was still the witching hour and the tavern sat quiet and still, as if the very walls were still sleeping.

Mila had never needed a drink more. She accepted the dark, pungent, amber liquid and gulped it gratefully.

"What the hell is going on?" a groggy and bleary-eyed Natalee said as she joined them at the bar, shaking her head at the pint Culis offered her. "It's four in the morning."

"You didn't see what we just saw," Culis muttered, drowning his upper lip under the froth again.

'What did you just see?"

"Do we think they were Children of Midas?" Mila asked Jahan and Culis.

"Absolutely," Jahan confirmed grimly. "I saw the group symbol on some of their cloaks."

He took a piece of chalk from the nearby dartboard and sketched a symbol onto the dark benchtop to show them. It looked like two snakes intertwining. "What's surprising to me is that I didn't know the Children of Midas had quite that kind of fortitude about them. At least, the group down in Traders Bay doesn't."

"They're different up here," Mila said softly. "More radical somehow."

"More *active*," Jahan corrected.

Mila shot him a sharp look. What did he mean by that?

"What did you see?" Natalee asked for the third time.

"A sacrifice," Culis said grimly.

"A murder," Mila corrected. "The Children of Midas reject Abbott's authority and want him to know it," she told Natalee. "They killed an acolyte tonight in Midas's name."

"They killed an *acolyte*?" Natalee gasped. "Are they trying to start a war? Are they trying to bring the jesu up here en masse?"

"The thing I don't understand is," Mila said, "I know the Children of Midas say they hate Abbott but surely this is just a squabble over some tiny doctrinal interpretations. Does it really warrant the butchering we saw tonight? And Midas is literally *here*. I know it's difficult to get direct access to him but why not just...clarify with him what he wants? Going to these lengths, killing...it's just..."

"Insanity," Culis filled in the word she was looking for. "It's what happens when lust for power meets lack of control, and we'd all be wise to remember it."

His words suddenly reminded Mila of Frank. The wild look in Frank's eye, the fear he'd exuded when she'd last seen him. That was a man who loved power and had little self control. She shuddered at the thought.

"So what do we do about it?" Natalee asked.

"Well, ultimately," Culis said pragmatically. "We don't have to do anything. We're not here for this. We're here to help Mila and bring down Midas."

"I think..." Mila said slowly, her brain running through options, "I think we need more information about these groups. We need to understand the anger, what's driving this level of extremism. If we don't, then we might discover that, when we finally expose Midas and bring down the Church, we still somehow end up with the Children of Midas in charge."

"If tonight is anything to go by, that could easily be worse than Midas and the Church," Culis agreed. "I hate to say it but, of the two of them, at least the Church has structure. Rules that most of the country seems to agree on. Back there? Whatever the Children of Midas were doing, that just seemed like...chaos. Like violence for the sake of violence."

"I could stay behind," Natalee offered unexpectedly. "I could infiltrate this local sect and learn more about who's stoking the violence and where they're getting their information from. I'm uniquely able to do that task."

"It's too dangerous," Mila protested. "What if you're exposed?"

"If she's exposed, I'll be there to protect her," Jahan spoke up, his voice hard.

"What?" Mila asked incredulously. "You'd stay too?"

Natalee beamed at him then looked back at Mila. "Just until you get back from your home," she said. "Give us a week to put our ears to the ground. You said it yourself, Mila. We need information about what's going on up here. How else are we supposed to understand it?"

"And," Jahan said, "as Culis so frequently likes to point out, he can protect you well enough himself." He gave Mila a dry smile. He clearly still didn't like her attachment to Culis but perhaps he was coming to terms with it in a bittersweet way?

She ran her power though him to check and instead of insights about his feelings for her, she found something else, something that astounded her. "You approve of what they did," she accused in horror. "You think that acolyte *deserved* to die."

There was a moment of stunned silence as Jahan processed what she'd said. Mila realised that she may have sensed something in him that he hadn't yet even admitted to himself.

"Not because I think the Heretical Behaviours is a sacred document," Jahan corrected slowly, thinking about his words carefully. "I...I guess I think they *all* deserve to die." His voice was flat. "Do I think it should have happened in the manner we saw tonight, and for the reasons they gave? No. But I'll admit, one less acolyte in the world only means I sleep a little easier."

Mila saw Natalee nod, and this prompted Mila to scan her too. She was severely disquieted to discover that Natalee's energy felt the same.

"I was a pawn at their heretical, bullshit ball," Natalee said, without hesitation, not a whiff of guilt surrounding her. "I was stripped naked and forced to kneel before the hand of a false god, waiting to be sent into oblivion. All for the sake of their control and power. All for the sake of a lie. I want them all dead too, Mila."

"Are you really the best two to ask to infiltrate a rogue religious sect?" Culis said with a disarming laugh. "With all this bloodlust against the Church that you've both worked up, you might decide to truly join them!"

The looks both Jahan and Natalee shot him were utterly devoid of any humour.

"I'm joking!" Culis threw up his hands. "Just trying to lighten a heavy night."

Mila tried to reign the conversation back in. "So...you two will both stay here." She clarified, suddenly unsure about their proposal, and more concerned than she wanted to admit that Culis might have a point. "Culis and I will go to my house with Tarett," she continued. "We'll get the things we need from there, and we'll meet you back here in a week."

"Sounds like a plan to me," Natalee said, with a light in her eyes and a grim smile at Jahan, who returned it.

Mila felt the roiling anger and fierce determination flowing from both of them, and for a moment, couldn't help but feel a deep flutter of worry that this was not a good plan but it was also true that they needed more information about the Children of Midas. If violence like they'd seen tonight spread across the country, then Culis was right. Bringing down one Church might just result in a new religious authority taking control, and one could make things ten times worse. They needed to understand how widespread this idea of vigilante religious justice was, and if there was a chance its flame could be extinguished.

***

The next morning, when the sun finally reared its head over the high mountains and began to heat the air mercilessly, Tarett stirred and brusquely informed the group that he had his own plans outside of idly following Mila and Culis to her house. Mila was shocked and shaken by the announcement, but Tarett was determined, despite the fact he was so hungover for the first few hours of the morning that he might as well not have had Midas's sand as his new emotional crutch at all. Mila waited for him to shower and force down a bite of toast before she challenged him on the decision but he still insisted.

"Now that my brain and soul are intact, I must go see my family. Besides, Lyndonberry isn't that far away from Bori, Mila." Tarett's manner was cool and sharp. Mila suddenly felt like a naughty child being told off by a strict teacher. "It'll take us both a few days to get to our destinations," he sniped. "I'll stay a night or two with my family, then be on my way. I'll still meet you at Bori and help to carry everything back. It'll be fine."

"You promised to help," she reminded him quietly, feeling cowed by his manner and suddenly unsure this new version of her old friend would remember his word.

"And I will," he said sharply. "I just told you that I'll meet you at Bori in a few days. But in the meantime, I'll be with my family." He said it with such finality that she could not argue. She also couldn't help but feel a corresponding pang of jealousy. Tarett's family had loved him and kept him hidden and safe, despite knowing about his powers. Of course he would want to see them and they him. They were unusual humans in that regard. She looked hard at Tarett and wondered if his mother would notice the difference in her son that Mila now noticed. What would she make of it?

After Tarett left for his own trip, the remaining four congregated in the bar room downstairs and ran through the plan one final time.

"Okay, so just to reiterate what we decided last night," Mila looked up at the strong, determined gazes that came back her way.

"Tarett is going home for a few days but will meet Culis and I in Bori, to help us. You two will stay here, you'll keep your ears to the ground and try to find out more about this group from last night. Do you know specifically what information you're trying to get?"

"I think we need to know who their key leaders are," Jahan said, nodding. "If we get that, then we can work backwards and find out what their ties are to Traders Bay and the branch of the Children of Midas that exists there."

"Okay," Mila said, nodding. "And you think you can do that in just a week?"

"Absolutely." Natalee and Jahan nodded fervently. "In fact," Natalee added, "I've already made inroads."

"How?" Mila asked, incredulous.

"Well, infuriating as it is to admit this," Natalee said with a sigh, "Culis and his uncanny ability to find cretins and gossipmongers has pointed me in the right direction."

Culis's grin broadened. "It pays to make friends in low places. And I told you, the gossip here is good."

"Wonderful." Mila rolled her eyes, "Another illustrious title for you. Christopher Culis, the gossip."

"A mere gossip?" Culis was indignant. "Is that what you think of me and my social arts?"

"I think many things of you and your social arts," Mila scoffed. "Gossip is just one of the more polite terms."

"Bah. I'm wasted on you."

"You're ridiculous."

"Alright, alright," Natalee cut in. "We get it." She stood up impatiently. "Come on Jahan, let's get moving." Mila stood up to meet her and gave her a hug.

"Please be careful," she whispered into the older woman's silvering raven hair. "Don't underestimate these people."

"You take care of yourself too," Natalee replied softly, then broke the embrace and turned her reproachful eye on Culis. "And you, take care of this one as if your life depends on it."

"Of course," he replied solemnly. "That needn't even be said."

Mila turned to Jahan who held out his hand to her. "Good luck."

She pushed his hand away and moved in to embrace her friend, hugging the hard planes of his body close, breathing in the smell of him, the clean linen of his shirt. "Don't do anything foolish, please," she whispered, fearful of his reckless anger, the one she could still feel roiling in him.

"I promise," he replied, his voice suddenly full of emotion.

When Mila stepped back, Culis moved in to shake Jahan's hand. Mila could see the vice-like grip that Jahan gave him and winced a little as Jahan pulled Culis close roughly and whispered something in his ear. Mila couldn't hear what was said, but Culis stood back and nodded grimly.

"Right," Natalee said. "Let's be off," and the two of them departed the tavern, leaving only Mila and Culis left standing at the bar.

"Well, little demon?" he said softly, turning to her with a wide, happy face. "What do you have in store for me?"

She turned and eyed him off. "I'm sure the gossips and fishwives of the city will be devastated to learn that you're still coming with me."

"Oh, am I?" His eyes sparkled. "I'm amazed you still think I'm going to blindly follow you into the wet, leech-ridden rainforest hellscape that I know exists between us and Bori without a single decent answer to any of my questions about this apparent quest in the first place. The audacity."

"Oh, come on." Mila said. "If your audacity has rubbed off on me, you only have yourself to blame. And what else are you going to do?" she teased. "Sit here looking pretty, flirting with gossips for a week? Alone?"

"I think not," Culis said with a smile and drew his rucksack tight over his shoulder. "I guess I'll have to suffice looking pretty and flirting with you on a death trail through the rainforest. Sound good?"

"Sounds good to me."

Mother

"S*ave him!"* Merry was screaming.

Her voice was the first sound that cut through the black and purple haze of unawareness Aidas had been floating in.

He rolled to his side, his body trying desperately to simultaneously heave in air and expel water.

He vomited.

He breathed.

He vomited again.

He breathed again.

He lived.

"Oh fates...Aidas." Alice's hands clutched his pounding head.

He blearily opened his eyes. All he could see were Alice's and Merry's open, wide, fearful eyes. Behind them, Talbot crouched in the dirt, dripping wet, wiping his mouth and rocking back and forth, hugging his knees. He looked pale and sick.

He saved me, Aidas's hands clutched to his chest. "I nearly drowned."

"When you didn't come back up..." Merry was crying now. "We thought... And then Talbot dived back down and you were... Oh gods, Aidas, we thought you were dead!"

Dead?

Aidas shakily rose to his feet, still clutching his pounding head. "I think...I think I'm going to go home now," he said quietly.

"Wait. Aidas, wait." Merry reached for him, but Aidas pulled away.

"Go away, Meredith," he snapped and she withdrew fearfully.

He didn't know where the anger had come from, but he was unable to look at Talbot or the girls. He wanted to be left alone. There was a deep, aching pit in his stomach, and he didn't think it was from all the water he'd inhaled.

He was frightened. Shaken to his core. He hadn't even known he'd been dying. Hadn't even been able to resist it. He'd gone towards the soft black pit of the end as easily as a lost pup runs to its mother.

His eyes burned. He wanted to cry – *knew* he was going to cry – and wanted to be alone when it happened. He didn't want the others to see.

He'd nearly *died.*

"Aidas!" Talbot called to him, but Aidas ignored him and continued walking.

I just want to go home. Lie on my bed. Eat dinner...I want my mother.

The rainforest parted for him with an ease it had never yielded before. He barely paid attention to it, could barely see it. His eyes were blinded by tears he was refusing to let out.

"I nearly died," he heard himself say again, this time to no one. He just needed to hear his own voice. "Drowned. I nearly drowned. I was almost not here anymore."

It seemed too big to be real. A big lie. A big impossibility. He couldn't imagine the world without him in it. He was out of the forest before he knew it and on the final stretch of road that led home.

His mother saw him coming, knew something was wrong just from his gait, confirmed when he got closer by the look in his eyes. "Aidas?" she called.

"Mother," he gasped, the tears finally escaping the tight hold he'd put on them. He gulped into them. "I nearly died."

"What!?" His mother ran to him. "Sweetheart, what happened?" She held out her arms and Aidas crashed headlong into them, burrowing himself fiercely in her embrace, his head desperately seeking the nook of her shoulder.

And then she was gone.

He was alone.

Standing there...he was covered in...golden sand?

Aidas spat some out of his mouth and tried to wipe his eyes clear of it.

"Mother?" He looked around, over his shoulder, spinning, desperately trying to see where she'd gone. "Where are you? What happened?"

A shadow of movement caught his eye from up towards the house. He looked up, expecting to see his mother. It was the only thing his brain could conceive of to explain what had just happened.

But he saw only his wretched father. Father, standing in the doorway, an aghast expression on his face, pale as a ghost.

"Mother!" Aidas called out, filled with confusion, a growing sense of dread settling in his stomach, beginning to spread to his heart. "Mother?"

He looked down at his hands, hands which were still covered in golden sand.

He knelt, reached for a tall poppy that was growing beside the fence post.

The poppy dissolved into the same golden sand at the merest touch of his fingers.

Aidas began to scream.

Scar Tissue

Come home, come home, come home.

The forest seemed to whisper to Mila as they hiked, beckoning her into its dense, wet expanse. She was drawn to the call in the same hypnotic way a small child is drawn toward the piper in a busy market, her stomach on fire with anticipation for what lay ahead of her. Before them, she could see the waves of humid mist rolling down from the mountains above, like a great, overheated waterfall. She basked in it gleefully, feeling the familiar pinpricks of sweat cover her skin.

"I'm going home," she whispered to herself, and even the sounds of the words were sweet to her ears as she and Culis followed the thin goat track that led from Ocianna towards Brewich, the inland rainforest city which lay between them and her home village, Bori.

Mila breathed in deeply as they walked, the smell of wet leaves, damp undergrowth, pungent orange flowers and thick mist was lush and intense. She wished desperately that she could bottle the essence of it. It smelled of freedom and adventure, safety and home all at once.

She also relished in the easy access she now had to plant life, to use her new power to drain the energy from a leaf or flower here or there. Every touch abated the discomfort of her symptoms more and more, until she nearly felt normal again. The relief she felt was palpable, and she pushed the worry about the long term effects away.

Another time.

To her delight and surprise, Culis seemed to be enjoying this journey far more than he'd enjoyed their previous rainforest adventure. While one could never have described him as *happy,* he at least did not look entirely miserable. And he did not even shudder when they made the inevitable stops to pluck leeches off their legs. Mila also noticed that he reached out and took her hand whenever the narrow paths widened enough to allow them to walk side by side. He seemed to make the gesture subconsciously. As though letting Mila read his innermost energy intimately was the most simple gesture he could have thought to do. She marvelled at the access the most private man in the world was determined to grant her.

They hiked fast and made excellent time, reaching the confusing, chaotic, and spectacular town of Brewich by dusk. As they left the goat track and stepped out onto the main street, Culis was almost hit in the face by a flock of rainbow messenger parrots heading to the trees to roost. Despite her exhaustion, Mila found herself laughing in delight at the discombobulation on his face.

"I'd forgotten just how wild this place is," he said, cracking a grin back at her. "You lead the way. I remain in your capable hands."

Although Mila was impatient to get to Bori, she knew they'd need to spend the night here. They needed sleep and she also knew that rushing through Brewich without sampling the bungle juice and having a quick look in a few shops would be its own kind of heresy in her book. So, she sought out a tavern, avoiding Bronnies for the sake of uncomfortable memories, and took Culis elsewhere. She led him to The Fungi, a loud and raucous tavern she knew was worth visiting.

When they arrived, the sun had well and truly set behind the trees. The orange lanterns out the front beckoned them eagerly and promised a warm welcome, good bungle juice and a hearty meal. Mila and Culis entered and breathed a sigh of relief, sinking eagerly onto a pair of high-backed, wooden chairs by the orange-glass windows.

They were exhausted. Despite her love of the hot climate, Mila could admit that this kind of weather made what would have ordinarily been a tough walk even more punishing. And, she reflected wryly, this was only the *dry* season. Had they attempted this in the humidity and heat of the wet season it would have made it a thousandfold worse. Although previously, she'd thrived in such conditions, now she felt that living in the far cooler south for so long had somehow thickened her blood and lowered her tolerance. That was at least how it felt, as though her body's natural cooling mechanisms weren't quite as effective anymore. It was a relief to enter the very dark, and unusually cool, tavern.

The building was perched on high stilts that were designed to help it catch the wind and allow airflow to weave around the floorboards and cool the patrons from underneath. Inside, several wind-powered fans sat in every corner, and when a particularly strong gust blew through them, tiny droplets of water were released from a pulley mechanism and sprayed into the fan blades. This resulted in an extremely pleasant and welcome cooling mist raining down on them.

As their bungle juice and meals arrived, Mila watched Culis dig in with relish. She took a sip of her drink and gasped when the sharp gingery flavour hit her tongue. Then the memory of the last time she and Culis had shared this drink came rushing back, unbidden.

It had only been a few months since they'd sat in Bronnies together and he'd chatted merrily with her for hours. She'd thought they'd been bonding and he'd been plotting to betray her if the plan didn't go exactly as they'd discussed. Which, of course, it hadn't.

While she'd never forget that day and to some it might look as though she'd put herself in a devastatingly similar situation again, in her heart she realised that this time things couldn't have been more different.

Over the last two months, he'd plotted for her, lied for her, and risked his own and his company's reputation for her. He'd sacrificed himself to Jezebel for her, then abandoned the Princess to come on this journey with her. He'd accepted that she kept secrets from him, accepted that she was powerful and not in control of that power. He accepted that with her touch she could accidentally drain his life's energy and leave him as a husk – yet had just spent the past twelve hours with his palm wrapped firmly around hers, giving her full access to him, showing her full trust.

"I think you might love me," she accused softly, playfully.

"Might?" His head turned sharply towards her

"Yes." She gave him a fond, close-lipped smile. "You do, don't you?"

"Might!? Mila. For the love of...fates, you are *infuriating*!"

"What? Why?"

"Mila, I..." For a moment he fought to collect himself. He lost the battle. His next words came out in a garbled rush. "Loving you has *ruined* me. Before I met you, I would wake each morning ready to take on plots and snares and spies and politics...Now my first waking thought is to wonder if your *tea* is the perfect temperature!" He ran one hand aggressively through his hair, the other gesticulating wildly. "I sit in robust negotiation with an angry pirate in Traders Bay, and yet find myself distracted by the way the sun discovers the fine red strands in the brown of your hair. I get jealous over the fact it is able to touch you, and I cannot, not without spies coming out of the woodwork! Imagine how it feels to have spent a lifetime honing my expressions, my words, my behaviours and to have all that come crumbling down, because of you." His breathing was ragged now and his voice drew quiet. "I cannot play pretend with Jezebel anymore, and she knows it. Everything I've ever worked for or prided myself on doesn't matter anymore because since having you in my life, something deep within me has shifted. There's no going back, and I don't want it to, but *god almighty*," the blasphemy was low but drove home his point powerfully, "I'd...Of course, I *love* you. I'd raze the world for you."

Mila took a deep breath and let the enormity of what he'd said sink in. She reached for his face, holding it gently, smoothing away the furrowed lines and feeling the earnest desperation of his energy, the aching sorrow and shame that swept through him. Her heart felt so full. She wanted to respond, to reciprocate the yearning openness she felt flowing like a full bodied river out of him.

She wanted to, and tried to, and couldn't.

He saw the hesitation that lingered like a shy cat in the back of her eyes.

"It's okay," he whispered in agony. "I honestly don't expect you to feel the same way." He meant it. "I don't deserve it."

He thinks he doesn't deserve love.

It made her heart ache even more to see him in that moment, as the boy who didn't believe he was worthy of love. Not unless he had something of value to exchange for it. These were the scars Frank Culis's brand of love had left upon him. She'd seen a glimpse of it now. Knew what it had done to him.

"Christopher," she whispered, "it's not...it's not that I don't feel that way." With shame she realised she couldn't quite say those three words.

Just say it, say it – I love you too.

She opened her mouth. "I..."

Suddenly it felt as though she was the one who'd taken the scar catcher potion. The words that sat on the tip of her tongue triggered unwanted images of that fateful morning years ago, which flashed before her eyes painfully. She hadn't said those words to anyone since that day.

But I love you.

She'd screamed those words at her father as his usually kind face had contorted in fear and horror. His response had been to lock the entire family in the house as he went to find the acolyte. Her lifelong sanctuary transformed into her prison by the swift turn of a key. Her words had been weak and useless.

I love you.

Her mother, generous to a fault, who used to plait flowers into Mila's long braid and tell her she was the prettiest, sweetest, best girl in the world, who now could not look at her and would *not* stop sobbing.

I love you, I'll love you forever. She'd told her every day of her life. It turned out, she hadn't meant it. The words had been a lie.

I love you, Mili.

Her sweet younger sister, Kendra, now screaming in fear at the sight of Mila's horns regrowing after she'd tried to cut them off, screaming at the slick blood all over her forehead and hands, dripping onto the immaculate floor, and slamming the door as she hid.

Mila choked, drowning in memories.

"Mila?" Culis's eyes came into view, coated now in concern. She was deeply glad that he was not holding a mirror to witness the scenes in her head play out.

"I...I can't. I'm so sorry."

"You never need to be sorry."

"No," Mila sat up, blinking away her tears furiously. "I want you to understand. It's important you understand."

Culis nodded, happy to wait in silence until she was ready to explain. Mila took a deep breath.

"The people who knew my heart more intimately than I knew it myself," she said, voice trembling, "who were supposed to love me unconditionally and without reservation...they changed their minds about me within a few hours on a cold winter's morning when I was fourteen."

Tears began falling again. This time she left them unchecked, and watched as they wet the table.

Culis reached for her, the agony in his expression mirroring her own. "Your family," he murmured. She nodded.

"That rejection," she continued, "It created this...scar of fear that lives on in me. When I try to access those feelings, the feelings I *know* I feel for you. I...I can't. It feels like they're lost in a prison that's inside me. A terrifying dark place that I cannot go and the words in my mouth feel...heavy and thick. I don't know how else to describe it."

She looked up at him mournfully. "I don't know if I'll ever truly be able to open myself to love again."

Culis moved his hand to her shoulder. It was warm and steadying. He said nothing for the longest time. He didn't try to convince her that he was worth loving, or that, if she just tried harder, she'd one day come to feel it too. He didn't make her feel like anything she'd said was wrong. He simply looked at her earnestly, allowing his sincerity and sympathy to flood through his touch.

"I'm so sorry that happened," he eventually said. His voice even and soft. "You didn't deserve that. They were your family. Religion be damned, they should have just loved you anyway."

They should have just loved you anyway.

The deep pain Mila had been carrying since that day reignited in her chest, sharp and hot as a poker. The tears roared to life again and there was no point trying to hold back the tide. Suddenly, she was grieving again, grieving for the thousandth time over a deep hurt that had been inflicted over a decade ago, but at least this time she was being held while she wept.

Culis drew her against his chest and stroked his fingers into the hair at the nape of her neck, holding her tightly to him as she sobbed.

And it didn't happen all at once, but slowly, in that dark tavern room, weeping for her young self, wrapped in the presence and energy of someone who loved her for who she was, an old wound finally began to mend.

The Art of the Game

Unfortunately, the quiet, powerful moment didn't last. Mila and Culis's embrace was soon interrupted as a loud and raucous crowd of people entered the quiet tavern without warning. The group emitted a playful yet warlike energy and the room quickly became a cacophony of talking and boasting and chanting. Something was about to happen here, and it truly ruined their moment.

"Don't go on their account," Culis said, shooting a look of annoyance towards the group as Mila pulled away from his embrace.

"Spies," was all she said in reply, and he gave a begrudging pout of acceptance. Even here, this far into the forest, they both knew they weren't totally safe from little birdies who could report what they'd seen back to Jezebel.

"What do you think is going on?" Culis asked and Mila assessed the energy and body language of the new guests to try glean that information. "A game of fenders," she concluded. "And an important competition by the looks of it."

"Fenders?"

They watched the members of the first two opposing teams set up on a large table in the centre of the tavern, each white-knuckling the cards they held.

"Explain it to me," Culis said into her ear, his eyes now glittering bright as they found seats that were closer to the action and settled in to observe.

He loved a game.

Fenders was relatively simple in its design, but more complicated in its execution. Two teams faced each other with three cards dealt to each of them and three cards placed face down on the table between them. There were two ways to win, and many more ways to lose face. The official goal was to trick the opposing team into guessing that your team either had no larks between the three cards you held or, before that, to ensure that every single card you held was of the same suit – a rose, a thief or a moon. The unofficial goal was to thoroughly embarrass your opponents and, in a setting like The Fungi, bonus points were usually awarded to whoever won the ensuing brawl that would undoubtedly materialise at the end of an embarrassing loss.

"There must be at least three people per team," Mila explained, "but teams do not have to be even and can field up to seven a side. Most professional teams usually set a minimum number, as it's far harder to crack just three people, but amateur tournaments like this usually have five."

"What do you mean 'crack'?"

"It's a game of bluffing," she explained. "Each team member's turn has three stages, but the stages are less important than the faces and body language of the nominated player. In the first stage, each team must take a turn peering at one of the centre cards. They can choose to swap any card out with one of the three that their own team holds in their hands, or leave it in place. Then they must pick up another card from the deck and add it to their team's hand. And finally, they can either discard a card in their hand or choose a card from the hand of their opponent to replace a card in the centre. The players on each team watch the faces and reactions of their opponents to determine what card combination they're trying to collect, where they're placing the ones they want, and when they've decided to relinquish the lark to try and collect the final card they need. And also, team members can't talk amongst themselves. It's a completely silent game. So, a team needs to be able to communicate their strategy with each other through body language alone."

"I don't know if you already deduced this, Mila," Culis said, cracking his knuckles. "But I can just tell that I'm going to *love* this game."

Mila laughed, delighted by his enthusiasm. And he was right. Culis only needed to observe two rounds before his understanding of the intricacies of the game were near perfect.

"Team on the right is going roses," he whispered. "And they already have two."

"How do you know?" Mila hissed back under her breath.

"The third player's irises...he hasn't put drops in them like the others have. They blew up when he picked up that last card, and since then he's been discarding like crazy trying to find the third."

'Discarding like crazy' was Culis's term for the slightly faster, almost undiscernible pace at which the third player had chosen to discard and pluck a fresh card from the deck. That was all the indication Culis apparently needed to confirm that the player had thrown out the team's lark and was now striking out on a limb, fishing frantically for the third of the set he needed for them to win.

And Culis was right. Two more rounds of that and the team on the left cottoned onto the new situation too.

"No lark," the captain of the left accused.

The team on the right visibly withered.

"Game goes to Mason's Monsters," the adjudicator announced with a slap on the table.

"I *knew it*!" Culis's smile was broad. "Ah, Mila. I want to play. I *need* to play!"

Mila went and ordered herself another drink, while Culis watched a few more rounds of the next game. Eventually, he left his stool, and she watched as he began working the room, talking to the other spectators and, eventually, recruiting three of them into a team that he put forward for a future round.

Pyrus, Gally and Tael were his chosen three – a treehouse builder, a school teacher and a banker, they said when they introduced themselves – and Mila watched in fascination as Culis drew them into his confidence prior to the game starting and sternly gave them his rules.

"No blinking for ten seconds after a card is drawn, do not touch your face with your hands at all. We all look once, and once only, after each card is shown, and that's it. No sidelong glances, no subtle nods or shakes. You're all skilled, I think, so play as you know best. Play with your instinct!"

They dominated.

Culis had chosen his teammates well, and despite the fact they were raking the floor and destroying any team that dared oppose them, Mila was relieved to sense the hum of violence within the room stayed low. Pyrus, Gally and Tael were each evidently well-liked members in their community, so no one felt particularly slighted or peeved that they were doing well, even if it was a foreigner captaining their team.

Mila let herself slump against the inner wall of the tavern and half-close her eyes, still watching in amusement, but undeniably tired. She'd almost dozed off when she was rudely jolted awake by the thud of a tankard being slammed down onto her table. She was so startled she nearly slid off the bar stool.

The energy of the man that stood before her was unpleasant – angry, drunk and controlling. It took her a moment to place him, but the recognition in his eyes as he glared at her was unmistakable.

Oberon. Cari's husband.

Mila's first instinct was to shrink away from him in fear. She didn't know exactly who had betrayed her to the authorities all those years ago, but she had strong suspicions it had been him.

"You!" Spittle flew into her face. "I thought we'd seen the last of you – demon."

He'd intended the last as an insult, but it had the opposite effect. Instead of cowing Mila further, it drove home how far she'd come since the time she'd been in the Highlands and publicly accused of being a demon. A year earlier, she'd have sprinted home in fear and isolated herself for months, hoping to be forgotten by time and fresh gossip. Now, the term carried no threat. She did not need to hide. The Church knew she existed, and she was under Culis's protection. She had nothing to be ashamed of, and she'd be damned if she let anyone drudge up that old shame again for the sake of intimidation.

"Nice to see you again, too, Oberon," she replied calmly, forcing herself to sip her drink with a nonchalance she didn't feel. She could see that infuriated him. "How are Cari and the boys?"

His eyes downright bulged. Too late, Mila sensed the desperation and the streak of violence that slipped through him. His hand shot out and seized the fabric of her collar, grasping it in a strong fist and wrenching her sideways. Mila was thrown across the table and down onto the wooden floor. A loud cry burst from her lungs as she hit the hard surface.

"Hey!"

She vaguely heard someone above her yell, but she had no time to focus on where the voice came from. Oberon's foot was already making its descent towards her face.

She rolled to the left. His big boot struck the board inches from her nose.

Fair enough, she thought, *I suppose I did seduce his wife.*

Culis's fist came out of nowhere, striking the man's jaw with a manic ferocity. Oberon tumbled to the side like prairie grass in the wind, clutching at his face in agony. He smacked into another of the tall, round tables and tipped it over, spilling drinks and glass all over himself.

"Righto!" the barkeep roared. "You three, *out!*"

Mila's underarms were quickly and roughly seized by a strong man, who must have been employed as security. She was hoisted to her feet and spun out into the now dark street, all but landing on top of Oberon. Culis followed shortly after.

Infuriatingly, despite the ungainly manner of their ejection, Culis still managed to only look vaguely tousled by the experience. He was angry, though. The angriest Mila had ever seen him.

"What in hell's name is going on?" he demanded.

Oberon ignored him, focusing solely on Mila, who tried to stand, but fell over her own feet and landed back on top of Oberon, who flinched and kicked her off him, his boot landing hard against her side and forcing a heavy *humph* of air from her lungs.

Culis wasn't having it. He hauled Oberon up by the collar and twisted the fabric until it choked the man. "If you want to live beyond the next ten seconds, I advise you to consider your next move very, *very* carefully."

Oberon was turning blue.

"Am I clear?" Culis's murderous, icy-calm tone was chilling.

Oberon frantically nodded and, with a look of utter disdain, Culis dropped him back onto the ground.

"Why are you back here?" Oberon croaked at Mila, scrabbling away from them and into the darkness, heaving for air and now clutching his sore jaw. "Haven't you caused enough ruin?"

"A jilted ex-lover?" Culis asked Mila, cocking his head towards the man.

"Hardly," Mila replied, while Oberon swore at the inference in disgust.

"Some of us don't soil ourselves with the spawn of the Muds," he said grimly.

"And yet," Mila replied sweetly, "some of us do. How is Cari, by the way? I don't think you said."

Oberon's face turned purple in rage again, but this time, Mila sensed something else beneath it. Grief. Deep grief. Something he blamed Mila for.

Mila gasped, feeling a cold hand grab her heart. "She's dead?" She hadn't known Cari long enough to love her, but she'd certainly been deeply infatuated with the woman, deep enough to risk putting her secret in jeopardy – and suffer the consequences.

"Worse," Oberon snarled and, abruptly, the fight went out of him. His head dropped, and he simply whimpered, "Nathaniel...he's...he's a demon."

Mila could see what it cost him to say the words out loud, to speak the dreadful secret he'd been bottling up inside. His shoulders shook, his fists clenched, his face screwed up in the epitome of grief barely masked by rage. The helplessness of a man who loved his son and didn't know what to do about this devastating news. Nathaniel was his and Cari's eldest son.

Mila stood up and brushed herself off. "When?" she asked softly. *When did his horns emerge? When did you find out? When did your world collapse?*

"Three days ago," he spat.

"And you haven't handed him to the acolyte yet?" she asked in amazement.

She could both see the war raging on his face and sense the tempest within him.

"Cari won't...I can't...But the other boys..." he spluttered, then gathered himself in an impressive display of composure. "I've made up my mind!" he said sternly, as if talking to Cari herself. "I'm doing it tomorrow."

So that's why he was here, Mila realised. Drinking his sorrows away at The Fungi. He'd waited three days. Far longer than her own family had. They'd barely given her three hours.

Her heart ached for the boy, for what was about to happen to him, what he was about to go through. She was suddenly seized by a wave of recklessness.

"Oberon..." She reached out a hand towards the anguished man, imploring him. "Give him to me instead."

Oberon swore at her and batted her hand away.

Culis stepped forward, prepared to intervene again, but Mila held up her other hand to him.

Wait.

She turned back to Oberon. "Let us take him. Listen to me. If he comes with us then you don't need to condemn him to the Church, and your family will stay safe. He can come with us, and we'll look after him. You'll never have to see him again, but you'll know he's safe. We'll take him with us. Won't we?" She looked up at Culis, who was clearly still confused about everything that was happening, but he trusted Mila. He nodded solemnly.

"You...you will?" Something in Oberon's chest lifted.

"We will," Mila said again. "Of course, we will."

Oberon found the strength to stand. The palpable relief showed on his face, illuminated brightly by the hundreds of tiny, coloured fey lights that had been laid by beetles around the outlines of the thick rainforest leaves.

Mila didn't really know what she was agreeing to, but the bursting pain in her chest told her the only truth she needed to know at this moment. She could not leave a demon child, Cari's child, to suffer what she'd suffered, or worse, to suffer the non-existent mercy of the Church's acolytes.

She and Culis found themselves following Oberon down the winding streets of Brewich. They were headed, Mila realised, in the direction of the terrace house in the lane that she remembered so well. Beautiful black mud bricks hugged majestic dark-green windowpanes and a small balcony was perched high on the second floor and bordered by lanterns on either side of its french doors. The place reeked of civility.

With a heavy breath, as if he couldn't believe what he was doing, Oberon gestured them inside. Once in, he shut the door behind them swiftly, and looked out the windows with a concerned expression. Mila appreciated that. Nosy neighbours were always a threat, no matter where you lived.

Inside was also dark, but decidedly homier than the outside. Small piles of books lay scattered about the space, and tiny coloured glass bowls, each with a small tea candle flickering inside, gave it a slightly ethereal vibe.

"Cari?" Oberon called, and Mila couldn't help but catch her breath. It'd been so long since she'd heard the name, seen the woman. Her stomach fluttered in anticipation.

Culis, if he noticed, said nothing.

But something was wrong. There was no answering call or patter of feet. Cari didn't answer, and the deafening silence of the house gave way only to the quiet *thud* of a door being pulled swiftly closed, elsewhere in the house

"No," Oberon hissed, running towards the sound, as though he knew exactly what that small echo meant.

Mila and Culis followed as Oberon flew towards the back door and flung it open, crying out into the night and the forest that lay beyond, "Cari, no! Wait!"

Mila stood on tiptoes and looked over his shoulder to see what lay beyond. Down the garden path, exposed by the sharp light of the full moon, dressed in cloaks, knapsacks, and determined expressions, stood the gorgeous, redheaded Cari, hand in hand with a teenage boy who could only be her son Nathaniel.

Running away, Mila realised. Cari was running away with her son, and Mila's heart cracked a little at the sight of it. What she wouldn't have given, at fourteen, for her mother to take her by the hand and tell her, "No matter what your father chooses to do, I'm standing by you."

"Cari, please!" Oberon's voice broke. "Please come back. Don't do this. Look..." He turned to Mila, grasping for her as though she were a lifeboat and he a drowning man. His grip on her forearm hurt as he thrust her forward into the moonlight for Cari to see her face. "Look who's come to get him. He can go with her. He'll be alright. We'll all be alright."

"Mila?"

Mila watched as Cari dropped Nathaniel's hand and her lips parted in shock. She paled, as though she were seeing a ghost. Perhaps she thought she was.

"You're...you were..."

"I'm back," Mila said, throwing her power out into Cari, desperate to satiate her curiosity and determine the truth that had haunted her for the first months after her capture.

And there she found it, the kernel of guilt and deceit that lay festering like a rotten fish amongst the turbulent sea of energy.

It had been Cari, not Oberon, who'd betrayed her.

Open Forest Worship

Mila had been powerless at many negotiating tables in her life. Now, for the first time ever, she was the one who held the power and it felt good. Intoxicating even.

Cari couldn't look at her. Oberon clutched Cari's hand so hard his knuckles were white. Nathaniel stared quietly at Mila from the corner, his eyes wide in horror and fear. Culis was just smiling bemusedly, in the grandfather armchair to the side, as though he were simply curious about the turn this adventure had taken. Mila was relieved that he hadn't seemed to find it necessary to get answers from her. Not yet anyway. It allowed Mila to focus solely on Cari.

"It was you," she said to the woman quietly, finally, after she realised no one else at the table was about to speak.

"It was," Cari confirmed softly, and then steadied herself and looked up at Mila with a defiant and steely eye, as if determined that she would not allow herself to feel guilty about it. "Yes, it was me," she repeated. "I told the Church who you were, and where to find you."

"Why, Cari?" Confirmation of the betrayal felt like a knife to the heart. Cari had been her lover this time last year. Just before she'd been dragged away by the mob and subjected to Trial by Cat. Just before everything had truly gone to hell. But, before their relationship had deepened into intimacy, the woman had, first and foremost, been a *friend*. Mila had helped Cari birth her third child. Their friendship had been an anchor for Mila in what had otherwise been a haze of loneliness and rubane smoke.

"Because I was falling in love with you, Mila." Cari's beautiful, cold voice snapped through Mila's pain, her features pulled tight. "I was about to give up everything, my family, my sanity...and then I found out you were...are...a demon." She hissed out the word. "And I realised you didn't love me back. How could you if you were prepared to let me unknowingly risk my life, the lives of my children, for your secret?"

"You should have told me," Mila whispered.

"No," Cari replied furiously. "You should have told *me*."

Mila felt her rage ebb away and shame take its place. It was true. If anyone had discovered their tryst, and known Mila was a demon, Cari and her family could have easily been tried for harbouring a heretic. They probably wouldn't have been sacrificed, as Abbott still did his best to keep that punishment specific to demons alone. But they would have certainly been locked up, or publicly whipped, or placed in stocks or perhaps even banished from Brewich altogether.

"I didn't tell you because the last time anyone found out," Mila said shakily, trying to explain, her father's furious face flashing in snippets before her eyes, "I was ostracised from my family and community. I was...terrified of it happening again."

"So you're not even sorry that you kept it a secret?"

"I...I can't be," Mila said truthfully. "I wanted to keep my life together. I wanted to keep you. It was a secret that meant my life."

"Well, in that case, I'm not sorry for reporting you," Cari replied with a sneer. "Typical demon. Selfish to the last."

If Mila hadn't been able to read Cari's energy, perhaps she would have been more upset with the woman. But, as it was, she felt the love that still nestled in Cari's chest and the way it had been warped into hatred and fear...by hurt.

"If I *had* told you," Mila said finally, "you would have reported me anyway."

Cari looked like she was about to snap back a nasty retort, but at the last moment, she bit her lips and contemplated the comment. "Perhaps I would have," she eventually said, her voice more even now. A shadow of the Cari Mila had once known was starting to show. "But things have changed." She looked to her left, to Nathaniel, and cringed. "I can't...It's impossible. I can't..."

"I know," Mila said gently, relieving her of the burden of trying to define how much a mother could love their child. "You shouldn't have to. Let me take him instead."

"And do what?" Cari rounded on Culis. "Sell him into slavery?" She faced Mila again with protective daggers in her gaze. "Oh, I know all about him and the Artor Trading Company's new venture. What happens to the demons you find? Do you sell them into slavery, into mockery and death? No. I'd rather take Nathaniel away myself. We'll leave Brewich and live alone, together. Away from people and the Church and the likes of you and your exploitative, greedy – "

"You have my word," Culis said, leaning forward, speaking for the first time since they'd arrived. "That the demon trade you're referring to is no longer operational."

Mila shot him a look of surprise. "What?"

Cari noted her reaction, turned back to Culis and scoffed. "You should get your lies in order before you start peddling them in my house, sir." She spat the title with derision.

"I mean it," Culis said quietly. "I've decided. There will be no more demon trade, not one I profit from anyhow. If demons wish to be employed by humans in the city, I will help them procure safe and protected work. If they wish simply to live somewhere away from the Church, in relative protection from these laws, I will manage that also."

"And how exactly will you do that?" Cari demanded.

"My family owns vast estates," Culis said with a shrug. "I haven't figured out all the specifics of it just yet, but I'm sure a small, secret demon village could be built, hidden and defended, if required."

Mila just stared and gaped at him. But Culis wasn't finished yet.

"Word of this can't get out, do you hear me? Not to anyone, lest the Church catch wind. They all have to believe that the demon trade is running exactly as I proposed it would." He looked at Cari earnestly. "I swear on my life, if you hand your son over to us, he will be hidden away safely, and well cared for and, most importantly, free to choose what his future life looks like."

Mila had tears in her eyes. Her chest felt tight. She reached out a hand to touch Culis's arm and felt his forthright, determined energy pummel her back in response. He was serious. This was happening.

"What about your father?" she whispered.

"I think it's high time someone reminded my father that, while he might control the Artor Trading Company, he does not control me." And then he added, more quietly, "Perhaps I also needed that reminder recently." He stared back at her fiercely.

Mila didn't know what to say. She was too astounded. A distant part of her registered that this was going to have terrible consequences for the already deteriorating relationship between the father and son, but at that moment she didn't care. Culis was finally choosing a side, and that side was hers.

Cari eyed Culis off beadily, sizing him up and weighing his words. Eventually she let out a deep sigh and nodded. She stood from the table and turned to hug her young son, who was trembling with unshed tears now. As soon as his mother's arms wrapped around his shoulders and he realised this was goodbye, perhaps forever, he burst into fitful sobs.

"I'm scared," he gasped.

Cari tried to soothe him, but she was crying too.

"Cari?" Mila said, after watching them for a long moment, her heart breaking for them, "we'll be coming back through Brewich in a few days. Why don't you...why don't you keep him here until then? Then you can take a few days to say a proper goodbye."

At this, Cari clutched at Nathaniel and sobbed even harder. Oberon placed a hand gravely on her shoulder and looked at Mila, his own eyes rimmed red and watery.

"Thank you," he said with false calm. "We'd be very grateful."

The family moment suddenly felt too private to be a part of any longer. Mila and Culis rose from the table and moved towards the front door. Oberon shepherded them out, with Cari and Nathaniel still desolate behind them.

"We'll be back in..."Mila considered the days in her head, "six days."

Oberon nodded, and when the door finally closed behind them, Mila turned to Culis with a look of exhaustion.

"Did I really just agree to adopt a demon boy from the woman who sold me out to the Church?"

"You've saved his life," Culis said softly. "Saved their family. Without a moment's hesitation. You're incredible."

"What about you?" she said, uncomfortable with the praise. "You'd get rid of the demon trade? Disavow Frank? Start a demon...sanctuary village?"

"No." He shook his head fervently. "There's nothing incredible about that. I've just found my spine, it seems." He looked at his outstretched arms and fingertips, as if feeling his blood running through his veins for the first time. "It feels incredible, like I've shaken off some yoke I didn't even realise was weighing on me so heavily. I feel...free."

Mila took his hand in hers, feeling his elation sizzling into her, drawing him away from the house and into the forest behind it.

"Come on," she said happily. "Let's go set up camp. I'm exhausted."

"I will follow anywhere you lead," he said simply.

When they hit the forest line and Mila was assured of their privacy, she shrugged off her rucksack, turned to Culis and pushed him up against a nearby tree.

He didn't hesitate for an instant, reading her need perfectly. He reached for her and lifted her. Her legs wrapped firmly around his waist as she raked her hands through his hair. She drew his head close and kissed him. Deep, claiming and determined. Mila was no longer confused, no longer hesitant. This man was everything, *everything* she could ever want. And despite her exhaustion, she felt invigorated by that knowledge.

She could trust him.

Christopher Culis had truly changed. Not only that...he saw her. *Loved* her. She leaned into him, wanting to give him everything, all forms of her. His feet tangled against the roots of the tree, and he fell backwards, taking Mila with him, barely pausing from kissing her to break their fall. They landed together in a small cove of soft ferns. It was as though the earth itself was drawing them both into her, urging them to reconnect with their core selves and to both let go of pain and fear and find that peaceful place one can only find in the embrace of the person that feels like home.

She loved him, Mila realised. Truly loved him.

And that terrifying and momentous thing struck her as resoundingly as a bolt of lightning. She wanted to tell him, wanted to bring him in and share everything, every part of herself. But her heart felt too full and her mouth too inadequate, so she appeased herself by kissing her way down his beautiful, slim neck, delighting in the way his breathing ran ragged for her. Lost herself in the heat of his roaming hands as they ranged her body and pulled her so close it was as if he wanted to fuse them together.

He rolled her over and, with her back pressed into the cool, clean soil, Mila was enveloped by the smell of sweet ferns and clear moonlight. And Christopher Culis. The smell of him was intoxicating. Leather and sweat and sea foam, intermingled with the lavendile of his soap and the smoked honey he sometimes used to try to tame the unrelenting wisps of his hair.

Mila felt the hard bulge of his erection push against her inner thigh just as his hands won their battle with her shirt and slipped inside it from the bottom up. The feeling of his hands exploring her breasts was exquisite. They were heavy and full and aching for him, and when he brushed his fingers across her nipples and tweaked them, she let out a low, guttural moan that echoed into the night.

Culis's ravenous expression froze, his eyes wild.

"What's wrong?" she whispered, aching for him to do more, to continue.

"You still have the necklace on," he said with a small, desperate cry of anguish in his voice.

"I don't care," she whispered, raising herself up a little at the waist and nipping at his ear.

Culis groaned again. "Ahhh, but damn me, I do. I can't take you like this. Wait one minute."

"For the love of all...how *do* you get the damned thing off?"

"The tool to do it is in my knapsack. I bought one in Ocianna. Hold on, I'll – "

"Too slow," Mila snapped with impatience, her body aching with desire. "You won't take me? Fine. I'll take *you*."

With understanding in his eyes, Culis allowed himself to be pushed back and for Mila to straddle his long, lean body, but not before working off his trousers and watching her face light up in delight and amazement as she surveyed all of him; bare, ready and straining for her. Mila placed herself over his hips and took his wrists, pushing them into the ground on either side of his head, noting how golden his skin looked against the chocolate black of the rainforest soil.

"Who do I belong to?" she whispered, holding her hips aloof from his, tauntingly low but not *quite* low enough.

"No one," he gasped back. "You belong only to yourself. Always. Forever."

She lowered her hips slightly, allowing the tease of his cock to sit right at her entrance.

"Wait," he said before she could lower onto him completely. "Ask me."

She leaned forward and kissed him deeply first, then repeated the question, a sultry whisper in his ear. "Tell me, Christopher Culis, who do *you* belong to?"

He smiled up at her and in that expression she suddenly saw all of him, laid out before her, far more exposed than merely his naked body. "I belong to you," he whispered. "Always. Forever."

She closed the torturous distance and slid down onto him, gasping as the wave of pleasure and friction and heat hit her all at once.

They were melded together, and Mila was able to finally ride out the red-hot arousal that had haunted her since the day she'd met him, the desire that had stalked her relentlessly since their first night together in Traders Bay, the unceasing yearning for his touch, for his eyes, his attention, that she'd had for him since the Dusk Ball. She'd wanted it all, for so long. And now she took it, claimed it as hers.

She moved on him like a woman possessed, feeling the decadent sensation of fullness building and building within her. As her orgasm came to her, she let it flow, uninhibited, finally, *finally* able to cry out, to scream her pleasure loudly into the hot open air of the night. She let it fill her body completely, felt it trickling like shooting stars into her fingers and toes and eating away what sense of scattered self remained

When she finally caught her breath and came back into her mind, she looked down at Christopher and smiled. He was staring up at her, the moon reflecting back at her from his impossibly green eyes, his expression one of open worship.

Home

The night before they were due to arrive in Bori, Mila lay in their hammock and watched Culis sleep under the light of the newly waning moon.

The trip had taken longer than it probably should have. For the last two days, Mila and Culis continued to find themselves...distracted, now that they'd crossed the final threshold. Since that night, neither of them wanted to do anything more than to revisit it, over and over and over again, and their days of walking had consisted of late starts, early nights and interrupted lunch hours.

After they'd recovered from that first time, Culis had quickly retrieved the small tool he'd bought from Ocianna from his rucksack. He'd lit the tiny, red-hot flame that could be used to unweld the vasium necklace from her neck, and formally freed her completely from the last shackle that artificially bound her to him.

She was free. Truly free now to choose him, and choose him she had.

I love him, she thought in awe as she studied his quiet breathing *and it doesn't frighten me.* She watched the way his face relaxed against the canvas of the hammock. They'd drawn their hammocks together, allowing them to sleep in one another's embrace, and her sleep had been blessedly dreamless.

She knew that for some, love felt like being struck between the eyes by a stone. Besotted and lost at first sight. Simple. But this love? This had been more complicated. It had been cloaked in layers, and had grown in the shadow of distrust, suspicion and persecution. The Culis she'd first met had been greedy and selfish. Too cunning for his own good and obsessed with pleasing his father. But even then, she remembered with a start, that wasn't quite correct. The bones of his character had always been good. The *very first time* she'd met him, he'd simply been a merciful man in the crypt. The man mourning his brother, who, despite having every reason not to help her, had hidden her from the pursuing priests and wished her luck in her escape. Ever since that low moment in Brewich, the night he'd let greed and fear of his father get the better of him, he'd been trying to claw his way back, aiming to be something different. And now, here he was beside her. Still arrogant and too confident for his own good, but now a man who actually valued others, and showed empathy and kindness towards them. A man who suddenly didn't always need to have an answer for everything, because he could trust those around him, who knew it was no longer just him against the world. A man who now knew that friends were more important than money. A man who now knew that he didn't need to always come out on top, so long as he came out side by side, with *her*.

And even, she thought grimly, if it turned out that this new power had indeed turned her into a monster, Culis would help her. He wouldn't revile her. She just knew it. He already saw her just as she was, and he'd love her anyway, just as she was.

He'd love her anyway, just as she was.

The building, relentless pressure inside her finally received her permission to unstopper itself, and it began to spill over its banks. It felt overwhelming, crushing her, a tsunami. A love so intense she could barely breathe through it.

I love him.

Despite everything. Despite the heaviness of their pasts, somehow, she and Christopher had found one another, truly saw one another, and in doing so, had found *this*.

She considered the casual abandon of his limbs, the way they draped around her possessively, the way his presence calmed and grounded her. "I love you," she whispered into the night air, wishing he was awake to hear it.

***

When morning finally broke, despite her excitement and the joy of the previous two days, Mila now suddenly found herself nervous as they left their camp.

All that lay between them and her old home was this final stretch of rainforest.

Would it still be as she'd remembered it? Would it still feel like home?

After a few hours of sweating and battling through the greenery, she finally shoved aside the final fronds.

She heard Culis's gasp from behind as the last of the vines fell away and revealed the clearing, and her home.

The tiny cottage was just as she'd remembered it, nestled between the sister-pair of bayan trees that dwarfed it, their huge roots arcing around it and their thick branches hanging low. The waterwheel on the western side still seemed to be in good nick and spun merrily with the catchment of dripping moisture from the tiny rock waterfall that provided consistent power.

She could see that the rubane she'd had come so far for did not disappoint. It was everywhere, growing all over the stone frontage of her house and beginning to spill out into the garden beds she'd carefully tended three seasons ago. Mila saw the hallmarks of rotting vegetables in gardens but could also see clear signs of animal tracks and digging.

Ah well, she thought as she surveyed it. *At least someone got fed.*

The cottage had yellow shutters, a green door and a tall stone chimney that ran up the eastern wall. The shutters were still open. Mila hadn't had time to close them when the mob came.

She hadn't realised she was staring in silence so intently until she felt Culis's warm palm in her own.

"Are you okay?" he asked softly.

"Yes," she replied breathily and took a shaking step forward. "I just can't believe...it all looks exactly the same, and yet also...quite different."

Together, they pushed the front door, which swung open easily.

One large room lay before her, the interior dark but not in a diminishing way. It was divided into segments by the hand-woven rugs on the floor and the tasteful positioning of furniture. The air inside was cool, and a number of weary fans still spun from the ceiling, powered ceaselessly by the waterwheel outside.

Against the back wall sat a number of small, round windows, each decorated with the stained-glass images of birds and plants. They kept out the majority of the heat but still let in faint streams of coloured light. The kitchen sat in a nook on the far right-hand side, beside the fireplace, which was integrated with a black iron stove. A long wooden benchtop ran under the window and still showed evidence of the last tasks Mila had been doing there before the mob arrived, cutting and preparing a tincture to heal the wound on the leg of a monkey from the family group that lived nearby. Mila assumed the troop had moved on by now.

She looked over at Culis and saw his eyes raised to the ceiling, inspecting the long, exposed beams, from which hung many bundles of herbs, now long dried and ready for use, accompanied by a number of wooden kitchen utensils, most of which had been hand carved by Mila.

"There's still some plants alive on the windowsill," she said in amazement, walking over to gently stroke the thick green leaves of the rosemayne plant she'd once been cultivating. The open windows must have allowed rain and sun to nourish them, even in their abandonment.

Culis still did not speak, just ran his eyes over the floor that was also a dark, polished wood. Mila looked at it too, seeing it again, as if for the first time, drinking in the colour, the way each board sat beside its counterpart. It had taken her a long time to individually size, cut and sand these boards. But it had been a labour of love. Worth every stroke.

Her eyes skimmed over to a round, woven rug, which lay in the centre of the room, inviting anyone who entered to stand and inspect the bookshelf that stood proudly behind it. There was a small, half-moon shelf built into the wall under the window where a fired clay mug sat patiently, another remnant of her old life, left behind on the fateful morning that she'd been taken. Culis walked over to it, picked it up and inspected it carefully. It had imprints of native flowers all along it.

Mila remembered picking the ones that had grown around the cottage at that time.

Culis turned to her, his eyes now wide with amazement. “You made most of this house and everything in it yourself, didn’t you?” His voice was soft, but there was a slightly accusatory note in it, as though he was confused that she’d never shown him this side of herself before.

“I did,” she admitted. She watched as his eyes continued to scan the space in awe.

In the back corner, a large bed was suspended from the ceiling by thick chains made from dried, woven vines. It was accessible from two wooden steps that she’d carved into an old tree trunk. Soft, wispy, white cotton sheets covered the thin mattress and hung fluttering in the air underneath it. The ensemble was adorned with a dark-green coverlet, embroidered with birds and plants. Next to the door hung a similar coverlet, although this one was red and embroidered with black and gold monkeys. Mila reached for it and drew it around herself, smelling it. It smelled like dust, rubane smoke and soapberries. She sighed deeply.

“This is extraordinary Mila,” Culis said, his voice full of awe. “The closer I look at everything, every tiny detail...the time, the energy, the effort...it’s the most extravagant thing I’ve ever seen.”

“I lived alone for a long while,” she replied simply. “I had a lot of time on my hands.”

“Mila.” Culis crossed the floor and took her hands in his. “This place and everything in it is...incredible. *You* are incredible.”

“Thank you.” She sincerely accepted the compliment. She was very proud of her house.

He bent and kissed her, then walked to the kitchen and filled the copper kettle with water. “Tea?”

Tea? In her own home? With the man she loved? Was she dreaming?

"Absolutely."

They sat down together on the smooth floor, resting their tired legs, and when the kettle whistled they sipped the homemade brew in silence and nibbled on their traveller biscuits.

"Christopher?" Mila turned to him, only half joking when she said, "Do we ever have to leave?"

He laughed and leaned his head on her shoulder. "You tell me. You're the one with all the answers these days. Seems more and more as though I'm just here for the ride."

Mila sighed. "I feel heavy with responsibility."

"Secrets can do that," Culis said in sympathy. "Maybe we can do something to distract you for a moment?" He ran his fingers lightly up her thigh and raised an eyebrow.

Mila laughed, and although she felt her body respond to his touch, she shook her head. "Insatiable man, will you give me no rest?"

"Haven't you heard? The wicked get no rest." He nipped at her neck gently, causing small shivers to break out all over her skin. Then he pulled away. "Fine, let's find something else to distract you." He walked to the window and seized the rosemayne pot that was now growing wild, bringing it back to her. "How about we try to figure out this new power of yours. Have you tried it on anything since that day back in Traders?"

Despite her firm assurance that he'd accept it without question, Mila found herself unwilling to admit to him that she'd been sucking the energy of plants from the moment they'd hit the rainforest. It would admit a fear of dependency on the small relief they gave her that she wasn't ready to even admit to herself yet.

"Yes," she said slowly.

"And?" he probed. "Anything? Is it reversible?"

"I don't think so."

"Try again now," he urged. "Let's learn your limits, make it all a little less frightening." He saw her hesitation and moved carefully towards her. "Mila. This power? It's *you.* You can't be afraid of yourself."

"Wanna bet?" Mila muttered under her breath, but she reached for the plant anyway, focusing hard on its energy, reaching deep down into its systems and commanding it.

"Less."

The two of them watched as the rosemayne's leaves began to wither and droop before their eyes. Mila closed her eyes in bliss, feeling the familiar, sharp sting of the plant's energy transferring to her. It felt like a small hit of pure adrenaline, pure happiness being injected directly into her heart. So good. Assuaging the symptoms she felt slightly and a small part of her registered that, for all the relief it gave her, it didn't feel *quite* as good as the energy from humans had felt...

Her eyes flew open in horror. "Oh fates."

"What is it? What's wrong?" Culis was concerned, but seemed hesitant to reach for her, as though he wasn't sure she was completely safe to touch yet.

"Culis." Her next words came out as a croak. "I might have figured it out."

"Figured what out?"

"The reason for...for *everything.*"

"What are you talking about?"

"Midas! The sacrifices!" She nearly laughed, but what came out instead was a hysterical heave of air. It was ludicrous, and yet...she suddenly understood it. All of it. In its horror and its simplicity. "He's chasing this feeling."

"What feeling?"

"Culis." Mila knew the time had come to explain everything fully. "Something I've never told you is...When I use my power like this," she gestured to the dying plant before her, "when I steal the life energy from another living thing, I get this...incredible rush. It's a high that I cannot possibly describe. It's the most powerful, insatiable, incredible feeling in the world. But it fades after a while and leaves a hole that feels...well..."

Terrible was an understatement.

"It feels bad. Anyway. It's just occurred to me that Midas must get the exact same rush when he uses his powers."

Culis took this information in silently. He leaned back on his palms and studied her, his eyebrows narrowed in concern. "So, you're saying," he said slowly, "that Midas proclaimed himself 'god' in order to provide himself with a steady stream of sacrifices. Because he's addicted to this...this feeling you're describing?"

"It's the most powerful sensation I've ever felt," Mila told him solemnly. "It wouldn't surprise me one ounce if it were true." And as she said the words, she knew in her heart it was. There was nothing else, no other reason, nothing that would drive an ikarei to do what Midas had done to their world.

"And Abbott and the Church? Where do they fit into this conspiracy?"

That question halted Mila's whirling thoughts. "Abbott must know," she said finally. "That's why he's so hell bent on choosing ikarei for the sacrifice instead of humans. He understands that more ikarei can't be permitted to discover that our powers can evolve like this. It'd change our entire society. If ikarei knew that we could all become so powerful, so destructive..."

"But surely others have discovered this in the past," Culis pointed out, his brow furrowing. "You and Midas are surely not the first ikarei in all of history to have evolved your powers in this way."

"No," Mila agreed, and then she thought of Reminisciary's secret dance room and the shrine it was to ancient gods of old. Tree gods, fertility gods, gods of fearsome and unusual powers...

"I think they've always existed throughout history," she said slowly. "And others have also fashioned themselves as gods. The gods of old. Midas is just the first to institutionalise it in such a way."

"He and Abbott invented the Rotting Muds," Culis said slowly, the cogs in his own clever brain turning as he began to figure it all out. "That's the difference. Previously, any so-called 'gods' of Artor were worshipped by choice, as part of the landscape of life." He sat up a little straighter. "But Midas and Abbott were the first to bring the afterlife into it and invoke a penalty after death for disobedience." He closed his eyes and shook his head. "Just goes to show that, when the conditions are right, when you mix devotion in with a healthy dose of fear and reward, you can convince anyone to do or believe anything. It's...it's genius."

He opened his eyes again, and they stared at one another, each feeling the horror sink in as they considered the world Midas and Abbott had crafted for themselves. Through their touching fingertips, Mila could feel Culis's energy going wild beside her as he tried to pick holes in the theory.

"This feeling. This sensation you describe," he eventually said, tentatively. "It must be incredibly powerful."

"It is," Mila admitted.

"Okay." Still cautious. "So how bad is 'bad'?"

"Pretty bad" she admitted quietly, unable to meet his eyes.

"Are...are *you* going to be okay?" The concern flowing from him had shifted now, from Abbott and Midas to her.

She felt...offended.

How dare he? Did he suspect she could somehow become tempted to be complicit in their ploy? That her own hunt for the rush could corrupt her too somehow?

"I'll be fine," she snapped. "This isn't about me. I'm not the enemy here."

"That's not what I – "

"Well then don't even mention it. I'm not Midas!"

"I never said – " he stopped himself, unwilling for this conversation to devolve into a fight. Mila hated his restraint in that moment. She wanted to yell, wanted to rage. Getting angry at Culis about this was a safe outlet. He could take it. Unlike her. She couldn't yet acknowledge that in the quiet moments, late at night, she'd been wracked by this very fear.

"I think the rest of the Church," she changed the subject, "the jesu and acolytes and other priests, I think they're all true believers."

"I agree," Culis said slowly. He didn't want to fight, but he wasn't ready to let this go that easily either.

"Christopher?" she said sharply, noting his train of thought. "Now is not the time. We have a false god to unmask. Don't make it more complicated than it needs to be."

She could tell he was still not satisfied, but to her relief, he accepted the placating kiss she planted on his lips, and responded when she deepened it. The way her body trilled with delight when his hands moved to her hips and drew her close was otherworldly. She'd never get tired of this, this feeling of light and the outpouring of love he was willing to give her. When she felt it, when their bodies joined and became one, and she could feel his energy, that love, flowing into her. It healed parts of her she didn't even realise had been cobwebbed and cracked over.

She drew back from him reluctantly, but with a smile. “Come with me.”

“We only just arrived! Where are we going now?”

“Not far, come.”

Shake the Dust

She led him out of the house, back into the searing heat of the day, and down a small overgrown track that veered to the left from her house. There, the rise of the landscape changed, and suddenly they were descending a series of grey stone slabs that had been arranged into a staircase.

"You *made* this?" he exclaimed in wonder, marvelling at the precision. "*How!?*"

"I called it, Viah's Staircase," Mila then gave a sardonic smile. "Needed the help of the evil one himself to get it done."

Viah's Staircase it might be, but it certainly did not lead into the Rotting Muds. It led to a round, clear pool that was fed by a waterfall that scurried down the high rock walls around it. The water was so clean and clear that the white pebbles that lined the bottom and the small fish that danced in the waterfall's spray were clearly visible, even from a height.

"What is this place?" Culis breathed in awe.

"Paradise," Mila said, as she unbuttoned her travelling shirt, slipped off the trousers, and walked, wholly naked, into the crystal waters. She dived under, nearly crying with relief from the heat and nostalgia of the sensation. This was what it meant to be home.

When she surfaced, she looked back at Culis who stared at her, his mouth on the forest floor.

"Well, come on!" she beckoned, splashing a little water playfully towards him. "What are you waiting for?"

"To wake up, apparently." He shook his head, and then slipped from his clothes so quickly he may as well have been made of liquid himself. He hissed with relief at the cool water against his overheated skin, and when he swam towards her and sidled up against her, his skin felt as smooth as silk.

She kissed him. He ran his hand down the length of her, exploring her hip, her backside, her thigh. He grabbed at it, seizing as much of her as he could in the palm of his hand, drawing her close. She wrapped her legs around his waist, and then he was inside her, pinning her to him before she could take another breath.

She realised in this moment that all she'd ever wanted in life was to be kissed into silence and submission. To be loved as loudly as a thunderstorm. Culis manoeuvred them to the edge of the pool and lifted Mila so she was half out of the water, lying with her back on the large, smooth boulders that ringed the little oasis. There, in the shade of the bayan trees, half in the cool, healing water and half in the life-affirming heat of the forest, he made love to her, every movement of his body worshipping hers, and every seize and sigh of hers adoring him in return.

Afterwards, they lazed on the hot rocks and let the radiant heat warm and dry them. Mila dipped her hair back in the water and allowed Culis to wash it, his clever, kneading fingers making her moan from a different form of pleasure.

When they finally returned to the cottage, he took her again on the hardwood floor, and Mila fell asleep in his embrace with just the blanket of embroidered monkeys covering their hips.

***

When she awoke, Culis was gone.

She wrapped the blanket around her shoulders and went outside, looking around, but unable to see him anywhere.

"Culis?" she called out after a short while, worried.

"I'm okay," came his calm voice from up in a nearby tree. "I just...just need to see the sky for a moment. Come join me."

"Okay." Mila climbed high out of the muggy humidity and into the breezy canopy after him.

Culis pulled her up to join him on his branch. The bayan tree he'd chosen still had branches thick enough to hold their body weight, even at this distance from the ground. When Mila reached him and saw his downturned mouth and dull eyes, she didn't hesitate. She pulled his shoulders in for an embrace. Culis didn't resist, leaning against her shoulder, breathing raggedly as he battled for control of his calm.

"I don't even know where to start," he admitted softly into her neck, answering her silent question. "But I don't feel worthy of this, worthy of having you."

Mila silently held him close in response. Eventually, she took his face in his hands, turned it towards her, and gave him a slow, soft and utterly fragile kiss. Through it, Mila felt him, his strong, familiar energy. That vigour and zest for life that always seemed to follow him around like a cloak was still present, but as she delved deeper, she sensed something unusual in him. Not something new, but in fact, quite the opposite. Something old that had been hibernating for a long, long time.

She kissed him more deeply, probing with her power, investigating him more thoroughly. Culis responded keenly and, for a moment, Mila forgot herself and became entangled in the kiss. But eventually, she remembered her intent and pulled away, still clutching his head between her hands, staring deep into his green eyes.

Something in him, a flame of some sort, had been renewed, Mila realised. Whatever it was, it was as small as a caraway seed, as likely to be blown away in a soft breeze as find root and grow. She studied it in her mind's eye, turning it over, wondering what it was, and then nearly burst into tears when the answer came to her.

It was the nameless essence that can be found in all small children. The innocence that exists before they're taught that the world around them is something to be fearful of, when they still see the creatures of the world as equally deserving of life and friendship and might cry over the inadvertent death of an insect.

When does that change? Mila wondered. *When is that recognition that we are all intrinsically connected and familiar to one another beaten out of us?*

That pure spark was here, now, inside Christopher. She could feel it, struggling to lift its head and grow in the light. Shaking the dust of its long confinement.

"You're an extraordinary man, Christopher Culis," she said softly to him.

"We'll see," he replied, kissed her gently again, and then began to descend.

Hunted

The next morning, Mila woke to the sounds of parrots on the roof.

She was utterly entangled with a sleeping Christopher, her head nestled into the crook of his neck, one leg strewn over his hips, and his arms wrapped possessively around her – tight despite his deep sleep. She could hardly believe she was in her old bed, in her own home, with this man. She felt a deep, utterly pervading sense of peace and was so relaxed she could feel her heartbeat sitting deep in her stomach. She lay there, luxuriating, debating for a long moment whether to rise or languish in his arms until he stirred.

Eventually, she decided that real life needed to resume. She'd be meeting Tarett in Bori later today and would bring him back here to help her collect the rubane. If she was going to get started picking the rubane, then she should do it before the full heat of the day set in.

With this decided, she rose reluctantly and dressed in her old Highlander clothes from her wardrobe – a dark-green singlet and shorts that allowed her midriff to remain uncovered, but over the top she donned a cream, loosely crocheted slip that draped around her like a corded spiders web and fell to her knees. She took a basket that hung from a hook on the ceiling and went outside with her scythe to begin harvesting the weed she required.

It wasn't long before she was soaked through with sweat and her hands heavy and thick with rubane sap. Culis was going to be miserable when he woke, she thought, and chuckled with a wry smile when she pictured his expression in her mind's eye. She also knew he was also going to put two and two together fairly quickly when he saw the bushels of rubane she was collecting, but she wasn't worried about that. Not anymore.

As she worked amongst the weed, her power was effectively blocked and the world muted again. It had been a long time since she'd allowed herself to rest in rubane's clutches and was surprised to find how comforting she found it. She hadn't realised how much she'd sometimes missed that all-consuming silence.

Before long, her basket was full, and she went back inside and placed it quietly on the kitchen benchtop. She needed to collect at least five times this much, and put all of it in oil but, just at that moment, she felt like she needed a break. Culis was still fast asleep, his mouth propped slightly open in abandon. She didn't remember another time he had slept so long, or so deeply. He was usually up at daybreak with the servants of the manor.

As she studied him, she realised she'd never seen him so relaxed either. The elastic tension he usually held in his shoulders had drained away, leaving him as soft and open as ripe fruit. She decided then against her initial plan to clamber back into bed and rouse him. Instead, she left the house again and made her way down to the waterfall to wash.

It was the first time she'd been any distance away from Culis without the vasium around her neck, and despite the fact that she missed his presence, the sense of freedom was utterly liberating. As it had been yesterday, the waterfall was clean and clear, and the water was cold enough to jolt the system, but not harsh enough to be uncomfortable. She gasped in joy as she entered and plunged under, revelling in the feeling of the water over her naked body, the liberation that feeling brought her.

She was home, and this was a life she might be able to reclaim someday. She felt so full of hope and optimism. Exposing Midas would be difficult, and fraught with danger, she knew this. And if they succeeded, the world would look forever different without his influence and tyranny. But right now, she was reminded that whatever the future held for her, time would eventually conquer everything. All successes and struggles would be forgotten eventually on history's breeze, but cool water on a hot day would always be sweet.

And I will always love him. She thought of Culis asleep in her bed and smiled. If she could somehow bottle this feeling right now and hold onto it, she was sure she could be reminded, even in the darkest times, not to be overcome by despair.

A stirring of birds in a tree a few yards behind her startled Mila out of her contemplation.

Birds didn't naturally blast fearfully into the air like that. Something had disturbed them.

Mila tried to push her power out into the direction of the disturbance, but felt nothing, and then remembered the sap that was still resolutely stuck to her palms. She swam over to a nearby boulder and began to scrape the sticky, waterproof mess from her skin.

Probably just a monkey playing a game.

But there was some urgency to her scraping. She knew deep down that it wasn't monkeys, or anything remotely natural that lived in the Highlands. Something intrusive and dangerous was intruding on the natural rhythm and flow of the surrounding forest, and it had arrived in her part of the forest.

Even without the use of her power, her skin was prickling. The cool water that had previously been so welcome now suddenly felt too cold. Her nakedness now just felt like exposure, weakness. She tried to steady her breathing and calm her suddenly racing heart but the fine hairs on the back of her neck stood up straight when another explosion of birds lunged into the sky, this time a little to her left.

Closer now.

Whatever it was, it was heading straight towards her. She could track its advance by the way all other forest noises fell silent around the one particular patch of vegetation where it lurked.

She scrubbed furiously at the yellow plant matter that had determinedly glued itself and dried mercilessly to her skin, seeking the answers only her power could give her.

Who is it? What is it? What do they want?

Were they coming for her? Or for Culis? How would anyone even know where they were? They'd been so careful, left no sign...

Realisation struck her like a cold hammer as she remembered something. The one critical mistake that they'd both missed while trying to get to Bori.

The stamp.

When he'd paid for Tarett's golden sand, Culis had signed a note with his personal stamp. That stamp would have told anyone who looked at it that Christopher Culis was personally in town, and that information might have been worth a lot to the right buyer...

Mila suddenly became absolutely certain that this *thing* in the rainforest near her, was not stalking her. It was here for Culis. Whatever this was, it was an attack on him, and she'd left him sleeping alone in the house, completely unarmed, his guard down. He would be helpless to an attack, caught completely unawares...

Go! Her inner voice screamed at her and Mila pushed up onto the rock wall of the pool, heaving her torso out of the water, preparing to sprint back up the staircase and wake him, but she was just one second too late.

The net that came down was heavy and thick. It forced her head brutally back down under the water and Mila could not pull herself back up.

She'd been completely wrong.

The thing had been hunting her, and her alone.

***

By the time she was finally pulled out, Mila was half drowned, spewing out water and bile, heaving in air when her burning lungs had emptied enough to do so. She coughed and choked on the ground, vaguely aware that a heavy pair of boots stood directly by her head. It took a long while before she'd regained enough air to feel she could blearily crane her neck up and identify her assailant.

Frank Culis stood nearly right on top of her, staring down with a face that was a mixture of rage and disgust, his eyes were narrowed into tiny prick-points and, Mila noted with alarm, ever so slightly unfocused.

"Frank?" she croaked in surprise, struggling against the weight of the heavy net around her to rise to her hands and knees. Part of her was relieved to see him. She'd been expecting something far worse. That relief was short-lived.

"Shut up." He kicked her hard in the ribs and sent her sprawling again. "You rise when I say you rise."

"Don't – "

He kicked her again. Mila groaned in pain then shut her mouth and breathed heavily through her nose.

"You think," he wheezed as he began to drag the net away from Viah's Staircase, down the hill and into the thick jungle with Mila still tangled in it, "that you...can work...with *my* son...to betray me?"

His face was red and grim as he dragged her, muttering to himself all the while. Mila's bare skin raked painfully across the coarse and unforgiving ground. She was still stark naked and completely exposed, but right now this seemed like the least of her issues. Frank was not only here, he was furious, and even more than that, the budding paranoia she'd sensed earlier in him had grown into madness. There was something animal and wild about his body language. He was not a man of sound mind. He'd become something far more insidious.

"Tasked by Abbott to track that wily, impervious bitch," he muttered through heaving breaths, "imagine what I find instead. The other demon and Christopher. *My Christopher.* In *love.*" He spat out the word, then stopped heaving the net and turned to glare down at her. "I asked *one* thing of you, demon. *One* thing and it was a *fair* trade. A fair, fair trade with a demon. What a fool. A fool I am."

Mila's blood turned to ice at his garbled words, and she realised right then that, despite the hopelessness of her situation and the pain Frank could inflict on her, this was a moment that she truly needed to fight for her life.

So she thrashed in the net as she screamed for Culis to come get her, to help her. She reached through the net for any part of Frank's body that was within grasping distance, his trouser legs, the back of his shirt, his exposed arms.

In a huge show of strength, she practically crawled up his body, still encased in the net, and scratched and clawed and bit at anything she could find, trying to rip the skin from his bones with her nails and teeth. Frank screeched at the assault and dumped the drawstring of the net roughly on the ground, shoving her away before turning and leaping on top of her, pinning her with his big body as he tried to reach for her wrists to bind them.

Mila fought underneath him like a wildcat. No part of Frank within reach was left unscathed. She bit at his fingers as he seized one wrist, earning her a punch to the mouth. He swore, and used his other forearm to pin her by the neck to the ground. But this time he pulled his weight forward and freed her knees, so she drove them up hard into his buttocks, hoping to hit something more tender. He grimaced but didn't pause. He had both her wrists now and was tying her arms above her head.

No, no, no, no, no.

Panic overrode her brain. "Help!" she screamed again. "Culi – "

Frank's forearm struck her out of nowhere, cutting her screams off with a sharp crack to the throat. Mila's eyes bulged and her world narrowed to a dim hum in her ears and a thin pinpoint of light.

Wheezing, heaving.

I'm going to die.

But she didn't die. And when she was finally able to breathe again, the net was gone, and Frank was tying a long rope around her bound wrists. In a last-ditch effort, she threw her fingers out towards his wrists, tickling his skin with the tips of them and desperately, desperately seeking her power, urging it to suck the strength and ferocity from the man.

Less, she cried desperately. *Less!*

She made enough contact with his skin to achieve it, but nearly cried with frustration to realise her hands were still stained with the rubane sap, rendering her touch powerless.

She satisfied herself by lunging again for his ear, trying to sink her teeth into it. That earned her another sharp blow to the head, which dizzied her enough to force her to stop.

"I'll wager you told him about the compass too, didn't you?" he snarled in her face, so close now she could smell his breath, his expensive cologne, his sweat, his rage. "Told him about it and now he's plotting to kill me first. Isn't he? Isn't he?!" He shook her, the whites of his eyes stark against the green of their surroundings.

"He loves you, you fool!" Mila spat blood at him, and Frank responded with another jaw-shattering slap.

She crumbled at his feet and didn't move, too exhausted, too broken, to keep fighting.

"I didn't want to hurt you, demon," she heard Frank say from above her, panting heavily himself. She glanced up and saw him looking at his fist with his face a picture of dark fury. "Not too badly anyway. That's for the Princess to do."

The Princess? Her brain was foggy with pain.

Jezebel.

Frank seized the rope that bound her hands and began to drag her again through the underbrush to where his horse patiently stood, waiting at the bottom of the hill. Mila cried out in agony as her naked body was dragged across the unforgiving jungle vegetation. She tried to scrabble to her feet, but the angle, her injuries and his speed, made it impossible. Tears streamed down her cheeks, mingling with the blood running from her nose and forehead.

When they reached the horse and finally stopped, Mila slumped, bloodied and lifeless, against the warm, concerned animal, while Frank busied himself with something at the saddle bag. When he approached her again, he was holding out another strip of fabric, torn from a spare shirt, and despite her feeble protestations, tied it firmly around her mouth. Then he practically threw her over the poor horse's back and tied her to the back of the saddle, tucking his long riding blanket around her so it covered her from head to toe. In her daze, Mila suspected it was less to save her modesty, and more because he knew riding through the countryside with a naked, bloodied woman tied to his horse would probably see him stopped at some point. Unless someone looked closely at the rug, they probably wouldn't know there was a person under it at all.

Above her, Frank clucked the horse on, and the last thought Mila had before she lost consciousness was to briefly wonder what Culis would think when he woke up to find her gone.

The Oubliette

Jezebel's attack started before Mila was even unstrapped from the horse. The punch to the face tore the skin against her teeth and caused even more blood to drip down the poor horse's flank. Mila cried out, but only softly. It was more a mewling noise than a human sound. She was unable to lift her hands to defend herself, and too exhausted from the way she'd been transported for days, to do anything about the assault. Frank hadn't even untied her to allow her to relieve herself. It had been a barbaric, humiliating, and painful way to travel. A part of her was relieved they had finally arrived at their destination.

Perhaps now Jezebel would kill her and then, at least, she wouldn't have to endure another second tied, bloodied and broken, to the back of a galloping horse.

The opportunity to languish in self pity didn't last long.

Jezebel swiftly cut the cord that held her wrapped around the horse's middle, and then seized Mila's hair, dragging her backwards off the tall horse's hind legs. The breath whooshed out of her when she hit the ground, and her bound hands and feet did nothing to cushion her fall. Mila lay where she landed and groaned, long and loud into the gag, as the pain from her fall met the stiffness and aching of her abused body.

"I will kill you, you little whore." Jezebel seized Mila's hair again, forcing her upright, only to punch her again and knock her down.

The rubane sap had finally worn away, and Mila could sense the black thundercloud of Jezebel's contempt for her. She was going to kill her – and Culis too.

"You know the worst part of all of this?" she hissed. "You were supposed to be different to the rest. I *saved* you, I *spared* you. I was the first to see your value, and this is how you repay me? By *stealing my betrothed*?" She'd worked herself into a hysteria. "You, out of everyone, you knew what it meant to me, what *he* meant to me. You knew and yet you still did this."

Slap.

"*How long* were you two conspiring to betray me? Did it *amuse* you to watch me trustingly – *obliviously* – plan this wedding?"

Slap.

The rage and hurt within the woman was overwhelming, and Jezebel was letting that pain ride her. She struck her again, and Mila realised dimly through the haze that she was about to be beaten to death on the cobblestones of the palace if she didn't do something right now.

Moving more on instinct than rational thought, she rolled swiftly towards the Princess, bumping hard against her feet. Once there, she reached out and touched her with the tips of her left hand.

In that split second of contact, she reached into Jezebel with her power and felt the vengeful jealousy the Princess held towards her. It was so clear, it stood out like a ball. A hot, red ball burning deep in Jezebel's stomach.

Mila was about to draw it out with her power when she saw something else. A different ball of energy, this one sitting in Jezebel's heart. One full of all the rage and betrayal that Jezebel held towards Culis.

Acting on impulse, Mila made a decision in that inch of a moment, and drew with all her might on the energy of the woman's murderous intent towards Culis.

Less, she coaxed, and felt Jezebel's fury towards the man draw out of her. For a heady moment, Mila was flooded by the exhilarating high of Jezebel's energy entering her own body, and then Jezebel kicked her directly in the stomach.

Mila's world reduced to a mere pinprick of light for a long, long, *long* moment.

When she came to and was finally able to heave in a wheezing breath, guards were dragging her by her armpits towards the kitchen. Jezebel was walking behind them. She was staring at Mila, waiting for the moment that she could see Mila was lucid again before she spoke.

"Do you know what an oubliette is, demon?" she snarled when she identified consciousness back in Mila's eyes. "It's a pretty word for an ugly thing. It means, 'the forgetting place'."

She let this linger between them for a moment, but Mila was too tired, too focused on sucking down air, to care much.

Jezebel continued. "I've never put someone in one before. But then, no one has ever betrayed me quite as uniquely as you have." As she spoke, the guards continued to drag Mila past the kitchen, towards an area of Jezebel's apartments that she'd never been to before. It was a small courtyard near the kitchen, with air that was ringed by the stink of rotting vegetables and befouled meat. It grew worse the closer they got towards a trapdoor in the ground.

Mila didn't struggle. She didn't have the energy, and there were too many of them for success to be remotely possible. Better to conserve her strength for whatever lay ahead.

A guard hauled open the trapdoor and revealed a ladder that led down into a dark, stinking hole below. The guard behind Mila shoved her forward, making her options clear. It was either go down the ladder willingly or be pushed and fall down the hole.

She chose the first option, grasping the firm wood of the ladder like a lifeline and praying her legs wouldn't buckle beneath her as she carefully lowered herself into the pit.

One guard followed her down as she descended. Both of them gagged as they entered the haze of stench.

It was the pit used for kitchen refuse.

There were probably a number of such waste-holes scattered throughout the courtyard. Each one was eventually filled in with kitchen scraps and a new one dug when needed. They were very narrow and chimney-like. Not wide enough for Mila to spread her arms out on either side of her and certainly not enough space for her to lie down.

When she got to the bottom, she discovered that this particular hole was evidently quite new, for the sloppy, liquid mess of rotten food at the bottom was only a few inches deep. Nevertheless, Mila was naked and barefoot and covered in bruises and open wounds. Standing in it was horrendous. The texture of the slime between her toes made her skin crawl. She couldn't imagine trying to sit.

With a shiny padlock, the young guard placed a chain around Mila's neck, looping it into a ring that formed a collar. Then, with a second padlock, he clipped the other end of the chain to the bottom rung of the ladder.

Mila was now locked securely at the bottom of the sordid hole, the oubliette – the forgetting place.

Hurriedly, gratefully, as though concerned he, too, might be forgotten down there, the guard clambered back up towards the light. Leaving Mila entirely alone.

She watched him go, and when he reached the top and his silhouette moved to the side, she found she could see one more shadow – Jezebel's shadow – looking down at her from above like a vulture surveys a carcass.

"I may remember to come get you at the end of the season," she crowed, then added ominously, "if I remember you're even down here at all." She let that statement hang between them and stared at Mila with eyes that were devoid of pity or humanity.

Mila refused to beg. She knew Jezebel would not change her mind about this punishment, and showing weakness or fear would only increase her pleasure.

"I expect that, if I do ever see you again," the Princess continued, "you'll be without your ears and nose. Maybe less a few toes too. I hear the rats around here are quite enormous. You'll be in good company."

And then the trapdoor closed, and Mila was plunged into darkness.

As dark as a grave.

Monster in the Family

Aidas knelt before his father, blood pouring from his head, into his eyes, into his mouth. His hands were clasped before him as though he were deep in prayer, except Aidas had never been religious. His hands were bound, palms pressed tightly together by a firm rope to keep them from opening, to keep them from destroying anything and everything they relentlessly destroyed at his merest of touches.

Mother.

Father stood before him now, grim-faced and determined. "Abomination," he whispered with exhaustion as he raised a sickly curved knife. "I will cut this curse out of you." His father had been trying for hours to cut the horns from his head. To unmake his son, remove his perverse powers.

Aidas whimpered in agony and fatigue. He knew he couldn't deal with much more of this, but he must endure it. On this lone issue, he unreservedly agreed with his father.

Get the horns out. End this curse.

But it wasn't working—the horns kept growing back. The pain? Indescribable.

"Do it," Aidas grunted again from behind his gritted teeth and aching throat. "Cure me."

On either side of him were Talbot, Alice and Merry. They held his shoulders and tried in vain to temper his uncontrollable writhing.

Merry's face, in particular, was right before his.

"Look at me, Aidas," she whispered. "Look into my eyes and don't look away. You are not alone. I'm here, we're here with you."

"Merry." He heaved, saying her name as though it were some sort of lifeline and then the knife descended again. This time, it was different, worse still somehow. His father was no longer slicing uselessly away at the horns. This time, he was cutting a circle into Aidas's very skull, right at the base of the horns.

Aidas saw Merry's eyes widen in horror. "No!" she whispered.

He ignored her. "This is how we used to do it with cattle." Father grunted quietly to himself as he ground the tip of the knife into Aidas's head, eyes deadly focused.

"You're going to kill him!" Talbot bellowed as Aidas' vision disappeared beneath a fresh fountain of blood.

But his father didn't hesitate, didn't even pause.

Aidas felt Talbot release his arm and the pain at his head ebbed for a second. Talbot was fighting their father! A loud, barking sound split the air. Dimly Aidas realised that his father had struck Talbot and sent him sprawling. Aidas tried to use the moment of distraction to crawl away, but hands were still bound before him and he didn't get far. He scrabbled along pathetically in the ground as the blood and dust mingled and tattooed his skin. The rock-solid figure of his father caught up to him easily, leapt upon him, and pinned him to the ground, straddling his neck and pinning Aidas's head between his knees.

"Let him go!" Merry's high-pitched, useless whine came from somewhere behind them. Alice was screaming.

His father didn't pause. Once again Aidas was blinded by blood and pain as his father drove the dagger into the base of his left horn, and then lifted, using Aidas's skull to leverage the blade as he literally digging the horns out of his head.

Aidas's world went black, then white, then red.

He was a floating spirit of nothing, a ball of energy without sensation. Was he dead? At least there was no pain. It was relief, blessed relief.

It didn't last long.

When his awareness came back into his body, all he knew was blinding hot heat, slicing through his head like glass. An alien noise was coming from his mouth, a guttural moan, like an animal in its final death throes.

"Aidas, Aidas," someone was sobbing over him, mopping the blood from his eyes, his nose. He couldn't tell who it was.

"Well, boy?" A far gruffer, more familiar voice pierced through the haze of pain. "You alive?"

"Urghhh," was all Aidas could manage in response, rolling onto his back, his eyes still tightly closed. The pain in his head was unbelievable. It was bad enough to send him back to oblivion. Surely. Any time now. Sweet mercy, take him.

He felt a strange sawing motion down by his hands and dimly recognised the ropes that bound him were being cut away.

"Well, boy?" the gruff voice said again. "You're free. I've liberated you."

Aidas forced one blood crusted eye to open a tiny bit. He saw the dark shape of his father standing above him, holding out his hand to help him up.

"Either this worked, or I died trying." His face was hard and expressionless, as if he hadn't just gouged the very roots of his own son's horns from his head, leaving two crater-like holes and a twitching, bloodied wreck of a boy on the ground before him. There was no love in his eyes, and no hope, Aidas noted.

He reached for his father's hand and took it.

His father disintegrated before Aidas even had time to feel the warmth of his skin.

No one said anything.

Eventually Merry stopped crying.

Alice brought Aidas some water and tipped it into his mouth from a safe distance. It splattered all over his chin and dribbled across his cheek.

"Kill me." Aidas moaned. No one replied. Talbot's gaze was fixated on the space, the scatter of golden sand, where their father had once existed, his expression a complicated combination of devastation and relief.

"Tal," Aidas eventually croaked out. "Bind my palms again." He placed them back in the prayer position.

Talbot didn't move.

Aidas turned to Merry, begging now. "Merry, please. I don't want to...I don't want to hurt anyone accidentally."

Merry nodded and moved as gracefully as a willow by a stream. Quietly and gently, she wound the ropes with efficiency around his wrists and fingers, ensuring they were immobile once she was done.

"How am I supposed to live like this?" he gasped eventually. "My horns are gone and it didn't even work. I can't...I can't touch anything without completely destroying it. I can't even feed or cook for myself. I'm helpless."

"We'll look after you Aidas." Alice said quietly but Aidas snarled at her words.

"I don't *want* you to look after me! I don't want to be a monster!"

No one contradicted him either. The silence between himself and Talbot was crushing. His older brother's gaze hadn't wavered from the place their father once stood. Aidas didn't speak. He just waited.

Eventually, Talbot's head slowly turned.

"There was only one monster in our lives. He's now gone."

"But...I... Mother." Aidas couldn't say the words. *I killed her.*

"You're powerful," Talbot repeated. "And you didn't mean to."

That simple sentence was all Aidas needed to feel an enormous wave of relief strike him. His brother didn't blame him for her death. The respite from his guilt was like an antidote to the poison that had been eating him alive. If his head didn't already feel so hurt and swollen, he would have burst into tears.

"You didn't mean to," Talbot repeated, placing a hand on Aidas's shoulder, a determined shadow crossing his face. "Little brother, a lot of wrongs have been dealt to us in this lifetime." His gaze swept across the gaping, open wounds in Aidas's head that still wept blood. "I think it's about time," he said softly, "that, from here on, we forge our own future, together."

"Talbot..." Aidas whimpered. "My power."

"I will protect you from it," Talbot promised. "I won't let you hurt Merry or Alice. I'll do anything it takes to protect you all. Whatever it takes."

He emphasised the last with such violence in his voice that Aidas was forced to blink and look at his brother properly. Talbot was trembling all over in anger, and a hard line sat above the cleft of his left eyebrow.

"What do you mean by *anything*?" Aidas asked slowly, unable to keep the note of fear from his voice.

"I mean," Talbot said, helping his brother stand and holding his bloodied shoulders as he looked him dead in the eye. "Anything."

The Three Stages of Fear

The passing of time was strange in the oubliette.

Mila experienced fear and despair in noticeable stages.

The first stage was sharp and primal. The fear sucked everything immediately out of her body and left her gasping and frozen, as though she'd been plunged into an icy bath. She stood in frigid paralysis, the instinctive response that the primitive mind has to being alone, underground and in the dark.

Mila clenched her jaw so tightly she thought she might grind her teeth down to the roots. She tried to hug herself for comfort. She rocked back and forth on the balls of her feet that were already ensconced in slime and bile. She tried to slow her breathing and calm her racing heart. None of it helped.

There was not a bead of light from outside that entered her deep prison, and the pitch darkness prevented her eyes adjusting to anything. She was trapped in a blackness that was so absolute she could not discern if she had her eyes open or closed. She felt paralysed, waiting in a petrified, frozen state for the monsters that live in such a consuming dark to strike.

One cannot exist in this state forever though.

Eventually, she was able to play a game with herself, one that helped her overcome her fear a little.

"It's light in here," she lied to herself, the words coming between her heaving, panicked breaths. "I'm just choosing to keep my eyes closed because...because the décor in here is so ugly. It's my choice. I want to have my eyes closed. I want it to be dark."

It was a silly game, but it gave her back the smallest sense of control. She was choosing this. Choosing to keep her eyes closed. Choosing to not see anything.

"I want my other senses to develop. I want to feel my power more keenly." She repeated it over and over until her breathing began to steady and her heartbeat didn't hurt her chest. "I'm choosing to keep my eyes closed. I'm choosing the darkness."

The second wave of fear, when it arrived, was a deeper, more pervasive kind. It was the sense that she'd just been buried alive.

The oubliette, the forgetting place.

Nobody knew where she was. No one was coming for her. She'd been left here to die, to be forgotten about. There was no future here. And Culis would never know what had happened to her...

This final thought broke her. The iron control she'd been struggling to have over her fear slipped again, and a heavy sob burst out, followed by a desperate scream.

"*Help me!*" she bellowed at the roof of her prison. "Please!" She screamed so loudly she felt her throat tear with the pressure. Her voice echoed uselessly around her. "Somebody! Hear me! Save me!" She yanked frantically at the chains that held her to the ladder and ripped at the one around her neck, scratching the skin.

"*Let me out of here!*"

It felt like she spent days crying out like that, alternating between begging for mercy from Jezebel, calling out for strangers, and sobbing at how close she'd come to having the life she'd always wanted and the fury and desolation she felt at having had it ripped away from her. For the love she'd just allowed herself to feel for Culis and would never get to explore with him.

She'd never told him she loved him.

The despair that accompanied that thought brought about a pause in the screams. She shuddered, exhausted, throat aching and ruined.

Culis. She sobbed quietly. He probably didn't even know that Frank had ambushed her. Was he now in danger from Frank too? She tried to stop the uncontrollable whirlwind of her thoughts. She was helpless to tell Culis about Frank, but she couldn't allow herself to think about that, about anything. It'd drive her mad. She tried to focus only on what she had been able to do. She'd tried to suck Jezebel's hatred for Culis away from her. Had it been enough? Would it keep him safe from Jezebel's rage?

The third fear, when it finally arrived, was a true physical fear.

She hadn't even realised that she'd fallen, kneeling in the slop, but a sharp bite on her ear jolted her awake.

The rat did not easily let go. Even when she flung her head forward with a yowl, the creature grimly hung on, gnawing at her flesh until she finally managed to punch it away and send it squealing into the darkness.

She groped in pain at her torn ear and could smell and feel the blood dribbling from it.

She heard them then, maybe a dozen, all skittering and scuttling around her in the darkness, their energy curious, wary and hungry. She roused herself and forced herself to stand up, stamping her feet and trying to yell. She felt the rats scatter back, but not far enough, and not frightened enough either.

Having now touched the liquid filth that pooled around her feet with her hands, it also occurred to her that she was now powerfully thirsty. She wondered how long it had been since she last had a drink of water. Her swim in the clear pool at her cottage seemed like a lifetime ago, and Frank had only given her a mouthful every few hours on their return trip.

How had he even found her? How had he known where to look?

She wondered if she would die of thirst down here, and then seriously contemplated drinking the soggy mess she stood upon.

There has to be something else.

She projected her power out and around her for the first time and realised something incredible. In this crippling darkness, she could use her power to see.

Projecting in this way wasn't a new evolution of her power. It was something she'd always been able to do with it. She'd used it this way to sense the assassins in Culis Manor all those months ago. She just rarely used it this way because it was too overwhelming to project her power out from herself and sense *everything* in her surroundings. But now, alone in this hole, it opened up new opportunities for information.

She could see. As her power touched things in the space around her it sent back information that she could use to make sense of her surroundings.

There were thirteen rats, one sitting to her top left was considering a leap onto her shoulder and tasting the flesh on her other ear. She pre-emptively reached out and punched it and was rewarded by the warm thud of fur against her knuckle and an ungainly squeak of pain as the rat dropped and landed in the muck at her feet. A small win, but a win nonetheless.

She tried to kick out at another one, tried to send them all a message that she was not food and any rat that came close enough would severely regret it. It worked, sort of. She could sense some of them shifting their attention to the watery scraps by her feet instead. But not nearly enough, and she knew they would try again eventually.

She projected her power out again, searching for anything else that existed in this hole, and was rewarded by the small life energy of the soft moss patches growing against the walls of the oubliette.

She leaned forward, cautiously licking a patch, finding it rich and full of clean moisture. She slurped the odd-tasting water down greedily. It was nowhere near enough, but she found another and another. Altogether there were six that she could reach, and she gratefully drank the tiny mouthfuls of relief they provided. It wouldn't be enough to sustain her long term, and who knew how long the moss would take to recapture the water she had stolen, but Mila decided to focus on just one problem at a time. And for the immediate future, both her crippling thirst was resolved and she could *see*.

Anything was possible.

She scanned her power out into the sludge below her. It didn't register anything live in the water, other than the scurrying rats, of course, but as she felt along the stone edges of her prison, she sensed the small hole the rats used to enter and exit her prison and marked it in her mind.

***

She must have fallen asleep at some point, because she dreamed of home and for a single false moment, she was safe and warm and happy again. In her mind's eye, she watched as Culis woke to find her absent. His confused and worried face looked more beautiful and golden than she remembered, and his disobedient hair was more romantically tousled than it had ever looked for a single day in his waking life. She watched the dream version of him rise and frantically begin to scour the entire forest in his search for her. She cried in her sleep as she watched him call out for her forlornly, and then a cold chill came over her as he eventually gave up, returned home and happily married Jezebel. Jezebel, who cruelly insisted on their wedding ceremony being held directly above the trapdoor of the oubliette.

Mila woke to darkness and the cold bite of hopelessness clutching at the corners of her heart. She wiped her cheek, forced it back and told herself that the real Culis would not give up.

What would he do?

There was no other way to occupy her time, nothing else to distract herself from her misery, so Mila spent the day exercising her brain, slowly imagining the steps she thought the clever, cunning and determined man she'd given her heart to would take to find her.

He'd wake alone in her beautiful bed, and he wouldn't be panicked. Not at first. He'd suspect she'd gone somewhere in the rainforest alone and he'd happily wait for her return. He'd potter about, tying his hair back into a bun with a strip of white linen cloth, recovering his clothes from where they'd been tossed the evening before. She could picture him so clearly, padding around comfortably in his long loose pants with his chest bare. Perhaps he'd boil water in the kettle and start to brew a tea. Which of her five handmade mugs would pique his fancy? Would he choose the rocking chair or the hammock to sit in? Eventually, at some point, perhaps when the heat of the day truly began to creep into the house, he'd realise that her extended absence was now unusual. Perhaps he'd suspect an injury or accident. He'd find the discarded basket full of rubane. He'd look around outside.

Would he know what the rubane was? Probably not, but he'd certainly suspect the purpose behind its collection.

Would he wait another hour before beginning to call out for her? Probably not. In the freedom of her mind, Mila saw her imagined Culis make a circle around the house as he looked for her. He wouldn't wander far into the forest. He didn't know it like she did, wouldn't want to get lost. Would he go back down Viah's Staircase though? Yes. He knew that place. He'd look there. And there he'd find her discarded clothes by the pool. He'd know then that something was really not right.

It comforted Mila to have this fantasy running in her mind. She felt as though she were alongside him, nudging him left and right with her mind.

No, don't go into the forest alone. Wait for Tarett. He'll come in a few days. He'll tell you about the rubane, about the plan.

She couldn't imagine what Culis would do in the days before Tarett arrived. He'd go mad just sitting around, worrying. But without Tarett to guide him back to Brewich and Ocianna, Culis was essentially stranded at Mila's house.

Would Tarett come? The horrifying thought suddenly rose in her mind. What if the coldness of Midas's sand overcame his nature? Made him disregard their friendship? What if he decided to abandon their venture?

No.

If Mila was good at one thing, it was forcing back useless, despairing thoughts.

Tarett will come. He will help.

Tarett and Culis would take the rubane back to Ocianna and meet up with Jahan and Natalee.

With Nathaniel too, Mila corrected herself. Surely Culis would remember the promise she'd made to Cari. He'd honour it on her behalf, she knew it. He'd retrieve Nathaniel first, then reunite with their crew in Ocianna, and then decide on what to do next.

With everyone together, they'd have all the pieces in place for the plan to succeed. For a moment, this brought her an incredible and unexpected rush of joy, but it was swiftly followed by a sinking heart. They didn't need her. The sabotage of the Spring Sacrament would still go ahead and the start of the Church's downfall would commence without her. Tarett would still be able to use his power to collect and transport the vast amount of rubane they required. Natalee knew how Mila had infused rubane into oil to save her at the Dusk Ball. She'd show the men how to do the same for this harvest. Jahan could get them, and the oil, past palace security. He'd get them access to the demons awaiting sacrifice, and Culis would use his status post the ceremony to really hammer home the damning evidence that the Church had lied, that Midas was a demon and a false god.

While part of her was happy that she was not the lynch pin to the success of this plan, she knew that it meant her own prospects were even more grim. It was only a few weeks until spring. The plan would need the crew's entire concentration to execute before then. They wouldn't be able to prioritise finding her. If there was even the slightest chance of her being rescued, it wasn't going to happen before spring. She was going to have to survive down here for at least a few weeks, if not months.

She shivered and felt the last of her hope ebb away.

It was freezing down here. There was no food. Almost no water.

She had nothing.

There was no one coming.

Anointing

Mila knew a lot about bodies and their limits. She knew her own even better. She knew most bodies could survive for a few weeks without food and she also knew she didn't have enough fat on her to go for much longer than that. She'd learned that whatever energy she'd sucked from the plants back in the Highlands had staved off the painful, uncomfortable symptoms of withdrawal for a long while, but that they were starting to return again now. She also knew that for the immediate moment, the key issue she faced wasn't food, or these symptoms.

Water was the element she'd be lucky to survive without for more than just a few days. The moss against the wall provided a tiny, semi reliable water source for her, but it wasn't a longer term solution. After a few more days had passed in the hole and she'd sucked the moss dry, she woke with a splitting headache and a bone-deep nausea rocking her body that told her it was not enough. She was withering.

She needed more water.

She couldn't drink the muck she was standing in. It was less water and more slop, and after a few days of her existing in it, it had become even more befouled. Drinking it would kill her before dehydration did. But there was nothing else. No other source.

Without water, her energy dwindled. She found she slept for longer periods of time, and when she woke she was often dazed for long periods of time after. Her mouth and throat ached, and eventually her tongue felt heavy and thick in her mouth.

She sucked desperately at the moss against the walls again but they had nothing left to yield to her.

No water.

When she woke on the third day without a drop, she resigned herself to death. Her eyes ached and she did not bother to try open them. As little movement as possible was the only thing she could try to do to conserve whatever was left of her energy. Unless something miraculous happened in the next few hours, she was going to die like this. Naked, alone, chained to the bottom of a garbage heap.

Forgotten.

In the end, the thing that saved her was entirely mundane.

It rained.

The sound of the heavy barrage of water pounding against the trapdoor woke Mila from her dejected stupor. A torrent of water poured down the sides of the oubliette freely and pooled at her feet. Mila could barely believe it. She forced her body to lean over and into its path, so weak she could barely lift her head to gulp it down. Instead, she had to remain satisfied with letting her head lean against the wall, letting the rain run naturally into her open, parched mouth.

She sobbed into it. Water had never, ever, ever tasted so sweet before.

She drank until she thought she might vomit and her stomach was swollen. And then she tried to drink more. There was no danger of the oubliette flooding, apparently there was a drain somewhere. Maybe the hole she'd sensed earlier. Probably. She didn't care. She had water. Blessed water.

The cold was the next serious issue. The rain didn't stop for days, and it brought with it cold air and dropping temperatures. Mila was still naked and found it almost impossible to stop shivering. When she was awake, she sometimes tried to warm her body up by performing some exercises. But her energy was so low she could barely raise her arms to do the punches.

The lack of food was also beginning to affect her body. The immediate painful pangs of hunger had transformed into a low, dull throbbing feeling, but she could still feel herself wasting away. Fighting off the rats was getting harder. Now she only swiped at them when they bit her. She couldn't muster the strength to try stop them running across her body.

For all the issues the rats caused her, it was true that they were good for two things. Firstly, they enabled her to tell the difference between day and night. During the day they would scurry away to sleep, but at night they would awaken and hunt for food. By this rudimentary system of keeping time, Mila estimated that two weeks had now passed. The second was that occasionally, in the rare moments when she was able to grab one by the tail, she could use her power to sap its energy, and that bolstered her immensely.

One rat's life energy could lift her spirits and motivate her to exercise and keep warm for a few hours. It was not enough entirely to survive on, but it was something. A tiny good, hopeful thing that existed for her in this place. For a day or so, she amused herself by trying to trap as many rats as she possibly could, but they were wily and quick, and unfortunately, the rats were also starting to become relentless in turn, in their hunt of her.

She'd been down here long enough that they'd lost any of the initial fear they'd had of her. They were also clearly accustomed to food being thrown into this hole, and now after two weeks of nothing, they'd apparently decided that, in the absence of new food, they would have to make use of the current offering. The only offering.

Her.

One cold night became entirely sleepless as the rats decided to test her. She tried her best to use her power and her fists to fend them off, but they came for her in droves. Every time she caught or punched away one of them, others dove onto her head or clung to her knees, nibbling at her extremities.

She screamed as she felt their sharp nails and teeth slice into her all night.

Is this how it ends? She thought, her mind wild with panic as she tried to thrash free of them. *Eaten alive by rats?*

She didn't know how long she'd been fighting them when the sound of movement from the trapdoor above her sent the rats scurrying. Her heart nearly flew out of her body at the sound. It had been so long since she'd heard anything except her own body slopping around in the darkness and rats squeaking.

She looked up and saw, for the first time in weeks, the night sky above her. Compared to the darkness of the oubliette, it looked blue and bright. The moon's stubborn sliver was still casting a brilliant light across the sky, despite the fact it was nearly all gone. It had been full just before she'd been captured.

She'd been in here for nearly three weeks.

She was so distracted by the knowledge that she nearly missed the silhouette of a tall figure looming over the entrance.

"Hello?" she called up, voice shaking. "Culis?" She hated the bubble of hope that rose in her chest.

No one answered.

Something hit her in the face, a cold, slick, oily liquid.

Mila gasped in anger and fear, wondering if it was an acid or a poison...but she checked herself after a moment or two passed and felt...nothing. She felt fine?

Must be kitchen slop. That servant evidently hadn't received the message not to use this hole, as the others all apparently had.

The trapdoor abruptly shut, and her mysterious visitor left, leaving Mila covered in liquid, very confused and alone again.

At least the rats had been scared away, for now.

She sniffed and tried to place the scent of whatever it was that was on her. It didn't smell bad. In fact, its smoky scent was rather pleasant and actually helped to mask the smell of the rotting garbage she stood in.

A brief flash of recognition crossed her mind and she remembered where she'd smelled something just like it once before. It had been a long time ago, but the occasion stood out to her meaningfully.

It smelled like the oil worn on the skin of the God-King, tephani oil.

She remembered shivering in his grasp nearly a year earlier, as he proclaimed, "I am immortal." The fragrant smell of his body oil at the time had been a symbol of his complete dominance and her abject fear.

She considered this fact for a long moment but could come up with no rational answers for the question of why someone had just poured that same oil over her, and then left, without a word.

***

Night after night, the same thing happened again and again: the rats attacked, the trapdoor opened, and a mysterious figure poured the God-King's oil into the pit.

Not a servant making a mistake after all. Something very deliberate was happening to her. But what?

"Stop *anointing* me. *Save me*!" Mila eventually cried up at the figure. But the door was always replaced before the sound of her broken voice could even rise above ground.

The week that passed seemed like an eternity, and as it crawled along, Mila began to feel a deep depression sinking into her bones. The rain that had fallen nightly for a few evenings had now stopped. She was beginning to feel faint again from lack of food and water.

One night she summoned what little remnants of energy she had left and cast her power out around her like a shield, sensing the rats and their impending approach, bracing for the battle that was about to come. She wondered what would happen when the day came that her power failed her. Would she simply sit down and let the rats strip flesh from her skin while she still lived, or would she lie face down in the sludge beneath her feet and try to drown herself in it first?

Once again, with supreme effort, she pushed the horrible thought away.

Focus on what you can still do now.

While she still had energy, she would fight.

Mila's wall of power pinged the first rat beginning to creep through the hole to her left. She braced herself for the attack she knew was coming. But then, something else, an entirely different energy, moved to her right, and Mila's head snapped in that direction. She threw her full power against the right-hand wall instead, probing ferociously in surprise.

What was that?

A cat, her power told her. There was a *cat* digging its way through one of the small drains on the other side of the oubliette.

Mila didn't hesitate, didn't let herself question it. She reached forward as far as her chains would allow, trying to move the majority of the slop away from the place on the wall that the cat's trajectory was bringing it.

A cat in this place meant another layer of defence against the rats. She would do anything, *anything* to have it here with her.

Mila probed out and energetically examined the cat as it dug. Its mind was determined. It was being pulled, drawn by something, and was relentless in its determination to reach whatever *it* was.

The rats could hear it coming, too, their ultra-sharp hearing catching the sounds of scratching and digging. And while it didn't outright frighten them, it disturbed them and made them more cautious, more careful. They didn't attack Mila that night.

Long after the night passed, the mysterious anointer came and went. Mila felt the cat continue its mission. Tired, but determined, almost to the point of obsession, it dug and scraped its way through the drain until it pushed away the final clumps of dirt and arrived triumphantly inside the oubliette.

"What on earth are you doing here?" With her eyes still clenched tightly closed, Mila couldn't see the colour or shape of the animal, but to her utter surprise, she sensed it as it walked directly up to her, through the sludge she stood in, and wound itself around her outstretched hand, bobbing its head happily against her palm.

"Oh my goodness, you beautiful creature. What are you doing in this place? Why have you come?"

If she'd had enough water left for tears, she would have shed them.

She wasn't alone anymore.

She hadn't been forgotten.

This cat had come, and even though she was a demon, somehow it could *see* her. Mila wondered if she was hallucinating.

She must be. It was the only explanation, but the cat's fur was so soft, and it's delighted and proud purrs so loud.

Then the cat pushed past her and to her great surprise, it began to clamber up the ladder behind her. Once high enough it leaned forward and determinedly rubbed itself over her oil-drenched hair.

The tephani oil, she realised in wonder. *The cat is drawn to the scent of the oil.*

A huge missing piece of the puzzle fell into place.

Midas had discovered this somehow. He'd used the tephani oil to trick the testing cats. He'd pretended they could see him and he'd used this to trick the Church and cement the lie of his divinity.

And then another thought struck her. Whoever was coming each night to pour oil on her knew about the rats, knew she was down here, and was trying to help her.

She hadn't been forgotten.

She clutched the purring cat to her chest and sobbed with relief.

Acceptance

More days passed.

Exhausted and now too weak to stand for more than just a few minutes at a time, Mila gave in to sitting in the sludge that reached her knees.

The cat, who she'd named Rastava, had shown no desire to leave. He'd perched happily and adoringly on her lap, seemingly unbothered by the stench and wetness of this odd place he had found.

Since Rastava arrived, no rats had bothered her, and as for those foolish enough to investigate the new situation, Rastava enjoyed them for dinner. A new, relative peace settled over the oubliette, punctuated only by the shifting of the trapdoor above and the regular dousing with the oil. Rastava's favourite time of day.

One day, as Mila sat in the darkness, with the peaceful hum of Rastava's contented purring vibrating under her fingertips, she realised, gratefully, that she'd reached a place of acceptance about her situation.

The panic and fear were gone.

She'd accepted her new reality, and in doing so, she was now able to somewhat separate her mind from the discomfort of her body. She also found that her power had sharpened considerably. She'd always been able to project her power and sense shapes and energy around her, but the shapes of energy from the creatures that surrounded her in the oubliette were now so clear in her mind that they appeared to her in colour.

Rastava, for example. The colour of his energy burned a deep orange in her mind's eye, but without being able to see him, she had no way to know if that was the colour of his fur or the colour of his soul.

And the rats weren't all grey. They were mostly a combination of a diluted yellow or green. When she looked down at herself, she seemed to be a blend of a shimmering purple and an effervescent silver. It was beautiful, and it comforted her considerably to be able to sit and watch her own swirling energy, while alone in the darkness. It was something she'd never done before, hadn't quite known she could do.

Eventually, with nothing else to do but either wait to die or wait for her mysterious, nightly visitor to decide to stop pouring oil on her and save her, she decided she was going to try and project her power and awareness out beyond the oubliette.

She forced herself to breathe in and out slowly. It felt good to project; it relaxed her and took very little energy. Mila tried to focus and send her awareness up and out of the hole and, to her exhilaration, it worked.

Her mind was out! Free from the oubliette, from this prison. She could see everyone and everything that was happening above her. At least now, even if her body was trapped down here, her mind's final moment would not be in this stinking, wretched place. She stretched her metaphysical legs and sent her mind running and leaping through the world above, ecstatic to be in it again.

She found Jezebel in her apartment quickly. The Princess's energy was so unique, and Mila was so used to monitoring it, that it drew her in like an insect to a light. Jezebel's energy was happy, thrilled in fact, and the yellow orb of her energy was prancing around her chambers. Whatever the cause, Mila didn't care.

She drew her awareness away from the Princess. She did not want to devote any of her carefully rationed energy to the hateful woman.

Instead, she reached her power further out, exploring the rest of the household. She felt the hundreds of maids and other servants buzzing up and down the corridors. They were stressed, anxious, exhausted. Jezebel clearly had everyone working overtime for some reason.

The entire building lit up in Mila's mind like a heat map. Bodies of rushing, frantic stressed people, orbiting around a yellow, glowing Jezebel.

And then another presence entered. A cool, blue-grey aura, as familiar and unmistakable to her as the back of her own hand – Culis.

In her prison, Mila's physical body suddenly sat up straight and, in a distant corner of her mind, she sensed Rastava lift his head at the disturbance.

Culis was entering the building, and Mila's heart flew to him. She wanted to wrap herself around him, to beg him to come find her, to save her. She couldn't believe he was only a few feet from where her body currently sat, shrouded in her own filth and misery. Completely ignorant to her plight.

Without touching him, the specifics of his energy, as always, remained a mystery, but even just seeing the humming, fuzzy outline of his presence brought her great peace. He was here. He was alive. Even if he didn't know it, they were together again.

She sat in the quiet comfort of Culis's presence all day, and it was the best day she'd had since she'd been abducted. Every now and then his path crossed with Jezebel's and Mila anxiously scanned the Princess, but to her relief she could sense no hatred or animosity in Jezebel towards him. Her last-minute effort to save him from that had evidently worked. She wondered if his presence here was part of the group's greater plan. It must be nearly spring now, surely. The Sacrament couldn't be far away. That comforted her too. Culis was doing what he needed to do to see the plan through to its dramatic conclusion, as she'd hoped he would.

Sensing him like this, knowing he was close, was enough. She could die now.

Only once during the day did she let her power leave him, and that was when she needed to scratch the itch of curiosity she had about Midas. She'd always wanted to see what Midas's energy felt like.

She sent her power shooting out in a wide circumference from her location. It flew across the vast expanse of the palace grounds, picking up everything in its wake – ants, lizards, servants, acolytes, priests. She wondered how far she could send it. She'd never really tried to push it far before but right now it seemed that as she was trapped in the oubliette without distraction, she was able to push it as far as she liked.

Eventually, she found Midas in what she assumed were his quarters. He mustn't have been wearing his gloves, because she could see his energy clearly. She was half expecting him to shine a brilliant gold in her mind's eye, but he did not. He was just a simple yellow bubble. As mundane as the rest of them.

Mila almost scoffed. How he would hate to know that.

She explored what she could of him from this distance. He was in pain, distressed, and dissolving the plants in his quarters into sand to try and appease the painful symptoms he was experiencing. Symptoms Mila herself recognised.

She'd been right. She knew she'd been right.

A part of her rallied in anger, but a far larger part of her simply looked on in apathy. She somehow...didn't care anymore. She was probably going to die alone down here. The one comfort she could give herself right now was not torturing herself over this situation that she could not change.

She pulled her powers back and returned to Culis. She followed him as he returned to his own apartment block and spent the day rotating between his office and his horses. Mila would have stayed with him all night if she hadn't been pulled back into her own body by the insistence of her powerful thirst.

It was overpowering now, and she'd again sucked the last of the moisture from the moss on the walls. How ironic to be dying of thirst again, when she also felt as though she was rotting from the bottom up. Her feet were sodden and painful from standing in the damp muck below her, and the feeling had been extending into her ankles of late.

That night the trapdoor was pulled aside again.

"Please," she begged, but her voice was dusty and hoarse, and she knew it didn't reach the hole above. "Please help me."

The oil came down as before, and Mila braced herself under the dousing.

"Please! I'm going to die down here." She forced her voice to rise a little louder. "I need water."

Nothing happened. No response. Mila didn't have the strength of will to look up and watch the lid of her tomb be replaced.

Then she felt an unfamiliar bumping of *something* against her left arm.

She reached across with shrivelled, clumsy fingers and grasped the item. It was a bottle, dangling by a string wrapped around its neck. She didn't hesitate and drank deeply. The bottle had been washed out and refilled with water. Sweet, sweet water, tinged slightly with the taste of hops and beer. She drained the entire bottle and while she could have drunk five more, this would at least keep her alive.

“Thank you,” she gasped, and held back tears of gratitude.

The bottle was retrieved, and the trapdoor was replaced without a word.

***

The next time the trapdoor opened, it was daylight outside.

The shock of its brilliance and the loud voices above struck Mila like a hammer, painful even through her tightly closed eyelids. She dared not open them, knowing that the sudden exposure to the bright sunlight after weeks of darkness could injure, possibly even blind her.

She felt the ladder vibrating above her as someone with a searing red energy walked down it, unchained her, then tried to push her up the rungs. Her feet were so ruined from standing in the muck for so long that they wouldn’t tolerate the wooden rungs with her body weight upon them. Mila cried out in agony when she tried.

The guard who had come for her had to wrap a rope under her armpits and drag her up the ladder behind him. Rastava meowed once, gently, in surprise at their visitor, but otherwise sat quiet and still in her arms during all of this, while Mila kept her eyes firmly closed.

She was too exhausted and disillusioned to be even the slightest bit hopeful that this was a rescue, but at least she was getting out of this hole.

When they got to the top, Mila didn’t try to stand. She crumpled to the ground when the guard put her down, wrapping her body protectively around Rastava as she breathed in the sweet, sweet smell of clean, dry dirt. The energy of those around her was terse.

"What's with the cat?" a male voice demanded. "Who put a cat down there with her?"

"No idea."

"Someone take it off her and give it a good meal."

And just like that, Rastava was ripped from her arms with a yowl, and she was left blind and alone. The sudden absence of her companion, her saviour, was like a gaping wound.

From then on, no one spoke again unless it was absolutely necessary. She was grateful that someone wrapped some sort of blanket around her, but it soon stuck to the filth of her body and chaffed more than warmed her. She couldn't walk, so had to be carried a short distance, before she was finally, blissfully, laid down on a soft pallet in a darkened room.

The relief of finally being horizontal, after weeks of being forcibly upright, was indescribable.

"We'll be back for her in two days," a male voice said to a third energy in the room. "Try get her somewhat presentable before then. She needs to be able to walk."

Mila felt the red energy of the guards' bodies leave. There was one that remained, though...a blue one. A nurse? Whoever he was began to sponge her down.

Mila managed to whisper in a desperate croak, "Water, please."

"Oh my, yes. Of course."

Her mind's eye watched as the blue swirl left the room and returned with a cup of water, holding it to Mila's lips. She drank the entire thing in two gulps and held out her hand for more.

"One more," the nurse said gently. "And a little food. But then no more, at least for a little while. You'll make yourself sick."

Mila swiftly devoured the small bites of pheasant breast that were held to her mouth. The food reawakened her dormant hunger, and she begged for more. The nurse acquiesced and found her some bread and apples, which he cut up into small pieces for her. She also ate those directly from his fingers, without pause.

He tsk tsked at her state but didn't say anything directly comforting. Mila spared a thought to wonder who he was, and if she'd known him at any point during her earlier stay at the palace.

He began to sponge Mila down again, and this time she laid back and tried to relax under the administrations. The act of lying flat on the pallet felt unbelievable, the ultimate luxury. She could feel the agonising tension in the key muscles that had supported her during her long stay in the oubliette and wondered if they'd ever fully recover.

She wondered briefly, exactly how long it had been. If she'd been brought out for the Spring Sacrament, which she suspected was the case, then it had been at least five weeks in the hole.

The nurse finally sponged his way down to Mila's feet, and at that point, couldn't hide his horror. Mila imagined the state of them. The skin was probably floating off the bone. Bloody and raw. She determinedly did not open her eyes.

The nurse abandoned the sponge at that point and, instead, switched to a powder – something to dry her feet out, and return their form somewhat.

It was at this point Mila heard him mutter, "Would have been kinder simply to sacrifice you immediately."

She accepted another cup of water, this time noting the taste of wattleroot lacing the drink. A sedative. Good. She wanted to sleep, to let oblivion take her. Despite now being out of the hole, the depression was holding firm. Her time alone in the darkness had reduced her to something small, something animal and scared, something that she barely recognised.

Yes, drug me, she thought. *I want to sleep.* And then she corrected herself.

Actually, I think I'd just rather be dead.

***

When she woke it was nighttime, but even with her eyelids shut it was not as dark as the hole had been. She decided to risk slowly opening them, and when she did so, she saw that the window beside her had been left open. The cool night air ambled slowly in, caressing her skin with a touch so gentle she cried at the silken, fresh feel of it. Beyond the frame lay the deep blue of the night sky and the brilliant stars that lit it up. After her time in the oubliette, she doubted anything would ever seem truly dark to her again.

She lay there, still exhausted despite the recent rest, and watched the sky for hours. As dawn began to creep in and taint the deep blue with a lighter sapphire, Mila heard the birds beckoning in the light, and began to cry again, despite herself.

Even though she was now out of the oubliette, her heart still felt like it was in its own dark hole. She felt numb. Completely unconcerned with her future – whatever may happen.

If the mission with her friends had gone as planned, perhaps there would be no sacrifice. And if for some reason they'd failed, well, at least the sacrifice would be swift, and probably painless. A far kinder death than withering away, dying of thirst, alone, forgotten in a deep black hole, with no one but Rastava for company.

Where was the cat? she wondered. She missed him. It was a small comfort to know that wherever he was in the palace he'd be treated well. No believer of Midas would ever dare mistreat a cat. But she did wish she'd been able to see what he really looked like, and thank him for being the light for her in her darkest moment.

The nurse arrived a few hours later and fed her a broth, which Mila drank readily. He then let her sleep again until midday, when he woke her for a more substantial meal of charred chicken and boiled, salted potatoes. He readministered the powder on her feet and nodded with approval at what he saw occurring in the healing process.

Mila still didn't dare to look at them. She focused instead on the cushion she lay on, and noticed dimly that it was familiar. It was the one she'd slept on when she'd been Jezebel's personal pet, all those months ago. She wondered apathetically if this had been done deliberately by the Princess, to remind her that, although away from her presence, she was never truly free from her altogether.

She didn't care.

Just let it be over. I'm exhausted. I'm ready for all this to be done.

After the nurse left, Mila lay back and let her power fly free through the palace again. She led her power to where she knew Culis's apartments were and found his reassuring, cool-blue presence quickly.

In her mind's eye, she saw him and leaned into his essence, wishing she could tell him where she was, wishing he'd feel her, could come to her. But he could not. And all she could do was sense him pacing back and forth in his room, moving swiftly, back and forth, back and forth, pacing the hallway. Pacing like a trapped panther.

Worried, she realised. *What was he so worried about?*

Searching for clues, she drew back from him slightly and scanned the palace grounds. This ability to scan her power through the world had grown so strong now after her stay in the oubliette, that it all but flew across the vast expanse.

Sensing everything. Everyone.

There were so many of them, so many people. Every wing, apartment, room and bunk was full.

Even down in the servants' village there were an unexpectedly large number of bodies. How unusual.

Mila focused on the servants for a moment. They were all emanating resentment and exhaustion.

What was going on? Surely this wasn't all because of the Spring Sacrament? Jezebel would never allow her death to receive this much attention.

In the late afternoon, the High Priest Abbott appeared by her bedside. Mila registered his presence but simply turned her head away when he darkened her doorstep. She closed her eyes again and reigned her power tightly back into her body. She wanted him to disappear. She wanted to be invisible. She did not want to feel the smug righteousness she was sure he'd be projecting.

"Well?" he asked the nurse in a brisk tone. "Will she be able to walk tomorrow?"

"It'll likely be painful," the nurse replied. "But she should be able to manage."

"It won't be painful for long," Abbott said firmly. And then to Mila's surprise, he turned and addressed her. "You'll be happy to know, demon, that it is not my intention to make you suffer tomorrow. In you'll go, and it'll be done swiftly. Your time on this earth will be done."

She determinedly ignored him but a lick of anger still flickered to life in her stomach. For a moment, a small kernel of Mila's old self reared its head.

She was so angry at this man, so angry at everything he'd done and had been allowed to get away with.

Take me to the Sacrament now. She thought to herself. *If only to get me away from this smug, evil man once and for all.* When the High Priest left, the spark of indignation was quickly extinguished by the looming cloud of her exhaustion. Mila closed her eyes again. She'd never felt anything like this in her life, such a bone-deep weariness of life. She'd never felt so utterly unpossessed of her own body.

The oubliette had changed her.

Not only had she been defeated, but she was tired of fighting.

Jezebel, she realised, had won.

Rubane

The nurse brought the evening meal around – warm, spiced rice with curried fish and a salad of bitter greens. Mila thanked him for his efforts.

"The spice concoction is my own," he said proudly. "An old family recipe of curry leaves and rubane."

Rubane.

The word registered with her immediately and, despite her hunger, Mila put the forkful of fish back onto her plate. She did not want rubane tracking through her digestive system, no matter how imminent her death was. It would only block her ability to use her power, not act as a barrier between her skin and Midas's touch.

The nurse noted the action with interest. "It's perfectly safe," he assured her, mistaking a fear of poison as the reason for her reluctance. "It's a plant from the Highlands. I grew up out that way, and my mother used to spice our fruit like this for morning oats. Lord Culis brought a number of bushels back with him a few weeks ago and left it in the kitchen to dry. I couldn't believe it when I saw it, and he said it was fine to take some for my own bottles. Made me quite nostalgic for home, it did. I've been drying it out and using it to spice my own meals. Although the amount he let me take will probably last me the rest of my life."

Mila lay stunned and as she ingested this news, a true flicker of joy fanned to life in her gut.

Culis had finished the job. He and Tarett had harvested the rest of the rubane. The plan was still going ahead. They were going to sabotage the Spring Sacrament tomorrow. They were going to save her and she was going to see Culis again!

Elated, she sat up abruptly. The nurse's mouth fell open at the unexpected movement and he firmly pushed her back down by her shoulders.

"None of that! You're not ready for such quick movements yet!" he scolded.

"I'm being sacrificed at the Sacrament tomorrow," she laughed in protest, although she obeyed him. "I think sitting up in bed too quickly is the least of my worries."

The nurse's energy shifted. He seemed uncomfortable.

"You're not being sacrificed at the Sacrament," he said slowly. "The Sacrament was held last week."

Mila's mind froze in shock.

Last week?

That made no sense. The rubane had been here? The nurse said that Culis had brought it back from the Highlands weeks ago. They were meant to use it at the Sacrament.

"And... and there... nothing went wrong with it?"

"...No?" She'd made the nurse uncomfortable with her odd, pointed question. She saw him instinctively glance over to check the restraints around her ankles.

She had a million questions.

Exposing Midas at the Spring Sacrament should have been the end of the lies, the end of the Church's reign over Artor. But...nothing had happened?

Something had gone terribly wrong.

Was something wrong with the rubane? Did they infuse it incorrectly? Was her theory about Midas all wrong? Had Jahan and Natalee been hurt in Ocianna? Mila's mind was buzzing as she tried to sort through each possible scenario of what might have happened, but the words the nurse said as he left the room made her entire world stop turning.

"You're being sacrificed tomorrow at the wedding, as the Princess's gift to her new husband."

Mila stopped breathing.

No.

With the click of the key turning in the lock, all the information she'd gathered about the palace that day clicked into place. The extra people, the overworked servants, Culis's worry.

The wedding is tomorrow.

And suddenly, it didn't matter that she was exhausted and tired of life. All that mattered was that the plan to sabotage the Spring Sacrament had failed, the wedding was tomorrow, and if Mila didn't figure out a way to expose Midas and bring down the whole corrupt system before then, she'd be sacrificed as Jezebel's last glorious triumph over her, and Culis would be tied to that monster for the rest of his life.

Adrenaline and rage surged through her, and she sat up so quickly it was as though an invisible hand had throttled her spine. She felt the blazing heat of her fury flow through every bit of sinew and bone in her body, powering her up.

She could not let this happen.

Her rage sizzled.

Jezebel had won everything, had taken *everything* that had ever meant something to Mila. She could not be allowed this. Mila would not give her the satisfaction of her death, would not permit her to *own* Culis.

Jezebel would not win. Mila wouldn't let her. Not this time.

Once she'd made up her mind to slip her bonds, doing so was easy. The nurse hadn't considered her a serious escape risk, and he'd evidently considered her ruined feet deterrent enough that, even if her spirit had been willing, she wouldn't have been able to get far. But Mila had also made no effort to hide her depression, and the nurse had witnessed her easy acceptance of her death. Therefore, the only thing keeping her tethered to the bed was a thin rope looped around her ankles.

And Mila had known, the moment she'd registered that she was lying on her old cushion, that there was a hidden shard of glass tucked into it. She'd put it there herself, in her state of desperation nearly three seasons ago. Back then, she'd been prepared to end her life with it rather than meet Midas's touch.

So much had happened since then.

Now she was going to use it to ensure that when she met Midas's touch, she'd be ready.

She found the sturdy, translucent shard quickly, and with a few flicks of her wrist it was little effort to slice through the rope.

It was the next part that was going to be hard.

Mila swung her legs over the edge of the pallet and looked at her feet for the first time.

She gulped back a horrified sob at the sight of them. They were paler than the rest of her. So white they could have belonged to a corpse, and so swollen she could see none of her usual bones as she experimentally wriggled her toes. It hurt to move them. Bits of skin looked like they'd simply floated off and peeled away during their time in the muck of the oubliette, leaving patches that seemed almost translucent. Her toenails had lifted and separated from their usual seats against her skin. Floating suspended in purgatory, still deciding whether to hold on or let go.

Would they bear her weight?

She sucked in a deep breath, anticipating the pain, then gingerly placed her feet down. She gasped as the pressure from the floor met the full weight of her body and pushed against the newly re-hardened skin at the bottom of them. It was agony. But bearable. Just.

She stood and wobbled, taking a deep steadying breath as she did so.

For a moment, the pain swelled, and Mila lost her resolve. The darkness threatened to rise and envelop her again. That apathy.

She could just lay down again and die tomorrow. That'd be so much easier than this. So much less painful.

There was a time, she recalled, that her mind had felt like a stone. That the madness of Jezebel's whims had crashed and broken upon it like waves vainly battering against a lighthouse. She recalled the way she had stood in stoic silence when Jezebel had cut off her hair, or when she'd been forced to witness and participate in extraordinary cruelty against Jahan.

Little by little, the darkness and rats, the loneliness and near death she'd experienced in the oubliette had whittled away at that strength. Now her mind felt like little more than a blubbery mass of offal. She felt teary and weak.

She started to sit back down on the pallet and pulled the thin slip dress she'd been given around herself. She could feel her ribs through the cloth. She couldn't do this.

Culis.

The name reverberated through her head, through her entire body. She reached out to him again with her power and felt his presence, still pacing his room.

I love him. I never told him that I love him.

Tonight, if she couldn't do this task for herself, she could do it for him.

She summoned her resolve. She stood up again, and before she let the pain of her feet register again in her head, she began to walk.

She was free.

And she was about to wreak havoc.

***

She only had a few short hours to accomplish her task.

From the window of the room she'd been kept in, she cast her power out from herself and found the guards patrolling nearby. There were only two in her immediate vicinity who could pose a problem. One stood on the corner of a battlement. He was looking out, not expecting the threat to come from inside. The other guard, however, the one pacing immediately below her, was going to be more of an issue. He'd probably been assigned to this exact location to prevent her from doing precisely what she was about to attempt to do.

She tuned her power into a fine beam and reached out to him, running it through him and him alone, sensing and scanning his energies. He was alert and determined. A keen, young guard who took his role very seriously.

He was going to do his utmost to stop her if he saw her. She'd have to incapacitate him. Be cold, calculated and determined.

Without another pause, Mila hoisted herself over the balcony and began to scale down the mature vine that grew directly beneath the window. She had never done a manoeuvre like this before, but she reached her power out to the plant and read it, as she had spent her whole life doing to the Highland vegetation. Tonight, she found the vine strong and willing.

She moved slowly and placed her feet only where the vine indicated to her that it was strong enough to bear her weight safely. When she reached the ground, she was trembling and exhausted from the effort, but she continued to clutch tightly to the beast of rage and love that was roaring in her chest, powering her on.

She turned to face the guard, knowing he was about to begin his approach towards her.

He spun. His eyes widened. Mila held out her hands to show she was unarmed and knelt in submission, dropping her head.

Don't cry out, she silently begged him, and he did not. She felt him walk over quickly. Curious and businesslike.

"You're the demon." He didn't grab her straightaway, sensing a trap. Clever guard.

"I was trying to find the healer and I got lost," she said, not needing to fake the pitiful tone in her voice. "I don't know how I ended up here. Please. I just want to go back to sleep. I'm in such incredible pain."

Mostly all true. The best kind of lie. She'd learned that from Culis too.

She pictured Christopher's smile as the guard reached for her. Without hesitation, she sent her power shooting through his skin and into his body.

Less, she commanded him and felt him buckle. *Less.*

Less of what? *Less of everything.*

Fuelled by the beast inside her, she didn't hold back. She sucked away at his energy like a starving beast, drawing in without restraint. She felt more than saw him fall to his knees before her and heard the small, involuntary cry of fear that gasped from his mouth, watched as he gave a bone-deep shudder. It was the shudder of a man whose life force was being sucked from him, and he could do nothing about it. She knew he was too weakened now to draw away, too paralysed by the process to fight back. She was killing him, and she felt nothing but cold fury, followed swiftly by exhilarating jubilation as his life energy entered her body and struck her heart like a lightning strike.

"Ahhh." Mila's eyes rolled back in her head as she let his body drop away. It hit the ground with a dull thump. She didn't know if it was a corpse now or not. Didn't care. She felt like her lungs were fully filling with air for the first time in her life. Her fingertips, toes and ears felt alive with white, hot, silver fire. She was...she was...

A god.

The insidious thought came to her without warning and brought her down a little from the unending high.

Not a god, she chided the thought and fought to find her own mind again. It was harder than it should have been. It was hiding away behind the mountains of energy and power she now felt sizzling beneath her skin. She felt incredible, amazing, indestructible again.

Unfortunately, eventually, she had to look at the body of the guard, because she had to hide it. With effort, she dragged it under the bed of vines that pooled upon the stone like a dark-green waterfall. She tried not to dwell on his shallow breathing, how his heart was thumping slowly and lethargically.

Perhaps she should kill him. Perhaps that would be kinder.

She shook her head to clear the confusion. She could decide that later. Right now, she needed to get moving.

She crouched in the shadows and took a few moments to steady her racing, jubilant heart.

“Easy now,” she whispered to herself, panting a little, willing her own racing heart to slow. It’d do her no favours to throw caution to the wind now. She needed to keep her head about her, and she needed her fine motor skills and sharp hearing for this next phase.

Keeping to the shadows and broadcasting her power ahead to avoid leaves or any garden debris that would make noise underfoot, she headed to the palace kitchen. The most harrowing part of the short journey was the quick dash she had to make across the open, exposed courtyard.

The thudding new rush of power she was riding distracted her completely from the pain in her feet, and she was able to run swiftly and smoothly across the cobbles, from one shadowy arch to another. It wasn’t a long journey, and there was no lock on the kitchen door. It was with ease and relief that she swung it open and stepped in.

Then she almost had a heart attack.

Spilling across the mosaic tiles of the kitchen floor, illuminated by the moonlight that flooded in through the window, was a long shadow. It belonged to a feminine silhouette, one that stood by the glass, face encased in darkness, arms crossed. Mila noted with a thrill of fear that there were horns extending proudly from a curly mass of dark hair.

A demon. Here. And whoever it was, they had been waiting for her.

The Lies of Midas

The figure stepped forward and the woman's face came into the light. Mila's breath stuttered in shock when she saw who it was.

It was Lady Meredith. Jezebel's trusted courtier.

She was an ikarei.

Through the shock of the moment, Mila tried to wrack her brain and remember the few times she'd been in the woman's company. Why hadn't she been able to detect her?

A fellow ikarei.

The first time she'd met her, it had been at the party at Lady Picory's manor, and Mila remembered now that she'd *known* there'd been a demon present, but her power had been too scattered and frayed to detect who it was. There had been other times Lady Meredith had been in her presence, but had Mila truly been so deeply focused on something and someone else that she hadn't noticed?

No. Impossible. It had to be rubane. It just had to be it, and Meredith nodded when she saw Mila making the connection.

"Yes, I used rubane to hide from you, as soon as Jezebel told us what your powers were."

"You're...you're an ikarei," Mila spluttered. "And you know about rubane."

"I know about many, many things. Some I know you've also figured out, because you're here."

Mila examined the image she had in her mind of her first meeting with Meredith. She'd been wearing peacock feathers. She'd also had a cat on her lap.

Something clicked.

"You're the one who poured the tephani oil on me in the hole, the one who sent the cat."

Meredith pursed her lips in confirmation. "The Princess should have never put you in there."

"You saved me."

"I did not." She waved away Mila's gratitude, as if uncomfortable or unable to accept it. "I was there on the day, all those years ago, when this all started. And it should never have ended with one of our kind being thrown in a hole to be eaten alive by rats. That's not how this...how *any* of this should have gone." She took a deep shuddering breath. As if she'd been waiting to talk to someone about this for years, and yet, was still afraid to hear the words come out of her own mouth. "Jezebel overstepped. This whole regime has...overstepped."

Mila read something important on her face. A mystery. A shadow of a history shrouded in pain. She couldn't read her though. The woman was clutching a large bushel of rubane in her left hand and it was blocking Mila's power.

"Who are you really?" Mila stepped forward with curiosity. Something else was afoot here. "What do you know?"

Meredith winced at the question. "I know that, to love someone, unrequited, for fifty years, is eternity in hell enough." She seemed to say it to herself, before saying. "We have no time to trade sad stories, Mila." She held out the handful of rubane and her voice became stern. "Are you going to do what you came here to do?"

Mila gaped at her, unable to believe what she was seeing. "You're helping me?"

Meredith didn't answer but wiped her face with the palm of her free hand, and Mila thought she caught the glimpse of moisture on the woman's cheeks. Lady Meredith was crying?

What is going on?

"Take it!" Meredith pushed the rubane into Mila's hands. "Quickly, before I change my mind."

Mila took it quickly, clutching the bundle to her chest. Meredith's energy suddenly opened up to her. She read it with interest, finding a complex blend of regret and acceptance. "Does Midas know about the power of rubane?" she asked as she scanned the older woman, unwilling to leave without more answers.

"He does not." Meredith's voice hitched, her energy was weary and sad. A woman who'd had enough.

"How did you know I was coming here for this?"

"I know that you used rubane, because you put it on that other demon at the Dusk Ball. The sacrifice that was meant to be you. I saw the mishap of Midas's powers that night, and was the only one who did not try to talk myself out of what I saw, because I know rubane. I know what it does. I also know that you know you're being sacrificed tomorrow." She continued. "So why *wouldn't* you be here, trying to get the rubane to save yourself?"

"If you know about the power of the rubane," Mila challenged, "then you also know what will happen when I wear it at the wedding tomorrow, or rather, what *won't* happen."

"I told you," Meredith snapped, her face a picture of pain, "I know many things."

"You know about the rubane," Mila repeated, mulling over the facts she knew. "You know about the oil that brings the cats...you gave that one to Midas."

It wasn't a question so much as a statement, and Meredith's silence was confirmation enough.

"Which means," Mila continued, her fear of Meredith ebbing away, her anger rising, "that not only do you know of the God-King's lie, but you *enabled* him." The accusation was soft but powerful as it echoed through the empty kitchen.

Meredith flinched but denied nothing. Her words from earlier suddenly rang in Mila's head, *fifty years of unrequited love...*

"You love him!" she realised.

"Once, yes, I did." Meredith's voice was cold.

Mila didn't miss the past tense nor the stony, unforgiving energy that radiated from her. Meredith carried a vengeful, toxic bubble around her heart, the type that forms when a true and sincere love rots, when it has suffered enough.

"I loved him throughout everything. All of it. Every sordid last detail." The older woman's voice was like steel, but her eyes had a faraway look about them, as though she was watching a memory in her mind play out before her, one that was more real to her than Mila standing before her. "Because of what happened to him," she said, "we all learned that ikarei power could evolve, could make us into monsters. So powerful. Capable of so much destruction. Aidas tried to resist it at first, tried not to use his power. But it was impossible.

Everything he touched...it was...his mother...it...Well." She shook her head. "You don't need to know all that. All that's important for you to understand is that, when his power changed, when the symptoms started, the withdrawals truly became unbearable. We tried to manage it for a while, but eventually, we knew we needed another solution, or Aidas would have died."

Mila blinked at the change in name. Meredith noticed.

"Sorry. Midas. Old habits."

"Midas was dying, so you invented the Church, invented the need for sacrifices, to save him," Mila said softly, feeling sick to her stomach.

Meredith nodded but her voice sharpened. "You don't understand," she snapped. "There was no other choice. The symptoms were so awful. Aidas was always in pain, screaming, agonising pain. He needed to use his power and eventually nothing appeased that need but human life. And so, Abbott and I...we came up with a plan. A plan where no ikarei would ever again be able to evolve their powers in such a way. A situation where Aidas could use his powers to dampen his pain, and...and it'd all be okay."

"You'd eradicate your own species to try and save him," Mila said with derision, her mouth filled with bile.

"To save all ikarei *and* humans! Could you imagine if forty, fifty ikarei evolved and needed to slake their powers on human lives? Can you imagine the carnage? The destruction that would cause? No, surely you can see, even now, that ridding the world of ikarei is the only sane thing to do once you know what we're capable of becoming. And besides...it wasn't meant to be like this forever!" Meredith didn't seem to be able to stop now that she'd started talking. "The Church? The Heretical Behaviours? It was only ever supposed to be like this for just a few years, just until we'd established the tradition. At least, that's what they told me. Aidas was supposed to forgive the populace, so long as ikarei were still brought to him as sacrifices. If the people could agree to that, then the other laws would be taken away. People would be free to live their lives however they wanted. But...somehow years passed, and Abbott and the Church...they didn't want to let go. It became bigger than anything it was ever meant to be, and Aidas...he...he can't be satiated anymore. Not even the seasonal ikarei sacrifices are enough. He's always in pain now, *always*. He exists in his own personal version of the Rotting Muds. Eternal pain. You cannot imagine it."

Mila could. Too clearly.

A cold stone of fear had been forming in her stomach as Meredith spoke, and now that Mila finally, finally understood the monstrous truth of it all, it seemed to envelop her entire being.

Midas was addicted to the rush that came from using his power, and suffered immensely from the withdrawals. Because they'd loved him, Abbott and Meredith had created this entire system, this lie that had taken over Artor and, ultimately, it still hadn't been enough. Midas had developed a tolerance. The Seasonal Sacrament was no longer enough for him and the Church's control was no longer enough to control the nation. Everything was falling down around them, and now Midas was losing his hold on everything, on reality.

Mila was frozen in place as she processed this.

This evolved power was a curse.

Was this to be her fate? To suffer immeasurably until she was driven to drain humans to slake the pain? And, she thought with horror, would history simply repeat itself? Would Culis become her Meredith?

In her mind;s eye, Mila saw a horrifying flash to an old, exhausted version of Culis, one with blood stains on his hands that would not wash clean. One who looked at her, as she sat upon Midas's throne, with eyes that beheld her with equal parts disdain and longing. In his desperation to save her from her fate, he would do terrible things, he would lose himself and hate himself, and her, for it. He'd live a haunted, half-life at the side of a monster, just to try save her from herself. She knew he would, and she couldn't let it happen.

It couldn't be their end. It just couldn't.

Was there truly no cure? Her mind whirred through options.

There had to be. The world was wide and there were plenty of strange, weird and wonderful potions, tinctures and tonics that had yet been introduced to Artor. Things that Midas didn't know about. There was plenty Midas did not know.

"You never told him about the rubane," Mila eventually found her voice. "Why?"

"Aidas was never...never quite the same after the day his power morphed," Meredith replied in a whisper. "Every now and then, he'd get a hard glint in his eye, one that...that I just didn't recognise," she said with a shiver. "The rubane is my insurance policy. I wear it every day I'm at the palace, just in case."

"In case the man you love might try to kill you?" Mila tried and failed to keep the scoff from her tone.

"Loved," Meredith corrected harshly. "Loved. Yes, I was a fool. But no longer."

"What changed?" Mila pried, wondering how far she could push this conversation. "You supported him for so long. Why change now?"

"That man," Meredith did not hold back. Her rage blossomed as if she'd been waiting her entire life to tell someone the truth. It came spilling out of her like a bursting dam. "That man has had *me* by his side through *everything*. I was there on the day it happened. I was there when he killed his mother. I held him as his father disfigured him. I stood by his side, even when his own sister rejected him. I have mopped his sodden brow through every anguished seizure of pain. I have kept his secrets, raised his daughter, enabled his *godhood* and all I ever asked was to be loved in return." Her voice finally broke. The cold exterior fell away to reveal the broken shell of a woman beneath it. "And all it took was a demon wearing some rubane to resist his touch, and he's turning the country inside out to find her, to marry *her*." She spat the words out. "That man will never, *never* make me his wife. He does not – *cannot* – ever love me."

The silence that fell between them was sodden with the weight of her regret and despair. Mila didn't interrupt, didn't move, didn't break it.

When Meredith was ready, she drew in another ragged breath and continued in a voice that was far more controlled. "And now that the Children of Midas exist? Well, it...it's all just become too complicated, too much. It needs to end."

With a heavy air of resignation, and sporting the open, throbbing wound of a bleeding, broken heart, Lady Meredith was handing Mila the key to bring down the entire establishment, and she knew it.

Mila didn't know what to say.

She was furious, she was frightened. She'd come here, was doing all this, to try expose the corruption of the institution and here it was, crumbling on its own from the inside. Rotten through by secrets and selfishness.

Meredith looked as though a great weight had been lifted from her as she retracted her horns. Mila spared an errant thought to wonder what her power was.

"We did terrible, terrible things. To ourselves and to others." Meredith breathed a heavy sigh, then muttered. "If I have any defence, it is only that I did it all for love." Then she turned her back, departed, and Mila found herself standing in the kitchen alone.

Mila forced her legs not to buckle from the shock of what she'd just learned. She gripped the bench beside her with white knuckles, willing herself not to fall.

This was too much information all at once. Too much to digest. What did it all mean for her, for Culis, for Artor?

Deep breath in, deep breath out.

Mila gathered herself and realised that, regardless of all she'd just learned, she couldn't spend the night contemplating it. Couldn't descend into a ball of panic over what might happen to her when this latest rush of her power wore away. She couldn't be caught here, in the kitchen of the God-King, on the eve of her impending death. She had to keep moving.

With great effort, she tried to push Lady Meredith's revelations away as she shoved the rubane into her pocket.

The plan. What did she still need to do for the plan?

The plan seemed to have both grown and shrunk in significance in her mind. It had always been about saving Culis, sparing him from his marriage to Jezebel. Now she wondered if she might spare him a worse fate by simply letting Midas's touch destroy her tomorrow.

It'd be so much easier.

How had that deep exhaustion, that overriding despair come back and found her so quickly? It was hard to convince herself to ignore it, to rise above the depressed fog of her mind that had miraculously reappeared so heavily, so cripplingly.

I want to live. She told herself firmly, fighting for clarity. *There has to be a cure. We will find it and I will live peacefully with Culis in my house in the rainforest.*

She closed her eyes and tried to remember what it had been like to be there together. A warm, dry house. Sweet smells of fresh fruit and dried tea. Culis with his damn smile, those damn eyes. The way he looked at her like she was worth everything.

Save him from this fate first, then worry about saving yourself.

It took great effort, but she managed to refocus.

She had the rubane now. What was next?

She needed oil.

Her feet remembered how to walk again, and she moved through the kitchen towards the room that served as a huge pantry. There on the shelves were a few large canisters of cooking oils of all varieties: grapeseed, rathsbane, fennyoli. Mila found an empty jam jar and filled it with grapeseed oil, then put the rubane into it, screwing the lid on tightly and shaking it vigorously. She wished she had time and means to heat the oil, which would guarantee a stronger infusion, but she couldn't risk staying in the kitchen for a single moment longer. It was such a high-traffic area, and with daylight on the way and the wedding in a few hours, it surely wouldn't remain empty for much longer.

She had intended to return immediately to her room and mull over Meredith's revelations. But now, with the jar of rubane oil safely in her pocket, and all these other oils lying before her, new inspiration struck.

Could she make it to Midas's rooms and steal his tephani oil? Replace it with plain cooking oil? Perhaps if there were cats present at the ceremony, which was highly likely, there'd be an opportunity to publicly reveal two lies at once.

Mila took a deep breath and turned a small jar over in her hands.

Did she have the nerve tonight to do such a thing? Something so brave, so utterly foolish? Hadn't she done enough already? Couldn't she go rest now?

Her mind drifted back to the thought of Culis again and it steeled her.

Save him from Jezebel. Bring down the Church. Have the life together that you've always wanted. A life full of love.

She reached for another small empty jar on the pantry shelf and filled it with plain oil, and then put a third jar, an empty one, into her other pocket. She ensured each jar was separated by a small strip of fabric so they wouldn't clink together when she moved. Then she went outside and returned to the vine at the foot of the wall she'd called down earlier that night

She stepped over the shallowly breathing guard, who remained stashed beneath the greenery, still undiscovered. She paid him no heed. Felt no guilt. She had a god to unmask.

With the cool green sturdy plant wrapped around her fingers and palms, this time as she climbed the vine the depression and apathy seemed to fall away again. She felt buoyed now, buoyed by the power of secrets, of exhilaration, of indescribable rage.

Burn the whole thing down.

She reached the window of her room but she did not stop there. She continued climbing, climbing, climbing...right up to the roof of the palace. When she arrived, she crouched low to keep her silhouette from betraying her against the brilliant night sky. She scanned for guards and once she confirmed she was alone, she began to slither across the rooftop tiles, more snake-like in movement than human. Eventually, she reached the eastern wing, the place where she'd sensed Midas's energy once before.

She'd made it.

She was at the God-King's quarters.

***

In the eastern wing, Midas slept with almost no security. His arrogance and incredible power had been such a shroud of protection for him for all these years that it must have seemed laughable for him to consider posting jesu or guards in his chambers.

Mila entered, unhindered, through the window and moved as silently as a shadow, holding her breath lest even the smallest noise betray her. She watched as his giant form tossed restlessly beneath his silken sheets.

As she began to slowly cross the floor, he muttered sharply, and she almost jumped out of her skin. He was wearing his sacred rubane gloves again, blocking his energy from her power, but even without being able to sense him she could see he was restless, angry, distressed.

Despite understanding the reason for his discomfort, knowing that this same pain may soon be visited upon her. Despite the fact that she saw more parallels between the two of them than she'd ever willingly admit, Mila stood over the God-King's writhing, sleeping form that night and found she had no sympathy for him.

May your rest always be plagued by terrors and horrors and guilt.

Part of her wondered what would happen if she simply grabbed one of the enormous heavy lamps from beside his bed and bashed his skull in with it.

Tempting, but no. His downfall needed to be public. His deception needed to be revealed to the people in an indisputable way, something the witnesses could repeat to everyone in the nation. She'd learned that from Culis too. The people needed to *see* Midas's downfall. They deserved nothing less. And Midas deserved nothing more.

She found the vial of tephani oil on a table that sat beside the bed, gleaming in the moonlight. She silently reached forward and plucked it from its seat, then drew away from the bed and to one of the far corners of the room where she crouched behind one of the many ornate armchairs.

There, she unstoppered the bottle and siphoned it into the empty jar she'd brought with her. She could smell the tephani as she poured and for a dizzying moment was taken back to the crushing darkness of the oubliette.

Her breathing rapidly increased and her eyelids fluttered as she battled for control. For a wild moment, as she fought down a crushing panic that nearly overcame her. Surely Midas could hear this? The screaming in her mind, the pounding of her heart, the way her breath had become ragged and animal. But he didn't stir, and eventually, she managed to calm herself.

She continued to pour. She did not falter. Did not stop. Clinical and pragmatic.

Once the exchange was complete, she took up the third jar and poured the cooking oil into the God-King's ornate tephani oil jar.

Would he notice? she wondered. *The different smell?* It mattered little if he did, she supposed. Even if he suspected something had gone wrong and chose not to wear the oil, the effect would still be the same. He wouldn't be wearing the tephani and the cats would not be drawn to him. That was all that mattered.

She was nearly done.

She began to creep back towards the bed to replace the jar. Step by step, she shifted her weight carefully along the stone floors, aware that if he woke he could quickly remove the gloves and kill her.

As she stood over him, it occurred to her to wonder what would happen if she touched him first on a safe part of his body. His shoulder or elbow perhaps? If she drained his life energy away from him

In some ways, that felt like a more fitting end for him than what she'd originally planned. Let him be the one to kneel before her and watch her hand descend. Let him experience, in some tiny way, a semblance of what he'd done to others. Let him be spiritually disintegrated...

Shivering with adrenaline and feeling more alive than she'd ever felt, Mila decided in the end not to spare the false god even a passing glance. She placed the jar back beside his bed and slunk away, retreating the way she had come – through the window and across the rooftop.

When she arrived back at her room, she took the pieces of rope that still lay on her pallet and tucked them amongst the vines, hoping no one would note the absence of any restraint on her legs.

It was done. She'd done it.

And not a moment too soon. Just as she lay her head back on the pillow, the first grey tendrils of dawn reared their heads up over the nearby mountain range. Mila stared at them with tired, dry eyes, ready to collapse with exhaustion, but there was one final thing she needed to do before she could allow herself a few blessed hours of rest.

As she felt the household around her begin to buzz, she knew she'd given the rubane oil all the time to infuse that she could spare. She quickly unscrewed the lid and lathered herself in it. Head, hair, neck, arms and chest. There wasn't enough to do her legs. This would have to be enough. The concoction was odourless, so she had no way to know how strong the infusion was, but time was up.

As the oil soaked into her skin, Mila prayed it would be enough.

She finally, *finally* lay back in bed, exhausted.

She was awoken a few short hours later when the golden rich sun burst with life and vigour into the room. In a sort of morbid accompaniment to the birdsong, she heard a woman's shrill voice from below echo up as she exclaimed in sing-song exuberance.

"What a glorious day for a wedding."

A Glorious Day

When the jesu came for her, it was mid-morning.

Mila wasn't necessarily expecting to be treated well, but she was also certainly not expecting to be roughly shaken from bed and placed in golden manacles.

"And apparently, *I'm* the heathen," she murmured angrily, refusing to allow herself to feel humiliated by their treatment. Her adventure overnight had restored something in her. She had taken back control, in whatever small way she could. And although she was nervous and fearful about what would happen today, she held a steady, hopeful bead of light resolutely within her chest. The depression was holding off. Perhaps the sleep had helped. The stolen life energy of the fallen guard helped immensely too.

As the jesu marched her towards the ceremony, she tried to visualise what would happen after Midas's touch failed on her. She tried to visualise how it would play out.

The touch would fail and the crowd would gasp. Midas and Abbott would be shocked. They'd have no words to explain the mishap. Perhaps they'd try invent a reason but Mila would call out to the crowd, would tell them all what she knew. Culis would be there. He'd stand firm and support her story. He'd draw on his friends and allies amongst the wedding guests to support him. Baird and the others would be there, surely? They'd support him, they'd support her story. They'd stand up and fight off any opposition or threats that would respond with violence to the truth.

The crowd would murmur in disbelief, and then someone would clamour for the God-King's arrest. It would take a moment, but eventually Midas would realise he'd been defeated. The guards would turn on him, take him and Abbott to the dungeons that Mila assumed existed on the grounds somewhere. And it would be over. Jezebel would have lost her power. She'd be disgraced. Culis would be released from his wedding vow. He and Mila would leave this cursed city together.

She huffed a laugh at herself and accidentally drew the raised eyebrow of one of the jesu escorting her. She quietened, and continued to slowly amble towards the Grand Cathedral

If this had been a children's story then perhaps, yes, it would pass as she'd imagined it, but Mila was not so naive.

Deep in her heart, she knew that even though she'd now decided that she wanted to live, she probably wouldn't survive the day. Abbott and Midas would not go down easily, and even if they were eventually arrested, they'd probably still find a way to kill her out of retribution.

At least she'd see Culis once more.

It wouldn't be pretty, and it might not be for long, but at least he'd know that she hadn't abandoned him at the first chance she had. She hadn't run away to Keras without him. She might even be able to convey to him that she now knew, without a shadow of a doubt, that she loved him.

"Move faster, demon," one of the jesu barked, shoving her forward.

Mila limped heavily, pretending to be more incapacitated than she was. When this day came to violence, as she suspected it would, it would be good if they underestimated her.

Mila saw the nurse who had tended on her way out, and had time to murmur "Thank you for everything" to him. He looked surprised at her acknowledgment of his efforts.

"I did nothing but prepare a lamb for slaughter," she heard him reply from down the corridor, but she couldn't tell if it was said with regret or indifference.

The jesu led her the short distance to the Grand Cathedral, which loomed around her, dwarfing her with its arrogance. Mila was grateful for the rubane oil on her skin muting her senses. With its help, the building that was usually energetically revolting to her was now simply visually impressive.

The jesu drew her into a side room, and Mila realised it was the place where she'd once waited, nearly a full year ago, with a line of other ikarei after her initial capture. Back when she'd slipped her bonds and run into Culis in his family crypt.

It felt like a lifetime ago.

Today, she was doused head to toe in the rubane, waiting patiently for her moment to expose the lies of the God-King and topple the Church.

She'd come full circle, and today was the day it all ended.

She trembled as she waited, trying to focus instead on the many voices of the guests on the other side of the curtain who were all chittering with anticipation and excitement. She listened for Culis but couldn't make out his voice. She didn't hear anyone she recognised, not Baird or Nemecca or even Arran.

They might still all be on the ship on the way back from Keras, she thought, realising that this meant Culis was well short of trusted allies. Her stomach scrunched even tighter at this thought.

Then, the deep thrum of a low bell chimed, and heavy vibrations hummed throughout the hall, as the voices of guests swiftly died away. String instruments struck up and began to play a processional melody, and Mila didn't need her powers to know that this was the signal for Jezebel to start walking down the aisle.

The wedding was about to commence.

The loud hum of rushing blood suddenly filled Mila's ears and dimmed the elegant etude. As she listened and waited everything suddenly narrowed down into one moment, into one single pinprick of time and she saw it all clearly. All of it.

Ever since the moment she'd woken to find herself with horns and powers and a new world that would never accept her, this fate had been hunting her. It had always been going to end this way.

She was always going to end up kneeling before him. Awaiting his touch.

No matter how much she'd tried to hide, or how much Culis tried to protect her, despite everything they'd done with the demon trade, no matter how they'd tried to change the status quo for ikarei, all of it had just been distractions, delays. She'd always been marching inexorably towards this very fate because she was a demon, and this is what happened to demons in Artor.

But not after today.

Never again.

As if he sensed her rising fortitude, one of the jesu behind Mila stepped forward and placed a knife against her back.

"I have orders to stab you where you stand if you so much as look like you're going to say or do anything to ruin this moment for the

Princess. I promise I will aim for your gut. It will be a painful and slow death. The God-King's touch will be a more merciful end. Do not resist it. Do you understand?"

She nodded grimly. "I have no intention to resist."

He prodded her forward. It was her turn to enter the now silent hall.

Mila pushed aside the curtains and stepped out into the magnificence of the Grand Cathedral again. The space was packed wall to wall, front to back, full of guests dressed in their finest attire. Jezebel and Culis stood at the far end, on a small podium, hands clasped together. Jezebel was wearing all white, her train dripping from her head like a snowy mountain made of white beads, extending halfway down the massive aisle, an icy river of fabric. Culis, on the other hand, wore just a simple black tunic.

He looked like he was attending a funeral, small and shattered. Like a broken man. It ripped at her to see him like this. Her proud Christopher, a shell of his former self, and Jezebel, either not noticing or not caring about her fiancé's decay, standing proud and victorious. She surveyed the scene with a revolving head, searching for something like an owl searches for a mouse in a field.

Jezebel's eyes caught the movement of Mila's entry and, even from this distance, Mila could see her bite down on a smile. Christopher must have noticed as well, because he followed her gaze and looked up.

When he saw Mila, her raggedy slip, limping and stumbling toward them, barely holding herself together, his face crumbled. All remaining colour drained away. Mila thought he might faint, but after a moment, he collected himself and Mila watched as fury infused into every fibre of his being,

She saw him turn and hiss to Jezebel, "What is this?"

"A sacrifice, to honour our wedding," she replied sweetly, before her voice turned to ice. "And the final proof I require of your love."

"No," he pulled his hands sharply away from hers. His voice, exploding in anger and desperation, echoed off the surrounding walls. The guests gasped.

Don't do it, Mila wanted to scream at him, seeing that rising need for action welling within him, his shoulders tensing, bracing for a fight. *Just wait,* she wanted to call out to him. *Wait until I reach Midas.* But the knife at her kidney reminded her that she couldn't call out, and Christopher didn't know her plan. He thought she was about to die here, at the altar of his wedding.

He turned back to face Jezebel. "This?" he said with revulsion, stepping further away from the Princess. "This is your wedding gift?"

"It's high time the demon met the end she was always destined for," Jezebel said with gravitas, her face caught in an ugly sneer. "It's long overdue, in fact."

The jesu behind Mila pushed her forward another step.

"No." Culis stepped further away from Jezebel and looked around him, whirling desperately, scanning the room with wild eyes, searching for anyone who might be on his side, might come to his aid. But evidently none loyal to him had been invited to attend, for no one stepped forward. Uncomfortable murmurs broke out amongst the guests.

"No," Culis said again in rising panic, "no, this cannot happen. I will not allow it."

"You cannot stop it," Jezebel hissed. "She dies today. You marry me." She stamped her foot for effect. "I win."

"No!" Culis cried out. A panic Mila had never heard from him before began to tinge his voice. "I refuse!" He turned away from Jezebel and began to move back down the aisle, towards Mila.

"Mila!"

Mila reached out her hand to him, tears streaming down her face. The hot, desperate love in Culis's gaze struck her solidly, reminding her suddenly of the way the waterfall's cool water had struck her on that hot day near her rainforest home.

So pure. So certain.

Home.

She realised it didn't matter if they never made it back to the rainforest together. This was it. To be with him, wherever he was, even surrounded by enemies, would always be home.

Cool water on a hot day will always be sweet, and I will always love him.

"Christopher!" she cried out. She twisted free of the jesu's grip and broke into a run, no longer caring how she died, recklessly desperate to reach him. She had to touch him just the once, had to tell him, had to have him know just how much she loved him.

"Guards!" Jezebel screeched.

Her cry was immediately answered. Six guards leapt towards Culis at the same moment that the hardened jesu seized Mila and easily held her back, putting the knife edge to her throat and drawing a small stream of blood. It all happened so swiftly, with such coordination, that Mila realised they'd been ready, waiting for exactly this, for his defiance.

Maybe once upon a time, Jezebel's intent to fulfil this engagement had been genuine, but that had changed once she'd realised the truth about the relationship between Mila and her betrothed. This spectacle had all been a sham. She'd never intended to go through with any of this. It had just been an opportunity to make them both suffer.

Culis, to his credit, realised the exact same thing at the exact same time and with nothing more than his bare fists and the rage of a man who believed the love of his life was about to be sacrificed to a mad god, fought the guards off like a cornered lion to try get to her. He was able to easily beat away two before engaging a third.

Mila watched on helplessly, in agony, as he tried to fight his way to her.

"Run, Mila!" Culis screamed, punching the third guard square in the jaw, but when a fourth clocked him squarely in the back on the head, he fell to his knees and Mila watched his eyes unfocus. He fell to his knees.

"Culis, stop fighting!" she tried to call to him, but the jesu pressed the knife deeper against her neck and the words caught she cried out in fear.

He's going to slit my throat right here in the aisle.

Culis roared at the sound of her pain, the sound of a raging bull. With blood pouring from his nose and mouth, his eyes wide and desperate, he tried to stand again and vault himself forwards, lunging for her.

Bam!

A heavy jesu boot caught his chest mid-flight, sending him sharply back onto the floor with an audible crack. Culis raised his head again and another guard punched him in the face. More blood sprayed across the floor. Someone in the crowd screamed.

Why is no one coming to his aid? Why is no one helping him?

Mila's blood was pounding in her ears. Culis's helplessness was gut-wrenching, and yet he continued to reach his hand out towards her, imploring for her to somehow not die. A jesu stamped on the hand.

Crack.

Mila screamed, her voice hoarse, her mind frantic.

They were going to beat him to death, here, on the floor of the Grand Cathedral, and all he cared about was getting to her.

"Save him! Goddamnit. Someone...please!" She fought against the jesu who held her, but he stuck the knife into her throat even further.

The pain was white hot. Mila froze and dimly wondered if he'd nicked her artery yet.

Culis was on his hands and knees again. He spat out blood. Mila watched as he slowly raised his eyes to the room around them and begged the guests to help him.

"Do *something*!" Culis screamed at the guests. A fifth guard now joined the fray, seizing him and pinning one of his arms behind his back, while a sixth grabbed the other. "Do *anything*. Please. Someone...*please*... I love her."

Mila's heart shattered into a thousand pieces.

I love you too, she was desperate, desperate to say the words, to scream them, but the jesu who held the knife tip at her neck was radiating malice and ferocity. He'd kill her right there if she'd said them. And perhaps Culis wouldn't have even heard anyway.

He was still fighting, but he was losing, and eventually he was subdued, overwhelmed by the sheer numbers of guards determined to beat him down and drag him from the building.

At least he is alive.

Mila watched helplessly as Culis was dragged away, and the hall was filled by the echoes of his frantic, desperate bellows of anguish. It made it all the worse knowing that she could have spared him if she'd just been able to tell him about the rubane on her skin. But he had not known, could not have known. He thought she was being dragged to her death. He'd nearly died trying to save her. Might still die, somewhere alone in a cold cell. Who knew what Jezebel's wrath would have in store for him once she'd finished with Mila?

As if she knew the direction of her thoughts, Jezebel looked over at Mila with a cold, expressionless face.

"Your turn, demon."

Sobbing and shaking, with a bruised body and soul, Mila knew the moment had come. With Culis's cries still ringing in her ears and her love for him churning throughout her body, Mila lifted her head and looked towards Midas's throne. The jesu who'd held her now loosened his grip and withdrew the bloody knife, allowing her to walk freely again.

Mila took a step forward and he did not follow. Perhaps he thought she was cowed. Perhaps he realised that there was no longer any wedding ceremony remaining for her to disrupt. Whatever the reason, he stayed back, and her distance from his knife gave her all the opportunity she needed.

No one was coming to save her. She had to finish this. Now.

She was thirty or so steps away from the throne. As she walked, it took a moment for her hoarse throat to find her voice, but as Midas began to ceremoniously remove his gloves in anticipation, and Culis's frenzied, despairing screams still echoed down the hall, it suddenly came to her in a rush of red-hot anger. When the words exited her mouth, they were fragile, but clear, like newly cooled glass.

"The God-King Midas is a false god," she proclaimed loudly to the guests who remained sitting in dumb, shocked silence. "You needlessly serve him. The sacrifices he demands are the whim of a mad man. There is no need for them to continue."

As she expected, her words were met with continued silence. Some of the guests glanced at one another in shock, still rattled by the violence they'd just witnessed, and others were simply startled that a demon had spoken at all. No one reacted to the content of her words.

She continued to speak as she walked. She was now twenty paces away from the dais where Midas sat.

"I can prove it to you," she called out to the crowd again. "Midas is a demon, like me. You have all been deceived, worshipping a demon this entire time. Your lives are a lie."

Still no one in the hall moved or responded. Jezebel almost looked embarrassed for her. But it was Midas's face, black with fury, that told Mila, once and for all, that everything she thought she knew about him, everything Meredith had revealed, was true.

"I'm beginning to think," the God-King hissed when she was fifteen paces away, "that, rather than sacrifice you, I will have you hung from the wall by your tongue. Too much of my divine mercy has made you grow bold."

"Where are your cats today, Midas?" Mila called out loudly, and for the first time she heard a murmur of voices from the crowd behind her as the room responded to her words.

Where were the cats?

The God-King made a point of having at least one cat around him at all times. Today there were none.

Thirteen paces.

The cats were in the room, of course, but one was winding itself around Jezebel's feet, the other sitting on the windowsill in the sun, and a third trailing behind Abbott in search of a treat.

"It's almost as if you are invisible to them, Midas," Mila continued, as she walked ever closer to the throne. "Almost as if the tephani-laced oil you wear every day to entice the cats to fawn about you...was tampered with."

Mila didn't need her power for her to feel her words land amongst the people listening. It changed the energy of the room. Frenzied whispers broke out around her. Questions were being asked.

Midas's furious eyes nearly disappeared beneath the frown of his heavy brow. Abbott's face didn't move an inch. Jezebel sighed audibly, as though bored, but Mila detected the note of anxiety about it.

Mila barrelled on, determined to make them all see. "It's almost as if," she said calmly, "without that oil, you're as invisible to the cats as I am – as if you are also nothing but a lowly demon yourself."

At that point, only ten paces away from the throne, Mila revealed the tiny vial of stolen tephani oil she'd been clutching in her palm. She poured it over her arm. The pungently sweet smell was unbearably strong, and the response from the cats was immediate. All three in the room turned their heads and, within seconds, they were at Mila's feet, rubbing against her and desperately trying to reach the source of the smell.

The crowd gasped. Jezebel's eyes widened in shock, in horror, in disbelief. She shot a sharp gaze towards her father whose furious expression now seemed frozen in place, his eyes bulging towards Mila.

"I am a demon, but the cats can see me when I wear this oil," Mila explained loudly, projecting her voice for the benefit of those in the furthest rows, who might not have seen what she'd done and were now craning their necks above the crowd. The cats' complete rejection of Midas, who was sitting mere feet from her, was deafening.

"This religion is a lie!" Mila bellowed, just as Midas roared and leapt from his throne, reaching for her. She felt the moment he touched her. The moment the skin of his palm closed over her windpipe and began to tighten.

But she did not disintegrate into sand.

She remained.

The entire room gasped. The shock of it stopping Midas dead in his tracks.

His hand slackened and dropped away from her. "What are you?" he whispered hoarsely. With him this close, his face an inch from hers, Mila could see him. Truly see him. And in his eyes was written a complex mixture of shock, fear and...hope. A mirror.

"I'm just like you," she whispered. "An ikarei. And..." her anger and fury at Midas fell away and was replaced with pity, with empathy. "I am going to help you."

His eyes opened in wonder and amazement. "Impossible," he said, but something fell away from him at her words, as though the energy of the God-King that he'd always adorned now dropped and he stood before her now just as a man. His voice sounded different. Smoother, younger somehow. "Impossible," he repeated.

"I know the pain you suffer." she told him. "I've felt it too."

"You? Can you..." Midas's eyes started to well with tears.

"Yes." Mila said softly in answer to the unasked questions she knew must be swirling through his mind.

Can a cure for the withdrawal symptoms be found? Can you take away my pain?

"I..." It came out croaking and soft. A plea. Then, suddenly, unexpectedly, he coughed.

And coughed again.

And then looked down.

Mila followed his gaze to his chest and caught sight of a blade's glistening tip poking through his sternum.

In disbelief, as one, they both raised their heads and looked over Midas's right shoulder. Behind him stood Abbott, the wielder.

"Sorry, brother," the High Priest whispered into the God-King's ear, so softly Mila didn't know if she'd heard him say it at all.

Abbott withdrew the blade, leaving Mila to catch Midas's huge body as it fell forward and his demon blood, his exposed mortality, bled out across the tiles.

Mila fell to the floor, crushed under his huge weight.

"Aidas!" Lady Meredith's scream rang out from across the room as she flung herself over the body of Midas. "Aidas! No!" she shook his huge, unresponsive shoulders. "No!" she cried out in anguish.

Mila clambered out from under the fallen body of the God-King and dodged the mourning woman draped across it. In the corner of her eye, she saw Jezebel standing to the side in shock, dead still. As if rooted to the ground.

Breathing heavily, Mila looked up at the High Priest and slowly regained her feet.

Brother?

She was still missing something here. Some piece of the puzzle.

"What did you *do*?" she demanded of him softly, then realised it didn't matter. Not right now. All that mattered was that Midas's power had publicly failed, the God-King was dead and they still had an audience of hundreds of dumbstruck, whispering guests. What mattered was that Mila now needed to do the task that Culis would have done best, but she now needed to try.

Sell it.

"It's over," she said to Abbott loudly, ensuring her words carried. "No more sacrifices. No more Heretical Behaviours. There need be no more fear, no more of the God-King's wrath to be avoided. We can all...coexist and go about our lives peacefully."

Abbott clearly didn't know what to say. He looked at the bloody sword he was still holding and Mila watched the full range of emotions playing across his face as his mind searched desperately for what to do next. He'd just lost so much, what remained for him now? The rubane prevented her from sensing the wheel of energies spinning inside him but she tried to push the truth of her words forward anyway, hoping that he would find purchase on them.

For a moment, a split second, it looked as though he might accept it.

But then she saw his face contort as he surveyed the body of Midas and the gathered crowd, saw that everyone was looking to him for guidance on what had just happened, and what to do next.

She saw it, the moment that he settled on a course of action that he pulled straight from within his own, personal hell.

When he next looked down at her, the smile he gave her was grim and evil.

"No," Mila hissed, and started to slowly back away from him.

Abbott followed, stalking her, calling out to his jesu as he moved. "Lock the doors!" he bellowed at them. "No one must know what conspired here today."

"No!" Mila cried out, panic rising uncontrollably. "You don't need to do this!"

Those in the crowd who registered his words began to murmur loudly amongst themselves. Confusion prevented them from taking action in the few seconds they could have used to prevent what happened next.

"The people can never know what happened here," Abbott shouted to his jesu and priests, who were already moving swiftly to obey him. He swung out wildly towards Mila with the same dagger he'd just used to slay his brother. She jumped back to avoid the arc just as he screamed. "The Church will retain control!"

His madness was catching. To her left, Mila heard a loud bang, and as she turned her head, she saw four jesu closing the doors to the Grand Cathedral.

Trapping everyone – herself, Jezebel, and all the guests and servants – inside.

Burn Them All Down

The screaming didn't start straight away.

It was so unbelievable, so nightmarish that it took some people a while to comprehend what was happening.

Mila smelled something pungent and acidic before she heard anything. She whirled and saw blades beginning to sweep smoothly through the crowd, as though the wielders were threshing wheat rather than bodies.

Then the screams began.

Flooded with horror, she turned to see Abbott still advancing on her, determined rage written all over his face. She ran. Not into the pews where the jesu were slicing through guests, but around the throne on the dais, towards the towering stained-glass windows in the thick, stone alcoves. Once there, she pressed one hand and one foot against either side of the alcove and scaled up as high up as she could. It was an effective way to move quickly out of reach of Abbott and his dagger.

"Can't stay up there forever, demon," he snarled, but then was forced to turn to block a lunge from another of the royal guards. There were so few guards here. Only Jezebel's private retinue of twelve to try and fend off the fifty priests and jesu, who were dutifully following Abbott's bloodthirsty command.

From her awkward perch in the alcove, Mila was temporarily safe, and from this height she had a perfect view of the bloodbath that was occurring below. At least thirty heavily armed jesu were making short work of the unarmed revellers. There was a literal river of red blood seeping across the floor of the Grand Cathedral.

Jezebel was shrieking, cowering in a corner, her magnificent dress ripped, her veil discarded. Two of her guards were standing in front of her with their swords drawn, while a third was fighting Abbott. Perhaps he would have even bested the aged High Priest, who only had his short ceremonial dagger, if another jesu hadn't joined the fight and plunged his own dagger into the guard's shoulder blade. The loyal guard went down screaming.

Jezebel looked up and away in fear, and her eyes met Mila's. She surveyed the temporary escape Mila had found for herself in the alcove, and it didn't take her long to try replicate the move in the alcove at her own back. It was harder for Jezebel than it had been for Mila, as she was taller and lacked Mila's physical history. But, inch by awkward inch, she shimmied herself up until she was eventually high enough to be out of reach from the swords flashing below. She achieved it just as her remaining guard was cut down by another swarm of jesu.

For a strange moment, Mila and Jezebel shared a look and were bonded in fear and disbelief about what was happening below them, the speed with which the madness had erupted and their world had turned inside out.

The moment was broken when a dagger flew past Mila, narrowly missing her head, and smashing the glass window behind her.

She gasped.

Abbott had thrown it and was searching for another.

The cool air crashed in through the window behind her. Fresh. Not reeking of blood. Mila stuck her head out and breathed deeply and then used the thick chain of her manacles to continue battering away at the heavy glass until she finally made a hole big enough for her to fit through.

Once she stuck her head out, though, she could see there was nowhere to go. The alcove didn't exist on the other side of the wall. The glass sat sheer against the outside of the steep, slick building, and a fall from this height would undoubtedly cripple her, if not kill her outright.

She was about to pull her head back in when she was almost hit by something that seemed so unbelievable she thought she was hallucinating.

The soft feathery body of Folly brushed the side of her head as he dived towards the ground, veering up at the last possible moment and landing securely on the shoulder of a figure that was running across the courtyard below.

She had to blink twice to confirm that she was indeed seeing reality.

Jahan.

He was here, she realised, he'd been observing the wedding in secret somehow and was now running to get help, reinforcements, other guards to help open the doors and put an end to the massacre now happening inside the Grand Cathedral.

"Jahan!" she screamed to him in desperation.

He halted, turning towards the sound of her voice, searching for her. "Mila?"

"Jahan help me!"

He looked up and saw her half leaning out the broken window. For a moment she saw the decision he had to make. To stay and help her would mean sacrificing everyone else inside the hall, abandoning them to their fate.

"Stay alive!" he called back to her, his face set. Decision made within the instant. "I'm coming for you."

"Hurry!" she screamed.

He paused, thinking for a moment, then nodded and ran off. Mila turned her attention back inside the Grand Cathedral, just as another dagger flew at her and nicked the top of her thigh. She cried out in fear, slipping a few inches down the alcove before she caught herself.

From below, Abbott looked pleased with himself. Some of the other jesu were around him now, handing him their daggers to try again. Some were laughing at her predicament, and Mila realised this had turned into some kind of game, a form of sport.

Jezebel watched on quietly from her own alcove with round eyes, not wanting to draw attention to herself. Wondering, probably, if she'd be next once Mila fell.

Around them, the screams of the dying guests were dimming. There were few still alive, and the butchers systematically continued their bloody work. It was evident that orders had been given to leave Meredith untouched as she remained draped and crumpled over the fallen body of Midas, kneeling in a pool of his blood, her shoulders heaving.

Mila suddenly felt a slap of fabric against her shoulder and heard her name being called from above.

"Mila!"

She looked outside the window again, and this time saw a length of thick cloth, a curtain by the looks of it, draped from the rooftop and swinging past her shoulder.

Without hesitation, she grabbed onto it and vaulted herself out the window, breaking the rest of the glass with her knees.

"Pull!" she screamed and she was elevated up the wall in one clean haul, not a moment too soon.

Mila watched as another dagger spun through the space in the alcove where she'd been crouched just a second earlier.

Behind her, Mila heard Jezebel's outraged screams as she realised Mila was being rescued, while she was being abandoned. Mila felt nothing for her. Felt nothing but sheer relief as, trembling, she clung to the fabric for dear life. Spinning high against the expanse of the courtyard far below her.

When Jahan came into view she saw that was standing on the rooftop and had wrapped the enormous curtain around the spire of the Grand Cathedral. He was using it as a pulley to support her weight and to avoid being dragged off the rooftop himself.

Once her feet were at the tiles on the roof, he wasted no time hauling her upright and leading her to the trapdoor he'd used to get up there.

"Servant's entryway," he said bluntly, checking her over to make sure she wasn't seriously injured before gesturing for her to follow him. "It doesn't lead to the hall. It'll come out at the courtyard."

Mila did not stop to breathe, did not stop to think. She just followed him, down, down, down the spiral staircase.

It was eerily silent.

They ran. Folly flew silently overhead.

"I need proper clothes," Mila panted as they got closer to the gates and she realised he intended to lead her straight out.

Jahan responded instantly, veering to the side and led her through another apartment. This one had evidently housed wedding guests. All of whom, Mila knew, were now dead.

She tried not to think about it as Jahan helped her wrap a green shawl around her shoulders and slip into a pair of loose, white trousers. The manacles still binding her hands slowed the process only minimally with his help.

"Good." Jahan quickly glanced over her new attire with approval. "Now. From here. We stop running and walk calmly, with purpose, out the servants' service doors and into the city."

With her heart pounding and near tears Mila shook her head. "I have to find Culis."

"He'll be okay for the moment," Jahan said. "I was watching from an alcove. He was knocked out and didn't see you expose Midas. He's probably in the dungeon right now, none the wiser to the bloodbath that's currently going on inside. It's probably the safest place he could be at the moment. But you? You have to leave. Now."

Mila's heart thudded into her stomach. "No, I can't leave him again."

"They're not going to kill him." Jahan seized her forearms with impatience. "They will try use him to validate whatever story they come up with to explain what happened here today. Mark my words. He's safe, for now. And we will come back for him when we can. When it's safer. I promise."

"You swear?"

"I swear."

And because, deep down, she knew he was right, she agreed to be led from the palace and into the city.

No one stopped them. The chaos of the slaughter in the Grand Cathedral had not yet spilled out into the rest of the estate. Perhaps it never would. In the back of her mind, Mila wondered dimly how Abbott would explain it, how he would contain the news of what had just happened. Every single prominent family in the country had either just been completely wiped out or lost a significant member. What would that do to the aristocracy? To the social order? And would he eventually kill all the priests and jesu who'd assisted him, tie up all loose ends? Would he kill Jezebel? Would Mila be hunted down as the lone witness to his madness? How could he justify so much death?

The questions that accosted her mind were ceaseless, and the pain of knowing that each step was taking her further and further away from Culis, who was probably lying broken and bloodied in a dungeon somewhere, was nearly crippling.

As her brain worked overtime, her feet mindlessly followed Jahan. To any observers, they were just two servants venturing to the city markets for kitchen supplies. It was almost a laughably peaceful day outside. Warm. Spring had started and the characteristic heat of the city was not far away.

Mila briefly wondered where Tarett was, and Natalee. Had they stayed in the Highlands? Had they come back with Culis? Why hadn't they sabotaged the Spring Sacrament? And where was Nathaniel? So many questions. For now, they'd all have to wait.

They wound themselves throughout the city and eventually hitched a ride on a farmer's cart leaving for Traders Bay. Once off her feet and able to lie down amongst the boxes and carpets, Mila found herself finally able to breathe and take stock of everything that had just occurred.

Midas was dead. Abbott had killed him. Abbott was his *brother*. Abbott was going to try to continue the Church's rule without Midas. For a dim moment, Mila wondered what the Children of Midas would make of it when they were no longer permitted to see their God-King in the flesh.

But truly, she couldn't think about anything other than Culis. She kept seeing his anguished, bloody, screaming face whenever she closed her eyes. He probably thought she was dead. That was the thought that finally broke the dam and permitted the tears to flow. She began to violently shake.

"Hey." Jahan reached for her and pulled her into him.

She let him, leaned into the connection. Fates, it was nice to just be hugged.

"You're safe," he whispered soothingly into her hair. "You escaped. It's okay. You did it. You're alive."

He was right.

She'd escaped. She'd survived. All of it. Frank, the oubliette, Jezebel, Midas's touch, Abbott's murderous rampage. She'd *survived*. And she would continue to. She knew she would. She was many things, but today she was a survivor.

She took stock of her chained, bloodied wrists, the sweat and filth that marked her body, the steady trickling stream of blood that still determinedly ran down her neck from the jesu's knife. Her torn, bloated, ruined feet. Her skinny, misshapen body. She surveyed it all, and she grinned. A mirthless grin. More of a baring of teeth than anything else.

This is what surviving looks like.

And Culis would survive too. She would ensure it.

Hell, if he had the audacity to die before they had a chance to live their lives peacefully together, she would go down to the Rotting Muds herself and drag him kicking and screaming back here into life with her.

She wouldn't lose him, couldn't lose him. How could she lose the person who felt so much a part of her, it was as though he'd been tattooed onto her skin, as though she'd be able to find pieces of his soul tangled in her hair? He was there with her, riding every exhale, his name written in the freckles and shallow lines that marked her face. He was everything to her. Everything. She would not rest, would do whatever was required, to free him. Anything.

They'd all called her a demon.

Perhaps it was time to live up to the name.

Epilogue

Jezebel was not, for one single moment, going to give them the satisfaction of seeing her fear.

She turned her nose up and stared down at the jesu who stood in front of her, as though there weren't bars separating them and she wasn't a prisoner in a filthy cell under the palace that had once been her dominion. As if her father hadn't just been murdered by his High Priest. As if her entire world hadn't just come crumbling down in a torrid storm of chaos, betrayal and blood.

"Let me out." She ensured that her tone was commanding, unwavering. The tone that had made servers quake in her path less than twelve hours earlier.

It nearly worked too.

She watched as the jesu narrowed his eyes and wondered for half a second if he was following the right set of orders.

"I am your *Princess*." Jezebel was determined to capitalise on his doubt. "Daughter of the God-King. Half-Divine in my own right. Did you not devote your life to him? You will release me."

The jesu murmured something and shuffled his feet uncomfortably.

"What did you say? Speak up, you rat."

"He *said*" – Abbott's curt and bold voice cut through the dim dungeon and saved the unfortunate jesu from his misery – "that he serves the true Church. And the true Church knows that while the God-King's body was corrupted, while his mortal mind had failed him, his immortal spirit lives on. This faithful jesu knows and understands that our God-King continues to guide our righteous path from his heavenly seat in Aluah, passing his high judgement and laws to us through his mouthpiece – his High Priest."

"What horseshit is this?" Jezebel hissed.

Abbott surveyed her calmly and did not reply immediately. His gaze felt voyeuristic. Under it, for the first time since she'd been thrown behind these bars, Jezebel felt like a caged animal.

"I will only say this once," he said, approaching the bars, his voice quiet as creaking ice. "Things have changed. You are no longer in charge. I am. I know that will be difficult for you, Jezebel." The absence of her royal title was deliberate. "But I'm sure you will find a way to...adjust."

She spat on the floor and Abbott's eyes flared.

"You will respect me, or I will make you regret it."

The promise of torture was so clear that Jezebel felt a rare streak of fear strike her square in the chest. Abbott was not playing. He'd just killed his god and ordered the murder of hundreds of innocent witnesses. He would have no qualms about torturing and killing her too, to achieve his ends, none in the slightest. In fact, she was surprised that she was even still alive. Only she and Lady Meredith had been spared the bloodbath that had occurred in the Grand Cathedral.

"What do you want from me?" She forced the words out in what could never be called a respectful tone, but at least it was somewhat neutral.

"Nothing...yet." He looked her up and down, sizing her up like she were cattle in a stockyard. "And then, when I'm ready for you, your unflinching, unwavering obedience."

Jezebel bit down on her tongue so hard she tasted blood. There was no response she could think of that wouldn't earn her his ire.

"Learning fast. I wouldn't have picked that," Abbott sneered, and then left, taking the jesu with him. She was utterly alone.

Actually, not quite alone.

She'd been deliberately ignoring the bloody lump that lay unmoving on the cold ground in the cell beside hers. The broken body of Christopher Culis.

She knew he was alive. The heavy breaths that wheezed out of his broken lungs was the only sound punctuating the otherwise all-consuming silence.

Silence.

It was so quiet down here.

Too quiet. In sudden panic, she understood that, if she was to stay indefinitely in this cell, she was about to get very bored. And when she was bored, her mind would force her to sit with itself. She'd be forced to sit alone with *herself.*

"Abbott!" She leapt up, terrified, and furiously rattled the bars of the cell. "Abbott, come get me, you filthy, stinking, slimy rat-ball. You pock-faced, mong-brained piece of shit. You vile, disgusting, heretic –"

"Jezebel," Culis's soft, weak voice groaned out from the floor of the cell beside her. "Stop."

Jezebel released the bars and moved closer to him, inspecting his injuries with disgust. Feeling no empathy. No sympathy. He deserved all his pain. Whatever agony he was in right now, it was only half of what he'd ever inflicted on her.

"Come join me in our new life together, Culis," she said with disdain, feeling nothing but apathy for the man lying broken before her. "One where you're suffering daily and nobody gives a shit. Oh, don't worry. I'm already well accustomed to it. It only sends you *half* mad."

Culis only groaned in response, then whispered something unintelligible.

"What did you say?"

"Mila?" The desperate question tumbled from his mouth.

Jezebel realised that Culis had no idea what had happened after he'd been dragged away from their *wedding*. He had no idea that their world had been turned upside down. Hadn't thought to ask. Didn't care why she was down here in a *dungeon cell* with him. All he cared about was that *demon.*

"Dead," Jezebel snapped. "Golden dust that was quickly swept away into the nearest fire."

The noise that came out of that man's body was inhuman, and Jezebel felt the smallest twinge of guilt as she sat down in the straw that lined the floor of her own cell.

She pushed it away. She'd be damned the day she ever spared Christopher Culis an ounce of her attention ever again.

She turned her mind to more important thoughts.

Escape.

Acknowledgements

A huge, resounding thank you to everyone who helped bring this story into the world and supported me along the way.

To my incredible Beta Readers – Danielle, Nessa, Eisha-Marie and Lora. Your insights and support gave me the fuel I needed to continue to with this work and make it the best it could be. To my editor Shannon Cave, you did a beautiful job again. I always feel like my work is safe in your hands!

To my online Author Support System. The dedicated new friends and supporters I have met along the way who have championed Heretic Behaviour to the high heavens and given me more success and traction as an author than I could have possibly dreamed of in my first year — Thank you, thank you thank you. And the biggest thank you goes especially to Nicole Rowles. Thank you so much for always being happy to take my frantic calls and texts. For brainstorming with me and calling me for writing sessions even when you were sick and exhausted. This author business is usually such a solo endeavour. To have your presence alongside me as we write together... I can't even begin to tell you how grateful I am.

To Oscar and Emma. You have both given me so much of your time and energy and skills over the years, and asked for nothing in return. The truest of true friends. I could not have done this without your support.

To Mum – who once again read this book in its different iterations at least 5 times and has remained bold and unafraid to tell me which parts she loved, and which parts needed work. Your love is all I need. And to Rick, for all your support and encouragement. For always making me feel like the time and energy I'm putting into this is just as valuable and important (if not more than) my 'real' job. I love you.

And Antonio, for just being himself. The world is a better place for having cats in it.

About the Author

E.C.Glynn lives in the Scenic Rim of Queensland, Australia. This is the 13329th time she's sat down to write a novel, and only the second time she's shown the attempt to anyone other than her cat.

www.ingramcontent.com/pod-product-compliance
Lightning Source LLC
Chambersburg PA
CBHW030341310726
48979CB00001B/132